Heart of the
Current

a novel by
CRISPIN YOUNG

Written and produced by Crispin Young
P.O. Box 1828, Hood River, OR 97031
Tahldia@gmail.com
www.tahldia.com

This book is dedicated to all of my friends for their kindness, encouragement, love, and inspiration. To Chase, for his patience. To the Eugene crew, for their confidence in my story. And a special thanks to Lauren Hougen for sharing her amazing editing talents, and Mandy O'Brien for her beautiful cover artwork.

And most importantly, I dedicate this book to my parents. Their ceaseless motivation, support, and steady gifts of fantasy novels and video games growing up helped hone my imagination.

Without the support of my friends and family, this book would not have been possible. Thank you from the bottom of my heart.

May the stars bless you always.

HEART OF THE CURRENT

CHAPTER ONE:

THE END OF THE WORLD

IT WAS THE same crimson dream Annie had suffered countless times before.

It always came to haunt her on the loneliest of nights, when she was curled up in bed with a bottle of whiskey and a mind clouded with ghostly memories. The emptiness seemed to gnaw at her the most after midnight. When she finally passed out, the dreams were always full of fire.

Annie ran through the dense forest. The sky was tinged red, and smudged with dark columns of smoke in the distance. Black ash drifted around her like fat, dirty snowflakes. She struggled to get her legs to work in the slow haze of the nightmare. Sometimes she would try and scream, but her voice seemed weak and distant.

More often than not, *it* was chasing her, screaming at her, tearing the forest down around her. It had the wide body and sharp face of a bird of prey, and its yellow eyes narrowed when it spied her. Sparks of white flame dripped from it like feathers. The creature wreathed in fire broke through the canopy and dove at her.

Annie dashed away through the tempest of ash and smoke.

She ran through the trees until she came to a cliff. She paused and looked back, clenching her shaky hands. The flaming bird was right behind her, screeching a terrible song that sounded like metal bending and scraping against itself. Her foot slipped and Annie lost her balance, and the world seemed to melt into a white void. The brilliance of the white abyss blinded her as she fell. She screamed and tore at the air around her.

Annie bolted upright in bed and blinked at the sunlight pouring through the window onto her crumpled sheets. She looked at the clock on her phone, and her eyes widened.

"*Shit!*" She tossed the phone down and wrenched the bedsheet off. Her large black Lab lazily eyed her for a moment before jumping off the bed and following Annie to her closet.

"This is the second time this week I've overslept, Tia," Annie told the dog absently as she rummaged through the messy closet. There were more clothes on the floor than on the hangers. After a few moments, Annie knelt down and inspected the clothes on the floor. She picked at them with a scowl, her brain too muddled from sleep to care what she wore. Tia nosed around, taking every opportunity to get in the way and lick Annie's face as she searched the mountain of clothes. After a moment she found a pair of jeans and a wrinkled camisole that passed a sniff test, gave them a shake, and slid them on.

Annie took a moment to inspect her reflection in the mirror and saw a pale, puffy-haired woman staring back. The jeans and wrinkled tank top hung loose on her thin frame. She wore little jewelry except for a simple silver ring with an amber stone, and a silver bracelet on her right wrist. The bracelet was old and scratched, but it fit so well that she never bothered to remove it. Whenever Annie was nervous, she rubbed absently at the raised silver bumps on the bracelet.

She grabbed a brush and tried to tame her long, sand-colored hair. It seemed to shoot in every direction, and brushing did little to give it shape. She gave up, grabbed a bandanna, tucked the wild, tangled hair behind that, and walked out of the room.

Tia had already run down the hallway and was waiting at the back door, her tail wagging furiously.

"Yeah yeah," Annie mumbled as she opened the sliding door and the dog bounded out.

Annie flipped on the radio as she set about finding breakfast. She poured herself some coffee that had been made the day before, added extra cream and sugar, and grabbed a stale bagel. The morning news was the usual mix of local crime and national drama.

Two men had been mugged at a Portland train station. A case of road rage left someone in the hospital recovering from a gunshot. Sunny and fifty degrees for the next two days, but more northwest rain coming on Sunday. The president was arguing with congress about national security threats. Russia is mad at us. North Korea is mad at us. The Middle East is pissed at us. Always the same old story.

Annie kept the radio on in the background to make the house seem more lively. More inhabited. She chewed at her plain bagel and looked at the photographs of her family on the fridge.

I really need to plan that trip home, she thought, feeling guilty whenever she saw the pictures of her mother. She had moved to the Northwest for a dream job, but her entire family was in Atlanta. She missed her mom, the fireflies, warm beaches, and the southern thunderstorms, but not the searing heat of the summers. She didn't miss the mosquitoes and fire ants.

Making a mental note to call her mom later, Annie finished the stale breakfast and quickly opened the back door.

"Tia! Get in here, puppers!"

Tia looked over from the corner of the yard and wagged her tail. When Annie called her name again, Tia gave a short, playful bow and picked up a tennis ball.

"No sweetie, it's not time to play! I gotta go to work!" Tia responded by rolling over onto the grass and scooting away from the door upside down, all the while furiously wagging her tail. The black Labrador wiggled and panted and let her tongue loll out the side of her face, giving her a maniacal and goofy expression.

"Do you want a *treat?*"

Tia's ears perked and at once she crashed through the doorway and easily shoved Annie aside. She went to the kitchen cabinet that contained her treats, and she patiently sat down.

"I see how it is. You only know how to behave if I give you a treat."

At the magic word, Tia whined and stood up high enough to meet Annie's eyes.

"Nope. You gotta sit." The dog immediately obeyed, eyeing the biscuit with intense focus. She grabbed the treat from her hand and devoured it greedily.

"I'm sorry I woke up late and I didn't have time to take you for a walk. You be a good girl and I'll take you on a good long hike after work."

Tia's large floppy ears drooped as Annie pulled a hooded sweatshirt from a pile of clothes on the couch and slid it on. It had a few holes, and the skull and ravens were fading, but it was her favorite heavy metal band.

"And leave the garbage alone."

She locked the front door, and stepped over a beer bottle and an overflowing ashtray on the front porch. As she walked to her car she saw her older neighbor, Ben Hawkins, pulling weeds between their driveways.

"Mornin', Annie!" He took off a dirty gardening glove and wiped at some sweat on his brow. "This is some lovely April weather we're having, isn't it?"

"It really is. I wish I wasn't going to spend a day like today in the office."

"Well, be sure not to work too hard." He pulled the glove back on and kneeled down among some sprouting tulips.

Ben was a hard man. He still wore a military crew cut, even though he had long since retired. He was thick, but not fat. His early morning runs had kept him in shape, as well as his numerous hunting trips around the world. Annie had been in his house only once, but she'd seen that Ben was an avid collector of guns and weapons. He never explained what he did for a living, but Annie had noticed several framed chemistry and engineering degrees on his wall.

He had let a few conspiracy theories slip in general conversation, and Annie thought of him as a little paranoid and strange. He was always quick to lend a hand when she needed help, and seemed kind and fatherly, but she felt that something was off about him. She chalked it up to numerous deployments to Iraq and Afghanistan that must have left a dark impression on him. *I'll probably never know.*

Annie was stuck in traffic most of the way to work. Living far out from the city center was nice since she preferred the outdoors to city living, but it meant a long commute every morning and evening. She chain-smoked and cursed other drivers, absently listening to the morning news. It was nearly 10 a.m. when she pulled up in the parking garage.

She took the stairs, hoping to evade conversation. Annie felt too tired and hungover to deal with pleasantries. She huffed up to the third floor, cursed her smoking habit, and gently opened the door to the break room. Fortunately no one was there. While the gaming company that Annie worked for supplied the employees with endless amounts of beer, video games, and even a pool table, no one had the leisure time to relax in the expansive room. Deadlines were looming and everyone was feeling frazzled.

She walked to the counter, slid a Nerf gun out of the way, and poured herself a large mug of coffee. She quietly walked into the main room. The cubicles buzzed around her as she discreetly took a longer route to her desk. It kept her from walking by the secretary and the creative director's office, and hopefully assured that no one had noticed her tardiness.

She slunk down into her cage, as she liked to think of it, and turned on her computer as she sipped her coffee. When she saw fifteen new e-mails, she turned to her second monitor, pulled out a tablet, and started drawing. The e-mails would still be there to read when she felt like dealing with them. She still felt half asleep, and her head still ached whenever she looked up at the fluorescent lights. She enjoyed relative peace for about fifteen minutes before her production designer poked his head over the grey cubicle walls.

"Hey. 'Bout time." He smiled gently, running a hand through his black hair. "I need those storyboards from you when you have a moment."

Annie winced. "I'm sorry, Matt. I thought I e-mailed them to you yesterday?"

"Those were for the battle at Osmek." His brown eyes were apologetic. "I need the storyboards for Fate's Touch. And . . . I also need the finalized character designs for Voltay as well. If you have them ready."

"Uh, yeah. They just need a few touch-ups. I can have them to you by the end of day."

"I needed them last week, Annie." His eyes were still kind. "I know you're swamped, but I really need to get started on the rendering."

"You're at the top of my list." She pointed her stylus at him and gave a wink. "I'll get them to you. Promise. After all, you're my favorite neighbor, Matt."

"I'm your only neighbor!"

"I know, and you're my favorite."

He blushed and turned to look over the cubicle walls, avoiding her eyes. "Be careful about Little Mike. He's on a tear this morning."

"I'm sure calling him Little Mike helps every bit," Annie mocked, still smiling.

"Well, let me know if I can help you speed along that design."

Annie scrawled on the tablet for another thirty minutes, enjoying the moment. Her headphones were blaring heavy metal, and she was engrossed in a painting of a tall man carrying a sword. He was by far her favorite to draw.

Simple, elegant lines shaped his perfect face. Long blond hair spilled out of the helmet and on the shoulders. His arms rippled with muscle, and he gave his foe a toothy grin. She paused for a moment while she examined his features, smiled, and gave a small sigh. She filled in the lines on his chain mail armor, careful to use her reference sheet for the house sigils. She drew him diving at a monster with long claws and curved teeth.

Annie became lost in the scene, sketching out the castle in the background and adding a few figures. Vague shapes in the sky would be more monsters, when she could get her stylus to it.

After some more detailing, she saved the document and opened up another art piece. This one was an older man with a narrow, solemn face. He had half a beard, and some quickly scrawled clothes. A hastily drawn house sigil with three moons decorated the plate armor. She had to fill the rest of his features out and hand it to Matt before it got too late.

She felt a tap on her shoulder. Annoyed at the interruption, Annie muted the song playing from her smart phone and pulled the headphones off.

"Hey, can I see you in my office?"

Annie turned in her chair to see her creative director Mike looking over her. He didn't bother making eye contact with her, but kept his eyes fixed on her latest drawing.

"What are you working on?"

"Voltay."

"What's wrong with his beard?"

"I, uh . . . I haven't filled it in yet?"

"Obviously. But don't you think that beard is a little too . . . cliché?"

Annie bristled at Mike's comment, but turned toward her monitor to hide the scowl. She saved her work and wordlessly followed Mike to his office. She turned back and saw Matt giving her an exaggerated sad face from his cubicle. She shrugged in reply and walked into the spacious corner office.

"Shut the door."

Shit, Annie thought.

"You were two days late with the dragon designs," he remarked as Annie sat down. He wasn't angry, but there was a cool tone to his voice that worried her. Annie blinked back at Mike. He was a short man, with a perfectly manicured beard splotched with gray. Dark circles ran under his eyes.

"Well?"

"I got backlogged with work for the battle at Osmek. They changed the script on me. It's not my fault."

Mike didn't respond, so Annie meekly added, "They changed which characters you can play for Osmek. I had to redesign some stuff to make it fit with the cut scene."

"You're constantly late, though."

Annie shrugged and absently started picking at her dirty nails while she tried to read the emotions on Mike's face.

Mike leaned back in his chair and scratched at his beard. "So, what's wrong with you?"

Annie frowned. "What do you mean?"

"You're late all the time. You're late with your work. You're late *to* work. I have people waiting on you. It's frustrating. God forbid anyone try to tell you what to do before you've had a cup of coffee."

Annie looked down.

"Listen, Annie, you're the talent on this right now. These characters, these places, it's all you, kid. You have a serious genius streak in you. But I'm trying to run a project schedule, and I don't like explaining why we, as a team, are late."

"That all?" Annie muttered, staring at her shoes. She realized she was wearing two different socks.

"You look like hell."

Annie's eyebrows grew together. "Um, thanks?"

There was a long pause. "I noticed you're not wearing your engagement ring anymore."

Annie pressed her lips together and scowled darkly at the floor.

Mike flattened his hands on his desk and said in a softer tone, "Look, I don't know what's going on in your personal life. But you need to get it together. It's affecting your work. You look like you could sleep for a week."

Annie just shrugged, not meeting his eyes.

"Hey, you don't have to tell me what's going on, I ain't a shrink. But I think you either need a break or another job."

Annie groaned. "You want me to work more, produce more, but then you say I need a break? I either take a break or get the fuck out? Is that it?"

Mike raised an eyebrow, "Take a long weekend. Get some rest. Go do one of your fishing trips. I see pictures of that dog of yours all over Facebook. Take it on a hike or something. You're pale as a ghost and you need some sun."

"Nerds don't get sun. We're allergic to it, you know."

Mike didn't smile. He focused on Annie and growled, "Go home. Right now. I'm sick of your sloppy attitude. Take a long weekend and figure your shit out. You act like you don't want to be here half the time, and I can find someone else to finish this project up."

"But they're *my* characters!" she whined. "*Tahldia* is mine!"

"Right now they're *our* characters, and if we want *Tahldia* to get out on time we work as a team. You make video games for a living, Annie. Some of the best RPGs on the market. Most folks would give their left nut to be able to say they designed a video game. You seem like you could care less about anything. Go home, think about what you really want out of life, and I'll see you here first thing Monday morning. Not a minute past eight and ready to work."

Annie sneered at the early time, "I still have to get my current deadlines out of the way. It's only eleven."

"Out. Deal with them later. I can probably take care of Voltay for you.

That beard of his is going to drive me crazy and I think I want to rework his armor. You really think Voltay should be Shafani? Don't we have enough bad guys from Shafan?"

"Dude, make him from whatever country you think best." Annie loathed other people getting their hands on her work, but she bit her lip and said, "I can't believe you're sending me home."

"I can't believe I didn't fire you." Mike tried to smile. "We need you. I'm giving you fair warning, and maybe a chance at recharging that brain of yours. I need you here, one hundred percent."

"Always nice to know I'm wanted." Annie forced a smile, but it felt mocking. "I apologize for being late with so many projects. Things haven't been easy at home, and you're right—I haven't been sleeping. I'll try and get that recharge for you."

Mike laughed. "I'd never have thought you'd apologize for anything. Duly noted. But I'm still pissed at you, and you should probably get out of my sight."

Not sure how much of the comment was a serious threat, and how much was just part of Mike's twisted humor, Annie quickly slid out of his office.

She sat down in her cubicle with a heavy sigh and started to collect her paperwork.

"Well . . .?" came the voice from the neighboring cubicle.

"He's sending me home. Can you believe this shit?"

"Why?" Matt's head poked over the cubicle wall.

"He said I need to take a break or get another job."

"What!?"

"I'm taking a long weekend, it looks like. He's so mad at me he doesn't want me around." Annie stopped shoving piles of drawings into a folder and turned to Matt. "Don't worry, I will work on the storyboards for you as soon as I get home, and e-mail them to you. If I don't get stuck in traffic again, I should be able to get them to you before end of day. They really only needed some minor tweaks."

"By tomorrow morning is fine." Matt gave her one of his shy smiles. "I know you prefer to work at night anyway. Go home and sleep that hangover off, and then give me some awesome storyboards by the time I walk in here tomorrow morning."

"How did you know I was hung over?"

"I just know, Annie." He hesitated, and then said, "Sometime invite me along for one of your parties, eh? We are overdue to hang out again."

She smiled and he blushed. He was always sweet to her. Too sweet for her, and she knew it. She had no idea what she was doing one hour to the next, and could barely care for herself or her dog. The last thing she needed was to try to care for a boyfriend. Matt hadn't worked up the nerve to ask her out again since making a fool out of himself after four drinks at the last office party. The poor man couldn't hold his liquor.

"Careful, the last thing this office needs is another party animal." She changed the subject. "Oh! And Little Mike wants to change Voltay. So go bug him for the character designs. He doesn't like the beard or gear I gave him. Oh, and apparently he is no longer Shafani."

"Oh, no." Matt rolled his eyes. "What's he going to do? Make Voltay a demon or something?"

"I don't know. I'm over it." Annie turned off her computer and patted Matt on the head. "Just remember, the creative director is God and he knows everything. He knows what's best for the game, and even what's best for his employees." She sneered. She tried to put a sarcastic light on the ordeal, but it just made her angrier.

"Seriously . . . How am I supposed to take a break and meet all these deadlines? It's just more stress that I don't need."

"You'll do fine. You always pull through everything." Matt gave her a grin and waved to her as she left her little cage.

Annie walked by Mike's office and gave a quick wave, happy to see he was on the phone and would not be able to give her any more "advice." He gave her a curt nod and pointed at the exit with his pen. She rolled her eyes.

As Annie walked by the secretary's desk, the petite blonde held up her finger as she talked on the phone, motioning for Annie to wait.

"Yeah, sorry, he is not in today. Listen, I'll transfer you to his voice mailbox and you can leave him your message. Okay. Thanks. One moment, please," she said in a breathless rush. She punched a few buttons, slammed the phone down, and focused her bright eyes intently on Annie.

"In and out today, huh?" Before Annie could reply, the secretary glared in the direction of Mike's office and said, "Hey, he's on the warpath today, so don't let him get to you. He was angry with me an hour ago because I let the ink supplies run low in the copy room. I mean, seriously? It's like, dude, I know how much ink we need, and when we run out I, like, totally get it. I know when to order it. It's, like, part of my job, ya know?"

Annie politely nodded her head and clutched at her heavy bags of file folders, hard drives, and sketchbooks. "Yeah, he likes to be a bossy boss, Karen. I know how you feel." Annie made a move toward the door, but Karen quickly waved her hand to stop her again. The phone rang, but she muted the call with a smirk. She twirled a strand of hair in her fingers and smacked her gum noisily.

"So, I wanted to tell you, me and the girls are going to that new bar down by the waterfront after work. Down near Belmont? Anyways, I hear all the hotties are going there, and well, you know, after Tim, I, like, figured it would be good to go scope out the scene, ya know? We're going to get all dolled up and head over at eight for a light snack and window shopping."

"Tim? I thought you were dating . . ." Annie faltered. She couldn't remember the name, but she knew this Tim guy was new.

"Oh, you're thinking of Chris. Noooo, Tim was so boring. And Chris was one of those conspiracy-theory nuts. Kept talking about all sorts of nonsense. Blah. How totally annoying, ya know? I don't want to think about war and conspiracies and, like, ya know, be a total downer. Anyway . . ."

Annie eyed the exit with a renewed sense of purpose and gave Karen an apologetic look. "Uh, I really don't know. It sounds fun, and—"

"Oh sweetie, you just need some girl time!" Karen interrupted, and threw herself into another breathless monologue about how Annie needed to just get cleaned up and join a bunch of women on the hunt for drinks and men. She waved her manicured pink nails around with every verb for emphasis. "Really though, you clean up good. Just put on a cute dress and some heels, it's, like, one of those fancier places, but it's a good time, I hear. You just need a distraction, like, one of those tall, dark, and handsome distractions, with hopefully a limitless bank account and good fashion sense. But ya know, it's all eye candy . . ."

"Really Karen, I have a lot of work to do. I'm going home to work, but I'd be glad to take a rain check and join you for a girls' night out another time."

I'd rather slide down a razor blade into a pool of salt before I get dolled up and go to some meat market, Annie thought.

"Well I'm holding you to it. I figured, you know, that you'd want to start fishing for some new fish."

"Gotta go. Bye." Annie held on to her last shred of politeness and shuffled out the exit with her bags. As she was waiting for the elevator, she heard her phone ring, but couldn't reach it with her hands full. She knew by the ringtone that it was her mother.

Oh, man, I really need to call her. Annie felt guilty. Her mother was retired, and spent most of her days watching television and calling family to get the latest gossip. Even with a three-hour time-zone difference, her mother seemed to forget that Annie was often at work when she called. But Annie was not in the mood to talk to her mom. If she let it slip that she was having trouble at work, or even a hint of any kind of trouble, her mother would launch into an hour-long monologue about how she needs to change this, or do that, and Annie wouldn't be able to get a word in. Even though she was twenty-six, her mother refused to treat her as an adult.

As Annie pulled out of the parking garage and headed toward the highway for the long drive home, she heard the familiar ringtone again. She reached absently with her hand for the phone, but realized it was packed too deep into her workbag to find and safely extract at eighty miles per hour.

Mom, it will have to wait until I get home. Sorry. Aunt Mary probably got you upset over something stupid again.

Annie listened absently to the news, noting that it was nothing but doom and gloom as usual. The president was holding a meeting with congress about some sort of threat. *Always the same old bullshit. I swear everyone has been freaking out since 9/11. I'm so sick of the sensationalism.* Annie turned the news off and put on a Swedish death metal band. *Matching music for a matching mood,* she mused.

Annie was pleased that she did not run into any traffic on her way home. *Probably the one benefit to leaving the city before two o'clock.* She smiled. Even without traffic it often took her close to an hour to get home. She broke every speed law, and weaved around the slower cars. She might have a horrendous commute, but at least she didn't have to deal with the city full time. She was quite all right with the skyline being in the distance.

She exited the freeway and drove up the rutted and worn road of the tiny wooded community of Cascade Falls. Thorny blackberry bushes covered empty lots and choked abandoned cars. Most of the houses were in varying degrees of peeling paint, moss-covered roofs, and moldy front porches. But the rent was cheap, and the dead-end street Annie lived on was quiet and lined with blue spruce trees. It had an overgrown nature trail and park on one side. Earl's house was the only well-maintained house in the cul-de-sac. The house on the other side of Annie's was empty and had been on the market for a year.

Annie pulled into her driveway and put the car in park, resting her forehead against the steering wheel for a moment. She still felt hung over, and decided a nap might be the best thing for her nagging headache. Her head itched, and her stomach felt twisted and sick. It was new for her hangovers. She chalked it up to being overworked, and drinking too much whiskey the night before.

She got out of the car and stretched deeply, inhaling the rich, damp scent of firewood and Oregon pine trees. She heard a hoarse cough and looked over at the dilapidated playground in the park across the street. There were several large, lichen-covered play structures shaped like animals. An old homeless man was crouched in the mulch under a rusted whale statue, a large paper bag in one hand, and the other hand scratching at his bulbous nose. He coughed again and stared at her intently. Annie felt a tinge of unease and pity touch her heart, but she turned her back to the man and walked to her door.

She pulled her phone out and saw that her mother had called a third time. That was unusual. Annie scratched her itchy scalp and frowned. She tried to call home, but got an automated message that said, "I'm sorry, all circuits are currently busy right now. Please try your call again later."

"Weird," Annie muttered as she unlocked the door, shifting the weight of her bags to find the right key. She barely had the door open two feet when Tia launched herself out of the house. The dog's exuberant greeting knocked one of the bags out of Annie's hands, and she dropped the others to pick up the artwork before Tia's bouncing paws damaged them.

"Nice to see you, too," she said dryly as Tia licked her face.

As Annie walked into the hallway, Tia maintained the "welcome home dance," as she called it, with whining and jumping. Tia stayed two feet ahead of Annie, jumping up and down like a black kangaroo so she could see eye to eye with her owner.

"Yeah, yeah." Annie shuffled down the hallway, dropped the bags on the kitchen table, and opened the back door so Tia could go outside. Once Tia was back inside, Annie dragged herself over to the couch and collapsed on the soft cushions.

"I'm sorry, I owe you a hike still. Maybe later?" Tia came over, laid her large head on Annie's chest, and stared at her with expectant eyes. "Mommy's tired. I'm sorry, baby." She patted the velvety ears. Tia jumped up onto the couch and laid her head across Annie's lap. After a heavy sigh, and an audible dog fart, Tia was snoring contentedly.

"We are some classy ladies, eh?" Annie glanced at the whiskey bottle on the coffee table, and rested her hand on Tia's head. She was comforted by the dog's company, as strange and excitable as Tia was.

She closed her eyes and realized she had left the radio on in the kitchen that morning. She could still hear the music, but she was so tired she couldn't bring herself to get off the couch again to turn it off.

She caught herself silently thanking Matt for giving her another day on her deadlines, and started to drift off into a daydream about a date with Matt. She quickly dismissed the daydream as too silly, and started to think about the handsome soldier from her storyboards as she drifted off into a light sleep.

The emergency broadcast system buzzer cut through the quiet house with its high pitched, abrasive tone. It always chilled Annie to hear it, even though they were always just tests. The only times she had heard it in an emergency was when a tornado came dangerously close to her parent's house in Georgia.

"*We can't . . . We're trying to understand . . . Oh, God . . .*" The fear in the announcer's voice was unmistakable and chilling. Annie's eyes flew open. "*The Secretary of Defense was last seen in Washington . . . We do not know if he was in the attack.*" The feed kept cutting in and out. Annie sat up and startled Tia, who bounded off the couch. She scratched at her head and tried to clear the sleep and confusion from her mind.

"New York City has been hit. Reports of Houston as well. We have unconfirmed reports that Paris and London . . ."

"Hit by what!?" Annie screamed. Tia slunk away from the raised voice. Annie scrambled over to the cheap radio and started tugging at the antennae to get better reception.

"We do not know who has launched this attack. At this point in time, we do not know if the President got out of D.C. in time. Again, if you're just joining us . . ." The reporter paused, and Annie realized the reception wasn't the problem, the reporter was choking on sobs. She could barely speak without her voice cracking. *"We have had reports of multiple nuclear explosions all along the east coast and in Europe. We do not know who is behind these attacks. We ask that everyone remain calm."* The voice broke at the word, and continued after a moment. *"Please remain calm until we can get further information. Again, if you're just joining us, multiple nuclear explosions across the eastern seaboard. Confirmed reports of nuclear explosions in the vicinity of New York City, Washington, D.C., and Houston, Texas, with multiple unconfirmed reports—"*

Annie's legs collapsed underneath her. She started shaking uncontrollably.

"Mom!" Annie gasped, and crawled to the phone on the counter. Her hands shook so bad she could barely hold the phone, but she hit redial and waited.

"I'm sorry, all circuits are currently busy—" Annie threw the phone down with an angry cry. She whimpered for a moment, not sure what else to do. Her body didn't want to move. Tia curled up in a corner of the kitchen and cowered, fearing that Annie was mad at her.

"Oh, Tia . . . baby, come here!" Annie motioned for Tia. As the dog carefully approached, Annie grabbed her. She pulled her into a fierce hug and cried into her furry neck. Tia whined questioningly, but let Annie cry. The dog licked her face and nuzzled her hair.

Annie tried to call her mother several times. And her stepfather's cell phone. And her Aunt Mary. She tried to call her grandmother. All the lines seemed busy. Or jammed. Or something. She tried another number, and he answered on the first ring.

"Annie! Are you okay?"

"Matt! Oh my god!" was all she could say before her eyes filled with tears again.

"We just heard. The office is emptying out! Where are you? Are your parents okay?"

"I can't reach them. I can't reach anyone on the east coast." Annie paused. "Are you still at the office?"

"I'm leaving right now."

"Your parents?"

"I can't seem to reach anyone in Japan."

"Matt—"

"Annie, listen to me. You need to leave. Get far away from the city."

"But—"

"Multiple cities! Annie! Listen! Who is to say they won't hit the west coast? Get Tia and drive out to that cabin you always tell me about."

"Come with me!" Annie blurted without thinking. "You don't have time to get to your apartment and get out of the city. Just get here!"

Matt sounded panicked, and he talked fast. "Are you sure? Okay, I'll meet you at your cabin. You said it's outside of Elkhorn, right? I know where that is."

Annie started blurting out every detail she could think of. "Exit 142. Go through downtown. Its just one blinking red light. There is a logging road two rights past the big green barn with the misspelled sign for corn. Some idiot spelled it C-R-O-N. Follow it and keep taking lefts when the road branches. You'll see green signs that say 'tree farm' on them. Near the river."

She stopped for a minute and shook her head. "What the fuck are we doing? This is fucking crazy!"

"Pack some whiskey, Annie. I'll be there as fast as I can. I'm worried the roads are going to be really crazy getting out of Portland. Just get out to your cabin."

"I can wait for you, Matt." She paused, and her eyes watered again. "I'm scared!"

"It's okay, Annie. Just leave now. Don't spend more than five minutes getting belongings. Exit 142, two rights after the green barn with 'cron' on it. Don't worry, I'll find you!"

"Matt—"

"Hey, I'm your favorite, right? I'll see you in a few hours. Grab food and blankets." The line went dead. Annie tried to call her entire family again. Still no service.

Chapter Two:

Tunnel Vision

ANNIE FELT NUMB. She tucked her phone into her hoodie pocket without thinking. She took a few wobbly steps across the kitchen. She no longer heard the frantic radio announcer, or Tia whining at her hip. Her vision narrowed and it seemed to her that something was blocking her hearing.

I'm going into shock. She pushed her feet to move into the living room, and she stared blankly around.

"I have to be dreaming," she told Tia. She felt sick from her racing heart and lurching stomach. Tia sensed something was wrong and stayed within inches of Annie to lick her hand and rub against her leg like a giant cat.

After a moment of pure confusion, Annie pushed herself into fight-or-flight mode. She scrambled down into her basement and grabbed at the camping gear along the shelves. She stopped, and realized with a start she was grabbing at the items blindly. She forced herself to pause and take a deep breath despite her shaking hands and unsteady legs.

"Get a grip," she muttered to herself.

She reached for the largest backpack she owned, a monstrous pack meant for several days and nights of hiking. She grabbed at the most important items she could think of: Her solar-powered USB charger for her phone. Rechargeable batteries and their charger, which plugged into the solar panel. Next she grabbed a water bottle with a specialized filter for streams and lakes. Her first-aid kit. An LED flashlight. Her spare headphones. Fortunately all her camping gear was stored in one place.

"Do I grab my fishing gear?" she asked Tia in a shaky tone. "We could be camping for a while. Might get hungry . . ." She left the hiking bag for further consideration, and ran to her car with the fishing pole, fishing pack, and a large sleeping bag, tossing them in the trunk. She ran back inside, with Tia at her heels.

"Shit! I need to pack dog food!" Annie opened a storage closet, pulled the nearly full bag of dog chow out and hefted it over her shoulders. She felt lucky to have purchased the thirty-pound bag of food just a few days ago. She realized she'd lost all sense of time, even though she'd told Matt she would be gone in five minutes. Had it been minutes ago that they talked? It felt like hours.

As Annie tossed the bag of dog food in her trunk, she kept making note of everything she needed. Somewhere down the street she heard a woman's voice wailing. The gut-wrenching sound chilled her.

"I knew you had brains! Gettin' the hell outta dodge is the smartest thing anyone can do."

Annie whirled and saw that her neighbor Ben was loading up his pickup truck as well. She noted that his truck bed was perfectly organized with coolers, tents, propane tanks, sleeping bags, and many canvas military bags bulging with various items. There were several cases of beer. He made escaping the end of the world look easy.

"Where you headed?"

Ben didn't stop moving. "Dunno! Game plan so far is get to the Idaho border. Maybe head north after that. Find some water and set up shop."

"I'm heading to Elkhorn with my friend." Annie hesitated, and then blurted out, "You can come with us! My cabin is a piece of shit, but there's fresh water and fishing. My ex Patrick put a solar panel on it six months back."

"Elkhorn?" Ben paused and scratched his head. "Annie are you fucking crazy? If they hit Portland there's a good chance Elkhorn will get fallout. Best bet is to go northeast, not east."

Annie's stomach did a few violent twists at the thought. "I'm meeting a friend. I don't know if I can get ahold of him again. Phones are being weird. I need to be at that cabin."

"Come back in a few moments. I'll have something for you," Ben called out as Annie ran into her house for more items.

Annie made two more trips with garbage bags of food. She had opened the pantry and threw everything she could into them. She put a box of her grandmother's hand-stitched quilts and a handful of photo albums into her car. She knew she was taking too long to leave, but she was convinced that she might not be coming back, and wanted to take as much as she could.

She grabbed a duffel bag and unceremoniously threw all the clothes on her closet floor into it. As she packed it full, she picked up a man's extra-large hoodie and frowned.

"Maybe Matt won't mind wearing Patrick's clothes. He might not have any spare clothes in his car." Pleased with herself to remember this sort of detail in the midst of her panic, she threw a few extra items into the duffel bag: extra-large workout shirts and baggy clothes that Matt's thin frame might fit into.

She lugged the bag to her car, and repeated the phrase, "This is fucking crazy," over and over again. She told Ben as much when he ran over to her.

"It was bound to happen, Annie. Those damned ragheads hate us."

She winced at the ugly words as Ben held his hand out and offered her a small packet of white pills.

"Here. I don't have many to spare. But if you insist on staying in Elkhorn, and there's a nuke, take these. Try to get more if you can."

Annie took the packet of pills and frowned. "What are these?"

"Potassium iodide," Ben said proudly. "It's for radiation sickness. Read the label. Don't take it unless Portland gets hit."

She swallowed her fear and put the pills in the car. How long would fourteen pills last for two people? "How sure are you Portland is going to get hit?"

"Pretty sure. There's some storage facilities there."

Annie paled, "Storage—?"

"Keep moving!" Ben barked. "I'm about to head out. We can caravan out of here for at least a hundred or so miles. If you hurry."

Suddenly feeling more frightened, and very alone, Annie lunged toward the house. "Wait for me! I need to grab one more bag!"

She grabbed her hiking pack and realized she could fit more items into it. She tossed in her glasses, her entire supply of contact lenses, tampons, a few toiletries, and some granola bars. She noted the bag still had dirty clothes in it from her last camping trip, but did not bother to remove them.

She emptied her carton of cigarettes into her bag and gave a wild laugh. "Ha, smoking *isn't* going to kill me after all." She counted five packs remaining. She wanted to smoke them all right then and there. And then take multiple shots of whiskey. And smoke more. *Fuck the end of the world,* she thought bitterly, *is this even worth it?*

17

She looked over the shelves once more. Annie grabbed a can of pepper spray from the camping shelf. She thought of Ben, and other strange men that could be out there, and prayed that the world wasn't going to go to hell. She had seen enough horror movies. As an afterthought, she grabbed a tennis ball from the floor and put it into the bag for Tia.

She gave herself a few brief seconds to look around the house. The radio had fallen eerily silent. She gazed at the picture frames of friends and family watching her from the walls. She winced when she saw the fish tank, and dumped extra food in.

"I'm sorry," she told them. They were only goldfish, but it still hurt to leave anyone behind.

As she gave the living room one final look, she eyed the whiskey on the coffee table and tossed it into the pack. She clumsily pulled the pack on and snapped the shoulder restraint closed to help her carry the bag. It was heavy, but not unbearable.

As she ran outside, Ben was waiting impatiently by his truck for her, his own hiking bag slung over his shoulder.

"I'm sorry, Annie," he said. When she gave him a questioning look, he frowned. "About Atlanta. You . . . you heard, right?" Suddenly he looked down, his eyebrows pinched together. He muttered something under his breath and scratched at his scalp.

She shook her head, her entire body shaking violently. She knew what he was going to say. She couldn't focus on that right now. She could only think of leaving. Escape. *Escape.* Shock was a funny thing. The world slowed down, and details got lost in the chaos. And yet other things Annie had long forgotten about bubbled up from her subconscious. Something in her brain seemed to be breaking.

Thoughts boiled over one another like competing notes in a symphony. Home. Family. Escape. Somehow, she had already guessed Atlanta was gone. There were military bases there. Her vision started to flicker and shimmer as her heart raced uncontrollably.

"Do you have a gun?" Ben asked her. Apparently he had been talking for some time.

She gave him a blank look. Her lips felt numb. Her nose was tingling.

"A gun, Annie. You need a gun." He waved his arms impatiently. "This is world war three! You need to protect yourself!"

She stood there, everything in her vision narrowing into a small tube. She fought to stand. She steadied herself by latching onto the pickup truck. Her legs were starting to feel numb. If she wasn't careful, she was liable to piss her pants. Tia was frantic from Annie's panicked energy, and ran between the two houses barking constantly.

"Don't worry! It's your lucky day. Bet you're glad you rented a house next to a survivalist." He pulled a gigantic duffel bag out of his truck. By the way he leaned into the weight, and the metallic sound, she guessed the bag was full of guns. It was nearly as large as Ben himself. She tried hard to fix her eyes on the bag and listen to Ben's harsh voice. He sounded far away, as if someone had placed their hands over her ears.

"I have a Glock I can give you, and a box of ammo, but that is all I can spare. It's enough to keep a few assholes away." He talked quickly, poking through the gun bag.

"I don't know what to . . . what to say," she managed to croak, still trying to get her eyes to focus.

"You've always been a good neighbor. And you remind me of my niece. She was a bat-shit crazy tomboy as well. Listen, we need to leave. We need to escape right now."

"Escape . . . ." Awareness suddenly flooded into Annie. Her face was completely numb, but sight and sound rushed back and she became acutely aware of the squirrel chittering in her oak tree. She heard the zipper on the duffel bag. The blue jay squawking on her roof. The wind rattling the new growth on the trees around them. And an odd humming sound, so far away her hearing barely registered it.

Her entire life flashed before her eyes. Intuition took over. She turned from Ben, her entire body bursting with energy and panic.

She started screaming, "Tia! *Tia!*"

She ran toward Tia and stretched her hand out to grab at her collar as a sudden flash of light erased all color in the world. Her hand stretched out before her, mere inches from Tia, seemed to disappear into a world filled with white. As her eyes felt like they were melting from the intense flash, she heard Ben scream and Tia shriek. And then she heard a roar that destroyed the world.

Chapter Three:

Ashes

THE WORLD KEPT flashing beyond Annie's tightly shut eyelids. Her mouth tasted like ashes and blood. Everything hurt.

Annie tried to move but her body seemed to have melted into the ground. It was all dead weight. Her mouth felt so swollen and dry she feared she was choking to death. She tried to swallow, but it hurt too much. Her head screamed in pain. The numbness her body had experienced when she saw the light had been replaced with a heavy feeling. Her blood might as well have been lead. Her wrist was burning as well, as if her silver bracelet had caught fire.

Flash flash flash.

That light, Annie thought weakly. Had she dreamed of falling through a white void with Tia? She opened her eyes. The world was awash with white and brilliant flickering rainbows. It made no sense, but it was beautiful.

She tried to sit up, and realized her camping pack was still hooked on her shoulders. She felt weak and exhausted. She forced herself up on one arm and looked in wonder at the world. Iridescent light flickered around her and bounced off the glass walls.

Glass? She rubbed her eyes and focused more clearly. The walls close around her were not glass. She gingerly reached out, almost scared to touch it. The light bounced from wall to wall, creating a vibrant display of hues around her.

Crystal? She stared closer, not believing her eyes. She ran her fingers along the cold, smooth surface. She had never seen crystal like this before. There were no cracks or scars along the surface. She numbly shook her head and looked around. She was in some sort of small box made of crystal.

What the fuck? She turned around, wondering if she was insane. Or dreaming. Or dead.

The flood of thoughts and emotions overwhelmed her. She turned to one side and dry heaved for several moments. Her stomach had been empty since her early morning bagel. She took several deep breaths, trying to focus. She felt a breeze on her right cheek and turned toward it. She had missed it at first glance, but now she saw it—a small hole in one glimmering wall.

She peered through the opening and saw green grass, dirt, and fallen leaves. She cautiously scrambled through the hole, and welcomed the cool breeze on her face. Before her, a beautiful forest rose up on all sides. The natural colors seemed incredibly bright and almost too vivid. She rose to one knee and looked behind her.

A giant crystal rose out of the ground. The trees swaying above cast dancing shadows and sunlight along the crystal's surface, which caused the flashing inside. From the outside it looked like a cone-shaped igloo.

Annie took a few steps back, and had to remind herself to breathe. The air smelled different. The birdsong around her was alien. Even the trees around her did not appear familiar. It seemed to be an ancient forest. It reminded Annie of her trips to the redwoods in northern California.

The trees appeared to be some kind of oak, but with towering canopies and trunks as wide as her living room. The ground was bare, and she could make out sharply sloped rocky cliffs to one side. It seemed that she was on a steep hill or mountain, but she couldn't trust her senses.

She took a few steps toward the rocky hill. There appeared to be more sunlight in that direction, and she wagered that she could get a better view of her surroundings from there. Small lights, like fireflies, danced among the leaves.

Strange. She had never seen red or blue fireflies. But there they were, in every color and the size of large bees, a dozen feet above her head.

She stopped and took another deep breath. It was the most beautiful place she had ever seen. The air was sweet and pure. Even the strange bird songs were lovely. There was an overwhelming sense of peace and tranquility that radiated in the forest.

"I'm dead," she said suddenly. "I'm dead and I'm in . . . heaven . . .?"

She had never believed in the concept of heaven. She reached out to a dancing blue firefly, but it zipped away from her hand with a sharp whirring sound like a hummingbird. The trees sighed with a fresh breeze; their leaves stirred and created dappled sunlight on the forest floor. A purple leaf floated down and lodged itself in her wild hair.

If I'm in heaven . . . She winced.

At that point, her brain seemed to break. Nothing made sense. Everything she knew was gone. Her parents were dead. Her friends. Her coworkers. Her dog. Even the flirty liquor storeowner. She had seen the flash. Heard the roar that drowned out their screams. Felt the heat.

I'm not dreaming. I'm dead.

Annie took a step but her shaky legs refused to hold her weight. She fell to the forest floor and ground the dirt in her hands angrily. She choked on a sob as she remembered Matt.

"You'll always be my favorite."

"I'll wait for you."

She gritted her teeth, tears blinding her.

"I didn't call my mom. I didn't–" She broke into violent sobs, her jagged breathing shaking her body. "Mom... No. Please..."

She convulsed and started wailing. "If I'm dead and in heaven, where are you? Aren't you dead, too? Mom? *Mom!*" Annie was twenty-six years old, but wanted to run into her mother's arms. She wanted to be held and reassured like a frightened child.

The thought made her scream again. Annie's anguished cries echoed across the woods. It reminded her of being in a canyon, the way the sound bounced back. It made her feel incredibly alone. She sobbed again, and helplessly punched the ground.

"If I'm dead, why does this hurt so much?" she asked the trees around her. "Why does heaven hurt so much?"

The trees did not reply. She glared at them angrily, and suddenly realized the forest had gone silent. The fireflies were gone. The birds were hushed.

Annie heard a branch crack behind her and frowned. She turned her head slowly to see two shapes approach beyond the clearing. She wiped the tears from her eyes. It was a man and a dog that could have passed for a Great Dane.

While he looked human, all the alarm bells in Annie's head went into a frenzy. Every instinct in her body urged her to run. Something was very wrong with the way they walked.

She stood on wobbly legs. "Who's out there? Ben?"

A hiss was the only response. It reminded her of the sound soda bottles make when opened, but the hiss lasted much longer. The hair on the back of her neck and arms prickled. The forest was completely silent except for the twigs breaking underneath the approaching feet.

She became aware of several sets of feet walking and shuffling through the forest now, and saw several more figures walking through the undergrowth. They did not seem to mind walking into branches, they just broke them as they made a straight line toward her.

The closest person entered the clearing with his hound, and Annie felt her body seize in cold panic. The skin had rotted on both man and dog, and hung in tattered pale green sheets. Something black dribbled from their mouths.

Hisssss.

Annie took several shaky steps backwards. She screamed and broke into a run. She looked around wildly, and spotted the rocky slope to her right. She was a horrible climber, but an even worse runner.

The undergrowth cut her face and clawed at her hair. She tried to shield her eyes with her arms but was more concerned with getting her legs to work. An ugly gurgling noise erupted behind her, and she realized that they could run too.

Goddamned fucking zombies! Monsters?! What the fuck! It was all her brain could scream as she ran. *I'm dead. I'm dead and in hell! I'm in fucking hell! Well that makes more sense than heaven . . .*

She was closer to the rock wall. She judged by the sounds of the forest cracking and breaking behind her that several *things* were chasing her.

If I'm already dead, why am I running? she asked herself. *I'm already dead, so I can't die again, right?* She didn't know what was going on, but she didn't stop running.

She found the rocky wall was made from hundreds of boulders that varied in size. Some were the size of her car. She lunged at the first rock and wildly kicked her feet to find a foothold. She pushed herself up to another rock, cursing the heavy bag on her back. She climbed several boulders before she allowed herself to look back.

The monsters were scrambling at the first boulder. For a brief moment, Annie was relieved to see that the monsters were as clumsy and helpless as TV zombies.

Then they started climbing.

They were slow, but they could grab at the rocks the same as her, and step on one another to get to the top of the first boulder.

Annie climbed up several more boulders before she realized there was a wall in front of her. She jumped at it and clawed at the rock, trying to find purchase. Each time she slid back to the top boulder.

Hissssss.

Annie tried to climb the wall several times, but each attempt became more painful and bloody as her some of her fingernails cracked and broke, and the jagged surface cut her hands. She shrieked at the pain and turned to look down at her pursuers.

They were only to the second boulder, and still had ten more feet to climb. Annie looked around for a branch or something to swing. There were several large rocks around her. She threw one as hard as she could, but it was not enough to knock the creatures back.

She hastily took her bag off and looked through all the useless contents before finding the can of pepper spray. She had always carried it for camping, but had never used it.

She leaned over her rock and found the closest creature three feet below her. It hissed in delight as it caught sight of her, and black drool oozed from its mouth. Its teeth were extremely long and sharp.

This zombie has never been a human, Annie thought with alarm.

She pointed the can at the creature's face and pressed down on the trigger. The reddish spray was a direct hit in its eyes, mouth, and what remained of its nasal cavity. It hissed in reply and kept scrambling toward her.

She cursed and scooted backward. She screamed again, and went back to throwing rocks uselessly at the monsters.

"Someone help me! Please!"

The strange zombies grew agitated at the sound of her voice, and Annie let the next cry for help fall out of her lips in a small whimper.

"Please ... someone."

The monsters seemed stuck, however, and could not climb up the last boulder. It was too high; Annie had needed to kick at surrounding rocks to make the last scramble.

They clawed at her rock, just out of reach. They could not climb over one another, since the rock they stood on was far too small for more than one monster. Instead they took turns knocking one another off the rock, hissing only at her. They seemed unaware they were knocking away their fellow monsters.

Fucking great. I'm dead and I'm going to die again. Welcome to hell, I guess!

Still gripping the pepper spray in one hand, Annie pulled her cigarette pack out of her pocket. Her fingers were shaking so horribly that she could barely take a cigarette out. Her hands convulsed with fear as she tried to work the lighter.

If you fuckers are going to kill me, I think I'm just going to sit here and smoke. She looked around. She could tell that it would take them a long time to get to her rock. *Maybe they'll never be able to reach me.*

"Fuck. You," she spit over the side of her rock at the hissing mob, and then leaned back to stare helplessly at the sky.

A terrible screech split the air. It sounded like the brakes on a train, with that terrible metal-grinding-on-metal noise. A second blast of sound split the air. Annie dropped her cigarette and cupped her hands over her ears. She timidly looked over the rock at the scene below. She saw two of the monsters writhing in black puddles on the ground, their mouths open and making that horrible noise. Even worse, an armored figure was standing behind the pile of climbing monsters.

A sword split the neck of the monsters on the ground and the shrieking stopped. But the armored figure was not finished. It plunged the long sword into the closest monster, creating another scream that filled the world. A second stroke and the zombie was silent. By this time, the monsters were paying more attention to the armored person than Annie.

Whatever this newcomer was, he was good with his sword. He danced out of reach, and then sprang close at the last second to slice the head off the nearest monster. His second swing took out the humanoid zombie and its canine companion. They did not even have time to shriek.

Annie felt shock coming back to remove her senses. She took several deep breaths and tried to focus on the armored figure. He looked like one of her knights that she had drawn. The armor was black and twisted down his shoulders. His sword hand was moving too fast for her to register any details about the blade. Within moments the knight had made quick work of several humanoid zombies and two doglike monsters.

He stood over the bodies and poked at them tentatively with the tip of his sword. Annie leaned farther over the rock to get a better look.

He whipped around and stared up at her, his hard yellow eyes burning in the open visor. She gasped and moved back a few inches.

She meekly raised a hand and managed to say, "Uh, hi . . . !"

The knight at once started climbing, his yellow eyes narrowed.

"Oh fuck! Come on!" she screamed at the world around her. She scooted back from the edge of the rock as an armored hand reached over the side. In panic, she grabbed her backpack and put it between her legs, trying to use it for a shield.

The top half of the knight was now visible, his sword in his left hand. His armored right hand grabbed at one of Annie's legs and she screamed and kicked frantically. She swung her right foot as hard as she could and knocked the sword away.

She squealed in pain and grabbed her injured foot. *Man that was like kicking a wall!*

Just as Annie picked up the can of pepper spray, the knight grabbed hold of her other foot and yanked. Her body dragged the backpack with her as she flew off the rock. Annie instinctively dropped the pepper spray and grabbed onto the knight's tattered cloak as she fell past him. He lost his balance and fell backward with her. She felt their bodies collide once as they tumbled, the hard armor crushing her left shoulder.

She tumbled roughly to the ground among the dead monsters, her bag cushioning her fall. A moment later the armored hands were at her neck, squeezing the breath out of her. She could only see the man's strange yellow eyes, and they were fixed on Annie with a deadly intensity.

Those eyes have so much hate! she thought with alarm. She kicked her legs, but he was far too heavy. Her hands tore at the helmet and tried to grab his neck, but the armor prevented injury. She punched helplessly at the breastplate with bloody fists, but he only squeezed tighter.

She tried to curse and scream but nothing could come out. *I . . . can't die . . . I need air!*

Annie's flailing hands found the pepper spray that had fallen with her. She wrapped her trembling fingers around the small can and felt for the trigger. She shoved the can against the visor's narrow eye slit and squeezed.

His hands released her throat and reached up for his helmet, clawing at the metal. Annie gasped wildly as air flooded back into her lungs in a cold rush.

The knight howled in pain. He stumbled away from Annie and tore the helmet from his head. Blond hair spilled out in a sweaty tangle. His left cheek and neck were covered in ugly scars.

The man staggered blindly, and his foot caught the edge of a rock. He fell forward onto one knee. He clumsily stood again, all the while rubbing furiously at his face with armored hands.

"What kind of spell is this?" he demanded, still unable to open his eyes. Annie scooted backward and looked around. The knight tried to reach for her, but cried out every time he tried to open his eyes. Annie ran to the nearest tree and hid behind the massive trunk. It could have easily hidden her car.

"Who are you?" she shouted.

"What are you?" was his anguished reply. "What did you do to me?"

She peeked around the trunk and watched him flail around among the monsters' corpses. It was a grotesque sight. A pale green hand covered in black blood crunched under the stumbling knight's armored boot. He pulled his gauntlets off and rubbed furiously at his eyes. Annie looked around at the forest. It was no longer the lovely place she had imagined just moments ago. The woods were growing dark.

The sun must be setting soon, she realized. *I could run. But where?* Her eyes darted from tree to tree. And then in the far distance she saw another monster, shuffling between tree trunks.

Oh fuck oh fuck . . . Okay . . . Can I even fight one of those? What happens when it gets dark?

"I know you are still there!" the knight raged, his hands firmly clasping his eyes.

"Who are you? What are these zombie things? And why the fuck did you come at me with a sword? I didn't do anything to you!"

"Trickery will not work!" The knight had followed her voice, and moved toward the tree Annie was hiding behind. She darted further away, relieved to see that the pepper spray's effects had blinded him. He stumbled after her and paused, listening.

"You attacked *me*! I won't hurt you!" Annie watched him from a safe distance, but glanced over her shoulder toward the distant figure in the woods. Then she eyed her backpack with dismay. The knight was standing too close to it for her to safely grab it.

"You say you will not hurt me?" The knight sneered. "What business do you have in these woods?

"I . . . I, uh . . ." Annie pulled at her hair. "Look, I really don't know! One minute I was packing my car, and the next minute there was a bunch of white light, and then I'm here! And there are fucking zombies everywhere and assholes with swords!"

"You make no sense!"

"*This* makes no sense!"

 What are you? A spirit?"

"What? No! I'm a woman! I think . . ." *Should I tell him I think I'm dead? Would that just make this situation worse? What the hell is going on? Is being dead supposed to be this confusing?*

The knight barked a laugh. "You *think*? You expect me to believe you just fell out of the sky? And you say you are a woman? Then why do you wear a sigil of death?"

"Huh?" Annie frowned. She looked down at her hooded sweatshirt and saw the skulls and ravens on it, and couldn't help but laugh.

"Oh my fucking god. Are you seriously kidding me? This is just an old hoodie. It doesn't mean anything!"

"You wear death on strange clothes and you have a foul tongue. I will not believe you a lady."

You're not the first to say that, actually. "I'm not lying! I really don't know how I got here, and what those *things* in the woods are. All I know is I'm trapped between a douchebag with a sword and a pack of monsters out in the woods. I think my best option is to climb back up on that fucking rock and stay the fuck away from everything!"

Annie peeked around the tree trunk and held up her bloody hands. "Do spirits bleed? Do they feel pain?"

The knight opened his eyes with an effort, walked to a rock, and sat down with his face in his hands. "Well, you do not seem smart enough to kill me. You missed your chance after you cast this curse on me."

"Thanks for the compliment, asshole." Annie edged around one side of the tree trunk to get a better look at him. The weird armored man looked familiar.

"You are strange. But I think you are the sign I was looking for."

"What do you mean?"

The knight didn't answer and rubbed at his eyes. "Remove this curse at once."

"It's not a—" Annie stopped. *I could pretend its some sort of curse. Maybe that could make me enough of a threat that he won't just attack me again. Or he could stab me in the back and kill me. Either way, I don't think I can fight this guy. Or those monsters.*

"It's not a curse. It's just pepper spray."

He groaned. "This pepper spray is horrible."

"Look dude, I don't know what's going on. I promise I won't hurt you. I pepper-sprayed you because you dragged me off a fucking cliff and tried to *choke* me. I don't know where I am . . . but I won't last two seconds out there in these fucked-up woods." She looked around in exasperation. "I just want to go home. But I don't know how to get there. I think I should stay here. Please—just leave me alone!"

The knight looked up in surprise and tried to peer at her with swollen eyes. "That would be unwise. It is not safe here."

Yeah, no shit, Sherlock. "Look, just don't try to hurt me again! Go away! Kill some monsters for me on your way out."

The knight laughed. "Well, I cannot do anything with this pepper-spray curse. Remove it at once."

"Do you have water?" Annie asked, daring to step closer.

"Is it that simple?" He laughed again. "I left my water skin at camp. I heard the plagarne making a fuss, and you screaming, and came over to investigate."

"Plagarne?"

"'Plagued ones' in the Shafani's ancient tongue."

Annie choked. "Wait, what?"

He gave her a hard look. "You are truly slow witted."

"I . . . I just, have heard the word Shafani before."

"Well, I would think so." The knight stood again. "Shafan is the largest kingdom on Tahldia."

Annie felt the tunnel-vision sensation flood back, and the shock numbed her senses. She placed a hand against her forehead and tried to steady herself.

"You're fucking with me, right?"

The knight looked offended. "Why would I jest?"

"Because there is no such thing as Tahldia. I made it up. For a stupid video game."

The knight gave her a suspicious glare. "You are mad. Absolutely mad."

"No, it all makes sense. I die, and I go to my heaven, right? I go to the place I made up in my mind that makes me the happiest. That's a heaven, right? And I loved drawing Tahldia." Annie heard wild laughter escape her lips. "I'm dead! And I'm in my dream world! I obviously am not using my imagination hard enough, or otherwise I could probably find my mom." She took a step toward the knight, suddenly fearless of him.

The man grabbed the hilt of his sword, and Annie stopped.

He said, "You are as mad as anything I have ever seen. You make no sense."

Annie stared at him as if for the first time. The sword. The yellow eyes. The peculiar armor she had seen hundreds of times before.

Fucking hell. I have drawn him.

Her heart seemed to start skipping beats, and she felt the world close in tightly around her. It felt as if a heavy soundproof curtain rolled over her, and she couldn't fight it any longer.

Annie fainted.

Chapter Four:

Hakayatas

ANNIE ONCE AGAIN woke to a world of pain and flashing light. Her left shoulder screamed in agony as she tried to move. Orange light danced in front of her as she tried to open her eyes and focus. She heard the soft crinkling sounds and smelled the nostalgic aroma of . . .

Campfire? Annie grunted and tried to move, but her body refused.

"What . . . where . . ."

"You were out. I could not rouse you," came the knight's gruff voice.

Annie tried to turn to the sound, but she still could not move. She became dimly aware that her hands were tied behind her back. Her legs and feet were also bound. She struggled for a moment, and realized she was trapped.

Great. This is just fucking great.

She opened her eyes fully and let them adjust to the firelight. Her contact lenses felt gritty, and her neck was sore. Her throat ached when she tried to swallow.

They were beneath the same massive oak trees that she had seen earlier. The forest was alive with the sounds of frogs and crickets, and a few strange noises she had never heard. Some reminded her of a squeaky swing set.

Other noises sounded like the delicate notes of a wind chime.

The tall man was sitting on the other side of the campfire. His sharp face was washed with the deep red and yellow colors of the firelight. He rested his hands on his knees and watched her carefully.

"Why am I tied up?" Annie asked weakly.

"Hmm, it was either your insane ramblings, or that pepper-spray curse. Hard to guess which seemed more of a threat while I tried to get some sleep."

"I see they have sarcasm on this planet, too."

"I almost wonder if you speak true," the man mused. "You have a very odd assortment of items in your bag. None of which I have ever seen before."

"Hey, where's my stuff?" she said with sudden panic.

He gestured beyond the fire. "It is here. I have not stolen from you. I wanted to know what you carry through these woods." His eyes glowed as he stared at the fire. His face was puffy and red, and very tired.

"These woods are not meant for most people. There is much magic here. And to find a helpless woman here alive? I thought you were a spirit trying to trick me. They have taken on human forms in front of me before."

Annie struggled to get more comfortable. Her left shoulder still hurt from the fall. She did not think anything was broken, but she wanted to stretch her left arm and massage it.

"Can you untie me?"

"No."

"I think my shoulder is pretty messed up. You kind of fell on me earlier. In your armor. It felt *great*."

"I will consider it. I still think you are insane."

"Maybe I am," Annie said after a moment. "The last thing I saw was a nuke. I should have died. I think I died. The flash seemed to erase the entire world."

"Nuke? What is that?"

"It's a giant bomb that you drop from the sky. It explodes. It can destroy everything. Kill everyone around for miles and leaves a poison that kills many more. It . . . erases cities."

"That is evil."

"Yeah. It is." Annie felt acutely aware of the soil pressed against her cheek. She stared at the firelight and felt her eyes burn with fresh tears. "I think my parents are dead. I think everyone I know is dead."

She started crying. "I had a dog, too. She was my life in so many ways. I was running toward her. She was the last thing I saw." She let the tears flow.

The knight stared at her suspiciously for a long while. "Is this why you wear a sigil of death?"

"Oh please, not *that* again. It's just a hoodie. With a silly design on it. It's not meant to be anything."

"What are you called?"

Annie laughed at the ridiculous question. "Oh, I'm called lots of things. Most people call me Annie."

He looked thoughtful for a moment. "Strange. What does 'Annie' mean?"

"I dunno."

The knight looked incredulous. "All names must have meaning."

"I think it means 'grace.' Or 'graceful.'"

"You are not very graceful."

"Thanks."

The knight poked at the fire, but kept his glare fixed on her. His chiseled face was covered in blond stubble and was very striking, except for a thick white scar that raced through his whiskers. His greasy hair was pulled back over his shoulders by a leather cord. Annie could see the tip of an even uglier scar snaking its way out of the armor at his neck. *He would be handsome if he wasn't covered in scars and such an asshole.*

She returned the glare. "Well?"

"Well, what?"

"Aren't you going to tell me your name? Doesn't a prisoner get that courtesy?"

"You are not a prisoner."

"Oh ho! You could have fooled me!"

"Hakayatas."

"Huh?"

"I am called Hakayatas."

"Hack-a-yah-tas." She spoke the word slowly.

"Hak. If it is easier for you to say."

"Is that another compliment to my intelligence, Hak?"

He growled, "That is what some call me," and stood. He began to remove his armor, and place it carefully on his side of the campfire.

Annie felt a tinge of fear squeeze her chest. *What if this guy is a freak? What if he hurts me?*

Hak finished removing his armor and unrolled a thin leather blanket. He had a simple tunic on, and brown breeches that appeared to have been made with rough cloth. Annie watched him carefully.

"Are you going to untie me?"

"No."

"Why the fuck not?"

"Silence. Tomorrow will be a long day."

"Oh, *fuck you.* I'm tied up and my arms are killing me. How am I supposed to sleep? Untie me."

"You do not make demands of me."

"Untie me or you won't sleep a wink tonight. You don't want to hear me sing. It's the best torture, I can assure you."

"Or I can gag you and leave you in the woods for the plagarne to eat."

"Or, you can leave me tied up right here by the fire. Okay, got it, I'll shut up."

Hak gave her one more angry glare and laid down on his blanket, keeping one hand on his unsheathed sword.

Annie sighed. *Nothing makes sense. The only thing that makes sense is I'm dead. But how am I here in this world that I made up? There is no way I survived that bomb.*

Annie's eyes shimmered with tears again. She felt them roll silently down her cheeks to the hard dirt. She wanted nothing more than to wake up in her messy room with her giant dog hogging her bed. She wanted to bury her face in Tia's black fur and cry. She had never felt so alone.

Annie woke the next morning to the sound of metal rattling. She opened a gritty eye and saw that Hak was suiting up in his armor. She struggled against her bonds, glaring at him.

"Do you wear that all the time, or just to superhero parties?"

"We are in a dangerous forest. Would you prefer I walk naked?"

Annie opened her mouth for a sharp retort, and then paused. She decided sarcasm would not be a good idea today. She needed to try another tactic. Her entire body was frozen with agony, and she had to get the ropes off her wrists.

"Hey, so, now that it's daylight, do you think you could untie me?"

Hak eyed her warily. "I think it would be best if you remain as little of a threat as possible."

"Dude, I've got to pee."

He simply stared at her.

"Seriously, please. I'm amazed I haven't pissed myself yet."

He moved to untie her hands. "Do not try to trick me or escape."

As the rope fell away from her wrists, Annie cried out as she finally moved her sore arms. She rubbed at the raw blisters on her hands as Hak roughly tugged down the rope on her legs. She winced at several broken, blood-crusted fingernails.

"Thanks."

Hak just stared at her.

Annie reached for her bag, but he held up a hand to stop her. "No, the bag stays here, lest you try and escape. I imagine you would not leave without this. Am I correct?"

"Leave? Where the hell am I supposed to go?"

Hak looked uncertain. "Well, I imagine you would not go willingly with me."

"To where? Seriously, where am I supposed to go? I don't know where I am, and I don't want to go wander around in the forest and become zombie food."

Hak stood by silently as Annie walked behind a giant tree trunk and dropped her jeans. She was filthy. And hungry. Her neck was bruised and aching. Her left wrist was burned and blistered.

My fainting spell might be connected to my crappy eating habits. I've been forgetting to eat regular meals the last few months.

After she finished her business, she tried to brush the dirt and grass from her hair and sweater. Falling from the cliff and rolling around on the forest floor had left her feeling like a ball of dirt. She walked around the side of the tree while picking helplessly at her tangled hair.

Hak didn't move as she approached. Annie walked up to him and stared at him closely.

He was incredibly tall—about two heads taller than Annie. His dark armor was mismatched, dented, scratched, and very dirty. His rough cloth pants were caked with filth and had a homemade appearance. He looked as if he had been living in the woods.

Even though Hak wore full armor Annie could see that he was lean, almost skinny. He was perhaps a few years older than her, but his beautiful yellow eyes looked ancient. The color of his long hair matched his eyes. His face was attractive even with the long white scar along his left cheek. She followed the line down to his neck, where the ugly scar grew and branched out from his armor in several places.

It's as if he has been mauled by a giant animal . . . or several swords, she thought. *How could he have such horrible scars and still be alive?*

As if sensing her unease, Hak held out a large leather pouch. She took it and looked at him questioningly.

"Water."

She gingerly fumbled with the tip. Hak sighed in irritation and showed her how to open the top. She drank greedily for a few moments, and then exhaled with relief. He watched her carefully.

Annie pointed to her hiking pack. "May I grab something out of there? Or are you going to bite me?"

He eyed her suspiciously, "What are you getting?"

"Food!" she hissed in exasperation. She knelt down and dug out two granola bars and began eating ravenously. She devoured the first two within seconds, and decided that a third would be a good idea. After a few bites, she hesitated for a moment, and offered the bar to Hak.

"Would you like a bite?"

"Is this a trick?

"This is a peace offering."

He hesitated. "No."

"It has oats, nuts, dried cherries, and chocolate." Annie's eyes grew wide in alarm. "Oh, please tell me you people have chocolate on this weird fucking planet."

Hak couldn't help but smile. "Ah, yes. It is a very sweet candy. Only for the rich, however. It is a rare delicacy."

"Well you don't have to be rich where I come from to have all the chocolate you want." She waved the granola bar at him again. "It's gooooood."

"Your people must be very fat, if anyone can buy as much chocolate as they want."

Annie laughed. "Yes, there are a lot of fat people where I live."

She waved her bar at him again. Hak took the granola bar and inspected it from every angle. He played with the plastic wrapper and took a long, hard look at the images printed on it. He took a small bite and chewed, as if it could be poisonous. After a few moments, he smiled. It was the first real smile she had seen, and he began taking larger bites.

She smiled with satisfaction. "Told you." The knight was far from harmless, and still frightened her. Yet she knew gaining some level of trust must be achieved if she were to survive for any length of time. And the monsters out in the woods frightened her more than this man.

Annie waved a hand dismissively. "Keep the rest. It's my peace offering."

"I was thinking about what you said." Hak gave her an odd look. "I think we should travel to a place where I can find some answers."

Annie looked up at him eagerly. "Maybe an idea of how I came to be here?"

Hak didn't answer her at first. His gaze swept the forest around them. "Keep your voice down. Yes, I need to take you to Meda. I will have some answers there, I think."

"Meda?" Annie's stomach twisted. "Wait. The Meda?"

Hak looked genuinely surprised. "You say you are not from here, but you have heard of Meda?"

"It's a city full of mages, right? Magical warriors and herbalists?"

Hak nodded slowly. "How do you—?" He stopped and looked at her.

"I told you. I invented this world! I made the streets, and the people!"

Hak gave her a hard look. "Must I tie you back up? You sound insane again."

"What? I'm telling you—"

"You insult me." Hak sneered. "It is best if you keep silent."

"But—!"

He whirled on her, his face contorted with anger. "Do *not* try my patience!"

Annie shrunk back from Hak in fear. "I'm sorry. I didn't mean to insult you."

He gritted his teeth and turned from her. He strapped on his black metal helmet and kept his gaze away from her. He reached down and grabbed his bag, and hers as well. Without another word he started walking.

They traveled for an hour without speaking. Annie kept scanning the forest for the next threat, but so far the day had been calm and peaceful. It was chilly enough that Annie kept her hoodie on. She fussed at her wild hair, trying to pull all the leaves, dirt, and twigs out of it. She discovered several large burrs she hadn't noticed before. They resembled thimble-sized pinecones, but were very sharp when she tried to pull them out. Her hands were swollen and sore from trying to climb the cliff the previous day, and she gave up after the third burr. She tried to keep her hair out of her face with the purple headband.

Hak walked quickly and with purpose. He stayed several yards ahead of Annie, still carrying her heavy backpack as if it were a sack lunch. The black armor made tinny sounds as he stepped, and outside of the bird songs, it was the only sound she heard. He stopped on occasion to survey the woods, and Annie would stop immediately, not daring to close the gap between them.

She was bursting with questions, but did not relish the idea of being bound and gagged. She sensed that Hak was very close to following through on his threat. When he looked back at her, it was a mix of annoyance and loathing. She did not doubt that he was strong enough to carry her bound over one shoulder and still carry her pack. She kept her hands tucked in the front pocket of her hoodie and tried not to bite her nails. She thumbed her bracelet nervously.

"May I ask a question?"

Hak didn't answer and kept walking.

"How far are we walking?"

"A few days."

"Must we walk in silence?"

"It would be preferred."

"I just want to know more about this world. I've never seen these kinds of trees or heard these kinds of birds. I don't understand the creatures that attacked me yesterday."

"This world is what you see. I do not see anything extraordinary about it."

"But these trees! They're so huge! And beautiful!"

Hak just kept walking.

Annie tried again. "I've never seen anything quite as lovely as them. We have redwoods, where I'm from. But they're some sort of pine tree. The trees here are much larger!"

"These are mana oak. Very old."

Annie let the words sink in. *I've drawn mana oak before.*

"What about that crystal igloo thing I woke up in?"

Hak froze. *"What?"*

"After I died, I woke up in this weird crystal thing. It was beautiful . . . about twice your height, shaped like a cone . . . kinda . . . Then I saw the monsters and ran . . . " Annie trailed off when she saw Hak's troubled expression.

"Impossible," Hak whispered.

"What is it?"

"Mana points. There are six that encircle this mountain, about a day's walk apart. But they . . . they do not do anything. They used to, but that was hundreds of years ago."

"What were they used for?"

"I have heard they were used by warlocks." Hak looked grim. "The warlocks have long since died out, and their knowledge with them."

"That's it? The crystals don't do anything at all?" Annie made a face at him.

"Some people take pilgrimages to them." Hak had an odd expression. "They are told to travel between the points for many turns of the moons."

"So you dudes just walk around and wait for them to do something?"

He shot her an annoyed look. "Nothing has happened in hundreds of years. You are surely insane. We need to keep our voices down or we will invite unwelcome guests."

She waited for Hak to say more, but he resumed his steady pace in silence. He had appeared troubled when she mentioned the crystal. Annie's questions were practically foaming at her lips.

How close is this to my imagination, I wonder? I had something like mana points in my video game, but they were little trinkets the player would pick up and add to their armor. They weren't as big as the crystal I found! And I've drawn a character like Hak, but this guy is not the same person from my game. My hero was smart, strong, charismatic, and a gifted magic user. He was kind and would have helped anyone who needed it. This guy seems like a villain. Even if this is some sort of dream, some things are just not making sense.

"Can you use magic?" Annie blurted.

Hak paused. She noticed that he clenched his fists as he shot her a furious glare. Without replying, Hak continued walking again, his pace faster.

"Is that a no?"

"Shut your mouth. You are like a child, brimming with annoying questions."

Annie was wounded by the response. "I was simply curious."

Hak kept moving.

And so they traveled most of the day in silence. Annie was glad that they did not run into any plagarne, but was also very troubled. Her thoughts kept shifting over her family and the nuclear holocaust that must have happened. She mourned her friends, family, and Tia. She felt so sad and alone. At one point the thoughts became too painful and she stopped walking, choking back sobs.

Hak looked back at her with annoyance. "Problem?"

"I just . . ." She looked helplessly at her scabbed hands. "I just miss my family. My dog. My old life. I can't get over the fact that I'm most likely dead and somehow trapped in my imagination. I saw the flash of light. I have to be dead."

Hak turned from her and only said, "We need to keep moving if we plan on getting to the village at the base of this mountain."

Annie sniffled and rubbed her dirty sleeve against her nose. She stared at him and didn't move. "Don't you have family, Hak?"

"No."

"I'm sorry."

"I am not."

"Your parents—"

"Gone."

"Do you have a wife? Siblings?"

He whirled, eyes burning. "I do not have time for idle chatter. Keep moving!"

She stood there, her eyes puffy from crying. Her wild hair, matted and dirty, moved in a breeze. She pulled her arms tight against her chest and cringed under his glare.

More gently, Hak said, "Please. We must keep moving."

As he turned, he paused suddenly and looked sharply to their left. The intensity of his gaze chilled Annie.

"What is it—"

Hak held up a hand, silencing her. He continued to stare at a copse of trees in the distance. They remained frozen for several minutes, Hak seeming to hear or see something Annie could not. Hak unsheathed his sword.

"Back up against that tree trunk. Do not move, no matter what happens."

Confused, Annie quickly obeyed. She was still staring at the circle of trees a hundred yards away. Shadowy images flowed from the trunks and moved toward them on the ground.

Hak hissed. *"Spirits."*

They were formless shadows without a figure to cast them. They appeared darker than the other shadows in the woods, and moved along the ground as if cast by an invisible group of bodies. They flowed like water toward the trail Annie and Hak stood on, silent.

Hak took several steps toward the shadows, his sword held at the ready in his left hand. The closest shadow was now only several yards away, and raised itself up from the ground and shifted into the shape of a woman with long, dark hair. It opened its mouth to scream. Hak darted forward and swung his sword through its neck.

The shadow fell apart like tatters of dark cloth and evaporated in the breeze. The sound it made as it disintegrated reminded Annie of grease hissing in a frying pan. The other shadows racing toward them raised themselves off the ground, took various human shapes, and lunged for Hak.

Annie's heart was racing wildly. She clung to the tree's bark, feeling the sharp grooves press into her scabs.

What the fuck is going on?

"Hakayatas!" one spirit hissed, ducking a sword blow. Hak and the spirit engaged in a dance that enthralled Annie. Hak ducked as the person lunged. The spirit had taken the form of a young woman, but as she swung her hand out, her fingers stretched into sharp points like daggers. She ducked at an inhuman speed as Hak swung his sword at her. Another shadow rose up behind Hak, taking the same female form.

"Behind you!"

Hak kept his gaze on the first woman, but arced his sword backward and caught the second figure in the arm. It darted from his reach without so much as a drop of blood.

"Annie," said a cool, familiar voice.

Annie gripped the tree harder and turned her head toward the voice.

A man stood a few feet away with a knowing expression. He had familiar jet-black hair and green eyes. Annie had once kissed those arms covered in the tattoos she had known so well.

"Patrick?"

"Annie," he said again. "I have missed you."

Annie's legs began trembling. "How—"

"Come with me, Annie. Get away from that man. He's dangerous."

Annie felt her hands release the trunk of the tree. She felt numb, as if she were only half awake. Patrick wore the same familiar clothes, and the necklace she had given him. His eyes were kind and tinged with worry. He held out a hand to her, the familiar tattoos snaking out of a shirtsleeve. Annie reached toward his hand. She was so scared and confused; she wanted to believe that Patrick had come to rescue her. Time seemed to slow down.

Hak was screaming.

As if in a dream, Annie slowly turned her head toward his voice. He was charging toward her, begging her to stop. His normally angry expression had been replaced with terror. She dully realized she had her hand outstretched, and gazed back toward Patrick's lovely face. He gave Annie a charming smile and motioned for her to come to him.

Hak's sword plunged through Patrick's head. At once his face crumbled into hissing black embers that dissipated in the breeze.

Annie shuddered, her outstretched hand dropping.

"I *told* you to stay still, girl!"

"But—"

"It is a trick!"

Annie refused to believe it. She didn't want to believe it. She stared at the place where Patrick had been standing and moaned quietly. There was no evidence that he had been standing there just a moment ago. She could not see footprints in the dirt or any remnant of black ash. Her vision swam, and she fell to her knees.

Hak caught her elbow. "Are you all right? Did you touch it?"

Annie couldn't get up. She was frozen in place, her brain still trying to register what she had seen.

Hak shook her arm and screamed, "Did you touch it!"

"No ..."

"We cannot rest here. Come." Hak was still holding her, and he tugged harshly. His armored glove bit into her sore arm and jolted her senses. Annie got to her feet, but stumbled when she tried to walk. Hak half dragged her down the trail, pulling her as hard as he could. After threatening to carry her, Annie forced herself to walk faster. They traveled about twenty minutes before Hak let go of her arm. Annie was too stunned to talk.

"Keep going. You can do it. There is a safe area to camp not far from here."

Annie nodded dully. They walked for what seemed like hours, the woods eerily quiet around them. Just when Annie felt that she would faint again,

Hak stopped and dropped the bags at his feet.

"Here."

At that, Annie dropped to the ground. She was thankful that years of hiking and camping had given her legs the strength to keep up with Hak. He busied himself with gathering wood for a fire while Annie rubbed at her shoulder and tried to stop herself from shaking.

"What *was* that back there?"

"Mana spirits."

"It . . ." She fumbled for the right words. "It knew me."

"They can see your memories."

Annie shuddered and let the words sink in. "He was wearing the necklace I gave him. The tattoos were flawless. I . . ." She stifled a sob. "I really thought it was him . . ."

"Your husband?"

Annie shook her head quickly. "No. Ex-fiancé."

Hak raised an eyebrow.

"Uh, it means we were going to marry. At one point. Didn't work out."

"You still think of him."

"No."

"Mana spirits seek your weakness."

"What the fuck, Hak? That *thing* looked just like him. Had his voice. The same smile!" Her stomach twisted at the thought. "I felt like I was in a dream."

"They seek to draw you to them. They take your mana and life."

"I don't have any mana."

Hak eyed her curiously. "Well, it certainly had an interest in you."

She felt a raindrop on her cheek.

"It will be dark soon."

Annie just stared. She felt like her senses had been robbed from her by the mana spirit.

"Can you gather wood?" Hak gestured at the woods around them. "We must make a fire. Not to cook food, but to ward off undesirable company."

"I'm not *that* helpless." She tried to smile. "I used to go camping all the time."

"Well, get to work." Hak began pulling items out of his bag.

Annie bristled at the command, but paused. *At least he's being more civil. At least he has not threatened to tie me up in the last few hours.* She set about picking up dried wood around the small clearing.

"Do not venture too far," Hak muttered, pulling a leather blanket and rope from his pack.

"Glad you care," Annie said dryly.

"I do not feel like rescuing you again."

"Same here."

When she carried an armful of wood back to the center of camp, she realized what Hak was doing. He had strung a length of rope between two mana oaks, and spread the leather blanket over it. He secured the cover against the trunk and a root the size of a small boulder. *A tarp. It's small, but will keep the rain off. I don't like sleeping that close to him, but what choice do I have? Ugh.*

As if reading her thoughts, Hak said, "Try not to lose your mind again this evening."

"I'm not crazy," Annie snarled. "I really believe what I said."

"I mean it."

"Look, I won't hurt you. I'm probably the most harmless thing for miles." She gave him a flat stare. "I know you think I'm crazy. I know I sound crazy." She paused, and looked at him sadly. "But I really feel like . . . like I'm dreaming. And I have a really hard time being quiet when my whole world has been turned upside down. I mean, nothing makes sense right now. How can you expect me to just sit here and take it quietly? Put yourself in my shoes."

Hak didn't reply. He busied himself with stacking the wood and prepping the kindling.

I hate being ignored, but I can't help feeling like he is ready to snap at me at any moment. I really don't know how to soften this wall between us. I just want him to talk to me, to tell me about this world. To tell me more about Meda, and his life. There's so much I want to know!

Annie sat down by the stacked pile of kindling and watched Hak work with some kind of stone and a metal box. It was an odd contraption, but she understood by the repeated strikes that he was trying to start a fire. A few sparks flew, but nothing ignited. He patiently repeated the process for a few moments when Annie felt the familiar hunger for some nicotine. As she pulled out her cigarettes and lighter, she smiled.

"Here, let me try?"

She flicked the lighter underneath the kindling and let it catch the dry tinder.

Alarmed, Hak jumped to his feet and stood back. "How did you do that?"

She smiled with amusement. "It's a lighter." She held up the red plastic lighter so he could see it.

Hak's eyebrows furrowed together. "I thought you said you could not use magic."

Annie laughed. "It's not magic. Here, take it. Check it out."

She tossed the lighter to Hak, but he stepped aside and let it fall to the ground.

"It won't hurt you. It's just a little plastic casing with fuel inside. When you roll the gears and press down on the lever, it sparks the fuel as it leaves."

Gingerly, Hak picked up the lighter and inspected it carefully. He smelled it, shook it, and rolled the gears slowly.

"Show me again," he said.

She carefully approached him and showed him the lever. After a minute, Hak was able to work it easily.

He laughed. "This device is amazing."

"It makes things pretty easy, doesn't it?" She took the lighter back and put a cigarette on her lips and sparked it.

"What is that?"

"It's a cigarette. Do you guys have tobacco here?"

"You smoke?"

"Yes. Is that a problem?"

"It is just that I do not know any woman who smokes," he said quickly.

"Who does smoke in this world?"

"Old mages usually. The occasional soldier will smoke a cheap enchanted herb that renders them useless." He watched her inhale the cigarette and shook his head. "You are not like most women, I think. It is not considered proper for a young woman to smoke."

She shrugged and sat down by the fire, occasionally poking at it with a stick to encourage the flame's growth.

"It smells terrible." Hak crossed his arms. "It does not smell like the herbs that people usually smoke."

"Oh?" *Damn. I was afraid there wouldn't be any tobacco here. I guess it's a good thing I've been hoarding my cigarettes instead of smoking them.*

"Well, it seems harmless enough. Other than that putrid smell. You are an odd one, Annie."

She sat back and realized with shock that Hak was actually trying to make conversation. Annie smiled. *It must have been the lighter. I wonder what he would do if I showed him my phone or flashlight. He'd probably think I'm some sort of witch and stab me on the spot. I'll have to break him in slow when it comes to the twenty-first century.*

"You have airships on Tahldia, right?"

"Of course."

Annie smiled triumphantly. "I knew it. What else, dude? Griffins?"

Hak looked at her uneasily. "Yes. That is a less comfortable way to get around, but quick. And less trouble in my opinion, since I do not have to deal with other people."

"Are you not fond of other people, Hak?"

He looked troubled and quickly turned his gaze to the fire.

Shit, I'm going to lose my chance at conversation. Way to go, Annie.

She glowered as the occasional raindrop turned into a downpour. They stood and silently agreed to share the covering of the tarp.

"Want to see something really cool?" she asked as they went to sit under the tarp. She pulled out her smartphone and showed it to him.

He took it from her carefully and looked at it. "Um, yes. I saw this when I searched your bag. What is it?"

"Watch!" She took the phone from him and pressed the button to get it out of sleep mode. She was relieved to see she still had battery life when the screen flickered on.

Hak watched in bewilderment as the screen lit up. Annie's fingers deftly swiped along the screen to pull up her photo album.

"I'm not surprised at all to not find a Wi-Fi signal, or any kind of signal. But I can still use my photo album. I have probably an hour left on the battery before I need to recharge it. Fortunately I have a solar-powered charger."

Hak just looked at the screen in wonder as she pulled up photographs from her old life.

"What I said probably made zero sense to you, huh?"

"You have the ability to see other places?"

"No, these are photographs I took with the phone."

"What are photographs?"

Annie thought for a moment. *Such a weird thing to try and explain!* She bit at her lip for a second and laughed. "I'll show you. Hold on, let me get to the screen. Okay, smile!" She held the phone up to take his photo.

Hak just sat there, speechless.

"No, you have to smile when someone takes your photograph." She waved a hand at his face. "Smile! Think of something funny, or something that makes you smile. A real, genuine smile."

Hak thought for a moment, and he smiled at something mysterious. Annie clicked on her phone, and then held it out for Hak to see.

He looked at the screen and his mouth dropped open.

"I know what you're thinking. But it's not magic."

"Then how?"

Annie shrugged. "Don't know. Science. Some really smart people realized they could make machinery do this. It's all miniature gears and wheels, really. Little engines, if you want to think of it that way."

Hak eagerly reached for her phone again and grabbed it with his metal gloves. "Be careful," she warned, "I know it's really neat, but you've got to treat it very gently. Pretend you are handling an egg. It's probably the only smartphone left in the world."

"Show me more," he breathed, looking down at the photograph of himself.

"Here, take your glove off . . . Okay, now use your fingertip to swipe at the screen. *Gently*. That's it. Now you can just swipe when you want to see a new photograph. That phone is stuffed with them, so it can keep you entertained for the full hour. You can use up the battery, it's not like I need to call anyone."

"Call?"

Annie chuckled and explained concepts about the telephone, and communications.

"Truly a remarkable invention, this photograph phone."

"Smartphone. Yes." Annie laughed, delighted with Hak's curiosity. *Now I think I can approach him with more questions. He will understand that the world I come from is much more different than he could have imagined.*

"Who is this?" Hak pointed at a photo.

Annie felt her heart freeze up. "That's my friend Matt. I worked with him."

Hak kept scrolling through the photos while Annie peered over his arm. Her heart was pounding painfully. "That's my living room. My old house. That was a flower growing in my backyard. That's Tia." She winced and felt her eyes burn. "Tia was my dog."

"She is a gorgeous creature. Tame, you say?"

"Yeah. She wouldn't hurt a fly. Slept in my bed, played with balls and sticks." Annie sat back for a moment, her eyes watering so much she could barely see.

Hak looked over at her, a mix of curiosity and annoyance on his face.

"Uh, sorry."

"No," Hak said. "It is I who am sorry. It looks like you spoke true. You truly seem to think your old life is gone."

"I think I'm dead," Annie whispered, giving him a pained look. "I really do. Hak, the last thing I saw was something that should have killed me. Then I woke up here."

He looked thoughtful for a moment. "And this is why you act so strange."

"I've been trying to tell you."

Hak was still looking at her photographs. "Yes, this is indeed something strange. Circumstances have been very odd here, so I cannot really be surprised anymore."

"How so?"

"Just know that my country is not at peace. And I am not who you think I am."

"Who do you think—"

"I do not care to explain it now," he said coldly.

Annie winced. *Time to change the subject.*

"Here, let's look at photos later." She took the phone from him and moved her fingers quickly to her music selection screen. *Heavy metal would probably not be a good idea.*

"This is called classical music. This was recorded in a place called Germany. Just be quiet for a minute and listen." She hit play and let the orchestra music engulf them. Hak breathed out in amazement.

Is there even a Germany left? I wonder if all these musicians are now dead, Annie thought sadly.

Hak delighted in the melody. They leaned their heads back against the massive mana oak root and let the music envelop them. The only other sounds came from the occasional crack or pop from the campfire, and rain softly padding on the leather tarp. Hak looked at peace for the first time since Annie had met him.

I find this peaceful as well, in an odd way . . . I could almost be sitting in the redwoods right now, camping with a new friend. She had missed the delicate aroma of campfire and wet earth.

After the song was over, Hak looked over at the phone with sadness.

"Don't worry. I have a lot of music. There will be another song any second."

"How is this even possible? Are the little gears inside making this music?"

Annie chuckled at the thought. "No, well . . . kind of. This is like a photograph, but for sound. You can record anything, and save it. You can transfer the audio to the phone."

"I hear so many instruments," he said breathlessly, staring up at the bottom of the tarp.

"Yeah, a symphony can have dozens of musicians. This was created in a large theater, and someone recorded it. I took that recording off a thing called the Internet, and put it into my phone." Annie realized just how exhausting it was going to be explaining her world.

The video-game world she had created was in the dark ages, with a touch of steampunk. There were airships, yes, and some siege vehicles built with steam engines, but it was a very simple world. There was no Internet, or cars, or gunpowder.

"Such strange instruments. Some sound familiar . . . the horns and drums, but others I have not heard before."

"That's a piano . . . You haven't heard Swedish death metal yet," Annie mused, smiling slightly.

"Sounds evil."

Annie chuckled. "My mom and stepdad thought so. But it's just a bunch of guys screaming and playing their instruments really, really fast. It's harmless music, actually. It gets a lot of aggression out. That can be a good thing . . . not be so bottled up all the time, you know?"

Hak just nodded.

"The hoodie you asked about earlier?" Annie tugged at her sweatshirt for emphasis. "This is a heavy metal band. Their sigil is this."

"Skulls and ravens. Why?"

"Well, to play the part I suppose. It's an aggressive, loud form of music, so you can't very well put rainbows and kittens on it."

Hak chuckled. "I suppose not. But why do you have such angry music?"

"Dunno. I guess I'm a bit of an angry person sometimes," Annie said thoughtfully. "But it's just freedom of expression. Where I am from, you can say whatever you please, and you won't get arrested for it."

"But that must cause much trouble."

"Nah. Well, sometimes. But I believe everyone is entitled to their own opinions, even if I don't like them or agree."

"You are very accepting."

She laughed. "Sometimes."

"Strange."

She sat there for a moment, daring to close her eyes as the symphony played a sad melody. "Speaking of strange . . . I have a strange question."

"Yes?"

"What did you think about that made you smile earlier?"

There was a long pause. Annie feared she had stepped into forbidden conversation territory yet again, when Hak smiled. "I was thinking about a friend."

"Oh?"

When he didn't respond, Annie dared to tease him slightly. "What kind of friend?"

"A very good friend. She always finds the positive in life."

"She sounds like a nice person."

Hak was still staring at the tarp, but his look became distant. "She is. Her name is Nivya."

"That's a pretty name."

"It is for the western star. It is too cloudy with the rain to see right now."

"Does she live here?"

Hak was quiet for a moment, and then nodded toward the trees. "She lives a long ways from here, in the south. She is an herbalist."

"I hope I can meet her someday. I would love to meet an herbalist."

Hak laughed.

"What's so funny?"

"It is just . . . I cannot imagine how shocked she would be to meet you. With your . . . smoking, strange words and cursing. You are very odd."

Annie felt her cheeks grow hot. "Dude, I'm not a freak."

Hak arched an eyebrow at her.

Annie bit her lip and said nothing. *Great. I'm as unpopular and freakish here as I was in high school. I bet everyone is going to want to throw rocks at me here. Or call me a monster. Or something . . .*

"I did not say you are a freak. However, you act different. And you curse like a drunken soldier on the eve of Saints' Day."

"Yeah, but most of the time I'm not aware of it. Bad habit I suppose."

"I have never heard a woman with such a foul tongue. I find it offensive."

"Sorry. I'll try to be more civilized. One more question."

"Yes?"

"What does your name mean, Hakayatas?"

"The kayata bird."

Annie gave him a blank look.

"In Shafani legends, it brought fire, destruction, and change. World builder, some call it."

"That's quite the meaning."

"Now it is my turn to ask a strange question."

"Shoot."

"What?"

"That means, 'go on, tell me quickly.'"

"Oh." Hak paused. "Shoot. What a funny way to say it. I like that."

Annie couldn't help grinning. "Well, what's your question?"

"What does *dude* mean?"

Annie woke to the sound of a man singing quietly. Her eyes fluttered open, and she blinked and rubbed them several times to adjust to the light of the dying fire. The rain had stopped, and a tiny patch of starry sky was visible through the leafy canopy.

Her eyes focused in the direction of the voice. Hak knelt thirty or so feet beyond the fire, his back to her, his left hand open and facing the sky. He was singing in a language Annie had never heard. All the words seemed to be glued together. The syllables slipped along like water, and the vowels rolled up and down in a strange fashion. Hak's voice was as soft as a father's lullaby, but there was a sense of passion and yearning there. He could have been singing to a lover or begging for mercy, she couldn't tell. Goosebumps ran along

Annie's flesh.

The song was over as quickly as it started. Annie watched him cautiously, unsure of his intentions. *He says he doesn't know magic, but what was that? That was a little weird, but also kind of cool. I didn't know he could sing.*

Hak bowed his head, and repeated something about a 'Yonael, and 'red dragon'. He stood and kept his gaze on the sky.

Annie propped herself up on one arm and wiped some dirt from her cheek. She was groggy and annoyed that she didn't have a proper bed to sleep in. "What was that?"

Hak started, and turned to look at her. "What?"

"You were singing something."

His expression was unreadable in the shadows. "I was praying."

"Who are you praying to?"

He took a few careful steps toward the remains of the campfire. "I pray to Yona'ela, of course."

Nothing in my video game with that name. Annie squeezed the space between her eyes. "Who?"

Hak stopped just a few feet from the fire. He cocked his head to the side and stared at her. He seemed confused that she would ask such a question. "The goddess Yona'ela," he said again. "Gatekeeper of Alhena. Alchemist of Fate. She is but one of the gods in the stars."

Gods in the stars? Annie choked on a laugh and pressed her lips together.

"You find humor in that?" His deep voice had frosted over.

"What? Uh, no. I just . . . the stars. Okay." *Whatever, weirdo.*

He didn't move. "Are you faithless?"

She made a spitting noise. "Does it matter? This is either heaven or hell, I'm not sure which. But I can promise you, some chick in the sky had nothing to do with this." Annie swept a hand at herself, the camp, and Hak.

She had meant to make a joke, but it had come out wrong. Hak was silent for a long time. The clouds rolled under the stars and rain tapped on the leaves around her. The silence stretched beyond comfort. *Great, I think I've offended him somehow. But really? He thinks the stars are gods? Or does he think the gods live on the stars? Should I tell him what NASA thinks about stars?*

Sarcasm tempted her, but Annie stifled it. Hak's tall figure loomed above the campfire. She barely made out his features in the soft illumination of the dying embers. His face was a twisted mask in the red and orange light. Disdain and contempt tightened his lips and furrowed his brow. Or maybe it was anger. She couldn't really tell. Whatever it was, his expression frightened her. All of the smart-ass retorts in the world shriveled under the weight of such a stare. Annie lay back down, closed her eyes, and pretended to fall asleep immediately. She didn't want to ask him about his religion again.

Annie woke the next morning and felt sore all over. She found that the previous day of walking had left her legs and feet aching, despite years of hiking and camping in the Oregon wilderness. Her bruised shoulder and swollen hands throbbed incessantly. Hak was already awake and packing his belongings.

Annie looked over at her phone. They had run the battery out listening to music last night. She pulled the bulky solar charger out of her pack and tried to think of a way to mount it to the top of the backpack, so she could charge the phone as they walked. While the charger was a useful device, it was very slow. It usually took eight hours of sunlight to recharge the battery, and within the deep forest, Annie was not sure if she could get enough light.

Hak walked over, knelt beside Annie, and looked questioningly at the charger's iridescent blue panels spread out on the ground.

She tried to explain such things as batteries, and electricity, and the need to get more. She was unsure how much Hak understood. He just watched her work as she created rigging with some nylon rope that would allow the magazine-sized panel to hang off the back of her pack.

"What odd plant fiber," Hak said, rolling the nylon rope between his fingers. "It's shiny."

"It's nylon. It's a form of plastic, like the lighter."

"How does this plastic grow?"

Annie laughed again, and Hak flashed her an annoyed look. "No, it's a condensed form of oil. It's hard to explain." But she tried to sum up the extraction and use of petroleum.

"Strange. I would like to see more of this plastic."

"It's in everything I own, to a degree. The soft cover on my phone? That's plastic. Even the elastic in my hoodie"—she tugged and stretched her cuff for emphasis—"is a form of plastic. We use it in everything."

"It must be a very bountiful resource."

"No. Well, it was . . . but it's a nonrenewable form of energy. Which means it can be used up, eventually. My country was fighting other countries for the rights to large fields of oil."

She paused, and cast her eyes downward. "I think we were bombed because of it. A lot of countries didn't like mine. There was a lot of political fighting going on. I would listen to the news, but I never paid too much attention to the details. I guess I'll never know."

Hak simply nodded. "Wars waged for the sake of resources. It has happened here as well."

"For what?"

He hesitated. "It is a long story. But it is for metal, not liquid."

"Gold?"

"No."

She waited for an explanation, but Hak simply turned to finish packing up camp.

Annie took stock of the food she had in her bag. *Three more granola bars, a bag of chocolate bites, a protein bar, a bag of beef jerky, a few instant noodle packs, and a mostly full bottle of whiskey. I threw most of the food in my pantry in garbage bags, and then tossed them in my car. Lame.*

Annie settled on a granola bar and tried to chew it slowly. She didn't know when she would see more food.

"Where is the nearest town?"

"Feldall."

"How long of a walk?"

"One more day if we hurry." He looked at her coolly, but a smile tugged at the corner of his lips. "We are moving much faster than I had originally thought. You travel well in the wilds for a woman."

Annie scrunched up her face at him. "I'm a pretty tough woman. You better deal with it."

"We need to move."

"Right." Annie zipped up her bag and started to pull it to her shoulder when Hak stopped her.

He picked up her heavy pack with ease and slung it over his shoulder.

"Hey, I can carry my bag today. I don't mind."

"No."

"Still don't trust me, eh?"

"No."

"Well, it's gotta face the sunlight. If you insist on carrying it, at least hold it right." She walked over and loosened the backpack's straps as much as she could so they could easily loop over Hak's armor. It was still a tight fit as she struggled to get the strap over the spaulders.

"I will not fight well with it like this," he protested.

"Well, you're the one who wanted to carry my bag." She stood back and looked the knight over. "If you want to hear more music tonight, we need the top part of that blue panel to be facing the sun as much as possible."

"Just keep quiet, and we should not have to fight. In the last fortnight, I have killed many creatures on this mountain, but there are still many more. And they would rip you to shreds."

Annie made a face at him. "Fine, I'll be quiet. But whatever you do, don't get anything of mine wet. It will break and never work again. You're carrying my treasure."

"I know all too well that I carry treasure," he said coldly.

Annie froze. *What if he steals this from me? What's to stop him from running off with my belongings, or selling me off?* She shivered. *I wonder just how similar this world is to the one I made up. Some stuff doesn't feel right, while other things . . . I can't explain that I've drawn his armor, or the fact I designed Meda, herbalists, or mana oak. If this world is similar to Tahldia, then I can count on one thing: honor.*

Annie looked at Hak as he picked up his helmet. "Are you a man of honor, Hak?"

He paused with the helmet halfway to his face. He looked at her with burning yellow eyes. "Why do you ask such a thing?"

"I want to make sure you won't hurt me. Or run off with my stuff. You're the only person I know right now, and I want to believe that you are a man of honor. Are you a man of honor, Hak?"

"I believe in honor, yes."

"Then you must swear to me, Hak, that you will not cheat me or hurt me. Swear it on your honor."

He hesitated. "I cannot make this honor vow."

"Why?"

"If I find out that you are evil, or have been lying to me, I might have to kill you."

Annie's eyes widened and she sputtered. "But, dude, I can't hurt you. And why would I lie to you?"

"You would not be the first."

"Okay, how about you promise me you won't kill or hurt me, or steal my stuff, as long as you think I'm harmless. If you find out I'm evil—and that will be a surprise to me as well—then the honor vow is off."

Hak started to shake his head, but Annie stopped him, "I need this promise, Hak. I'm scared shitless right now, and . . . and in your world, I *know* you guys have these honor vows. I know you can't break it. I need some piece of mind. I . . . I'm scared you're going to hurt me. Or lead me into a trap. I'm placing my life, or afterlife, in your hands."

"I would never do that unless—"

"Then *vow.*"

"I have made too many vows as it is—"

"Then what's one more? I mean, seriously, dude, this one doesn't seem that big of a deal. Just promise not to hurt me. If you don't, I'm going to think you're a giant asshole."

Hak sighed. "I vow on my honor that I will not harm you, Annie of Oregon, nor will I hurt you or steal from you, as long as your word remains true, and you do not threaten me first. If you threaten me, deceive me, or try to sabotage my quest, this vow will cease to be binding. By my honor in front of the sun, stars, and wind."

Annie gave him a bow. She had meant it as sarcasm, but Hak responded by nodding his head, and he placed his hand over his heart in a regal manner.

"Do not deceive me," he whispered coldly, putting his helmet on. Without another word, the knight started walking. The bright green and white hiking pack looked ridiculous on the huge figure.

They had traveled only a few hundred yards when Annie tried to ask, "So, what kind of quest are you on? That means you're definitely a knight, right?"

Hak only made a hushing noise.

"You said I can't sabotage your quest, but I didn't even know you're on one. Can you tell me about it? What is it you're trying to accomplish? Can I help?"

Hak turned quickly and gazed down at her, his molten eyes shining. He clasped both of his hands on her shoulders.

"Annie. Be quiet, for the love of the gods. Your incessant chatter is going to draw more spirits to us, and *that* would be sabotaging my quest. Keep. Your. Mouth. Closed."

Annie felt a hundred questions foam at her lips. *Oh my god, he is on a quest! I wonder if it's a quest line I devised. How freaking cool is this!*

Annie eagerly stared back at him. She was suddenly less afraid of Hak. The last two days had shown her that he wasn't a bad guy. At least, compared to the other things she had met so far. "Will you tell me sometime soon? In exchange for a song? Pretty please? I would love to hear about it. I might know something that can help—"

Hak's hands were still on her shoulders, and they squeezed just enough to pinch at her bruises. Annie gave a little yelp, and Hak released her.

"Maybe. Now be quiet. Or I will shove a rag in your mouth. I made no vow about that."

Annie sneered and kicked at the ground. Hak had already resumed his pace. She followed a dozen feet behind him, trying to be as quiet as possible. She noted that the tinny sounds of his armor were not exactly the quietest sounds in the world, but decided that she was better off not pointing that out.

Instead, Annie tried to take note of every tree, bird, and insect that she saw. The forest path was very narrow, and had been more or less a deer trail in the last two days. The mana oaks became fewer and fewer, and disappeared altogether. Younger trees and bushes started to choke out the path, and the undergrowth scraped at Annie's face. The going became trickier for a few hours, and at one point Annie felt that they weren't on a trail at all.

Midway through the day, they came to a large path. Annie dared to think of it as a road. They walked out of the thick underbrush and right onto a large, heavily worn stretch of dirt that was wide enough to hold two cars side by side. She turned and looked at the way they had come, and was not at all surprised to see a wall of dense foliage. She pulled a few leaves out of her hair.

Hak raised his visor and looked down the road, a smile tugging at his lips. "You have done well. We are very close to Feldall."

They took a break to drink some water and have a quick meal. Annie lit a cigarette as soon as she sat down, and ignored Hak's sour expression when the smoke wafted past his nose. She gave Hak a few pieces of beef jerky, and enjoyed his delighted reaction to the spicy snack. He waved his hands at his mouth and choked out the word "Hot!" but kept chewing. She tore off a small chunk from her granola bar, and in return Hak let her try some of the dense bread she had been watching him nibble.

"Small bites. It is very nutrient rich. Herbalists make it for travelers. It is imbued with magic so that it does not spoil."

To Annie's amazement, the bread seemed to expand in her mouth. It was similar to a very dense shortbread cookie, but with a honeylike sweetness to it. It was incredible.

"Are these expensive? I'd like to buy some."

"No, not terribly. But Feldall will not have an herbalist. We can find food there, however."

Annie dug in a side pocket on her backpack and pulled out a handful of change and a few dollar bills. "I would imagine that my money is worthless here."

Hak took the money from her and inspected the coins and bills with intense interest. "The detail on these coins is truly remarkable!"

"That's called a penny. This is a dime ... quarter ... and nickel."

"The artwork on these coins could be enough to interest an auctioneer. Or a collector. But I think that a baker will want my type of money."

"Can I see what your money looks like?" Annie asked eagerly.

Hak pulled out a leather pouch and put two coins in Annie's hands. She could hear the heavy jingle of many more coins in Hak's pouch, but did not press her luck with more questions.

"This is a copper din. And a silver nic." Annie grinned and rolled the handmade coins around with her fingers. They resembled the ancient Greek coins that her mother had loved to collect. There was a vague image of a person on the silver coin, and an eye on the copper one. They were very crude, but without more coins to compare them to, Annie was unsure how uniform they were in design with other coins.

I wish my mom could see these. She would love this old medieval stuff! Annie thought sadly.

"We need to keep walking. And hope there is room at the inn for the two of us. You could use a bath."

Annie stuck her tongue out at him, but inwardly rejoiced at the thought of cleaning up. She knew that she had one spare change of clothes on her. It was the camping clothes she had in her backpack from a trip to eastern Oregon a few months back. They still vaguely smelled of campfire and had been filthy the last she had worn them, but they suddenly seemed pristine after the last few days in her current garb.

Oh man, to sleep in a bed again! A nice hot bath, and a nice soft bed. And maybe some fresh food and other people to meet! I'm going to a Tahldian inn!

She skipped happily at the thought.

"What is the matter?"

"Oh, just excited to be sleeping inside tonight."

"We have to hope there is room."

"You know what's funny?" When Hak didn't respond, Annie laughed and talked anyway. "I used to go camping for fun. To relax. Get away from everyone. Well, I think I've had enough camping to last a while. Staying at an inn sounds wonderful."

Hak began laughing.

"I don't like the sound of that laugh," Annie said uneasily.

"To get to Meda, we have much more camping ahead of us. This will be our only inn for a while. Meda is two weeks south."

"Oh fuck, are you *serious?*"

Hak kept laughing as he headed down the trail.

CHAPTER FIVE:

FELDALL

THEY REACHED THE edge of the town by dusk. Annie tried to absorb everything she saw as the road grew wider. Long, rolling pastures and quaint huts dotted the foothills, and the occasional figure worked in a field, too far away for her to get a good view. She saw horses with plows, and a small group of children running by a barn. The land seemed peaceful, if very antiquated.

The town itself seemed to be mostly wooden houses with thatched roofs; the road held deep ruts from countless horses and carts. It reminded Annie all too well of the ancient homes she had drawn for her game. The streets were dark and sparsely populated, and Hak seemed pleased that they had arrived at nightfall. He had asked her to not make a sound or talk to anyone, under any circumstances. She had to pretend she was mute.

They approached a large building just on the inside of the town wall. It was a large two-story structure with a finished wooden roof, numerous windows, and a bright lamp burning on the porch. Another lantern off to the side lit the walkway to the stables next to the building.

As Annie approached the front entrance, Hak grabbed her wrist and led her around the side of the inn toward the stables. They found a bored young boy sitting on a large oak barrel. His face lit up when he caught sight of Hak, and he rushed forward to give him an enthusiastic greeting. Hak smiled kindly and tossed him a coin, and asked him to get his father. The boy nodded eagerly and ran inside. A moment later a very large man with a thick brown beard and a dirty apron appeared.

"Well, then. Welcome back, finally."

"Do you have a room for us, Odal?"

"Us?" The huge bear of a man turned to look at Annie. Hak's tall frame had hidden her from sight.

Odal gave them a confused look. "Hakayatas, you know we don't take Vinder here."

"She is not Vinder. As far as I can tell." Hak paused to glare at Annie. "She takes commands from me. She will cause no trouble while she is here."

"What strange clothes," was all Odal could say, giving Annie a disapproving look. His wandering gaze swept over her, and paused at the bruise on her neck. His eyebrows wrinkled together, but he said nothing.

"I need to take her to Meda. Let us stay."

"Fine. Use the side stairs."

Odal ushered them inside. They walked through a warm, bustling kitchen and Annie glimpsed a common room through a small opening above the cookstove. A large woman was chopping onions as they passed. She gave Hak a knowing nod, but saved a scowl for Annie. Two younger women curiously looked up from kneading bread, and blushed when they saw Hak. The older woman smacked a spoon in front of them and they quickly returned to their work. Annie's mouth watered at the smell of cooking meat and vegetables.

Odal picked up two lanterns, led them up a narrow staircase from the kitchen, and down a small corridor with several doors on both sides. A larger staircase was at the far end of the hallway. He led them to the second door and unlocked it.

"You are sharing a room?" he asked, a bit incredulous. He gave Annie another unreadable look.

"I am fine with the floor. She must be guarded. For her own protection," Hak added hastily.

Odal shrugged. "Suit yourself, Hakayatas. I will bring you something soft to sleep on." He gave Hak a lantern.

They walked into a small room that contained a dresser, basin, small mirror, and a large, lumpy-looking bed with a quilt. Hak set down their belongings at the foot of the bed and removed his helmet. A moment later, Odal knocked at the door and handed Hak a stack of quilts and a pair of towels.

"Shall I have Marta prepare some water for baths?"

"That would be kind."

"I'll let her know." Odal lowered his deep voice and gave Hak a sour expression. "Be careful of the fools that have the room at the end of the hallway. They appear to be copper knights."

"Thank you, Odal."

"Your strange companion have a name?"

"Annie." She smiled and gave a small bow.

"Ah, she is tame!"

Hak stiffened. He had forbidden her to talk.

Well, screw him, Annie thought. She was eager to meet other people in this world.

Hak moved to close the door, signaling to the innkeeper that he was through with questions. "Thank you for your hospitality, Odal. Maybe have Marta send up some food as well."

"Not coming down to the common room? We have a fiddler visiting from Osmek this week!"

"No. We will eat in here."

Odal shrugged, "Suit yourself. It should be some grand fun when he gets warmed up." He closed the door as he left.

"Wow! Hak!" Annie grinned. "This place is so cool!"

He sighed and pulled his gloves off.

Annie walked to the bed and threw herself on it. It was not the soft cloud she was hoping for, however. Bits of straw poked out of the bedding and pricked at her sore hands.

"Beds are not as soft as I thought they would be."

"What were you expecting? Feathers?"

Annie laughed. "Actually, yeah."

"Well. Suddenly you are quite the princess."

She gave him a flat look. "Oh, come on, relax a little. Don't you want to go downstairs and hear the fiddler?"

"Odal is a nice man," he said warily, "but his inn can be a . . . challenging place. It would be best for us to stay up here."

Annie cocked her head and looked over at the closed door. "What's a copper knight? Is that supposed to be a mercenary or something?"

"Yes. Soldiers who swing their swords for a few dins. They are not known for their honor. We should not talk to them."

Annie rolled her eyes. "I'm sure you're the biggest, baddest guy here. Let's go have some fun!"

"I am filthy. You . . ." Hak shook his head. "You look as if you have crawled out of the zythil pits. It is no wonder Odal thought you were

Vinder."

"What's a Vinder?" Annie had not created anything in her video game with such a name, but the word seemed familiar. She lit a cigarette and found an empty bowl to ash in.

"A wild person. Someone who lives in the woods and preys upon travelers. They are dangerous, unruly people. It is not a flattering thing to be considered a Vinder."

Annie walked over to the mirror and gasped. Her blue eyes were red and puffy, with heavy bags underneath. She looked like she hadn't slept in a week. Her hair was a wild mat of burrs, leaves, and dirt. A light reddish bruise ran along the front of her neck. She took off her hooded sweatshirt to expose an ugly bruise on her left shoulder. She pulled the thin blue strap of her camisole off her shoulder to get a better look.

"Annie, that is not proper!" Hak turned away from her.

She burst out laughing. "It's just a tank top!"

"It barely covers your . . ."

"Stop. It's fine. It covers me just fine." She returned her gaze to the mirror and noted with amusement that Hak had turned bright red. "Look what you did to my shoulder when we first met!"

Hak slowly looked up at Annie and let his gaze settle on the massive purple bruise that swelled along her shoulder. It still amazed Annie that a man wearing full armor had fallen on her and not broken anything.

"I apologize. I did not realize how badly you were injured."

"Well . . . at least you didn't kill me. And you did save me from those plagarne things."

There was a knock at the door. Hak opened it to one of the younger kitchen helpers. She was standing a bit bashfully at the door, her arm around a basket.

"Mum thought it best to offer this for half a din—" The girl craned her neck curiously around Hak and caught sight of Annie standing there in her slim tank top smoking her cigarette. The girl's eyes grew wide and she began to stammer, obviously scandalized. "Uh, her recipe for honey soap, if you want—" She quickly pushed the basket into Hak's hands and darted away, her eyes staring at the floor.

Hak sighed and took the basket, shutting the door.

"What is it?"

"They try to sell extra items to guests. To get more money. I have no use for this flowery stuff, however." He showed her the basket. There were a few vials and lumps of white stuff inside.

Annie picked up a lumpy piece the size of her lighter and inspected it closely. "Soap?"

"Yes. And oils. For the bath."

"Dude, I'll take them!"

"It costs money."

"I'll let you take some of my change. Like you said, you can probably sell it to someone."

"Fine." Hak handed her the basket. "Go across the hall. I will wait for you here."

He pointed her toward a door with a swan on it. Annie brought the basket, a towel, and her spare set of clothes. There was a circular metal tub in the small room, a lantern, and a bench. The tub was full of steaming water. Annie set down the basket and quickly removed her clothes. She opened the various bottles, unsure of what each was supposed to do. *Maybe one is for the hair, and one is for after the bath? I wonder which one is the soap? The lumpy thing? They all smell wonderful!*

She carefully set herself down into the tub, hissing with delight at the heat. At once she could see a film of dirt float to the top of the water. The tub was not large enough to stretch her legs out, so Annie set about washing as much as she could in the confined space. She rubbed at her hair and scrubbed at her fingernails. The water quickly turned brown and filthy, but Annie still felt cleaner than she had in days.

After what may have been half an hour, the water had cooled considerably. She stepped out of the tub and looked around. *Do I drain it? How? Is it considered rude to just leave this filthy water here?*

She scrubbed at her body with the coarse towel and wrapped it around her head. She pulled on her second pair of jeans, and a short-sleeved green t-shirt. She noted that the jeans were much looser than the last time she had worn them. The sweater was simple, and a bit thin, but would hopefully cover enough skin to keep Hak from feeling scandalized again. There were no decals or art on the sweater, which Annie thought might be a good thing.

She picked up the clothes she had been wearing for the last few days and was disgusted at how stiff they had become with sweat and dirt. As she opened the door, she caught sight of one of the young serving girls waiting in the narrow staircase. The girl blushed and quickly turned her eyes to the floor.

Annie walked back into the room and found Hak sitting at the window, looking at the quiet town.

"Is this appropriate?" she asked sarcastically, spinning once so Hak could see her clothes.

"Strange leggings, but it is passable, I suppose. The tunic is a bit low cut, and odd looking . . . Your towel is not meant to be a hat."

Annie laughed. "I know that, silly. Just trying to get my hair dry."

She found a small tube of leave-in conditioner from her bag. She couldn't remember packing it, but she was thankful she had. She applied a small amount to her hair to make the brushing easier. After much cursing and impatience, she finally had all the burrs removed. And her hair smelled like gardenias. For one painful moment, she was homesick.

"What's a nice hairstyle here? Up? Or do women here wear their hair down?"

Hak laughed. "I would not know where to begin with you."

Annie looked wounded, "C'mon, seriously. I don't want to be considered a Vinder."

"Let it fall and dry. I cannot help but think that anything we try to do will make you look less like a Vinder."

Annie let out a "Hmph!" and turned back to the mirror. She brushed her wet hair out straight, and pulled on the purple headband she had been wearing.

"Close enough," was all Hak said.

"Marta will be by with food soon. I am going to go get cleaned up, and then find a horse for tomorrow. Do not leave this room for any reason."

"Oh, c'mon, please?"

"Stay," Hak said coldly, and closed the door behind him.

"Stay"? I'm not a dog!

Annie waited a full five minutes after Hak left. She scrunched her hair in her hands and let it dry to its normal, puffy shape. She cracked open the door in the hallway and looked around. The inn was bursting with noise and exuberant energy. She could hear someone tuning a fiddle down in the common room below her.

How bad would it be if I went downstairs? Just for one beer? Oh god, they had better have beer on this planet!

She waited, her mind racing with possibilities. She heard the gentle slosh of water coming from the room with the bath. She began to walk out, but thought better of it. She crept over to the bed and scrunched the hay inside up into a passable mound, and set the sheets over it. If Hak looked too closely, he would see through the ruse. She turned the light down on the lantern and moved it to the dresser, away from the bed.

If he just peeks in, hopefully he will think I'm asleep. Better to ask forgiveness than permission.

With that, Annie crept out of the room and toward the large staircase at the far end of the hallway.

As she walked downstairs, her senses were pleasantly shocked with the boisterous noises of the bar. Men barking laughter, women squealing in delight, and so many conversations going on at once Annie could not absorb them all. A man with a fiddle was standing at the front of the room by a large hearth, and he was just finishing his first song. Annie guessed that there were two dozen people in the room, and noted a few dark alcoves along one side that could have easily hidden more.

Her wandering eyes found Odal and a young man standing behind a large bar at the far end of the room. Annie spied a few empty seats and made her way through the crowded room. She avoided the questioning looks a few men gave her.

Odal nodded to her as she sat down, "Aye, you clean up well, Lady Annie."

"Just call me Annie." She smiled. "What do you have to drink?"

"We have a berry wine from Osmek—"

"No wine, please."

"Beer?" Odal tried to conceal his shock.

"Yeah."

"We have a brew on tap my eldest made. Has a pleasant bite to it. However, most of the ladies here prefer the wine. It's one din."

"The beer sounds amazing. I'll have a pint. Or whatever size you have. And Hak said he would pay for everything."

"Okay." Odal said, giving her an odd look. He worked a spigot on a very large oak barrel and poured a very generous amount of beer into a mug. Annie grinned. *Yes, this is just what I need after the last few fucked-up days. A din can't possibly be a lot of money. Maybe the equivalent of five dollars. I'm sure Hak won't mind.*

Annie eagerly lifted the mug to her lips and began drinking. It was a rich, amber-colored beer. It was not as nicely filtered as some of the beers she could buy in a grocery store, but it was on a par with some of the homemade beers that Patrick had perfected in college. She didn't like how warm the beer was, but she felt thankful to have something to numb the anxiety that had gnawed at her. She took hearty gulps until she had emptied half the mug.

"Amazing!" She sat the mug down on the counter.

Odal laughed. "I am happy to see that you enjoy it . . . so well. Did Marta send up food? And does Hakayatas know you are down here?"

"No, she did not. And I'm starving. The food smells great."

Odal eyed her for a minute, clearly not missing the fact that Annie hadn't answered his second question.

After a moment, Odal shook his head with a bemused smile and turned to the hole in the wall that led to the kitchen. He motioned with his hands and a moment later a tray with bread appeared. He placed the steaming rolls down in front of Annie. There was a yellow, thick glaze and a lump of something pale on the plate.

Honey and butter! Annie was ecstatic, and began pushing torn hunks of bread into the honey and butter to make a paste. She wolfed down several mouthfuls and then chased it with a hearty chug of beer.

"Someone has quite the appetite," a man next to her said. Annie didn't stop eating, but turned toward the voice. It was a young man, roughly her age, in a travel-worn cloak and nice garments. Some of the clothes had fancy embroidery, and the man wore a few rings of silver.

"Their bread is delicious," Annie mumbled as she chewed. The man arched his eyebrow at her disapprovingly, and turned back toward his own meal. Annie didn't give him a second thought as Odal lowered another plate of food in front of her. It was covered with peas, onions, carrots, and a large bird leg.

I hope that's chicken.

As Annie wolfed down her dinner, she kept her eyes on the common room. She asked Odal question after question when he passed by her seat. Annie knew that people loved to hear themselves talk, and she was glad that Odal, unlike Hak, was all too happy to talk about his life and share gossip. He had married at fifteen, and began raising a family immediately. He was happy to talk about his children and Marta. Annie gracefully dodged any questions pertaining to her odd clothes and origin, and kept the conversation centered on Odal and his business.

As she took a third mug of beer from Odal, he took her empty plate and said cautiously, "That beer is strong, Annie. Do be careful."

"Oh, I'm fiiiine." She giggled, feeling slightly tipsy. "You should have seen what I would drink in college."

Odal cocked his head at the word, but did not say anything further. The common room was a flurry of dancing by now. Annie enjoyed watching the revelry. There were men gambling at a long table with dice and a pile of copper coins, and the fiddler led the dancers with an upbeat tune. *I feel like I'm in some sort of crazy medieval movie! There's magic! And knights in shining armor! And common rooms! And such good beer! Maybe I'm in heaven after all.*

The fiddler frantically tapped his foot while he played, and eight people took turns trading dance partners across the floor. Annie watched their steps with a keen interest. It was similar to square dancing. Folks jumped into the center to bow to their partner, then they twined their arms together and they twirled back and forth in a circle three full times, and then parted arms. Then if the couples wanted, they would jump in the middle again, and turn to the person next to them, and continue the dance. Some couples did not trade partners at all. It was dizzying to watch.

Annie felt her head itch suddenly, and scratched furiously behind her ears. It felt like an insect was running along her scalp. A man walked up to the bar next to Annie with an empty mug and asked for more. She guessed he was a few years younger than herself. He had a long face, sharp hooked nose, and beautiful blue eyes. His cheeks and nose were ruddy from drinking, but his eyes shone with happiness. It was a welcome emotion for Annie to see. When he looked over at her, she couldn't help smiling in return.

"Well, hello there, my lady." He gave her a small bow. "Why are you not dancing?"

"I can't dance," Annie said, tipping the mug to her lips and taking a deep swallow of beer.

The man watched her drink, and laughed with drunken delight. "I want to see if you can dance as you can drink ale!"

Annie hesitated. *Oh, why the hell not? He* is *cute . . . and this is way better than any bar Karen could drag me to!*

Annie took another swig of beer and set the mug down, and then she let the young man lead her to the cleared space in front of the hearth. She caught a few disapproving looks from the people seated nearby. They were clearly eyeing her jeans and T-shirt. The two women at the table ducked their heads together and whispered while watching. Annie looked around and realized she was the only woman in the building without a dress on. *Oh, fuck it!* She gave a drunken laugh and let the man pull her into a spin.

"You dance just fine, my lady!" the man said after a moment.

"That's the beer!"

The man barked a laugh. "Delightful! Where do you come from?"

"Place called Oregon!"

"Strange!" The man spun her about and let go. After a moment they jumped back into another slow spin. "Is that near Taui?"

"You could say that!"

"So your first time at the top of the world, then?"

"Yeah!" Annie slurred, far too tipsy to care. She had forgotten how much she loved a good drunken dance. "This place is awesome!"

They were both laughing hysterically as they talked. His name was Tomas, and he was from Meda. His face was young, but very attractive. He was witty and kind, and Annie let the ale ease her social anxiety. The man seemed harmless enough.

As the song ended, the man gave her a small dip and pulled her back up. She saw Hak's face as she gazed over Tomas's shoulder.

Hak was seething at the top of the stairs. He was dressed in a plain blue tunic and brown leather breeches, and wore a brown scarf that hid the scars on his neck. She could see by the way his lips moved that he was uttering a torrent of curses.

"You will have to excuse me," Annie whispered urgently to Tomas. He reluctantly let go, and Annie dashed toward the bar. She found her mug freshly filled, and motioned for Hak to join her. She could see he was furiously grinding his teeth.

"Aye. He did not know you were down here," Odal muttered, shaking his head.

"Hak's a bit uptight, isn't he?"

"You'd better take him this, and go back upstairs. I do not know his reasons, but I have not seen him that upset." Odal handed her a second mug and shooed her away.

Annie walked quickly over to Hak and offered him a mug. "You gotta try the beer! It's awesome!"

His yellow eyes burned, and his lips were tight against his handsome face. Annie began to push the mug of beer at him, but Hak put a firm hand on the back of her neck and squeezed. He turned Annie to face the stairs and began pushing her upward.

"Owwww dude, what the fuck—"

"I *told* you—"

"Ouch! Let go!"

Annie could feel several sets of eyes following them as they walked up the stairs and out of sight, Hak's fingers digging painfully into the back of her neck.

Hak did not release Annie until they had walked back into their room. She quickly set the mugs on the basin and whirled on him.

"Seriously?! What the fuck!"

"You swore you would not leave the room!"

"Did not!"

Hak sputtered, then pointed at her. "You swore you would not talk to anyone," he shouted, "and yet I find you drunk and groping some mercenary like a ship's whore!"

Annie's eyes bulged with fury. "You take that back, asshole!"

Hak took his mug of beer and sunk to the ground in front of the door. Annie glared darkly at him and balled her hands into little fists. After a moment of consideration, Hak took a few swallows and sighed heavily. "This is going to be a very long two weeks."

"Well you know what? Fuck you. I'm not going to Meda with you. I'll stay right here." Annie sneered and walked over to her pack of cigarettes. She lit one, grabbed her mug of beer, and stared angrily at Hak.

Hak twitched at her words. "You will come to Meda. You must. The answers will be there."

"That's what you keep saying. But you know what? You're an asshole. I don't need to go with you. I can go by myself!"

"So you just think that wandering about by yourself is smart? You will be raped by Vinder before the second day."

Annie made a spitting noise. "Fine. Then I'll just dress like a man. Seems to be my thing here, anyways."

"Then they will just kill you and take your belongings."

Annie faltered. *Fucking hell.*

"Why can't I dance? Why can't I be seen? No one down there threw stones at me or called me a freak, so why worry so much?"

"Because it might not be good to let . . . certain people know I am here."

"Why?" Annie drunkenly sat on the bed. "Why are you so scared and angry? What's your problem? You don't want us to be seen, you won't let me talk. Are you hiding? Is someone trying to kill you?"

"Shut up!" Hak snapped.

Annie winced and stared at the floor.

Hak looked around a bit, as if listening to the hallway outside. The common room was loud enough that no one had heard their shouting.

Hak whispered, "Yes."

"Wait, *what?* Someone *is* trying to kill you?"

"Keep your voice down! The miners in the zythil pits can hear you."

"Is my life in danger?"

"Keep acting a fool, and you will surely get me killed."

"Why are you hiding?"

"I must."

"Are you a murderer? Are you dangerous?" Annie whimpered, her eyes wide. The room spun.

After a moment's thought, Hak gave her a cold look. "Yes. Now shut your mouth."

Annie felt her stomach do a twist. And then another. Suddenly, three mugs of beer seemed like a bad idea.

"Where's the bathroom?"

"Why do you want to take another bath?"

"Ugh, no . . . Where do you guys pee and stuff?"

Hak waved at the hallway in disgust. "There is a room next to the washroom." Annie leapt off the bed and stumbled out into the hallway. Hak was close at her heels.

"Are you going to watch me every second?" Annie asked, suddenly terrified of the tall man.

"I will wait outside."

Annie opened the heavy door and a horrible stench assaulted her senses. Even with a large window open, there was no mistaking the putrid smell of shit and piss. She saw that there were a few large pots on the ground under a bench with a hole cut in the wood. Some of the pots looked rather full.

"Fucking hell." Annie felt her beer threaten to jump out of her stomach. After a few drunken moments, she found a way to safely hover over one of the pots without touching anything. *Well, I've been to rock concerts and outdoor music festivals with bathrooms worse than this.*

After she relieved herself, she peered out the window to see if there was any means of escape. There were no handholds, and the drop appeared to be too steep. Annie knew she was too drunk to attempt escape, and Hak had her backpack. She was trapped.

Annie woke the next morning with a pounding headache. In a strange way, she relished the old familiar feel of a hangover. *I feel pain and hangovers. I can feel drunk, and happy, and sad. Hah. Maybe I'm somehow still alive. Or maybe the hangovers in hell are really this bad.*

She slowly sat up in bed and saw that Hak was gone. The night before had been a blur of tearful, drunken fighting. Annie had been sufficiently drunk, while Hak had sat on the floor with his back to the door. Somewhere in the middle of arguing, Annie had become homesick and emotional, and had cried herself to sleep. Hak had slept in front of the door on a pile of blankets. He had seemed horribly frustrated and annoyed with her drunken sobbing.

Somewhere in the middle of her emotional breakdown, Annie had come to the sour realization that she couldn't trust anyone at all. Even an honor vow from Hak might not be enough to protect her. He treated her like a *thing*. Despite all that, she had no choice but to travel with Hak to Meda. She hoped that after she arrived in the large town, she could lose Hak once and for all. She was determined to find a powerful mage who could give her the answers she wanted. Perhaps Hak could prove useful.

Annie stretched and stood on wobbly legs. She coughed and looked at the pile of cigarette butts from last night in dismay. She had been trying to conserve her tobacco supplies, but after three large mugs of beer, she hadn't paid attention. *Might as well have one more*, she thought.

A tray of food and water was resting on the dresser. She noted that Hak had placed the solar panel against the windowsill.

Pity he didn't know he has to plug it in to something, Annie sighed. She plugged in her smartphone and left the charger to its business.

She poured herself a glass of water and took a few sips. The water was surprisingly cold and sweet. She finished off a second glass and began to pace the room while absently chewing on some bread. She was not hungry in the slightest, but she didn't know when she would eat again, either. Despite a pounding headache and an upset stomach, she was determined to finish the entire loaf.

She found a small pitcher with water and poured it into the empty basin by the mirror. She scrubbed and cleaned her hands as best she could, and carefully removed her contact lenses. She blinked several times, and carefully opened a new packet of lenses.

Man . . . I have a few months' worth of contacts left. What will happen when I run out? I won't be able to see at all! At least these are the kind of lenses I can sleep in for up to a month. I have to be careful, or I'll be blind and helpless.

Annie walked to the window and surveyed the town as she ate. *This place is right out of a fairy tale. It's just so quaint. The children play barefoot between passing horse-drawn carts. A woman stands at a simple booth yelling out for people to try her vegetables. There are shop signs along this side of the road, although I have no idea what any of those symbols mean. It's just a simple village. Right out of my sketchbooks. No cars. No people yelling at each other. No one lugging a laptop to a soul-sucking job. This is their reality.*

She leaned against the window frame and watched the town. She caught sight of Hak walking down the road with several bags. He was unarmored, clean shaven, and had the same peculiar scarf hiding his scar. She almost didn't recognize him. He seemed peaceful enough, and patiently sidestepped a pack of children scurrying after a ball. He smiled at them. Then he turned, looked up at the inn, and caught sight of Annie in the window. His expression darkened.

Annie returned the glare as he walked up to the building. He handed one of his bags to the stable boy and walked inside. A few moments later, he opened the door to the room and dropped a large bag on the floor.

"What's that?"

"Provisions. Enough for the two of us for two weeks."

"Are we carrying all this to Meda?"

"No," Hak said sharply. "I have a horse, remember?" He gathered his belongings and added them to the pile of supplies. "I also found a horse for you. An old mare too lame to haul a plow, but strong enough to carry a reed like yourself. The farmer was too happy to sell her."

"Oh." Annie paused. She could not remember the last time she had been on a horse. Her mother and stepfather had given her horseback riding lessons as a treat when she was sixteen, but that had been nearly ten years ago. She was unsure how well she could ride an old mare. *I'm not going to let him see me sweat, whatever it takes. I'm not some frilly helpless lady like he's used to. I'm sure it's just like riding a bike.*

Hak looked over at her and arched an eyebrow. "You do know what a horse is, right?"

Annie forced a laugh, "Of course I do. And we ride them around in my world, too."

"Good. We leave in a few moments. Do what you need to do, and meet me in the stables. Do not distract yourself." Hak reached down, took her bag, and then left the room.

Annie growled in exasperation. *I'm not ready to leave yet. There are shops here I want to see!* But she did not yell this at the open doorway. She was learning to keep her mouth shut around Hak. She would be rid of him in two weeks.

She had one more cigarette and watched the town below. She fumed at the thought of two entire weeks with a person like Hak.

He's no fun. He yells at me. He's rude. Ugh . . . Annie scratched with irritation at her scalp, and glowered at the reflection in the mirror.

"Why the angry face?"

Annie jumped and turned toward the doorway. It was the man she had danced with the previous night. She grasped for a name. She had been quite drunk last night.

"Tom?"

"Tomas. Yes." He gave her a huge, glowing smile. His eyes flickered to her cigarette for a moment, but he didn't say anything about it.

"Are you already off? I thought you had just arrived, Annie of Oregon."

Annie laughed, despite her pounding headache. "Just Annie. Please. And yeah, we're leaving."

"Ah. As I am." Tomas looked sad. "I hope that our paths will cross again. You were a true delight to dance with."

Annie felt her face grow hot as she blushed. "Thanks. You weren't so bad yourself."

"Where might you be traveling?"

"I, uh—" She paused and scratched at her scalp. She remembered the fight last night. Hak had been worried about being seen or followed by someone. Something deep within her foggy mind cried out a warning. Annie couldn't tell if it was Hak's warning, or her own, but she listened to her intuition. "Uh, not really sure."

Tomas raised an eyebrow. "No? Just casting off into the winds?"

"Yeah." Annie put her cigarette out in an empty mug. Tomas watched quietly, his face unreadable.

"Will you be joining your big friend, or would you like company?"

Annie bit her lip. "I think it's just going to be me and . . . my big friend."

Tomas nodded, and gave her another warm smile. "Well, my beautiful Annie, I do hope our paths cross on the road again." He walked up to her, took her hand in his, bowed down and kissed it. Her face grew unbearably hot.

He gently dropped her hand and turned to leave. There was something about the conversation that bothered Annie. *I'm not sure if it's the hangover, or if that guy is a creep. Or maybe he is just really some cheesy knight that chases after all the ladies. Bowing and kissing my hand. Ha! I wonder what Karen would think of the men here?*

Annie poked her head out into the hallway, but Tomas had disappeared. She made her way downstairs and walked through the empty kitchen. A large cauldron was stewing over a fire, and several loaves of baked bread sat out on the counter, but no one was around. She quietly ducked outside.

She found Hak in the stable talking with Odal.

"—yes, it's very strange," Odal was saying. "Very loud noises. Quick and sudden, like thunder. But there were no clouds in the sky."

"What direction would you say?"

"Man last night said he heard it on the western flank of the foothills. Spooked his horse a bit. Second report of the noises this week. Just be careful out there."

"Fair enough. Thank you, Odal." Hak glanced over at Annie.

"Odal, thank you so much for your hospitality. I loved your inn. I hope to come back and visit again." Annie gave him her warmest smile.

Odal bowed. "My lady, you just about set the place on fire. I dare to say, I think you impressed some young men last night. Your dance partner looked so forlorn after Hak took you upstairs. I *even* had a woman ask for beer shortly after your dancing."

"I had a wonderful time. It's important to let your hair down and live a little. Or else you walk around with a face frozen like that." Annie jerked a thumb at Hak. "This guy is no fun, you know."

Odal nervously glanced over at Hak, and then whispered to Annie, "Do be careful, Lady Annie. He is one of the best swordsmen there is. But try to stay on his kind side."

"He has a kind side?"

Odal dared to grin at the comment, and gave Annie one more bow. Hak silently led two horses out of the stable and watched Annie impatiently. She decided not to mention her conversation with Tomas. *Hak would probably just scream at me again for talking.*

She walked over to him and noted that he had tied her backpack on his horse. The gray mare he had found looked quite bedraggled, and hairier than any pony she had seen, but seemed kind enough when she reached out to stroke her muzzle. Hak's horse was a large black stallion, and nipped at Annie's hand when she tried to pet him.

Just like your owner. She scowled.

"I would not do that if I were you," Hak said.

"What's his name?"

"Shadow."

"Hmmmm, how original."

Hak looked wounded. "He is a good horse."

"Does my horse have a name?"

Hak shrugged. "I did not ask. I am sure you can think of something."

"All right." Annie paused, and then asked, "So, where are we going?"

"South. And quickly."

"Hey. How come you didn't have Shadow when you found me?"

Hak snorted. "That mountain is far too dangerous for anyone, let alone a large, noisy horse."

"But not dangerous enough for you?"

"I needed to be there. I had my reasons," he said coldly. The tone in his voice made it clear he did not wish to discuss it any further.

They carried the reins for a bit and walked to the edge of the town. Annie thought she heard something familiar.

"Tia?"

Hak stopped. "What is it?"

Annie shook her head sadly. "I think my hangover is playing tricks on me. I thought I heard my dog."

"I can hear many dogs right now."

"Yes, but I thought I heard *my* dog."

"You can act strange later. Come." Hak mounted Shadow and watched Annie expectantly. She eyed the old stirrups and the mare looked at her with a sense of unease.

"Uh, I feel like walking for a bit. Is that okay?"

"Just get on the horse, Annie."

After two clumsy attempts, she pulled herself up into the saddle and took the reins. In a way, it was like riding a bike. The mare was calm and responsive, and Annie felt hazy memories of trail riding come back to her. They traveled for about five minutes before Annie saw a group of five children running though a field next to the road.

There were two girls and three boys of varying heights, with dirty brown hair and chubby cheeks. Their clothes were filthy and patched in several places, and their skin was tanned a dark brown. Annie guessed they were between the ages of four and ten. They were squealing with delight as they played with their dog, which was barely visible in the tall grass. The tallest boy reached down, picked up a large stick, and heaved it as far as he could. Annie saw the grass give way to a figure bouncing through it. The black dog leapt high and caught the stick easily from the air. The children cheered.

"Holy fucking shit," Annie breathed.

Hak whirled his head around to look at her in alarm. "What is it?"

Annie sobbed and hastily dismounted from her mare, nearly losing a shoe as she slipped from the saddle. She fell to the ground, and a heartbeat later jumped up and ran toward the children.

"Annie!" Hak shouted in alarm.

She didn't listen to him, and ran with tears streaming down her cheeks.

"Oh god, Tia. *Tia!*"

"Stop this nonsense!" Hak jumped off Shadow, hastily tied the horses to a tree, and ran after her.

The kids stopped laughing and cheering when they saw Annie approach. She knew she must be frightening, in her strange clothes and screaming in an unladylike way.

"Tia!" she shouted again. The grass stopped moving around her. The children stared at her with large green eyes and open mouths.

"Annie, what is this madness of yours?" Hak reached for her neck, but Annie was knocked down by a huge black dog.

"Oh god!" she wailed, and wrapped her arms around the excited dog. Then she cried some more. The dog was just as frantic, whining and crying while trying to lick Annie everywhere at once. Annie sobbed louder. The dog was so excited Annie could barely hold on to her.

"How is this possible?" she heard Hak say.

"We found her," said the smallest child. "She's ours!"

"The dog knows this strange lady, Nic. Look at it. The dog is going mad!"

Annie ignored everyone around her and blubbered into Tia's neck. *Every moment of every day since I lost you, I missed you. I needed you, sweet pooch. I heard you yelp, I thought you were dead!* Annie sobbed harder.

Hak knelt down next to Annie and stared at Tia. After another minute of licking Annie's face, Tia turned to Hak and began licking him. Hak actually laughed.

"It's the nicest dog we ever saw," said the tallest boy. Annie wondered if he was the older brother of the other children. "Never seen one that tame. Momma let us keep her because she wouldn't touch the chickens."

"You big baby . . ." Annie kissed the dog and wiped tears from her eyes, "You were always such a big wimp."

"This is . . . a miracle?" Hak shook his head. "There is no way this is your dog."

"This is definitely her. This is her collar, for fuck's sake!" Annie pointed at the green collar and the small, bone-shaped metal plate with Tia's name on it. The children giggled at the foul language.

"See this number? This is the number you call to reach my phone. It's in case she ever got lost." She hoped Hak understood that.

"I still find this impossible to believe—"

"Tia! Do you want a treat?"

At the phrase, the dog immediately sat down and licked her lips. She stared from Annie to Hak and back to Annie again.

"Lay down."

Tia obeyed. The children cheered.

"Roll over."

Tia just looked at Annie expectantly.

"She can roll over, I swear."

"I believe this beast is yours." Hak stood and scratched at his chin. "She does match the photograph you showed me. But . . . this is just madness."

"I don't know how she's here and I don't care." Annie embraced Tia again. Fresh tears burned her eyes. "Such a happy dog, yes you are. You missed me as much as I missed you, didn't you, baby girl."

"Where did you find the dog?" Hak asked the children.

"We found her by town, trying to steal food," said the tall boy.

"She was scared," said the smallest child.

"But she liked us. She followed us home," said the young girl. "She looked really hungry, so we fed her."

"Are you going to take our dog?" the smallest boy asked. He fidgeted and sucked at his thumb. Hak looked down at the children. They all stared sadly at Tia, except for the tall boy. He watched the large man and nervously eyed the sword and armor.

Annie looked over at Hak and gave him a sad, pleading look. "This isn't even an issue, Hak. You know she is my dog. She *has* to come with us."

"It will be dangerous on the road."

"I need her. And she behaves. Mostly."

"But—"

"I'll never forgive you."

Hak sighed heavily and shifted his gaze from a desperate Annie to a group of forlorn children.

"We can buy her from you," Hak said gently. "I might have a few copper —"

The smallest child burst into a long, loud wail. His older sister tried to soothe him, but glared angrily at Annie. The oldest boy looked unsure.

"I don't want money," sobbed the youngest, pointing at Tia. "I want my Sapa!"

"Sapa—" Annie began, but Hak raised a hand to silence them all.

"I will give you a nice, shiny silver piece." Hak tenderly offered the small coin to the children.

The oldest boy jerked at the price, but hesitated when that failed to make his little brother happy.

"How about a bag of chocolate?" Annie asked. At once, all the children hushed and stared at her.

"Chocolate? Is this a trick?" the tall boy asked.

"No. No trick. I have lots of chocolate. Hak, go get my backpack. *Now*."

Annie was surprised by how quickly Hak jumped at her command and obeyed. He did not question her. He returned with her backpack and wordlessly dropped it on the ground next to her.

Annie dug out a plastic bag full of chocolate bites and waved them around. "Take this bag of chocolate, and let me take my dog."

The smallest boy grabbed the bag of chocolate from her greedily. "Mine!" he screamed at his siblings. Tia was already forgotten. The older girl snatched the bag from him and said, "We have to share." The kids shook the plastic bag, confusion wrinkling their eyebrows. They began fighting over the bag. Finally, the plastic ripped open and small chocolate bites littered the ground. There was more arguing as the children grabbed up the candy and pushed at each other.

"Smart," Hak whispered, watching the children argue.

"Yep. Let's say goodbye and get Tia out of here."

The oldest boy blinked at Annie and Hak, then gave them a shy smile.

Hak bowed to the tall boy and exchanged a few grateful words, and then he and Annie hurried back to the road where he had hastily tied the horses. Tia froze as they neared the big animals, but Annie ushered her along with praise.

"I need to walk with her for a moment. Until she gets used to the idea of horses."

"I thought you said you had horses?"

"I knew what horses *were*. I never said I owned one. I don't think Tia has seen one up close."

With a growl of annoyance, Hak picked up the mare's reins and led her along with Shadow. Annie skipped along happily with Tia, and the dog bounded in enthusiastic circles around her. Every few moments she knelt down and rubbed the dog's head, or made kissing noises at her. Her entire outlook on life changed with this one hopeful sign.

Chapter Six:

Past and Present

"I'M NOT DEAD!" Annie said suddenly.

"What?"

"There is no way I can be dead, right? Tia is here! Maybe . . . Maybe somehow we got here . . . I don't know. I just can't explain how she's here. She looks and feels real!"

Hak shook his head in frustration. "You are not dead. You are just insane. You have looked and felt horribly real the whole time."

Annie stuck her tongue out at Hak. He looked very troubled. His eyes were focused on the road ahead of him, and when he turned to look down at Tia, his eyebrows furrowed together.

He is just as confused and amazed as I am, Annie thought. She was too happy to question the miracle.

She walked alongside Hak and the horses for a few hours, until the excitement had worn off for both of them.

"Will your beast be able to travel for two weeks?" Hak asked her doubtfully.

"Sure. I might make her some booties if her paws get raw. I think I have a needle and thread in my backpack."

"You do," Hak assured her. "In a little white box with a red cross on it."

"Ha. I forgot you searched my stuff thoroughly," Annie said dryly. "But I don't think I'll have to make dog boots. Tia and I hiked the Pacific Coast Trail for a week once. She had more energy by the end of that than I did."

"Good," was all Hak said.

"If she senses that I'm in trouble, she will do anything to protect me." Annie gave Hak a grave look. "Don't try to grab me or look like you're hurting me. She might attack you."

"Do not give me reason to do so," Hak said.

They walked in silence and Annie bit at her lips nervously. *I want to know what this guy's story is. He confirmed last night he's a murderer, and dangerous. He acts as if he's a wanted criminal. I need to know what is going on in that brain of his. My survival depends on that.*

She gazed at Hak and smiled at the odd scene. Here she was, alone in Tahldia with a knight in full armor, riding horses to the mage city of Meda. The solar panel had been placed at the top of Hak's bedroll to catch the most sunlight.

A knight with a solar panel and a smartphone. What the fuck kind of afterlife dream is this? How did I get here? Truly? Did I faint and die, or did I somehow push myself here? I remember hearing about dragons and knights growing up, but I just thought they were stories. Tahldia is real . . .

"We need to talk. Is it safe?"

Hak looked down at her from Shadow. "Yes, I suppose. Just do not begin screaming."

"I just . . . I just thought of something." Annie scratched at her head and tried to think of the best way to tell him. She fumbled with the silver bracelet on her wrist and bit her lip. "I didn't make up Tahldia."

Hak began laughing, making Tia jump excitedly and the mare shy away nervously. It was a loud, happy noise that Annie had never heard from Hak before.

Here you are telling me not to make noise and you're laughing so hard you're going to fall off your horse.

Annie watched as Hak bent over in the saddle laughing for several moments. There were tears in his eyes. He lifted the helmet off his head and wiped at his face carefully with his gloves.

"Oh, Annie. You are truly a funny person."

"Are you done laughing? I'm sure Odal heard you back there."

Hak looked at her and shook his head, his face red from laughter. Despite her annoyance at how he handled her, Annie was pleased to see that Hak could laugh and act somewhat normal. His deep throaty laugh was a pleasant sound.

"You were saying—" Hak suppressed another fit of laughter. "—that we are all real after all."

"That's not what I meant, really." Annie shoved her hands into her pockets and kicked at a small rock. She had to think back to how she had organized her thoughts before she continued. "I just . . . I didn't make up Tahldia for my game. It was never my original idea. Sure, I told the CEO of one of the biggest video game companies that it was all my idea, but it wasn't." She looked at the ground, ashamed.

"It's a big deal, to rip off someone else's idea. So you're really the only person who knows, Hak. But when I was little, there was a guy who lived next door to my parents who told me about Tahldia, and the people here."

"*What?*" Hak stopped Shadow and looked down at Annie. "You just now thought of this man?"

Annie shot him a scathing look. "Sorry. I guess I was in shock. You know, from the nuclear bomb, the zombie attack, and thinking I was dead. That sort of shit can be distracting, you know." *Crap, I wonder what's next. Unicorns? Dragons?*

Hak let out a deep breath. "Tell me about this man, Annie."

She shrugged. "He lived next door to us when I was growing up. Joe Wilson. He was awesome. Strange, but really cool."

"Joe Wilson? What an odd name." Hak thought for a moment. "You say he knew of Tahldia?"

"He had tons of stuff in his house . . ." Annie felt her heart beating heavily as certain things from her past begin clicking together. "He was an artist and could play the most amazing songs on his piano. He had all these amazing oil paintings of people and . . . dragons. Mana oaks. Knights. Every inch of Mister Wilson's house was covered in art. That's how he made his living. He painted a lot of things for comic books . . . background art and world-building stuff.

"I'm a complete creative failure. In some ways, I was doodling Tahldian knights since I was ten. I just took his idea and made it my own. It was just a silly fantasy world, right? It wasn't supposed to be real!"

"What happened to him?"

"He died from cancer when I was fourteen." Annie gave Hak a sad look. "I used to go over to his house and watch him paint. He had a gorgeous atrium inside his house and he had plants everywhere. He was always listening to classical music on the radio.

"My stepdad didn't like him much. He thought Mister Wilson was strange. But my mom adored him, and she thought that our neighbor would be a good influence for me. So mom signed me up for painting lessons with him when I was six. He used to tell me stories as we painted together. Stories about this world."

Hak's face seemed to be made from stone. His expression was unreadable, so Annie nervously continued her story.

"What can I say? My whole life I thought about your world, Hak. I drew knights, dragons, and griffins. Kids picked on me all the time. You see, girls like me aren't necessarily popular where I'm from in Georgia. You have these Southern belle types who like to dress up and have fancy hair and clothes. I was happier reading comic books and drawing dragons.

"I didn't really have any friends because I was such a nerd." Annie laughed bitterly. "I loved to draw, so I kept doing it. It was my escape. I wanted so badly for Tahldia to be real. It was all I drew. I guess I eventually forgot Mr. Wilson had created the place to begin with. When I was in college, I decided to put together a portfolio and pitch it as an idea for a video game. I had a friend in the industry who pulled a lot of strings in order for me to pitch it to a boardroom full of —"

"What did this Joe Wilson look like?"

Annie shrugged. "It's been a long time. He was older . . . I dunno, I guess in his sixties when he died? Short and skinny, with a bald head. Had a big nose. Light brown eyes."

Hak shook his head. "Any scars? Tattoos or sigils?"

"He had a limp. But that was from a car accident. I was only a few months old when it happened, but my mom told me about it. What does it mean, Hak?"

"Not even the best warlock can travel across planes. And all the warlocks are dead. I do not know what it means. Perhaps this Joe Wilson had somehow dreamt of us or seen us in a vision. That can happen."

"I guess." Annie was doubtful. "Why are all the warlocks dead?"

"They were wiped out by the Shafani hundreds of years ago. They were too powerful." Hak looked troubled. "It sounds like your neighbor had a vision."

"I've dreamed of you, Hak," Annie said faintly. She looked up at the knight's face and stared deep into his yellow eyes. "Or of a knight a lot like you. Maybe it was because I was drawing knights in general so much. But I definitely had a dream of a knight with yellow eyes. And your eye color is extremely rare in my world."

"Yellow is not a very common color here, either," Hak said. He looked down at his hands for a moment, and then turned his gaze back to Annie. "It is very odd you say you dreamt of me. Or dreamt of a knight with yellow eyes. When was this?"

"When I was twenty maybe? But I turned what I saw into a character design . . . and he ended up being the hero of my video game. Remind me when we camp tonight to show you my sketchbook. I think I put one in my backpack."

"I saw it," Hak said, his voice hard. "You have a talent with the arts, Annie. But I was very disturbed by what I saw."

"Why?"

"Because . . ." Hak seemed to search for the right words. "I saw the people you had drawn . . . There are some uncanny resemblances to some people. People who want me dead." He said it very carefully, as if trying to keep Annie calm.

She felt chilled by the words. *I've drawn people trying to kill Hak? What the fuck!* "Like who? Who would want to kill you?"

"Voltay."

Annie almost fell over. "But . . . Isn't he . . ."

"The king of Shafan."

Annie felt sick. "Oh, Hak . . . What did you do to piss off a *king*?"

"It was what I saw." Hak growled. "Do you not understand why I hated you when I first talked with you? Do you not understand why I thought you were evil?"

Annie sputtered. "I'm not evil!"

Hak stiffened in the saddle, his face grim. "You know too much. And yet you seem to know nothing. I do not understand this at all. Yet it seems that you always speak true. When you showed me photographs, and now this dog is here." Hak waved a hand dismissively at Tia. "I do not know what to think about you at all."

"Well, I have been telling you the truth!"

"I hope so, Annie," Hak said quietly. "I want to believe you. I truly do. But this is just so strange."

"Agreed," Annie said.

"You seem like a harmless woman. You are loud, rude, and you have an extraordinarily foul tongue. But you do not seem evil. And yet you have seen Voltay's face and house sigil."

"Mr. Wilson drew him several times."

"I wonder why."

"He said, 'We must remember when evil happens. We must face the villains.' But he said that about a lot of things. Like I said, he was a bit of an odd duck."

"Strange way to put it," Hak said.

"Hak, something else doesn't make sense. I was little when I saw my first image of Voltay. I liked drawing him because he had that really funny pointed beard . . ."

"But . . . ?"

79

"But how is he still alive? The guy must be ancient by now."

Hak hesitated, and chose his words carefully. "He does not age like a human does."

"Not like a human? So what is he, an elf? You guys have elves and dwarves and shit here, right?"

"No . . . Well, we do have elves *and shit*." Hak growled, shocking Annie. She had never heard him curse before. He sighed and squeezed the bridge of his nose. "There are things not many here know about Voltay and Bingen. Things that would be considered blasphemous."

Annie waited for him to say more, but Hak prodded Shadow into walking again. He looked around uneasily, one hand squeezing the helmet resting on the saddle's pommel.

"What is it, Hak? Please don't ignore me or tell me to shut up. You *have* to tell me what is going on with you. Please? I'm begging you to tell me the full story."

Hak grimaced as if Annie were physically hurting him.

"Can this wait until we make camp for the night?"

"Please quit dodging my questions!" Annie pleaded.

"It is a very long story," he replied gruffly. "It will take some time to tell. And I am not sure *how* to tell you. Or even if I *should* tell you."

"Why?"

"It is dangerous to know me, Annie."

"Is this one of those if-you-tell-me-you-have-to-kill-me sort of things?"

Hak laughed bitterly. "Perhaps."

Annie's heart beat painfully in her chest. Her intuition screamed at her to get away from Hak as fast as possible. And yet, there was something about Hak that sparked every fiber of Annie's curiosity. She felt oddly safe around him. In another time, on another planet, and with a haircut, Annie would have been attracted to a man that looked like him.

But Hak is a giant asshole. He's five types of asshole all rolled up in plate armor. And yet why am I finding myself more and more curious? Why do I feel like he could actually be a good guy under all that cold mental and physical armor? This guy seems to have issues, but maybe there's a good reason. What kind of reason would make him a murderer and wanted by a king? I'm trying to put myself in your shoes, Hak, but it's really hard. There is so much I don't understand about you.

Hak caught her gaze and said gently, "Get on your horse and ride for a while, Annie. We must distance ourselves from Feldall."

Reluctantly, Annie agreed. She climbed into the saddle a little more gracefully this time. Tia kept her distance but did not let Annie out of her sight.

They traveled south until the setting sun cast a soft light on the forest, giving everything a golden glow. After a spending a few moments looking into the forest on either side of the path, Hak decided to make his own trail.

He led them far from the main road to ensure no one saw their campfire. He found a very small clearing with a stream, and they dismounted. Tia drank eagerly from the cold water and then slobbered all over Hak. He laughed and gave the dog a gentle pat on the head.

Annie gathered firewood while Hak tended to the horses and made camp. She had bristled the first time he ordered her to gather wood, but she enjoyed it tonight. It allowed Annie to collect her thoughts and digest everything that had happened that day. Tia helped pick up smaller sticks and ran about the campsite trying to start a game of fetch. Annie set the wood down in a large pile and saw that Hak had set out two large bedrolls.

"You bought me a sleeping bag?"

"Yes. You needed one, correct?"

"Yeah. Thank you."

Hak grinned. "You are welcome. I actually purchased a few things for you, to make the journey easier for both of us."

Annie raised an eyebrow. "Such as?"

Hak reached down and handed her a canvas bag. Annie unwound the twine and pulled out a bundle of fabric wrapped in a simple brown belt. Hak looked very pleased with himself. Annie gave him a confused expression.

"Clothes," Hak said, smiling. "Proper traveling clothes for a lady. I am hoping they fit. Shoes are expensive, and we will need to fit you in Meda."

"I have shoes. I actually wore my best pair of hiking boots out of the house. They'll last." Annie inspected the bundle of clothes doubtfully. There was a light blue tunic, similar to what Hak wore but with a flowering vine embroidered along the hem. *Oh god, my grandmother would love this. But the pants . . . ?*

Annie held up the heavy, brown leather pants. They looked about four sizes too large. The brushed leather was faded with heavy wear. *Oh man, straight out of an adventure tale . . . All I need is a feathered hat and a bow and arrow and I'll fit the part.*

Hak was still watching Annie, a smile playing at his lips.

"Uh, thank you, Hak. These are . . . a nice gift."

"You are most welcome. I would like you to start traveling in these clothes. The sigil on your . . . hoodie is a very odd thing to wear on the road. You need to fit in. You draw looks everywhere you go."

"Thanks," Annie said dryly.

Hak did not miss the bite in her response. He sat down near her and began stacking wood into a cone shape. She helped him light the kindling, and before long the sky had grown dark. Annie looked up in amazement at the stars and gaped for several minutes before looking at Hak.

"Wow! That's so cool! I have never seen so many stars in my life!"

"Truly?"

"Yeah. Where I come from, there is so much smoke in the sky that you can't see all the stars. We call it *smog*."

"That sounds terrible."

"I don't recognize any of these." She continued to stare up at the night sky through a large opening in the leafy canopy. There was a red nebula smudged across the blue and purple sky. The more Annie looked at it, the more stars she began to see within the crimson stardust. It took her breath away.

"No? You have never seen the Dragon's Eye?" Hak leaned over and pointed at a brilliant red star at the edge of the nebula.

"What is that? A planet?" Annie squinted her eyes at the flashing ruby.

"That is what some mages say. I always thought it was a star."

"Hey! Do you guys really have three moons here?"

Hak gave a deep, throaty laugh. "Of course! How many are we supposed to have?"

Annie shrugged. "Three. But there's only one moon where I'm from. I want to see them!"

"Only one moon? How odd."

Hak pulled out enough bread and cheese for the two of them. Annie gave Tia the rest of her jerky, knowing the spicy treat wouldn't phase the dog. *If she can eat three pairs of my shoes, she can eat beef jerky.*

"You will see the moons soon. This dense forest will begin to thin out quite a bit. We are at the edge of a mountain range, heading to another range. We will pass through a stretch of grasslands before reaching Meda. The grasslands will be a great place to watch the cosmos." Hak turned his gaze to Annie and all humor had vanished. "It will be very dangerous on the plains, Annie. You will need to do everything I say, without questioning me. Your dog will need to obey me as well.

"There will be creatures on the plains who might make a meal of us. We will have to be very aware of our surroundings, and respectful to the wild. If we respect the creatures of Tahldia, they will respect us in kind. If we anger them, we will find ourselves in trouble. And I cannot use a sword against all of them."

I wonder if he means dragons. But Annie was too scared to ask. She pulled Tia toward her, wrapped her arms around the big dog, and leaned into her for comfort. When they sat side by side, the dog seemed to dwarf Annie. Hak gave them a small smile.

"How do we protect ourselves?"

"Have caution. Do no harm to any creature. Even swiping at what could be a harmless bug might incite an entire colony of driddle flies to swarm us for days."

Annie nodded, watching Hak's tired face in the firelight. *Those eyes seem so ancient. Those scars are so horrible. What has this man been through?*

"Hak," Annie said carefully, "I think it's story time."

Hak grimaced and stared sadly at the bread in his hands. His gaze shifted to Annie, and he suddenly seemed much older. "I worry that telling you will put me in danger, or yourself."

"I need to know. You're the only person I've hung out with on Tahldia. And . . . well, you saved my life. I might not have made it five more minutes without you that day you found me. I feel indebted to you for that, Hak, but I also wonder what the fuck is going on with you. You've been really mean to me . . . but for some reason I still think there is good in you."

Hak gave her a sad smile, but said nothing. He looked into the fire for a long time, while Annie watched him patiently. She could see that she had made Hak upset somehow, but this time he was not yelling at her. She thought she saw his eyes water a few times as he watched the flames dance. Just watching him made Annie feel depressed.

"The stars have cursed me. I am broken, and I have nothing." He spit the words out, startling Annie. "I am fallen, a reject of my kingdom, if you will. I have no king. No family. No home. I should be dead." He gave a bitter laugh.

Hak's eyes watered again, and he glared at the fire furiously, as if he saw a spirit. Annie slowly reached out to Hak and tried to touch the thick scar that snaked its way along his neck. Hak gave her a pained look and leaned away.

"What happened to you, Hak?"

"I was a general in the Shafani army. I led many men to their deaths. I sought out men and killed them with my magic, in the name of my king." Hak's face twisted angrily. "His majesty, Voltay Oosberick the Fourth, wanted to own all the zythil in the world. The mines in Shafan are nearly barren. The dwarves and warlocks fought Voltay at every turn, and he in turn eradicated almost all the dwarven cities in the western world."

"I thought you said the warlocks are all dead? You said they died hundreds of years ago."

Hak snorted. "They did."

Annie leaned back and whistled. "Just how old is this Voltay dude?"

"He is at least six generations old."

"How?"

"They tell us . . . in all the stories, that Voltay and Bingen were imbued with the divine power of the stars. That they kissed the gods and their blood became pure mana." Hak sneered. "All lies."

Annie leaned forward. Hak winced and said in the softest whisper, "They are half-breeds, Annie. Blood of demons. They feast on others to grow in power."

Annie sucked in her breath as Hak continued. "During my twenty-ninth summer, I had received word that a dwarven regiment was going to attack an outlying Shafani city. I had enough soldiers to wipe them from the land, but I was given no orders. I demanded action, but the other generals would not listen. After many days, I grew tired of waiting for the command from the dragon general.

"I went to the regent's tower. I interrupted a feast." Hak shivered. "Apparently Bingen preferred to eat serving girls instead of roast boar."

Annie nearly choked on her bread. "They were eating *people*?"

Hak nodded. "Blood sacrifice. It . . . it is truly an evil deed. Once I had laid eyes on the grisly scene, they did not give me a chance to escape. You see, once you see demons in their true form, the enchantments and charms cast to look human no longer work. They took me to a dungeon hidden beneath the castle. The guards down there were not human. Some sort of strange spirit I had not seen before. At first, I wondered why the demons let me live . . ." Hak was shaking. "But then I wished they had killed me."

Annie tried to place a reassuring hand on Hak's arm, but he jerked away from her.

"They are torturers, Annie. Demons. They . . ." Hak closed his eyes and took a deep breath. "They robbed me of my mana. They took from me the one delight I had in life. They sucked it out of me until I was as dry as the Tauian desert." He made no move to wipe at the tears that silently slid down his rough cheeks. His voice was filled with barely subdued rage. "I wish they had killed me. They tried."

"Why didn't they?" Annie asked timidly.

"Mana energies can spike when the body is distressed. Demons get energy from that pain and fear. They delight in torture. They have this . . . crystal. It's about the size of a silver piece. They cut me and rested it inside my wound as the blood poured out, and removed it after the blood ceremony was complete. With some spoken words it drained my mana." Hak shuddered. "They cut me several times, and jabbed the gem deep inside of me. It burned and froze me at the same time . . . *Gods* . . . You see, I had a lot of magic. I was ripe for the taking."

"Oh, Hak," Annie whispered, placing a hand to her mouth. "How could someone do that?"

"For power."

Hak wiped at his eyes and took a few deep breaths. Tia sensed his distress; she walked over to Hak and leaned against him. She licked his cheeks for several minutes despite Hak trying to brush her away.

"Does she always do this?"

"She knows when people are upset. It's her way of hugging you."

Hak sighed and rubbed one of Tia's ears.

"How did you escape?"

Hak made a face and let his hand fall from Tia's head. "I do not know how long I was imprisoned. The half-breed demons know how to erase memories; they stole many happy memories from my childhood. I cannot recall what my parents looked like, or if I had siblings. But I remember all the torture.

"I think I was captive for close to a year. It was summer when they captured me, and it was spring when I escaped. Time ceased for me. When I lost my ability to use magic, I begged for death every day.

"After a particularly grueling day of torture, I heard the alarm bells ring throughout the tower, but I was too broken-spirited to move. I had given up hope."

Annie's eyes burned with tears as she tried to envision the scene. It broke her heart to imagine anyone going through such torture. Tia nudged Hak's chin with her wet nose, but he didn't push the dog away.

"The dwarves had apparently spent years digging toward the capital from the nearby mountains. Even with the aid of magic, it was still quite the feat. No one expected the ground to open up in the middle of the city and thousands of dwarves poured out. It was the last surviving host of dwarves in the western world. Their wives and children fought that day. They *even* had three dragons and half a dozen elite mages. Old bards will tell you there were warlocks, too. Everyone talks about the siege of Falishan to this day.

"I heard the cries of the dying. I heard the dragons screaming. I knew it was hopeless for them, and all I could do was pray to the gods that their deaths would be swift. It was only when I heard the spirits slain in the hallway outside my cell that I dared to hope.

"The dwarves opened all the cell doors. It was then that I realized how fortunate I was. So many prisoners were unable to escape because their legs and arms were gone. Their eyes were missing and their faces covered in scars." Hak took a deep breath and shuddered. "Are you sure you want to hear *all* of this, Annie?"

"It might give me some nightmares, but that is nothing compared to what you have been through. I'm so sorry this happened to you."

His face twisted for a moment, but Hak leaned into Tia and absently petted her. "The other prisoners begged for us to kill them. My dwarven rescuers gave me a sword when they saw I could still stand. I gave mercy to three men and a woman that day. You do not want to know their details, Annie. I can still hear their tortured screams every time I think about it.

"Before I gave mercy to the woman, she told me to 'protect the last warlocks.' She begged me to tell the kings in the eastern kingdoms of the horror in Voltay's castle.

"The men and dwarves who opened my cell door ordered me to run and fight. I believe that they felt a newly freed and armed group of prisoners would aid in the distractions of a city under siege. They were right. I was happy to slay anyone who tried to stop me. Even though I was weak from imprisonment, my thirst for revenge drove me forward.

"I ran up to the entrance of the tower and saw daylight for the first time in a year. The sky was choked with smoke, but it was a welcome sight. I also saw that the dwarves were losing the battle. A dragon was dying in the courtyard, and there were so many bodies . . . I did not know where to run but I knew I would not have the energy to fight my way past the city gates. I grabbed a better sword from a fallen soldier as I ran, and I felt blessed that he had a small bag of dried meat and a full water skin on him. May Alhena shelter his soul.

"Then I found one of the tunnels they had used to invade. It was a great opening in the ground, as if an earthquake had rent the courtyard in two. Everyone was busy fighting, and dying. There was no one in the tunnel, but there were several lanterns near the mouth. The dwarves must have left them when they reached the end of their march.

"I took two lanterns for myself and I ran for hours, until the lanterns ran out of oil. At that point I walked as fast as I could, holding a hand against the wall and feeling my way through the tunnel. I do not know how long I was down there. I do not know how I found the energy to escape that day, but I did. I ran out of what little food I had, and thought I would die of thirst. I felt like I traveled for days, but I was so weak from being imprisoned that I did not have a decent grasp on time.

"It was when I felt a cold breeze on my skin, and saw a beautiful shaft of sunlight, that I knew I would live. I crawled out of the ground near the northern mountain range, very far from the city. There was only a small party of dwarves waiting at the other end. I told them of the battle, and the dead dragons. They gave me water and bread out of pity, and let me pass. Then I stowed away on a ship to this continent.

"I have been wandering the eastern world ever since. It has been two turns of spring since I escaped, and I have been trying to find a way to get my magical abilities back. I want revenge."

"The siege failed . . ." Annie said sadly. "But you're alive, Hak."

"Half of the dwarven race was wiped from Tahldia that day. But the dwarves knew that if they did not go to war united, they would all die eventually as Voltay searched for zythil. He would just pick them off as he found them."

"That's awful." Annie wiped her eyes. Hak watched her for several minutes. His face betrayed a mix of concern and sadness.

"Annie, you must not breathe a word of this to anyone. I am like a diseased wretch on this side of the world. Anyone who discovers that I am Shafani will want to kill me. I have been attempting a quest to clean my honor with the mages of Meda. Until then, I am an outcast. It is like trying to lift a curse. Right now, no one trusts me."

"I know that feeling." Annie shot Hak a wry smile.

"I am being very serious." Hak poked at the fire with a stick, staring deep into the coals. "I need my magic back more than anything. They say there are ways to revive the mana current within a soul, but the council will not tell me anything useful. They have me bouncing around the eastern world doing stupid quests. I feel that they are merely trying to keep me busy and out of the way.

"Meanwhile, Voltay grows in power. I have tried to warn the elder mages of Voltay's true form, but to no avail. Their arrogance could be the end of them. We are all running out of time. And I have reason to suspect that Voltay and Bingen have sent men after me."

Annie shook her head, trying to digest everything that Hak had told her. "I feel like you are telling me the truth. I really want to believe you."

Hak stood up very quietly, and removed his gloves to work at the buckles on his armor. He slid the spaulders off and carefully followed with the breastplate. The chain mail underneath glittered in the firelight. Hak removed that as well, until he was down to his blue tunic. Wordlessly, Hak took off his tunic and was bare from the waist up. He was lean and well-muscled, but a great tangle of scars riddled the entire left side of his body.

"Why would I lie about torture?" he asked sadly, and raised his arms so she could see the full extent of his scars.

Annie tried her best not to cry at the sight. *Oh god, it's like a monster chewed him up and spit him out.* The deep scars ran from Hak's waist all along the left side of his body, curling around his left nipple and clawing down his back. The scars covered his left arm and crossed over his veins in a strange pattern. Near the center of each long scar was a large, round welt. Annie reached out and touched the large mark on his arm carefully. Hak did not pull away from her.

"That is where the gem was placed. My skin never healed well in those places." Annie followed the thick lines up to Hak's neck and she reached out and touched the scar there. Her finger traced the bumpy line over his main artery and her vision swam with fresh tears. Hak flinched and gently grabbed her hand.

"How did you live?" she whispered, her voice cracking.

"They healed me just enough, so that I could not bleed out in time." He said it so quietly Annie barely heard. "I was no use to them dead. Apparently you cannot harvest mana if you have a quick death. It takes time to drain magic, Annie. I was very powerful once."

"You say they drained you, but they still kept you alive."

Hak nodded slowly. "I have the smallest amount of hope that there might be something left inside of me. But I cannot reach out to my magic. It is like I am a plant, and the sun has set forever. I feel as if all the light and nourishment has gone from my life; when I reach out for the current of magic, nothing happens."

Annie gazed at the broken man in front of her. She believed him. She understood now. Annie's heart hurt to know that anyone could have endured so much. Hak stood there and watched her sadly.

Annie put her arms around him. Hak tried to jerk away but she fiercely told him to be still. For a long moment, Hak stood there stiffly while Annie hugged him. She placed a cheek against his scarred chest and sighed. *Poor thing. We've been so mean to each other.*

Hak tried to wriggle out of her arms.

"Haven't you ever had a hug before? Relax."

"Not . . . proper . . ." Hak managed.

"Shut up and quit fidgeting. You need a good hug." She squeezed him for another moment, even though he kept his hands stiffly at his sides. She released him and stood back to get a good look at his face in the firelight. *He is so much taller than me! My forehead barely comes to his chest. I wouldn't want to be on his bad side.*

"I owe you an apology, Hak. I'm really sorry for the way I treated you at the inn. And all those times I called you an asshole."

"You no longer think I am an asshole?"

"Well, you *acted* like an asshole. But I forgive you. And I'm sorry for making your life more difficult than it already was. Please forgive me."

"Fair enough." He reached down to pick up his tunic. "Now you know everything."

Annie sat down on her sleeping bag and curled up against Tia. She was suddenly very sad. "We are more alike than I ever imagined."

Hak sat down near her on his bedroll and gave her a curious look. "How so?"

"We've both lost everything." She turned her head away from him and buried her face in Tia's side. "We're alone in this world." Annie felt a tear slide down her cheek into the dog's soft fur. They did not speak again for the rest of the night, and Annie quietly cried herself to sleep.

CHAPTER SEVEN:

LESSONS LEARNED

ANNIE WOKE UP to something long and hairy crawling on her face. She sat up and swatted at her face frantically. A green moth the size of a tennis ball fluttered away from her. Shuddering, Annie pulled the soft hide of her bedroll to her chest and looked around.

The air was cold, and there were only smoldering embers left of the campfire. Annie looked over at Hak curled up tightly in his bedroll, his face peaceful as he slept.

Poor thing, Annie thought again. She looked sadly over at him for a long time, watching him sleep. He was handsome to her at that moment. Anger and sadness were gone from his face as he slept, and he almost looked happy.

Her thoughts were a cluster of confused and conflicting emotions wrapped up in fear of the unknown. *Someone is chasing him. I could be in danger, even if the threat isn't from this guy like I originally thought. I'm all alone in this world, and he is the only guy I can count on. At least I have Tia.*

Annie rubbed her eyes and looked around. "Tia?"

The dog was gone.

Annie pulled the blanket off and stood, shivering in the cold morning air. Her heart beat painfully and a sudden fear nibbled at her. "Tia?"

Hak's eyes flew open and he focused on Annie immediately.

Annie looked around the clearing and called Tia's name once more. Hak stood and had just opened his mouth to hush Annie when Tia came bounding out of the forest with half a squirrel in her mouth.

"Oh, *grooooooss.*" Annie gagged. "Tia! Drop it!"

Reluctantly, Tia spat out the carcass. The dog grinned at them and wagged her tail.

"If she can catch her meals, it will be easier on us and our food supplies," Hak said matter-of-factly.

"But . . . it's a squirrel!" Annie whined in revulsion. Tia began sniffing at the carcass again. "It's so nasty."

Hak gave Annie an odd look. "Annie, what did you feed Tia in your old world?"

"Dog food," she said slowly. Hak folded his arms and gave her an exasperated sigh.

"Not wild meat. She had kibble. Little bits of dried food."

"Well, a squirrel is probably much tastier, and will give her plenty of energy to run with us. And there is not *dry kibble food* here at this moment."

Annie sighed and waved a hand dismissively at Tia. "Fine. Eat it." Tia wagged her tail again and licked Annie's hand. "Gross!"

Hak laughed at them. It was that pleasant, deep laugh that Annie enjoyed. *He is still human. He was tortured, and had his life ruined, and he can still laugh. Maybe Hak is a good guy after all . . . .*

"You should probably find some way to tie her at night," Hak said as he picked up camp. "I would not want her to get into trouble."

"Agreed. I'll make a leash out of some rope. I'm just happy she is behaving so well. And honestly, I'm shocked she managed to catch a squirrel."

"She was probably very hungry," Hak said gently. "I would have purchased extra dried meat in Feldall if I had known she would turn up. I am somewhat decent at using a bow. I might be able to catch dinner for all of us tonight. I will have to keep my eyes open. It is very annoying to hunt without magic."

"Hak . . ." Annie started to open her mouth but the words wouldn't come out. She still felt awful about what happened to him. He looked at her, waiting for her to finish her thought. Annie shook her head and rolled up her blanket. "It's nothing. Never mind."

He looked at her quizzically, then bent to retrieve the bundle of clothes she had left next to her bedroll. An ugly black leather belt tied them together. "I will turn away to give you a chance to put on your new garments." Hak pushed the clothes at Annie.

She sighed and unfurled the pants and tunic. Hak walked to the edge of the clearing and turned his back on her. She chuckled at his modesty, and removed her clothes quickly. The air was cold and she hurried to put the leather pants on. Without the aid of the belt they would not stay up. The woolen tunic had long sleeves and was surprisingly warm. It had a neckline that ran along her collarbone, and puffed up around her shoulders. It was trimmed with embroidered flowers and vines along all the edges. It reminded her of German Oktoberfest clothes. The wool was itchy, but Annie felt grateful for clean clothes.

She walked up to Hak and playfully poked his shoulder. "Ta-da!"

He turned and looked at her for a long time. She felt ridiculous. Finally, he gave her a small smile. "You look nice, Annie."

"Thanks."

"I was going to say 'you look normal,' but I think that would have offended you."

Annie snorted and shook her head. *Men. Different planet, but the same inability to communicate with women.*

Hak suited up in his armor and carried the last of his belongings to Shadow. Hak had to remind Annie how to saddle her horse and buckle the straps. She watched silently as he tied her backpack to Shadow and climbed onto the horse. Her muscles felt incredibly sore, and it took her a few minutes to get comfortable in the saddle. They made their way back through the thick undergrowth until they got to the main road.

The woods were cold and foggy, with the occasional songbird piercing the silence. She looked down at her hands and inspected her remaining scabs and broken nails, her thoughts continuously drifting back to the previous night.

"I would give anything for an extra-large mocha right about now. With whipped cream and caramel on top," Annie mused, lighting a cigarette. "Do you guys have coffee here?"

Hak frowned. "What is that?"

"Damn it!" Annie let out a sad breath and explained to Hak the magic of a coffee shop. She tried to describe how espresso, milk, caramel, and chocolate were mixed together to create a wonderful treat. Hak marveled at the thought of chocolate every morning, and explained that most Tahldians drank tea. Annie was glad to know there was tea, at least. They listened to music as they traveled. They spent the morning talking about the differences between their worlds, and tried to find common ground.

Annie spent the better part of an hour explaining what a car was, and how it was used. Suddenly Hak was bursting with questions for her, and she talked until her throat became sore.

Annie smiled. *Okay, this is nice. We can actually have something close to a normal conversation. In some ways, I'm just off camping again. Yeah . . . that's what I'll keep telling myself. I'm just off on another backpacking adventure with*

Tia and a friend. I always wanted to go horseback riding again, right? If I keep telling myself this is just like camping, it's going to be a lot easier to cope with the whole mess. At least I'm good at being outdoors. Karen wouldn't have lasted a night without diet soda and a manicure set.

No matter how Annie looked at the situation, she was still a bit stunned by it. But she was determined to be a better traveling companion for Hak. Last night had made her realize just how deep Hak's troubles ran, and she found herself sympathizing with him.

And Hak seemed more relaxed around Annie. Yet he still became frustrated at explaining certain Tahldian customs. He did not want to talk deeply about Falishan, but he offered her the best explanation he could on the differences between Shafani culture and the eastern kingdoms.

She was not at all shocked to hear that the Shafani were a deeply religious, modest culture. Women stayed at home, while the men worked, fought, prayed, and traveled. The eastern kingdoms seemed more liberal to Annie as Hak described them, but she sensed that all of Tahldia was much more conservative than she was used to.

She enjoyed the day, listening to Hak talk about the various plants and animals of the world. Annie had seen or heard of most of them from her old neighbor. She was enamored with the stories of fairies, hummingbirds that glowed, and tree nymphs that supposedly lived in the larger trees.

Annie noted that Hak avoided certain topics completely. She did not ask him about his weird religion again, but she pressed for other details of his personal life as a Shafani. He would not talk about his childhood, or what he had done to become a mage. From the stories he told Annie, she gathered that he had been a very powerful mage while in the military. Every time she asked him specific questions about spells or mana usage, Hak would more often than not shake his head and change the subject. It was similar to the reaction she received from her old neighbor Ben when Iraq was mentioned. *War can really fuck with a person's head,* Annie mused.

It frustrated Annie when Hak refused to elaborate, but she understood that she had to respect Hak's boundaries. And Hak also touched on subjects Annie didn't feel like talking about. He asked her numerous questions about Patrick and her personal life. Hak found it difficult to believe that a woman as old as Annie was not married and settled down already. He offended her when he said she would never be able to raise a large enough family. *As if marriage and children are necessary for women. I lose respect just because I haven't settled down.*

Those were the worst questions Hak asked. And he learned that asking questions about her love life would cause Annie to sneer and lapse into a cold silence. After a day of conversation, where each had clumsily danced around many uncomfortable and painful questions, they began to understand each other a bit better. *It's funny how I'm happy to talk about my childhood, and Hak makes that twisted-up face every time I ask him about his. But at least we haven't fought at all today. He hasn't even snapped at me. This is some kind of record!*

As the sun touched the top of the distant horizon, Hak began looking for a place to make camp. Once more they walked away from the main road for several minutes, until Hak felt comfortable and found a water supply. He told Annie how to bed down the horses, and he walked into the woods with his bow and arrow.

He was gone for a long time. Annie had plenty of wood gathered and a warm fire going by the time Hak returned with a small deer.

"Aw. You shot a baby!" she said, teasing somewhat. The more she examined it, the more she knew it wasn't any sort of deer that had lived in Oregon. The deer was the size of a small dog, and covered with black lines like a zebra.

"It is an adult," he reassured her. He walked to the edge of camp and began to skin the deer. Annie felt her stomach perform an uncomfortable twist at the sight, but she tried to remind herself that it was another way to camp. *Personally, I would rather have hot dogs and s'mores. But at least Hak is cleaning it.*

Hak made a small spit over the campfire and roasted the deer for a long time. The smell of cooking meat made Annie's mouth water. Tia kept walking around the campfire, her eyes eagerly watching the deer roast. Hak pulled a leg off of the spit once it had cooled, and handed it to Annie.

She sank her teeth in and felt hot grease run down her chin.

It's delicious! Even without any spices, she enjoyed the roast deer immensely. It reminded her of lamb, and she helped herself to a second leg. Tia happily ate the remaining scraps. The deer had been just enough for the three of them.

"Thank you," Annie said after a time, staring at the fire.

Hak seemed surprised, but smiled. "Hunting will be more difficult on the plains, but there are plenty of ground squirrels."

Annie bit back a sarcastic *yay.*

"A good dinner calls for a celebratory drink," she said suddenly, and reached into her backpack. She pulled out her phone, cigarettes, and her bottle of whiskey. "I'm going to introduce you to Irish punk music and good Irish whiskey."

"That sounds . . . dangerous," Hak said uncertainly.

Annie let out a long laugh and smiled as she found one of her favorite bands on her playlist. Hak shook his head at the music, but listened eagerly all the same.

"It is so fast. And loud. Why do they have to scream?"

Annie chuckled as she twisted the cap off of the whiskey bottle. "Just listen. This is a great song about four men who go out drinking after their wives leave them."

Hak listened with an odd look on his face. Annie couldn't tell if he enjoyed the music, so she handed him the bottle.

Hak took it from her, sniffed it, and made a face. "Oh Annie, what is this?"

"Just try it."

Hak took a delicate sip and winced slightly.

"You gotta take a bigger drink than that. That's Irish whiskey! You'll never have another chance to have some. That is probably the last bottle in the entire world."

Hak looked thoughtful for a moment. Annie doubted he would take another sip. Suddenly, Hak raised the bottle to his lips and drank for several seconds.

Annie gave a deep laugh and clapped her hands together. "Wow. Good job!"

Hak wiped his mouth and gave her a shy, goofy grin. "It is strong."

She nodded and took another shot. She placed the bottle on the ground and set about tying Tia to a nearby tree, giving her roughly ten feet of lead. Her ears drooped slightly, but she did not resist the restriction.

"There. Now I don't have to worry about you."

"She will stay out of trouble that way," Hak said.

Annie sat down again. "She's a good dog. She's never run away before, but I'm scared she would try to make friends with a plagarne."

She passed the bottle back to Hak. He sighed. "Are you trying to get me drunk, Annie?"

She felt her face grow hot. "No. I'm trying to make peace with you. And besides, when I went camping, music and drinking were always part of it."

"It is strange to see a woman drink like you do." Hak scratched at the blond stubble on his cheeks. "Just do not try to trick me. Do not try to run off if I drink too much."

"You know, I used to think about escaping . . . but not anymore. I feel more comfortable around you knowing what you went through. When I first met you, you thought I was a spirit, and I thought you were some sort of monster, too. You *choked* me, for fuck's sake. I wanted to get away from you as fast as I could. But I saw how you treated Odal, and the children who found Tia. You acted kind to everyone except *me*, and part of it was, we weren't communicating. After hearing your story last night, and seeing those scars, I can honestly say I feel a lot better about being around you.

"Now I know you're a good guy, and I want to make peace with you." *Oh god, I hope he's a good guy. Am I already drunk? Did I ramble on like a complete idiot just now? Man, that sounded dumb.* Annie felt her cheeks burn.

"It is forgiven, Annie. We both misunderstood each other greatly." Hak took another long swallow from the bottle. Annie watched the precious liquid disappear with a bittersweet smile. *Well, we might have enough for one more night. Maybe when we get to Meda.*

"Do you still think I'm a complete and utter weirdo?" Annie blurted.

Hak eyed her for a moment and then shifted his gaze uneasily to the fire. "I, uh . . . I think you are harmless, and you have a good heart. You have a foul tongue, but you are full of fire and energy, which is a good thing, mind you, it is just that . . ." He looked embarrassed. "I-I think you are different, Annie, but that is not a bad thing . . . ." He scratched at his head and focused intently on the fire. "Uh, you are smart, and very strong for a woman . . . ."

Annie chuckled and shook her head ruefully. *I'm just going to take that as a compliment.*

"I feel like listening to some acoustic guitar music now . . . really give myself a camping flashback." Annie thumbed through the playlist on her phone. "My friend Ryan used to play guitar for us around the campfire. It was always so relaxing."

Hak watched her with an odd expression. "What would you do on these camping quests of yours?"

Annie giggled. "Nothing. That was the beauty of it. It was just a good excuse to get away from the city and enjoy each other's company. We often went on long hikes, cooked good food, told stories and played music. Some of my best memories are when I was camping with my friends."

Hak leaned back and gave Annie a tipsy smile. "Tell me your best camping story."

Annie laughed and thought about it for a moment. "Well, there was this one time me and about seven of my friends went camping on the Oregon coast."

Annie described the long, rolling sand dunes that covered a small portion of the Oregon coast. "We ended up climbing over a few dunes and realized that the sand stretched on forever. We dropped all of our stuff and made camp just out of sight of the road, and then decided to walk around on the dunes. You can roll down them. It's a lot of fun when you're drunk." Annie smiled at the memory and felt a pang of sadness for her friends.

"You climbed mountains of sand? For fun?" Hak asked, incredulous.

"Yeah. We were just out having an adventure. We walked for so long we actually lost track of where our camp was. It was very surreal, but we were drunk and we let our imaginations go wild. We could have been in the middle of an enormous desert on an alien world. We didn't bother using any lights to find our way. The moon was full and everything was tinged silver. It was so beautiful.

"We joked about fighting monsters and dragons and creatures that only exist in myth on my world. We could climb to the top of the tallest sand dunes and pretend we were dodging an attack. We would roll all the way down to the bottom. Just like children. It was a lot of fun."

Annie fingered the silver bracelet around her right wrist and looked at the small burn scar it had left on her from the day of the bomb. "At one point during our rolling adventures I realized I had torn a giant hole in my pants and lost my bracelet. I was terrified I had lost it forever. We used our flashlights and found it after some drunken searching."

"What is that bracelet made out of?" Hak asked suspiciously.

"Silver."

"Are you sure?"

"Positive. Why?"

"It looks like zythil." Hak said, leaning closer to look at her bracelet. He was close enough that Annie could smell the musky sweat in his hair.

"We don't have zythil on my planet." Annie held out her wrist so Hak could look at the bracelet all he wanted. "What is zythil? You said Voltay wanted all the zythil mines in the world, but I don't understand what could make it so special."

Hak took her hand gently and ran his fingers over the old silver bracelet. It was scuffed and scratched from a decade of wear. "Zythil is the rarest metal on Tahldia."

"Right. But what do you guys use it for?"

"It is hard to explain. It can be used as a sort of magic amplifier." Hak dropped her wrist quickly and leaned back onto his own bedroll. "Zythil does not scratch. That bracelet must be silver." He said it more to himself than to Annie.

"So you guys use zythil to increase magical power?"

"Yes."

"Can you make an entire suit of zythil armor and just fuck everything up?"

Hak let out a loud gush of laughter. "Ah, no. Zythil is so rare that a suit of armor would be priceless. An entire country could not pay for that. It is so rare that it is never combined and made into items larger than jewelry. The way that nations fight over it means that the amount of zythil in one object can never get too large. The largest piece that I have heard of was a pair of chain mail gauntlets. But half of the links were iron, and half zythil.

"For every ton of gold mined on Tahldia, a small bit of zythil is found. It is often found within black crystals."

"Have you ever owned zythil?"

Hak nodded. "I had a small necklace and two rings that were zythil. Bingen took them from me when I was imprisoned."

Annie was intrigued. "How much stronger were your spells with that jewelry?"

Hak thought for a moment. "It is hard to describe. Without zythil, I could make a fireball that could kill ten men. With zythil enhancing my mana currents, I could easily have destroyed five times that many men. It also helps a spell caster with energy. If a person uses magic for a long time, they get very tired. With zythil, I could fight in a battle all day without fatigue."

Annie shuddered.

"The crystals that are mined in the zythil pits are worth almost as much as the zythil itself. They do not boost energy, but they sap it and store the energy." Hak touched the large, circular welt in the middle of his cheek scar. "The same crystal that did this."

"It works sort of like a battery, then."

"What is a battery?"

Annie was about to explain the concept of batteries to Hak when Tia gave a low, brief woof, followed by a growl.

Annie grabbed her smartphone, turned the music off, and listened. "Tia heard something."

Hak grabbed his sword and quietly pulled it from its scabbard. They froze and watched Tia. The dog focused intently on a tree directly across the campfire. The seconds slowly ebbed into minutes, with Tia giving the occasional uneasy growl. Annie saw Hak's intense stare and did not dare to talk first.

After a few moments, Hak gently put his unsheathed sword on the ground in front of him, keeping his eyes alert.

"Maybe it was a squirrel or something," Annie said at last, giving Tia a light pat.

Tia responded with a maddened frenzy, pulling hard at the rope that tied her to the tree. Not a half second later three men jumped into the clearing, dressed in black and brandishing swords. Annie had just enough sense to dart away and pull her furious dog with her as a sword crashed down into the spot Hak had been sitting just a moment ago.

Annie curled up in the small hollow of the large tree and blinked. *Hak?*

Suddenly, a metal boot kicked hot embers into the face of the man who had swung his sword at Hak's bedroll. He screamed and dropped his sword to clutch at his face. Hak wasted no time, darting forward and beheading him. The horses reared and screamed in panic. Annie thought Tia was going to burst with rage. The dog was frantic now, but unable to jump into the fray. Annie struggled to keep the large dog from choking herself on her leash.

The other two men circled behind Hak. One wildly raised his sword and swung it down at Hak. Annie screamed.

The sword glanced off of Hak's armor in a shower of sparks. Hak grunted, and turned so fast his attack was a blur. He caught the man's outstretched sword arm and sliced it off in a spray of blood. The man fell backward; his screams joined the cacophony of panicked horses and the snarling dog. The third man lunged forward, but his outstretched hands were empty.

Hak arced his sword over his head and threw his weight behind the swing. The sword glanced off some sort of bluish barrier around the third man. Annie caught a glimpse of his face in the firelight and felt horribly ill.

She had met him at Odal's inn.

Tomas.

He leered as Hak tried to take another swing, only to have the blow somehow deflect a foot from Tomas' head. Tomas did not flinch as the sword came at his face, and he seemed indifferent to the strange shower of sparks the invisible collision produced.

"Zyl Magi?" Hak asked in astonishment.

Tomas grinned triumphantly, reached out, and grabbed Hak's arm. A ring on his finger flared as if it reflected sunlight. A blast of blue light, as painfully brilliant as a welder's torch, filled the space between the two struggling men.

Hak screamed in agony. The terrible sound tore at Annie's heart. A sudden surge of adrenaline made her dizzy. Without thinking, she grabbed the bottle of whiskey and lunged at Tomas. She roared and slammed the thick bottle against the back of his head. He stumbled, and she jumped on his back and pounded her fists against his head as hard as she could. Pain shot through her hands. Tomas released Hak and turned to grab Annie's arms. She looked defiantly into his eyes and growled fiercely.

Tomas gave her a menacing smile that appeared half mad. "Oh, my dear Lady Annie, we meet again."

He pulled her close so that his face was just an inch from hers, and he gave a hiss. "Shall we dance?"

The world flared with sudden brilliant blue light, and fell into darkness.

"Annie!"

The world exploded in pain. Annie groaned and gave a small whimper. She felt Tia licking her face. Her skin prickled at the touch. She became dimly aware of the ground underneath her as feeling burned back into her legs and arms. She couldn't move her fingers.

"Hak?"

"Oh gods, Annie."

"I c-can't . . . open my eyes . . ."

"Give it time, it will wear off."

"Tomas!"

"What?"

"That man. Ungh . . ." Annie felt sick. She tried to roll over but everything burned.

"You knew that man?"

"He was at the inn," she tried to say. She could hear the fear and suspicion in Hak's voice through her cloud of pain. "He was the one . . . we danced . . . that's all—unnngh!" Annie cried out at a sudden flash of fresh pain. "I think I'm going to be sick—"

Hak rolled her to one side so she could vomit. A moment later she felt cold water splash on her cheeks.

"You were hit by lightning magic."

Annie continued to convulse and dry heave for several moments. Tia licked her face again, and Annie tried to wriggle away from the dog.

"Don't move."

"Unngh . . ." Annie tried to give a weak laugh, but it came out in a choppy gurgle. "Don't worry, I can't . . ."

She felt Hak's armored hands slide underneath her and pick her up as if she were an infant. A moment later he gently lowered her again. She felt the bedroll slide over her and she cried out as her skin prickled with pain.

"Drink." She felt the water skin at her lips.

Annie forced herself to open her eyes. The world spun wildly around her and she closed them again. She let a few cold drops slide down her throat and choked as she tried to swallow. She vaguely remembered swinging the bottle like a baseball bat.

"I can't believe . . . Is the whiskey okay?"

Hak gave a small chuckle and sighed. "You have strange priorities. You are lucky to be alive." He gently brushed the hair out of her face.

"That . . ." Her fingers began to tingle. Her blood felt like liquid fire, tearing through her muscles as she tried to move them. "That lightning . . . was some crazy shit."

"How did you break his barrier?"

"Huh?" Annie tried to open her eyes and see past the vertigo of five Haks leaning over her. She couldn't tell which one was real.

"I saw you. Hitting that man *Tomas* in the head. How did you break his barrier?" He sounded so far away.

"I just jumped at him. I didn't try to do anything . . . except stop him . . . he was hurting . . . you." Annie began shivering uncontrollably.

Hak tightened the bedroll around her. The many faces that stared down at her were tinged with worry.

"Hak?" Annie shook and squeezed her eyes shut. *Everything prickles and burns!*

"Yes?"

"How did you . . . get shocked . . . and still . . . where is Tomas?"

"You broke his barrier. I cut him on the shoulder, but he got away."

"But he shocked you . . . how are you still standing?"

"Training."

She tried to process the idea of Hak training with such powerful magic. The world heaved; Annie felt like she was sprawled out on a quivering water bed, not solid ground. "I don't feel so good," Annie whimpered.

"It is all right. He will not be back tonight, I think."

Annie opened her eyes for the third time. She focused on Hak until he became a single image in front of her, and then turned her face to the shattered remains of the campfire. Even with most of the embers scattered, there was still enough light for Annie to make out the headless remains of a corpse a few yards away. After another dizzying moment of looking, she found the other corpse close by. Bile rose in her throat.

Hak sat down next to Annie and scanned the woods carefully. He kept his sword ready in his lap.

"We have to get . . . out of here," she managed. Tia licked her face once more and lay down against her right side.

"It is too dark to travel in the woods," Hak said. "We would risk injuring a horse trying to walk out of here in the dark."

Annie felt a cold terror seep into her mind. "But what if he comes back . . ."

"He will not. At least, not tonight. They know who I am, and must have thought I was powerless without magic. They underestimated me."

"Water," Annie croaked. Hak quickly placed the water skin at her lips. She drank greedily for a moment, determined not to choke. She felt cold and hot all over.

"You are very lucky, Annie," Hak whispered, wiping a sweaty strand of hair from Annie's face. "Get some rest. You will feel better in the morning."

She tried to thank him, but fell into a black, dreamless sleep.

Chapter Eight:

The Road to Meda

ANNIE WOKE THE next morning feeling better. She had a raging headache, but she was unsure if it was from the alcohol or the close call with her first magic spell. The painful tingling she had felt the night before had mercifully vanished. She made a face at the faint taste of vomit in her mouth. Hak sat motionless next to her bedroll, his alert eyes scanning the woods quietly.

She pushed herself up into a sitting position and looked around. There were charred logs around the camp, and dark spots littered the ground where blood had sprayed.

No bodies.

"How do you feel?" Hak asked gently.

"Like I beat myself in the head and stuck my tongue in a light socket." Annie grimaced and rubbed her temples.

Hak gave her a questioning look, but she did not feel like explaining what a light socket was. She grabbed a cigarette from the crumpled pack on the ground. It had been stepped on during the fight. She bent the cigarette back into shape and lit it with shaky fingers.

"Where are the bodies?"

Hak nodded toward the trees. "I moved them out of sight. They will be duzrak food when we leave."

Annie didn't feel like asking what a duzrak was. She picked up the water skin Hak had left by her side and took a long drink. She caught a grin from Hak out of the corner of her eye and gave him a flat stare. The smile shrunk back from his lips, but played around the edges, as if he found something incredibly amusing about her but didn't want to laugh.

"What?"

"Pardon?"

"What are you grinning at?"

"Apologies, Annie." Hak quickly looked at the sword on the ground in front of him.

"No, what is it?"

He hesitated, and then the grin teased his lips again. "Your hair."

Annie made a face and reached her hand up to her hair. She found it dry and sticking up in all directions.

Hak allowed himself a small chuckle. "You look like a puffball flower."

Annie was too tired to make a sarcastic retort. She frowned and tried to smooth her wild hair back down to her shoulders. "Who were they?"

"Mercenaries." Hak's smile was gone. "Most likely paid by Bingen to find me."

"And that one asshole, Tomas, what happened to him?"

"I managed to strike his shoulder. But it was a glancing blow. I doubt he bled out from it. He panicked and cast a vanishing spell. . . . He will be back, I am sure."

"Greeeat." Annie threw the cigarette butt into the firepit. She pulled a brush out of her backpack and sadly noted the bag had been singed in several places during the fight. She tried to ignore the dark splatters along the fabric.

"You say you knew him. You know his name."

"Oh . . . he was just that dude I was dancing with, back at Odal's inn. He told me his name and made small talk. That was when you showed up and had a rage fit and dragged me up the stairs."

Hak nodded. "He looked familiar. Did he say anything to you?"

"He said he was a merchant of some sort. Silk, I think. And he said he was from Meda. He asked me to come with him. He was being really cheesy. He didn't say anything exciting like, 'Oh, I can cast lightning spells and I want to kill this dude named Hak.'"

Hak shot her a glare. Annie ignored it, stood, and shuffled out of the clearing. He called out, "Where are you going?"

"I need to rinse my face off."

"Don't walk that direction!"

Too late! Annie felt her stomach heave when she saw the two bodies stacked on some rocks. A head was placed on top. A bird pecking at the face flew off when it saw her. The eyes were open and glazed, the jaw hanging from its socket. She quickly turned her head from the grotesque sight and took several deep breaths. She heard Tia whine back at the camp, and Hak's footsteps charging through the undergrowth. He caught her arm as she swayed.

"Apologies. I should have dumped the bodies farther away."

She jerked away from his hand. "Ugh. It's fine. I'll just walk upstream. Nothing like dead bodies staring at you first thing in the morning."

She began walking the other direction, and heard his footsteps behind her. She turned on Hak and waved him away. "I don't need your help. I need a few minutes to myself."

Hak looked down, and walked away without another word.

Annie knelt on a rock hanging over the stream twenty or so yards away from the bodies. She plunged her face into the frigid water and held it there for a moment.

What have I gotten myself into? Fucking hell, I should just drown myself right here and now. She pulled her face out of the cold water and took in a deep breath. *I just want my own damned bed. And maybe a cup of coffee. Is that too much to ask? Why am I here? Why didn't I die? And why am I surrounded by crazy assholes?*

Annie held her breath and dipped her head in again, this time up to her shoulders. She scrubbed her hair as best she could. She pulled her head out and began brushing the wet hair down. *Why? Why is this happening to me? I almost died again last night. Jesus tap-dancing Christ. This sucks.*

She glowered as she walked back into camp and sat down on her bedroll.

"Are . . . Are you well, Annie?"

Annie closed her eyes and took a deep breath. "I'm . . . just very freaked out right now. I've never seen a dead body before. And the fact that I'm not a morning person isn't helping."

"Apologies. Are you able to travel?"

"I feel like I could sleep for a week."

"We must go. It is very dangerous here."

The cold, familiar tingle of fear coursed through her suddenly. *I'm tired and I feel like shit, but no use in feeling sorry for myself. The sooner I get out of here and get to Meda, the better.*

Annie stood without comment. Hak readied the horses, Annie looked over the bloody campsite one more time and shivered.

Seriously? What the hell? She untied Tia from the tree and gave the dog a long hug.

"I never thought you could be so vicious," she told the dog in a soothing murmur. "You were amazing last night, Tia."

"She would not let me near you at first," Hak said softly. "After you fell. She guarded you well."

"I think we're both in the same boat. Last night was fucking nuts."

"Yes. I think that would be an accurate description."

Annie snorted and mounted her horse. She gave Hak an impatient glare as he secured her backpack to Shadow.

Hak walked up to her and took her hand. He put it carefully under his chin, held it there, and gave her a sincere look. "Annie . . . thank you for saving my life last night."

"What?"

"If you had not jumped into the fight, I would be dead. You broke Tomas's barrier somehow. It was a distraction that gave me the upper hand. If you had cowered like a frightened maiden behind that tree there, I would not have been able to break free of his spell, or find a way to strike him. You were very brave. I thank you, deeply and truly."

Annie let him rest her hand under his chin, his stubble brushing against her fingertips.

This must be some sort of cutesy honor thing, she thought with mild irritation.

He held her hand there for a moment longer, then gently dropped it. Without another word, Hak turned and mounted Shadow. They rode for several hours in a thoughtful silence.

"Hak?"

"Yes, Annie?"

"Would you teach me how to use a sword?"

She thought he would laugh at her, or say no outright. But Hak contemplated for several minutes before agreeing. "Yes. It would be good if you knew how to defend yourself. Ordinarily, I would not imagine teaching a woman how to fight. But . . . I think you could be quite vicious and effective, if you knew what to do."

"Um, thanks?"

Hak gave her a small smile. They spent the day riding as fast as they could, but had to take several breaks because of Tia. The dog kept up well, but Annie worried that the fast pace would somehow hurt her. She knew deep down that Tia was a hunting dog, but it didn't help. She would always see Tia as her pet, prone to goofy moments and cuddling. It was hard to believe that the dog would fare better in this new environment than Annie.

When they made camp the following night, Annie did not play any music. They were very paranoid about Tomas sneaking up on them again. Hak talked to her about the basics of swordplay and handed Annie his sword. He seemed hesitant to do so, but laughed when they both realized it was too heavy for her to lift. After Annie spent a few embarrassing moments trying to simply pick up the sword, Hak gave her a long stick. They spent the next hour sparring with sticks, and Hak tried to explain defensive and offensive styles.

She never got her stick anywhere close to Hak's armor. He deflected every blow with ease, and gave her a few good smacks. He was careful to avoid her shoulder, but gave her an especially strong slap on her thigh. She felt like a child trying to fight an adult. After an hour, she was exhausted and gave up.

"Not bad for a woman who has never fought."

Annie grunted; she felt like he was just trying to make her feel better. *Admit it Hak, I suck. Just give me a shotgun and let me at that asshole Tomas!*

Hak insisted they take turns sleeping and keeping watch. Annie groaned and protested at the thought of only sleeping half the night. Hak reminded her that it was in their best interests in case more mercenaries showed up. He took first watch and let her sleep late into the night. She growled and flung her arms at him when he tried to wake her for her turn to keep watch.

"Annie, you must. I will need to sleep at least a little tonight." With a small apology, Hak pulled the bedroll off of her and exposed her to the crisp night air.

She cursed and groaned at him. She stood and paced around the dying fire, trying to wake up. Hak curled up in his bedroll, one hand on his unsheathed sword, and promptly fell asleep. Tia watched Annie curiously as she paced around the fire. Finally, Annie sat back down and put her arm around Tia. She held the stick she had used for sparring in one hand for a long while as she nervously scanned the forest.

Eventually she became bored. She played a video game on her phone for two hours, and rubbed angrily at her face when sleep threatened her. She stood and stretched and stared at the stars for another hour. As the sky began to lighten, she finally nodded off while sitting upright.

Large calloused hands grabbed her mouth and kept her from screaming. She jerked awake and tried to move but she was securely pinned. Tia whined questioningly behind her.

Annie panicked and tried to let out a shriek, but the large hands muffled it. A moment later she felt a warm breath in her left ear, and a familiar voice whispered, "You can't fall asleep while on watch. Or this is how you could wake up. Or maybe they would stab you in your sleep."

Motherfucker! Annie tore Hak's hands off her mouth and swung her hand up to punch him.

"Whoa! Hey!"

"You *asshole*! How can you scare me like that?"

"How can you fall asleep? You are supposed to be keeping watch! If you fall asleep and Tomas sneaks up on us, we could be dead! He could bring more people next time."

Annie gritted her teeth so hard she thought she would break them. She picked up a small stick next to her and threw it at Hak's face. He deflected the stick and it landed in front of Tia. The dog jumped up and wagged her tail, thinking it was a new game. She picked up the stick and dropped it in front of Annie. When Annie refused to remove her glare from Hak, Tia picked the stick up, walked it over to Hak, and dropped it at his feet. Hak returned Annie's cold stare. Tia looked from one person to the other and gave a confused whine when they both ignored her.

After a moment, Hak turned away from Annie and said, "Get your belongings. We will eat on the road."

"Asshole," Annie muttered, and they left without another word.

The next night Annie did yoga on her watch. She stretched and took in deep breaths while she stared up at the dragon nebula with its curious red planet for an eye. The trees were thinning out now as they traveled. Annie was amazed at all the new stars she could see. The following night they camped in a meadow, and she saw the three moons in the horizon. It took her breath away. One moon was a faint pink color, while the other two were larger and tinged with brilliant blues and silvers. They were in various stages of waxing, with the pink one the slimmest.

The next few days held many wonders for Annie. As they entered a great grassland, she could see mountains rising up against the southern horizon. The way they had come was much the same—rolling foothills rose up around a large mountain covered in snow. She guessed that Hak had found her somewhere in the shadows of that great mountain. It was the first of several snow-capped peaks that ran into the northern horizon and disappeared into the distant clouds.

The days were flooded with Annie's questions about the various flora and fauna of the plains. Annie saw curious creatures that looked like miniature giraffes, only with tiger stripes. Their tall necks and bulbous heads poked out of the grass in great herds. When they ran from the approach of Hak and Annie, the grass churned wildly with the sudden movement of hundreds of bodies. She saw strange birds shaped like swifts, but they were a brilliant mix of red and white feathers. Their slim tails were three times the length of their bodies, and the great flocks joined in acrobatic dances that swirled in unison. The clouds of birds flowed like a red shadow above the plains and made Annie smile. They were beautiful.

Suddenly, Annie thought she saw a dragon. It looked like a snake with wings. She screamed and startled the horses and Hak. When Hak followed her finger to the distant flying shadow in the horizon, he laughed.

"No, Annie. That is a wyvern. Not a dragon. Dragons are much larger, and have bigger bellies."

"A dragon is bigger than *that* thing?" She swallowed uneasily.

"Much bigger."

"Damn." She tried to get more comfortable in the saddle. "Do people ride dragons on Tahldia?"

Hak laughed deeply. "No. That would be suicide. A dragon is too proud and intelligent to deal with a human."

"Will they bother us?" she asked fearfully.

"Only if we bother the dragon first. We are like fleas to them."

"So . . . dragons never hurt people?"

"Only if a very talented warlock knows the right spell. Only then can a dragon be controlled."

"You said dragons were fighting on the day of your escape."

"Yes. Three dragons fought at the battle of Falishan."

"Why did they fight? Who controlled them?"

"The dragons fought on their own accord. Voltay was killing anything that stood in his way when it came to zythil mining. The dragons had as much right to that battle as the dwarves did. Voltay destroyed their nests, and their eggs. Dragons prefer mines and caverns, you see."

"So Voltay destroyed their natural habitat."

"Yes."

"Can they talk?"

"Yes, many know our language. They speak with their minds." Hak pointed at his head. "They are the oldest living creatures on Tahldia. It is said that they come from the small red moon."

"Cool. How many dragons live on Tahldia?"

"Not many. Perhaps fifty or so. Most are in a long slumber. Wyverns, however, are another story."

Annie looked back at the horizon in the direction of the wyvern.

"Why's that?"

"Well, for one thing, they are not as smart. Secondly, you can train them and ride them, if you raise one from a hatchling. They are a mischievous creature, and they will attack a traveler if they are bored. Or hungry."

Annie shivered. "So do a lot of people ride them?"

"No. They are a difficult beast to tame. If you slight them in the smallest fashion, they will remember."

"Wyverns can hold grudges."

"Yes. Which makes rearing them and training them very difficult. Some magic is usually necessary to placate the creature and ride it."

"But they can't talk?"

"No. But they can understand commands and words, if trained to do so."

"Huh. Interesting."

"They are a formidable mount in battle." Hak looked thoughtful, as if remembering some strange detail. "But they can be prone to throwing their riders, and turning on them in a fit of bloodlust."

"Ever ridden one?"

"Once. But she had been abused too much as a hatchling." Hak looked sad. "They are fearsome creatures, but every animal deserves respect. That is one of the first things you learn when training with magic. *All life is sacred.*" Hak snorted contemptuously. "That poor wyvern was half mad due to rough training. Anyone who approached her had to cast soothing and controlling spells. I would not ride her a second time.

"When you control a creature or a person with magic, Annie, you can *feel* that creature. It is a very unsettling feeling. You are inside their head, and susceptible to their thoughts, emotions, and pain. That is why it is often a last resort for a mage to try to control another person's mind. Even a common non-magic user, such as yourself, can affect the magi in unpredictable ways."

"Like, breaking their spell?"

Hak nodded hesitantly. "That was a strange stroke of luck on your part. I still do not understand how you did that." His face was unreadable for a moment, and he looked over at her. "You should learn how to block and deflect mind spells. It takes decades of training to properly master, but you should know the basics.

"I do not have a connection with the current. So I cannot properly train you as a master mage could. However, I can at least tell you what to look out for, in case someone tries to read your mind or control you. You should know what to expect. You may need that knowledge in Meda."

"Really?"

"As I said, Meda should be safe for us."

"Should?"

"Yes. And remember that a control spell is a fickle thing. Most people find it extremely unpleasant to enter another's mind. It is not used very often. However, I believe that the council may want to probe your mind."

"Great."

Hak gave her a slight grin. "To be honest, Annie . . . if I had had the ability to read your mind when I found you, I would have. I did not believe who or what you were at first. I still find . . ." Hak bit his lip and appeared tongue-tied. "I still find you a very interesting lady."

Annie laughed. "Oh, I'm a lady now? Shit, I've been promoted."

Hak smiled and shook his head. "We also need to work on your language before we reach Meda. And manners."

Annie snorted. "I can clean up well if I need to. Don't worry."

"Please try it around me. I find your language distasteful, and a little rude."

Annie gave Hak a mocking bow. "Aye, m'lord. I can curtsy and act like a tame human. I promise."

"Now. As for blocking a probe or control . . ." Hak looked thoughtful. "A mind is open and closed at the same time. You have the potential to expand your mind out of your body, as well as receive the minds of others. In the most basic way, this is how dragons communicate.

"With proper training, and a skilled teacher, a person can learn control. It takes a lot of mana, and a very intricate form of magic to force their will upon someone. However, you do not need to even *know* magic to feel someone probing your mind. If someone reaches into your mind, you can feel something just on the edges of your consciousness. For example, you might suddenly feel a different emotion, or have a very strange thought.

"When minds connect, there is a channel of energy that is shared between the two people. In training, we used the idea of water to communicate this basic theory of magic. I want you to imagine, for the duration of this training, that your mind is like a lake or pool of water.

"I want you to imagine two separate pools of water, Annie. Alone, the waters do not touch. If you add a river or stream between them, the water will flow freely and mix together. That is like your mind, and that of the caster. You will sense strange things. It also tickles. A little."

Annie laughed. "It will tickle like I have a bug in my brain?"

"Yes! That is a very good description. It will be as subtle as an ant."

"Crazy. But . . . wow . . ." Annie was speechless. *Okay, I've read enough comic books and watched enough sci-fi movies to know about magic and such . . . but I never thought it truly existed! This is some crazy shit. But . . .*

"Can anyone learn to use magic? Can *I* learn to use magic?"

"No."

"What! Why not?"

"You are too old."

Annie scrunched up her face at him. "Oh, don't be rude!"

"What? I am being honest. You must train your entire life to understand how magic works and how to use it. Furthermore, you need a natural affinity for it. Not everyone who trains from childhood can effectively cast magic. Most herbalists are a form of failed magi. They know enough to get by, and they earn a living imbuing small items with enchantments and such."

"Like that bread we had outside of Feldall?"

"Yes. But back to your lesson."

Annie was brimming with questions, but she knew better than to interrupt Hak.

"Now, Annie, if you feel someone in your mind, there are a few things you can do. The first thing you should do might be the most difficult for you, since you have no magical knowledge. The first tactic is to push the person out of your mind."

"How do I push?"

"I cannot teach you that. Apologies, but it requires someone to push you first. And I am unable to do that. My year in the torture chamber broke that skill."

Annie gave him a sad look, but Hak continued, "While I cannot teach you how to push with your mind, I can tell you another tactic. It requires you to flood the other person's mind with imagery.

"Go back to the first thing I said about the pools of water and the river that connects them. Imagine kicking up a great cloud of debris in the body of water, at the mouth of the connecting river. Imagine dirty water flooding that connection. It would be very difficult to see anything."

"Interference. In a weird sort of way, it makes sense," Annie mused. She had a small flashback of playing on the beach when she was little. She remembered the sand castles and the moats that she would build, and all the connecting channels of water that she dug out with her hands. *This is so weird, but it does sort of make sense. Hak is a good teacher.*

"Now Annie, it is not enough to cloud the mind. While flooding the mental connection with debris, you must also put up walls. You must be able to guard your water from further connection with the stream. This is where it becomes difficult, and requires a lot of training. Imagine flooding the connection with cloudy water, and simultaneously building a wall at the mouth of the river. You can block the connection from coming back. Water will eventually clear, and flows back with more force than before.

"The last tactic is to send pain. If someone is controlling you, you could be in a situation where you are also being hurt. Your pain will flood their stream, and send shockwaves back into their pool of water. You will be in pain, but so will the person controlling you. It is the easiest tactic, because you do not have to cast anything, or try to push anything. The pain is real, and the effects on both people are instant. It is the most unpleasant way for someone to try to break control of the spell.

"However . . ." Hak trailed off and looked down at his saddle. "Demons are the one exception for that tactic. They feed off the pain they create and gain strength from it."

Annie winced and looked at the scar that trailed under Hak's left eye. After a long silence, she said, "Thank you. These are important things to know. I appreciate your patience explaining them. You're a good teacher."

Hak seemed pleased. "You are welcome, Annie. I am glad to share this knowledge with you."

"Hak? Does mind reading hurt?"

"No. But it is unpleasant." He sighed. "It is uncomfortable to have someone else in your mind. They can see your memories."

"Like spirits," Annie said.

"Yes. Exactly like a spirit. Do not be afraid if the council wants to probe your mind. I have a feeling that they will not believe your story outright. But the process should not take too long. They did it to me when I first arrived."

"Really?"

"Yes. They knew I was Shafani. You stand in a room and seven people enter your mind at once."

"That's a lot of water to mix up."

Hak laughed. "Yes, it is. But it was a good thing they looked into my mind. They saw what I had gone through at the hands of Voltay and Bingen."

"But . . . you said they didn't believe you that they were demons."

"Yes. That is the odd thing. They probed my mind for a good hour, and yet they seemed dissatisfied with what they found. Ultimately they released me, and trusted me that I would do no harm to the council, or anyone in Meda for that matter. However, I am an impatient person, Annie. I want them to do more than sit on their hands. The eastern countries could be inundated with a Shafani army, and yet Meda does nothing except plan festivals. It is very strange."

"You said you are on a quest for the council."

Hak looked uneasy. "Yes."

"What do you need to do?"

"I cannot tell you that, Annie. It is for the council to know."

Annie gave an exasperated sigh. "Not even a little hint?"

"I cannot tell you."

"Is that why you were in the mountains when you found me?"

"Annie," he said harshly. "Please, do not try my patience."

"Ugh. You can be so difficult sometimes."

Hak barked a laugh and shook his head. "So can you."

They traveled for two days in relative peace. The mountains that had seemed so close in the south did not seem to grow any closer. Annie was getting impatient to get out of the grasslands. She felt exposed to anything that could fly. She worried Tomas would attack them every evening.

Hak sparred with her every night before they ate, and tried to teach her about Tahldia as they rode during the day. On the tenth evening since leaving Feldall, they made camp a day's ride from the edge of the southern foothills. Hak had been very strict with Annie the entire day. He had taken on the harsh and calculating tone of a professor, asking her many questions about what he had taught her so far.

Annie missed several of them, which frustrated Hak. She did not dare admit to him that she had taken to daydreaming when he had rambled on about a particular subject. She had never liked politics and history all that much.

As they made camp for the night, Hak kept asking her questions about the kings and queens in the eastern world. She forgot all the names, and gave a casual shrug when Hak asked why she didn't pay attention.

"Sorry. I guess I have had a lot on my mind."

Hak gave a heavy sigh. "Do you remember who Halona is?"

Annie thought about it for a moment as she tied Tia's rope to a heavy rock. "She's a queen in Taui?"

"No!" Hak snapped, which startled Annie. "Gaeric Halona is the king of Medalia, and his throne sits in Meda. Gods, Annie, pay attention. You are going to embarrass yourself."

"So what, Hak? Halona is not my king. Why do I care about your politics?"

"We will reach Meda in a few days. Have you given much thought to where you will go or where you will live?"

Annie shook her head fiercely. "All I care about is getting home. I need to see what has happened to Earth. Even if . . . even if my parents are gone, I need to know if any of my friends are still alive. My whole life was there. This place has been fun and all, but I'm tired of running from crazy mages and sleeping on the ground. I miss television, burritos, and having a hot shower every night."

"You miss whiskey."

"That, too." She laughed. "I still have enough for a few drinks tonight, and some to share with you if you want. We never had a chance to finish it off. There's not much left."

"It might not be wise to drink and risk being unable to defend ourselves."

"Well, I'll drink your share then."

Hak looked annoyed. He set out their belongings and got the horses settled in. They nibbled on stale bread and dried meat as they worked. He grabbed the two long sparring sticks and tossed one to Annie. She clumsily caught it.

"Annie, you need to really focus tonight."

"What are you so nervous about? I can't learn to be a master with sticks. Shit, I doubt I'll ever be halfway decent with a real sword."

"Language, Annie. And yes, you will learn to defend yourself. I will not be as gentle tonight, so defend yourself as best you can."

Annie held her stick out in a defensive posture. *Ugh, why did I even suggest this in the first place? I don't feel like practicing tonight.* Her hands had layers of blisters on them from practice, and her body was riddled with small bruises from failed defense.

Hak walked around her, his posture tense and ready to strike. He lunged forward, faster than Annie was used to. She barely dodged the attack.

"Be alert, Annie. I will not be so easy on you tonight."

She gritted her teeth and thrust her stick forward. Hak deflected the blow and hit the side of her leg. It stung like hell. Annie flung herself to one side, trying to open up space between them.

While she lacked brute strength, Hak had encouraged her to use her small frame to dodge and parry as much as possible. She was much faster than the first time they sparred, but still too slow. Hak's next blow landed on her ribs.

"Ow!"

Hak didn't give her time to recover, and Annie barely deflected the next blow.

Geeeez, this guy is serious tonight!

She dodged the next two attacks, and deflected another blow. It was encouraging progress. She struck the left side of Hak's armor with a heavy metallic thud. She was so excited about landing her very first blow that she was not prepared for the counterattack. Hak swung his stick out, hit her on the leg once more, and prepared to strike again. Annie raised her stick to try to deflect the blow, but she overestimated the distance.

Hak's stick crashed into her hand, and bolts of pain shot up her arm. Annie cried out and involuntarily dropped her stick. Hak grabbed her by her outstretched arm and swept his leg against her calves. She fell on her back and Hak was on top of her. He did not grab her, but gently pinned her against the ground. Annie felt tears sting her eyes as pain and embarrassment coursed through her.

"Are you all right?" he whispered.

She whimpered. "I think my finger's broken."

Hak placed a hand against her back and eased Annie into a sitting position. Tia whined and pulled at her rope.

"Apologies, Annie. Let me see your hand." Hak reached out and carefully took her left hand in his. His scarred hand dwarfed hers. Annie sucked in her breath as Hak gently touched the bleeding finger.

His blond eyebrows were pressed together with concern. "Can you bend your fingers, Annie?"

Annie tried to curl her fingers against her palm, but the pain was too great. She was acutely aware of Hak's other hand still resting against her spine. He stroked her back gently for a moment, and Annie felt her face grow hot.

"You will be okay, I think. I am very sorry. I wanted to challenge you this evening. You have been doing very well."

Annie pulled the bleeding finger to her lips and sucked at the wound. "Well, thanks for not babying me. But I think I'm done sparring for the night."

"You earned your drink, Annie." Hak stood and offered her a hand. She gratefully took it and pulled herself up. Hak cleaned her hand with cold water and wrapped it in a sliver of cloth.

Annie took a deep drink of whiskey and settled back against her bedroll. The stars were coming out, and the nebula seemed to glow brighter with every passing minute. The two larger moons were almost full, and produced plenty of light. The smallest moon was barely a sliver touching the horizon. Annie pushed the bottle of whiskey at Hak.

"It's the very last of the whiskey, Hak. I'm going to finish it off in a second."

"If you insist." He gratefully took a small drink and handed her the bottle.

Annie looked at the last half inch of whiskey sadly. *Two more cigarettes. One last drink of whiskey. And all my creature comforts and tastes of home will be gone.* It made her want to cry.

Annie held the bottle out in front of her. "A toast. To Hak, for saving my life and teaching me that Tahldia is real." *Or maybe, just maybe, I really am dead. Maybe this is all some sort of strange afterlife dream.* She silently added the thought to her toast. She drank the rest and relished the sweet burn of whiskey in her throat. It was just enough alcohol to give Annie a pleasant buzz, and it removed some of the pain that gnawed at her left hand.

"Tell me a story," Annie said. She felt the need to be distracted from her sadness. She lit a cigarette and lay down to stare up at the stars.

"Would you like to hear a story about the stars? You seem very interested in them."

"Yeah. That would be cool."

Hak told her the myth of the moon brothers and sister. The larger moons, Maule and Saiso, were originally the great silver dragons that had created Tahldia. Their mother, the sun, watched over them all. Maule and Saiso had to protect their younger sister, a small pink dragon named Ikti. She often

114

liked to play pranks on her elder brothers, and would hide from them and tease them.

Hak gestured to the nebula. "One day, a great red dragon fell in love with Ikti, and chased her around the universe. He took her, and they created many beautiful eggs." Hak pointed out the constellations in the nebula that represented Ikti's eggs.

"Maule and Saiso were enraged that their sister had left Tahldia. They kidnapped Ikti from the great red dragon, and slew him as he protected their eggs. The smear of red you see across the sky is his blood." Hak pointed to the white stars underneath the red eye. "Even dead, the dragon weeps for his mate, and the eggs. They never hatched without their mother present."

"That's so sad!"

Hak gave her a sly smile. "When the brothers Maule and Saiso brought Ikti back to Tahldia, she was more stubborn and rebellious than before. They fought viciously. They eventually turned themselves into moons out of spite and anger with each other. As the smallest of the moons, Ikti still tries to hide from her brothers to this day. That is the legend of why the moons change phases at different times. So Maule and Saiso cannot catch her. And her mate, the red dragon, mourns above."

"It sounds like some sort of myth we would have back on Earth. We had tribes who described the cosmos in similar ways, I think. It's been a long time since I studied up on mythology."

Hak walked over to her and inspected her hand once more. He gently removed the cloth bandage. Annie lay very still and stared up at him as he held out her hand.

"You will have a very large bruise, and you may lose that fingernail, but I do not think your finger is broken. Apologies, I should have controlled my swing better."

Annie bit her lip as Hak wrapped her finger up again. "It's okay. I'll never learn if you baby me. You're not used to women fighting, are you?"

Hak shook his head. "Some cultures have women warriors. The Taui, for instance. I know it can be done. But Shafani do not think it is proper."

"You grew up in a pretty strict society. But I didn't. Where I'm from, women can do anything men can. And I think it's important to know as much as I can."

"I do hope that you will not have to defend yourself. But I worry."

"Don't. I still have that pepper spray. And I'll be safe in Meda, right?"

"I hope so, Annie. I just worry."

She shot him a questioning look, but he ignored it and went to his bedroll. He seemed distracted by something. He removed the outer layer of armor, but left his chain mail on. He lay down awkwardly and placed his unsheathed sword at his side. She wondered, not for the first time, how he could be comfortable sleeping like that.

"It is your turn for first watch, Annie." Hak pointed northward. "Please wake me when Saiso is over that mountain there."

"Which moon is Saiso?"

"The one with more blue along the center."

"Okay. Sleep well, Hak."

He yawned and tucked an arm under his cheek. Within a few moments his stern face had grown soft and Hak's breathing became slow and steady.

Annie wished they had made a fire, but she knew it would draw attention on the open plains. She sat up and pulled her knees to her chin, and looked out at the three moons. She tried to imagine them as a family of dragons.

Annie kept glancing over at Hak. She couldn't help herself. He seemed peaceful when he slept.

I wonder what it would be like to kiss him?

The thought simultaneously frightened and intrigued her. *Why did I just think that? Holy crap . . . I must be drunk.*

Annie lit her last cigarette and stared up at the stars, avoiding another look at the sleeping man. She savored the curls of smoke that ran from her mouth to her nose, and she closed her eyes. *I wonder if Patrick is still alive? He might be a cheating asshole, but I hope he's okay. I wonder if I am ever going to trust another guy again. I just don't understand them.*

She felt the familiar emotion of desire and curiosity playing at the edges of her mind. Every time she tried to banish the thought, it came back.

Did I ever truly think Hak was ugly? The scars aren't so bad, especially when he smiles. He has a nice face, and a pretty awesome six pack.

Annie stopped and blushed, then shook her head. *Hak is five hundred times worse for me than Patrick ever was. He's killed people. He has some serious issues from being tortured. He doesn't see women as equals. Why the fuck do I want to kiss him? I need to ditch him in Meda. I have to find a way home. The insanity of this whole situation just seems to get worse. I'm in some sort of strange world with zombies, knights and a mage trying to kill us. The last thing I need is to . . . what? Do I want a relationship? Do I want a one-night stand? Am I just really lonely? Have I been alone with this guy for so long that I forget my priorities?*

Annie shook her head again and looked at her empty pack of cigarettes. She sneered and chewed at a nail. She knew she would be irritable and unpleasant to be around for the rest of the journey.

That's it. It's official. I've lost my goddamned mind to be thinking even half the things I am thinking about.

Disgusted with herself, she continued to watch Hak sleep. She gazed at his handsome face and loathed the new feelings she was discovering for him.

It's been a long time since someone kissed me or held me. I need to get laid. Or something. What the hell is wrong with me?

She was frustrated with herself, and the primal emotions that gnawed at her common sense. *God . . . think about something else, Annie. Stop being so stupid. Just shut up, brain. Just stop.*

But Annie, another part of her mind said, *You're only human. It is only natural to want companionship, desire, and sex. Hak is not a bad-looking guy; he is young, healthy, and very handsome. It could be fun to kiss him. It feels good to be around him. It's only natural to wonder what's in his pants—*

Annie silently pulled at her hair in frustration.

Tia sensed her unease and pushed her head under Annie's arm to get a hug. Annie embraced the dog for a moment, and then stood up straight, ignoring the stiffness in her joints. She was too frustrated to sit still.

She turned her head toward the northern horizon, and thought she caught a glimpse of something large flying in the moonlight. She blinked, and it was gone.

Maybe it's a good thing that was the last of the whiskey, she thought ruefully.

The next three days were cloudless and surprisingly hot. Hak was kind to her, and helped dress her wound in the evenings. He did not push Annie to spar again, but instead treated her to a new myth every evening as they ate. Annie tried her best to ignore the strange feelings that had crawled into her mind, and focused on the trip. Hak preferred silence most days, and Annie was content to put on her headphones and distract herself.

Even Tia seemed exhausted, and Annie worried about the dog collapsing. The heat of the day kept them silent and weighed down. Annie rejoiced when they saw a huge forest before them.

Hak did not remove his armor as they rode away from the grasslands and entered the hilly forest. She could tell that the rest of the journey would lead them into the mountains. A great snow-covered peak rose above the trees far in the distance. The trees were not as tall as mana oaks, but Annie was glad for their shade.

"How can you wear that stuff in the sun?" Annie asked as Hak lifted his visor to take a drink of water.

"The armor? I just do not think about it. You get used to it."

"Ugh. I'm sweaty as hell and I just have this stupid sweater on. I don't know how you do it."

"There will be a small hot spring on the other side of this hill, if I remember correctly. We are almost to the mountains. Meda is nestled against a great cliff. There is a waterfall that plunges through the center of the city. I think you will like it, Annie. It is very beautiful."

"How many people live in Meda?"

"I do not know for certain. Perhaps as many as fifty thousand people."

Annie sucked in her breath and felt her heart beat rapidly with excitement. "How come we haven't seen any other travelers?"

"We will join the main road soon. I have taken us on a small detour in order to avoid notice. We will camp early tonight at the hot spring. It is a safe place, and it will give you an opportunity to clean up before I present you to the council."

"I can't wait to find out why I'm here. I'm so ready to go home."

"Do not forget your manners," Hak said. "Do not use foul language, and give a slight bow to anyone I introduce you to. And remember what to do when you meet a council member."

Annie placed her hands over her heart and gave a deep bow in the saddle. "Peace of the stars be upon you."

"Correct. And don't speak unless spoken to."

"Yeah, yeah. Don't worry, I won't start running around naked and dancing on tables."

"We will most likely have an escort from the gates. However, I am not sure what will happen next." Hak looked very uneasy and wouldn't make eye contact with her. Annie didn't like it one bit.

"You're worried about something and you're not telling me," Annie said, crossing her arms.

"It is difficult to be Shafani in Meda," Hak said quickly.

Annie squinted her eyes at him, but he kept silent. "You still have that honor vow with me, buster. You can't hurt me."

"I will not hurt you."

"Something's wrong. I can feel it."

"I am just worried about the council," Hak said, not looking at her. "I am worried about my quest, and if they will be pleased with me."

His eyebrows furrowed together and his lips were tight against his face as he stared at the trail. Annie recognized the sour expression and knew she wouldn't get another word out of him.

Annie changed the subject to the forest around them. She wanted to know everything she could about the strange creatures she saw in the trees. They appeared to be brown bears the size of house cats, curled up against branches in the canopy. They made hushed, chirping noises like birds. The little bears froze and watched them pass with small yellow eyes. Tia growled at them and stayed close to Annie.

The forest grew thicker around them, and the trees became taller. They had been walking up the steep slope of a hill for the better part of two hours. When they finally reached the top, Hak turned to Annie and eagerly motioned for her to join him. Annie's heart felt as though it stopped when she took in the view.

The late afternoon sun cast a golden hue over the great wooded valley below. Along the western and eastern edges of the horizon, massive cliffs rose out of the forest and grew into a small mountain in the southern distance. They were entering the mouth of a V-shaped valley.

She saw a distant waterfall cascade down the cliff face like ghostly hair shimmering in the wind. A large group of spires rose from the forest around it. The water glistened in the late afternoon light. Several small rocks on the cliff face shimmered brightly in every color as the fading sunlight fell on them. It reminded Annie of reflecting glass, and she felt her heart beat faster.

I can't wait to see it up close!

The deep shadows from the cliff slowly blanketed the valley below. The eastern cliffs seemed much larger than the western ones, even though Annie had a hard time figuring out just how large the valley was. She guessed it might have been wide enough to hold all of Atlanta, with room to spare. The snow-covered mountain loomed at the other end of the valley.

"We will walk along the eastern cliff. Meda is there at the far end, near the foot of the Dohl Mountains." He didn't sound relieved. Hak pointed to a thin trail of waterfalls along the cliff. "There are hot springs near those falls. It will be a nice place to camp. And you can have a hot bath."

Annie let out a happy squeal. "Well, what are we waiting for? Let's go!"

Hak urged the horses toward the eastern cliffs. The sun had passed behind the western mountains by the time they reached a small river. There was still enough daylight to walk up a road hidden from the main trail.

"Most merchants do not bother with the hot springs. This path is too narrow for their carts, and most travelers do not know about this place. We might be lucky enough to have the place to ourselves for the night. However, do not be surprised if we share camp with someone. Try not to talk to them."

"Don't worry. Tomas taught me a lesson," Annie said dryly.

They reached a hollow in the cliff wall. An outcropping provided suitable shelter from the elements. A trail snaked away from the clearing toward the sound of bubbling water.

As they made camp under the outcropping, Annie tied Tia to a heavy log and helped Hak start a fire. They were down to dried meat and an odd mixture of seeds and grains that reminded Annie of granola. It was not toasted or flavored with any sweeteners, and she found it disgusting. It was as tasteless as eating raw oatmeal. She still tried to eat a few bites at Hak's insistence, but it made her mouth feel like a cotton ball.

"Go wash up first. Clean all of your old clothing. I will hang them by the fire."

Annie scrunched up her nose at him in confusion. "You want me to wear my old clothes tomorrow?"

"Yes."

"Why?"

"Just do it, Annie."

"Whatever." She carried her crusty hoodie, jeans, and tank top toward the springs. She found several warm, steaming sapphire pools. She plunged her clothes into the smallest pool, and was delighted with the heat. The hot springs did not smell like the sulfur springs she had visited in Oregon.

Annie's finger was still too swollen for her to scrub her clothes thoroughly. She mashed them against a rock for several minutes with her good hand, and hung them on a low branch near the hot springs. She slipped out of her clothes and carefully stepped into one of the larger pools. Annie hung on to the side as she tested the depth of the dark water. It came up to her neck. It was perfect.

She stood against one side of the pool and took in several deep breaths. She had loved going to hot springs in Oregon, but had never had the opportunity to enjoy them alone. There had always been groups of college kids and old hippies, and usually it was too noisy to hear the frogs and crickets.

Annie listened curiously to the noises in the forest. They were strange and alien, but also very soothing. *The melodies of the forest at night must be beautiful everywhere,* Annie thought. It was one of her favorite parts of camping.

Two small blue lights flickered in the canopy, darting behind branches. Annie froze. It was the same thing she had seen outside the crystal when she had first woken up in Tahldia. She had believed they were fireflies, but now she was not so sure.

The lights chased each other over the water and along the side of the cliff, oblivious to her presence. They would dart around each other and suddenly pause. *Just like hummingbirds.*

One of the blue lights changed purple, and then red. It gave a high-pitched chirp and darted at the other light.

Okay, maybe not quite like a hummingbird.

The two lights swirled around each other, both bright red and chirping frantically, then they whirred out of sight. Annie smiled. *I know I need to get home . . . but man, this place can be so cool sometimes.* She took in a deep breath and let the magic of the forest hypnotize her for the better part of an hour.

Hak's voice called out from the nearby trail. "You are being very quiet. Are you all right, Annie?"

"Yeah. I'm pretty much done. I'll be there in a minute."

Annie pulled herself out of the hot water and sucked in her breath at the temperature change. She wished she had soap and a towel. She slipped on the sweater and leggings that Hak had given her and carried her wet clothes back to camp.

He pointed to a line hanging between two rocks near the fire. "You can hang your clothes there. They will be dry by morning."

"Thanks." Annie hung her clothes and settled down in front of the fire to brush her hair. She added some of the gardenia conditioner in an effort to detangle her locks.

"I will take first watch tonight. Get some rest. I will not take long at the hot springs."

Annie gratefully curled up near the fire and used Tia for a pillow. The poor dog was exhausted.

"Hak?"

"Yes, Annie?"

"What will you do when we return to Meda? After all the stuff with the council and when I get to go back home. What do you plan to do with your life?"

Hak seemed startled by the question. "It depends on what the council wants me to do."

"What do *you* want to do?"

"I . . . I am not sure. I will most likely return to Falishan and try to find some way to destroy Voltay."

"And then?"

"I do not think I will survive beyond that. I said I would *try* to destroy Voltay. It may be the last thing I do in my life."

"And . . . and you're just okay with that? You know it's a suicide mission and you're just like 'whatever' about it? Don't you want to live? You know, go out and dance and find pretty girls?"

"That is not the life I am meant to have," Hak said brusquely.

Annie folded her arms and sneered. "God. Aren't you being a bit melodramatic? You need to ease up a bit, Hak. Enjoy life."

He growled at her and pointed at his scars. "How, Annie? How am supposed to lead a normal life?"

"By not giving in to all these horrible, angry emotions! You're still a good person, Hak. Don't go throwing your life away because you feel some sort of revenge is necessary."

"It is the only way."

"You were given a second chance for a reason, Hak."

He shook his head angrily at Annie. "You do not understand anything. I was given another chance at life so that I could warn others. I have done that deed, and now I must find a way to get my magic back and destroy those demons, or die trying."

"Ugh, I wish you didn't value yourself so little!"

"It is easy to be worthless without honor, Annie." Hak walked toward the hot springs without another word.

She wished there was something she could say to make Hak feel better. Annie found it very difficult to fall asleep.

Her dreams were full of cliffs and falling helplessly into a white void.

Annie woke to one of Hak's armored hands clamped firmly over her mouth. She jerked awake and tried to pull his hand off of her face. Hak put his other hand up to his mouth and motioned for her to be silent with one finger. At once, Annie stopped squirming and tensed. They stared at each other for a few seconds, and he gently took his hand off her mouth. She was suddenly aware of Tia growling next to them.

Annie sat up and looked around wildly. *It's almost light outside! Did he stay awake the entire night? Is someone out there? What the fuck is going on?!*

"I think we have company. Not sure. Be ready for anything," Hak whispered next to her ear, so quietly she almost didn't hear it. "I wish I still had magic. At times like this, I feel so powerless."

They sat and waited, listening to the quiet woods. The sky lightened to a soft blue. Annie looked around and realized Hak had already packed up their camp, but had left her pepper spray by the fire. She grabbed it nervously. The horses were saddled and ready to go. It didn't make sense.

"How long have you been aware of something out there?" Annie hissed.

"Tia began growling. I walked around the forest but saw nothing. Still, your dog is convinced something or someone is nearby. I figured we needed to be ready to go as soon as we have enough light."

Tia gave another deep, low growl that seemed to go on for many moments. They heard a stick snap in the distance. Far away, the birds stopped chirping. Then another crack split the silence. Something was walking toward them. Annie checked Tia's leash. She was unsure what was safest.

Should I untie her and be ready to run, or should I leave her leashed to the log and keep her out of trouble?

Hak gripped his sword tighter and held a hand in front of Annie, as if telling her to stay. He slowly edged out of the small hollow in the cliff where they were camped and made his way toward the horses. Shadow whickered uneasily.

"It's their horses," said a gruff voice.

"Shut up, Mel," said another voice.

Two men emerged on the trail, holding swords and shields. They wore dark leather armor and tattered black cloaks. They were caked with dirt.

"Who are you?" Hak demanded.

The two men froze at the sound of Hak's thunderous voice and turned to stare at him. They held their shields up carefully. Two more men appeared behind them.

The man in the front squinted. "Are you called Hakayatas?"

"Who would like to know?" Hak growled.

One of the other men pointed at Hak. "It is him. Look at the scars."

"And he has the Vinder with him." One of the latecomers pointed at Annie. Suddenly all four men were staring at her.

Annie felt cold all over. She gripped the can of pepper spray in a shaky hand. Tia barked angrily. Hak lowered the visor on his helm.

"Take him and kill the beast. Leave the girl alive. Tomas wants her."

The mention of Tomas removed all doubt about their intentions. Hak roared and charged, not giving the intruders a chance to say more. Annie crouched, preparing to spring away.

"Zully! The girl!" barked the first man. "Do not let her escape!"

The apparent leader of the group raised his shield and deflected Hak's blow. He thrust his sword at Hak, but it glanced off his armor. Hak used his enormous size to keep charging, and he knocked one of the other men over. He turned, ducked a blow from the first man, and brought his sword against the back of the man's legs. The blow found the small space between the pieces of the man's armor and a spray of blood rushed out. The leader fell to his knees screaming. The horses reared wildly against their restraints. Tia went into a frenzy and tugged violently on her leash.

Hak rolled out of the way as two of the other men spread out around him. The fourth man leered at Annie.

Shit! Tia could get hurt! I better get away from her before this dude hurts her! Annie broke into a run toward the hot springs. The man charged and jumped in front of her, his sword and shield between them. Annie could hear the crash of steel behind her and hoped Hak would be all right.

The man gave her a cold stare above the tip of his dented shield. "Aye, wild one. Where do you think you are going?"

"Stay back!" Annie screamed. *Is that dried blood on his shield? Oh shit . . .* She heard Hak yell something, but it was cut off by a loud, metallic clang.

The man grinned and walked toward her.

"Fuck you!" Annie growled.

The man almost fell over laughing. "My, my! I just might!"

He pushed his shield at her. Annie gave a wild kick at it and stepped back, evoking more laughter from the man.

"I like a spirited woman!"

Annie inched backward until she felt the cliff behind her. She turned her head to the right and watched helplessly as Hak fought the other two men at the same time. A line of black blood oozed from underneath one of their breastplates. Hak swung wildly to keep some space between him and them.

Annie's distraction cost her. Zully thrust his shield against her and pinned her to the rock wall. All the air was pushed from her lungs.

"Aye! I have your Vinder, Hakayatas!" He called out, pressing Annie into the rock wall. She was dimly aware of Tia barking, snarling, and yelping. The man dropped his sword, but kept his shield pressed against Annie. She struggled for breath as the man's hand wiped the hair from her eyes. She tried to suck more air into her lungs, but it was like breathing through a straw.

If only I could move my arms! I'd spray this asshole in the eyes!

"Aw, poor thing. Such a pretty face for a Vinder. Shame it is turning blue."

"F-f-f-f-!" she tried to breathe and curse him at the same time. His face was riddled with acne scars, and several of his teeth were brown or missing. He leaned up against Annie, pressing his body into the shield. He was only a few inches from her. The hobos by her office had been downright beautiful compared to this man. His breath smelled like rancid meat.

"Want to give me a kiss, sweet lady?" He tilted his head towards hers.

Annie's head jerked forward and slammed against his fat nose. White stars flashed in front of her eyes, but she felt the pressure on her lungs ease. She gasped for air as the man took a step back. She felt liquid trickle down her face. Annie wiped it away from her eyes and found blood on her hands.

"You bitch!" he roared, raising his fist to punch her. Annie stumbled, held the pepper spray in front of her, and aimed. The red liquid hit home. Zully screamed in agony and flailed around wildly. His shield smashed Annie in the right shoulder, and the pepper spray flew from her hand as she hit the ground.

Despite a direct spray to the face, the man grabbed one of her legs and yanked Annie toward him. She kicked and shouted, but he held on savagely. Panicked, Annie looked over to see Hak engaged in his own struggle. He was focused on the last man in front of him. She saw blood oozing down one of Hak's leg plates. His opponent seemed to be in much better shape.

Zully pulled Annie underneath him. She was overpowered despite her opponent's temporary blindness. He rested his knees on either side of her body and pinned down her arms with them. Annie kicked and bucked her body, but she couldn't force him off of her.

"You miserable cunt! I will make you pay for that little fire curse!" Zully roared, spit flying from his mouth. He was unable to open his eyes, but his flailing hands found Annie's head and grabbed her hair. She jerked and struggled fiercely, but Zully slammed her head against the ground and began punching her.

Stars shot everywhere and Annie's vision blurred red. She felt a tooth crack and tasted blood. She closed her eyes against the pain and begged Zully to stop. She felt her head explode over and over.

Then she heard Zully scream, and more weight fell on her. She felt him struggle wildly with something else. Her vision was dimmed and blurry, but she could make out Tia tearing into the man's face. She tried to focus on the fuzzy scene. Annie felt hot liquid pour on her. She heard her heartbeat throbbing painfully in the depths of her head.

Even though Zully was no longer punching her, her head was still pounding as if the beating had never stopped. Human screams and panicked horses began to blend together in one horrible cacophony. She crawled a few feet away and vomited.

Hak! she thought with terror. She tried to focus on the two figures dancing in the clearing. Everything was dim, as if she was trying to watch the world through thick gauze. She realized with alarm that her contact lenses had been knocked out.

She saw one of the men fall. The other stumbled but caught himself. Annie couldn't tell who it was. The figure ran towards her. She held up a shaky hand and begged for mercy. *I'm done for!*

"Annie! Oh gods, Annie!" She felt large hands encircle her trembling arms and turn her over onto her back. She couldn't stop shaking.

"Where are you hurt?"

She knew it was Hak, but part of her brain seemed unable to register the familiar voice.

"Annie, answer me! Where did he stab you?"

She looked down and realized she was covered in blood. She looked up at Hak and tried to focus on his face. She blinked and felt one of her contact lenses slide out of the corner of her eye. She closed her eye and rubbed gently at it until it fell back into place. The other contact lens was definitely gone. Annie squinted and tried to focus her one good eye on Hak.

"Say something!"

"Rocks!" She frowned. That wasn't the word she had meant to say!

Hak pulled her shirt up and inspected her chest. Annie was too dazed to feel embarrassment. Hak pulled at her clothes until he realized there were no stab wounds. He removed his gloves and combed his fingers through her hair.

He pressed a hand against her forehead.

"Hik," she tried to say. "Hok . . . H-H-Hak . . ." *Fuck, what is wrong with me? I can't say what I need to!*

Hak looked down into her eyes. His face was wild and full of fear. It frightened her. He eased Annie into his arms and gently pulled down on her cheeks to look into her eyes.

"Can you understand what I am saying, Annie?"

She nodded. Suddenly Tia was there and licked her face.

"Back, dog!" Hak yelled, and waved a hand.

"No . . ." Annie moaned. She wanted Tia at her side. *Oh god, Tia saved my life!*

"Your beast is covered in blood, Annie. You do not want her licking your face, I think."

Annie felt her heart squeeze in fear. She turned and focused her one good eye on Tia. The black Lab's muzzle was covered in blood. An ear was torn and bloody, and fur was missing around her neck. But the dog seemed to be in good spirits. *She must have pulled the leash off and . . . oh, the poor thing . . .!*

Annie tried to reach for Tia but Hak stopped her. She looked over at Zully on the ground. His face was gone and his throat had been torn out. His fingers twitched slightly.

It was too much for Annie. She wailed suddenly, a long, childish noise that echoed along the cliff. She cried and choked on sobs for several seconds before burying her face against Hak's cold breastplate.

Hak did not try to hush her, and gently cradled her until her wail became a low, confused moan broken by wracking sobs. *I just want to go home! I just want my mom! I just want this to all be a bad dream! Oh god, Annie, wake the fuck up!*

"Annie," Hak whispered into her ear, as if comforting a distraught child. "Annie, we need to get to Meda. You are hurt. You need a healer."

Annie ran her uninjured hand against her nose and wiped the tears, blood, and snot from her face. "Home . . ." she whimpered.

"Can you stand?"

She nodded dully. Hak helped her up and let her lean on his arm.

"Oh!" Annie cried out, pointing at Hak's leg. Blood was slowly dribbling out from underneath Hak's breastplate. She felt sick again.

"It is just a small cut. Here, let me take you to the hot springs. At least let me wash the blood off you. Your old clothes are dry . . . can you dress yourself?"

Annie wanted to stand up defiantly and walk off to do it herself. Instead she swayed for a moment and Hak caught her.

She gave him a weak nod and said, "Y-yeah." She growled and shook her head, fighting the confusion bubbling at the edges of her mind.

"Are you sure you can do it?" Hak asked doubtfully.

Annie nodded again. She didn't trust herself to speak once more and risk gibberish pouring out. Hak walked her to the hot springs and eased her down to sit by the water. Tia jumped in the smaller spring and swam around. The dog seemed unperturbed by the fight, or killing Zully.

Fuck . . . I guess Tahldia makes everyone a murderer. Even my sweet puppy! I wonder if I'll be forced to kill someone?

"I will be back with your clothes. You need to change, and we need to leave immediately." Hak disappeared down the trail.

Annie clumsily sunk her arms into the hot water and washed the blood off. She rinsed her face and watched as small red drops trickled from her forehead into the water below. Her face felt swollen and her teeth hurt.

She cupped some water to her face and rinsed her mouth. She spit out blood and bits of teeth. The sight chilled her.

Hak appeared with her clothes and left them next to Annie. He turned and stood at the top of the trail, his back to her to give her privacy.

She very carefully eased out of her bloody clothes. She was still dizzy, but she managed to remove her leather pants without falling over. She did not bother trying to unhook her bra or remove her underwear. Annie took a small dip in one of the shallow pools to wash the rest of the blood off. She found that taking several deep breaths helped steady her racing heart.

"You all right?" Hak asked, not looking.

"Y-y-yes." Annie struggled to say the simple word. The lie was obvious. She rinsed the blood out of her hair and wiped at her arms. The heat of the water made her feel sick. She remembered the heat of Zully's blood when it had poured over her. She shuddered, and quickly climbed out of the shallow pool.

Tia pulled herself out and shook hot water on Annie. She came up and licked Annie's face when she reached down for her old gray hoodie and jeans. After a few awkward moments, Annie pulled the clothes on and walked toward Hak. He led her back to the horses. Annie looked around and saw the four bodies strewn about the campsite. There was blood everywhere.

She threw up.

"Easy, Annie." Hak pulled her wet hair out of the way as she retched.

"S-s-sorry," Annie whispered.

"Do not worry," Hak said, but she could tell by the catch in his tone that she should worry. Hak sounded terrified. "We will get you to Meda. There will be a healer there."

Hak untied the horses and looked at Annie doubtfully. He quickly removed his bags from Shadow and tied them onto the mare. He tied the mare's lead onto Shadow's pommel.

"Hold still, Annie. I do not trust you to ride right now." Hak placed his large hands around her waist and hoisted her up onto Shadow as if she were a toddler. She curled up against the front of the saddle and didn't say a word.

Hak eased himself up into the large saddle behind Annie and shifted his weight until he was comfortable. He gave a grunt of pain as his breastplate pushed against Annie's back.

"We must ride fast. You have a tough beast, Annie. Tia will be able to keep up with us, I think. Do not worry."

Annie squinted her one good eye at Tia and felt like crying. Her dog's right ear flopped unnaturally against her face. Despite the blood oozing from the tear, the dog seemed delighted to start a new adventure.

I envy your stupidity, you lucky dog.

Hak pushed the horses into a trot down the trail. When they reached the main road he urged them to run. To Annie's relief, Tia kept pace. The dog seemed determined to never let Annie out of her sight again. She felt her vision swim and she closed her eyes. Her head tilted back to rest against Hak's armor.

"No falling asleep, Annie. Stay awake."

"Toored."

Hak whispered into her ear, "Tell me a story."

Annie didn't want to talk; her thoughts and words were not syncing with her lips. Finally, she said, "No . . . you."

"Stay awake, Annie."

She felt the horse bob wildly underneath her. The front of the saddle was uncomfortable, as was Hak's armor pressing against her. He kept one hand on the reins and held her in place with his left arm.

Hak pulled her closer. "Annie, I am sorry. I am so sorry."

His voice rose softly behind her in a song of prayer. It was that strange language again. His voice was calming, even though the words slipped together in one long mess. She tried to focus on the song, but nothing made sense.

"Hnnngh?"

"Everything will be all right," Hak said, more to himself than to Annie. She let the world flow by her in a green and brown blur. She was too dazed to think clearly.

"Would you like to hear the story about the faeries of Dohl Valley?"

Annie murmured a yes. Hak's words flowed over her and eased her confusion. She tried to stay awake and focus on his words, and listen to the story about how Meda was created. The story wasn't making sense. Annie kept forgetting what Hak said moments before. It frustrated her and she struggled to keep her eyes open. His deep voice soothed her battered mind.

They rode hard the entire day. Annie felt as if part of her brain was missing. She couldn't tell how much time had passed, or think clearly. She kept looking back fearfully at Tia, but the dog kept up. She was foaming at the mouth from running, yet every time Annie turned to check on her, the dog was still there, and her eyes never left Annie.

The main road was large enough to hold four cars side by side. Annie couldn't be sure, and fought every second to keep her brain working. She dimly became aware of a great river that flowed alongside the road beyond the trees. The current seemed swift, but Annie thought she saw figures riding the tops of the white water.

They passed people on the road itself. Horses, carts, and entire groups of people were traveling in and out of the valley. Annie tried to look at the strangers with her good eye. Everyone seemed to gape in shock as they rode past. An old man called out to Hak, and Annie saw the concern in his eyes. Hak ignored them all and kept the horse at a fast trot.

Hak had grown quiet and was leaning heavily on her. It worried Annie, but she couldn't talk, either. Her mouth felt broken and swollen, and her throat was parched. She moved her tongue around and found the bits of shattered molar poking back. She wanted to cry again. She felt for Hak's arm wrapped around her waist, and gave his hand a tight squeeze. He quietly squeezed back.

The road widened and the trees fell back. The dense canopy had hidden the sky from them for most of the day. Annie was not prepared to find a city sprawled out before her. She gaped and closed her bad eye so she could take in the amazing view. The fog in her brain cleared slightly.

They had reached the end of the valley where the two cliffs met. In the center, a huge white-and-gray city sprawled out against the cliffs, and beyond, an enormous mountain that dwarfed anything Annie had seen in Oregon.

A great waterfall poured from the top of the cliff, and seemed to plunge straight into the heart of the city. A clear river poured out to the right, and ran along the road in a frothy white torrent. The city rose up sharply on all sides as it ran the length of the hill into the cliff. It looked as though San Francisco and ancient Hopi Indian tastes had been combined. The buildings were stone, and some of the small ones burrowed into the cliff had ladders snaking out of the bottoms.

A large wall was built from one cliff to the other, with a great iron gate at the center. The massive doors were open and people passed freely by a group of men in armor. They crossed a small moat connected with the river, and there they found city guards.

A man wearing polished armor and a crimson tabard ran up to them. "By the red dragon's tears! What has happened to you? Vinder? Bandits?"

"Bandits. By the hot springs near the end of the eastern wall. We need to see a healer. Immediately." Hak grunted with pain and said, "We need to see Saiso if it is at all possible."

We need to see the moon? Annie thought weakly. She fought back the pain and confusion with a great effort.

"Right." The armored man turned and motioned at another guard standing nearby. "Kyrl, I need a hand with the lady."

"No. She is fine . . . we need to get to Saiso. Now."

"I will give you an escort. Blasted festival down by the falls has the streets pretty clogged. I will take you up the back way."

A second guard walked up with a horse and handed their escort the reins. The man climbed on the horse and pointed down a street to their right. Hak uttered his thanks.

They rode up the winding streets toward the right side of the city. They ran across a beautiful stone bridge that arched over the pounding river. The noise was deafening, but Annie found it soothing. It reminded her of Oregon rivers, and the sweet smell of wet earth, and days at the beach. Her parents would take her to the carnivals so she could play all the games——

Focus. Brain, don't fail me now. Annie shook her head and clenched her teeth. The sharp bite of pain from her broken molar jolted her. In her confused haze, she had forgotten her tooth was broken.

Their escort called out to the people milling on the road ahead of them. They stepped out of the way and let Hak pass. For some reason Annie thought this would be the difficult part.

Hak was so nervous about something, but the city guards aren't asking questions! They're totally helping us right now. What is he so worried about with Meda? This city is just unbelievably beautiful!

After what had seemed like an eternity, they stopped at the top of a narrow road lined with tall stone buildings built into the cliff. The guard dismounted and hurried over to Hak and Annie.

The cliff cast a deep shadow on this section of the town. Hak picked up Annie by the waist and carefully dropped her into the arms of the waiting guard. As she turned, Annie was stunned to see the entire town and valley spread out before them. She couldn't believe how far they had traveled!

It had only felt like a few hours! But the sun is getting ready to set! How did the entire day pass?

Tia trotted over and collapsed at Annie's feet. The dog gave her one small lick and sprawled out, panting at a frightening pace. Hak pushed himself from the saddle, but instead of landing on his feet, he simply fell.

Annie cried out and went to him. She was horrified to find both dried and fresh blood trickling down the side of his leg armor. *Oh my god . . . I had no idea he was bleeding behind me!* Guilt tore at her as she gently pulled the visor away from his face.

"I-i-idiot," She managed to say, running her hands along his breastplate. She couldn't figure out how to find the wound under all his armor.

The guard ran to a large wooden door at the end of the alley and banged at it fiercely.

"Wise Saiso! You are needed!"

There was no answer. For what seemed like eternity, Annie watched the wooden door and willed it to move. Deep within her damaged mind, she knew they were seeking help. She knew, for some reason, that the door *must* open.

Finally the wooden door flew out and made a loud *crack* as it hit the wall. An old, wrinkled man in green robes glared angrily at the soldier.

"What!? I am having dinner!"

"This man said he needed to see you, Wise Saiso. I apologize for the intrusion."

Saiso glared in the direction of Annie and Hak and his wrinkles seemed to squeeze together as he took in the sight. He was short, but lean. What little silver hair he had left was tied into a pointed ponytail at the back of his head. He walked forward to look down at Hak and Annie, and gave a start when he saw Hak's face.

"By the *stars*. What the hell have you done now?" Saiso turned to the guard and snapped his fingers. "Help me get this idiot in the house."

The guard swallowed uneasily, but obeyed. Hak leaned on the guard, and Saiso led them inside. The first room was small, and riddled with shoes, jackets, and an odd assortment of items Annie didn't recognize. Some could have been children's toys, but she was not certain.

Saiso led them through several rooms, each darker and more cavernous than the last. Annie had the suspicion that his house went deep into the cliff. They passed a brightly lit room with several people eating at a food-laden table. There were two small children, and several men and women about Annie's age. They barely looked shocked to see two bloody people walk by their kitchen.

Saiso waved a hand in irritation as they passed. "Do not wait on me. I will be busy for some time."

Saiso took a lantern from the wall and said loudly, "Gwen! Kosh! Get in here!"

He led them into a dark room. The light from the small lantern did not touch the walls. Annie felt like they had walked into a giant cave.

Saiso pointed at the walls and said, "Firiel!"

To Annie's amazement, four torches on each rocky wall burst into flame, lighting the room. There were two stone tables draped in cloth in the middle.

"Lay him over there on that table. Girl, go sit on this one." It took Annie a moment to realize that Saiso was talking to her. She jumped when he clapped his hands at her. "Go! Sit!"

Annie mutely made her way over to one of the stone tables and sat on the edge. Tia quietly followed her and laid down in a huff at her feet. The dog was no longer panting, but Annie had never seen her so exhausted. She realized Tia's paws were bleeding. Annie knelt down and ruffled the fur by Tia's uninjured ear and watched the guard. Hak grunted as the man helped him up on the other table.

"Help me get his armor off," Saiso told the guard. They worked at the buckles and armor and lifted the breastplate off of Hak, followed by the chain mail he wore underneath. His blue tunic was soaked with blood. Annie winced.

Hak gave her a sad look. "It will be all right, Annie."

"Now. Lay down." Saiso gently pushed Hak against the table and put a towel under his head. Then Saiso turned to the guard and pointed to the door. "You did well, soldier."

"Wise Saiso?" The guard asked in confusion. "You do not want me to stay?"

"No. You were never here. You never saw this man or this woman." Saiso waved his hands at the guard's face and murmured something under his breath.

Without another word, the guard walked out of the room. Two children appeared at the doorway and watched Saiso carefully.

"Gwen, boil some water. Kosh, get the herbs." The children stared at Annie and didn't move.

"Well?" Saiso clapped at them. "Move it!"

The girl jumped and ran toward the hearth. She poured a bucket of water into a large kettle and said, "Firiel!" The wood in the hearth exploded into flame. The boy ran to a wooden cabinet and began pulling out jars and bowls. Annie gaped at them. They couldn't have been older than thirteen.

Saiso crossed his arms and looked down at Hak. "By the gods . . . what happened to you two, Hakayatas?"

"We were attacked just north of Meda. By the eastern cliff at the end of the valley," Hak said weakly. He winced as Saiso lifted the bloody tunic off the wound.

"Gwen! I need some towels over here!" Saiso snapped impatiently.

She ran up to Saiso and handed him a wet towel. Saiso sighed with irritation and said something at the cloth. Suddenly steam radiated from it.

"You need to work on that," Saiso told her, not unkindly. "Keep practicing."

He dabbed at Hak's wound with the towel and gave a small chuckle. "How did I know you would come back with trouble at your heels?"

Gwen tentatively walked up to Annie with a steaming white cloth. She fearfully dabbed at Annie's forehead, as if she would suddenly bite. Gwen was petite, and dressed in a simple dark green robe. Her large brown eyes took in Annie with a mix of curiosity and worry. Annie tried to smile at her, but her face seemed too swollen to move.

Saiso took a bowl from the young boy and pinched some sort of herb from it. He sprinkled the brown-colored powder on Hak, who gave a pained groan.

"Where else are you hurt, Hakayatas? Were there any spells?"

"I am fine."

"Do not feed me horse shit and tell me it is chocolate."

"See to her first," Hak said weakly. "She took a blow to the head."

"I can see that," Saiso said dryly as he worked on Hak's wound. "Her face looks like a popped melon."

"I can wait a little longer."

"No, you cannot. Kosh, finish this." Saiso handed the bowl back to the boy. "Now remember, make sure the wound is completely cleaned before you close it up. Infections do not happen on my watch."

"Yes, Wise Saiso."

The old man turned to Annie, and then stared down at her dog. "What is this? What is this mongrel doing in here? It looks half dead."

"The dog stays," Hak growled.

"Fine. Whatever. More germs. I am surrounded by crazy people." Saiso irritably put his hands on Annie's shoulders. She winced at his cold touch.

"Hold still, woman. I need you to lie down." Annie obeyed and lay down on the hard stone table. Saiso held his wrinkled hands an inch above her body and slowly waved them around. He smelled like lavender, thyme, and other herbs. She felt a prickling sensation where his hands traveled, even though he did not touch her. His hands hovered over her heart, and then her neck, and finally over her head.

Saiso paused and his frown deepened. "Hmmmm. Yes. The brain. A finger. A tooth. The cheekbone is fractured, too. It feels like there might be a cracked rib or two. Can you talk, girl?"

"She cannot talk or see very well. I noticed she had a hard time focusing."

"Concussion. Bah! That is simple. I can heal this in no time."

Saiso motioned for his young assistants. They brought him a steaming bucket of water with knives poking out of the top, and a tray with burning incense and a pile of bones. Annie stared at the knives and bones with terror.

Great! What kind of freaky voodoo shit is this? Saiso pushed her head back against a pillow. She felt her heartbeat accelerate and her hands trembled. Annie had never been fond of doctors or hospitals, and suddenly she was terrified of what this old man might do.

"Hik!" she said in panic.

Saiso rolled his eyes. "Hold still. You will be fine. You cannot move when I do this."

Annie felt the young assistants gently hold down her arms and legs. Panic seized her, and she tried to scream.

"Oh for the love of the gods! Was she struck dumb as well?" Saiso asked irritably. "Siliern hazen!"

Annie felt her entire body grow heavy. It was as if Saiso had paralyzed her. She couldn't even move her lips, and she gave a frightened whimper. The old man placed both of his hands on her cheeks and she felt heat and ice envelop her senses.

Hak's face appeared above her. "Annie, look at me."

"Get back to your table!"

Even though Annie felt disconnected from her body, she saw Hak pick up her hand and clasp it. "Everything will be all right," he told her.

"Go lay down, you big idiot."

"Saiso, please. Just put her to sleep. She is scared out of her mind."

Annie tried again to scream but nothing came out. The old man's icy hands were hurting her. She felt as if her teeth were breaking all over again.

"Baaah! You people!" Saiso touched his fingertips to Annie's forehead, and the world disappeared.

Annie woke in a soft bed in a cavernous room. A small lantern hung on the wall. She moaned and brought her hands to her face. The swelling was gone, and nothing hurt. She poked at her cheeks experimentally, trying to find any pain.

"You slept for a long time," said a deep voice next to her.

Shocked, Annie turned and found Hak lying next to her.

He gave her a smile. "I was so worried about you."

"Oh, Hak! Are you okay?"

"I am fine." He propped himself up on an elbow and looked down at Annie. "How are you?"

Annie tried to shake away the shock of finding Hak in bed with her.

"What are you doing here?"

"I was worried about you. I did not want to leave your side. How are you feeling?"

"Good, I guess." Annie looked up at Hak leaning over her. "What are you doing, Hak?"

He gave a deep chuckle and smiled at her. "Just keeping watch over a beautiful lady."

Annie felt herself blush, and she couldn't look away from Hak's strange yellow eyes. They seemed to glow in the dim light.

"But . . . isn't this considered . . . this isn't proper, right?"

Hak smiled gently and ran his hand through her hair, pulling a strand away from her eyes. "I am sorry. Do you want me to leave?"

Annie shook her head. "No. Please don't leave me."

Suddenly, Hak leaned down and kissed her. She felt her body burn with delight as his lips met hers. Her body surged with newfound energy. His hand cradled her neck as his tongue found hers. They kissed for many moments before Annie managed to break away long enough to murmur his name.

Hak kissed her cheeks, and his lips trailed along her neck. His hand slowly moved down her body and a finger caressed the inside of her thighs. Annie gasped as Hak slid a finger between her lips and pressed inside of her.

Annie stared at Hak with shock. He gave her a sly grin and began pressing harder. Annie moaned with pleasure. She had forgotten how wonderful it felt to be caressed in such a teasing manner. Hak's energy seemed to melt into hers. She could almost see their auras glowing and blending together.

It felt right.

It felt good.

"Hak . . ." she moaned, feeling her body throb with each stroke.

"Annie . . ." he breathed into her ear, and ran his tongue down her neck. He was on top of her now, kissing her breasts and running his fingers between her trembling legs.

"Annie . . ."

"Annie?"

Annie jerked and opened her eyes. She was on the stone table, with several woolen blankets on top of her. Hak was sitting next to the table, giving her an odd look. They were alone in the strange healing room.

"Annie? Are you all right?"

"Oh god . . ." Embarrassment poured through her like a cold shower as she remembered the dream.

"You were saying my name. You seemed to be having a bad dream."

Annie jerked the blankets over her head to hide her face. She felt like her cheeks would melt from the blushing. She let her face contort with every emotion imaginable under the blanket. *Healed only to die of embarrassment,* she thought.

Finally, Annie pulled the blanket down to her nose and gripped it against her mouth. She gave Hak an uneasy laugh. "Yeah. It was a really crazy dream. Pretty fucked up."

"You can talk again."

Annie paused, and realized she felt much better. Her mind felt clear and refreshed. She ran a finger over her forehead, but could not find the wound from headbutting Zully. Her cheeks weren't swollen. She carefully poked her tongue around in her mouth and was sad to discover a molar was missing. She looked around the room and realized her vision was still messed up.

She blinked irritably and rubbed at her eyes. *It's like my other eye is the bad one now! I know I lost the contact lens in my right eye and I had it shut most of the ride here, but now it's fine! And my other eye is so blurry!*

Annie gasped.

"What is it?" he asked with alarm.

"My eyes!"

"Saiso said he healed you completely," Hak said, giving her a concerned look.

"Yes! He fixed my eyes!"

Hak watched, a look of fascination on his face, as Annie pulled the remaining contact lens out of her left eye. She blinked and looked around the room. "Oh my god, I can *see!*"

Tears burned her eyes. *I've been wearing glasses since I was a little kid! I never thought . . . I never imagined that I would be able to see this well again! How did Saiso do it?*

"You seem well." Hak sounded relieved.

"And you! You were hurt so bad!"

"No. It was a simple cut. Saiso patched me up very quickly."

"You were bleeding everywhere!"

"I am fine. Do not worry." Hak lifted the clean tunic he was wearing and showed her his ribs. "See? No new scars."

Annie leaned back against the pillow and let out a deep breath. Tia's head popped up at the end of the table and the dog eagerly licked her face.

"Saiso appears to be a bit of a rough old man, but he is kind. He even healed Shadow and Tia's paws when he was done with us."

"I was so scared, Hak. That was the worst thing I've ever been through."

"I am sorry. I should have been more careful at camp. I should have known that Tomas would send someone after us if he could not catch up."

"Do you think Tomas found a healer?"

"Oh, undoubtedly. Although, it would not be anyone nearly as talented as Saiso."

"Will Tomas be here? In Meda?" Panic twisted Annie's stomach.

"No. I do not imagine he would be here. You will be safe."

"Hak, he wanted me alive. He told his cronies to take me alive."

"Yes . . . I heard that as well."

"But why?"

"I do not know, Annie. But you are safe now."

Annie sighed and wiped a stray tear from her eye. She was tired of being frightened. She was tired of crying. *I just want to go home.*

"Pardon, Master Hakayatas," said a small voice. Annie lifted her head to see Gwen standing at the doorway. She had a bundle of cloth in her hands that Annie recognized as her clothes. "My aunt Mari wants to know if you are hungry. We have fresh bread and tea, if you would like."

"Oh god," Annie breathed. "Tea would be awesome!"

The girl cocked her head at Annie and set the clothes down on a chair next to Hak.

"Saiso wants you both to drink some of this as well." The girl dropped a small vial into Hak's hand. "Both of you take half. It will prevent fever, and offer some energy."

The girl gave Hak a small bow, shot Annie an odd look, and left the room.

Hak popped the cork off of the vial and drank half of the contents. He handed Annie the vial as he wiped his mouth. Annie hesitantly took a sip, and was delighted at the sweet taste. It was a mixture of vanilla and peppermint. She gratefully downed the contents. Her body tingled slightly.

The girl returned with a tray of bread, three cups, and a teapot. Saiso was at her side. She set the tray on the table at Annie's feet, gave a small bow, and left. The old man watched as Annie began stuffing the warm bread into her mouth, nearly choking.

Saiso gave a small laugh. "So what are you? A Vinder? You act like you have never been healed before. Never met such a pretty Vinder, though. Your energy levels are very odd."

Annie paused, a chunk of bread stuffed in her mouth. Hak shot Saiso a strange look. "How so?"

Saiso sat back in his chair and waved a hand indifferently. "She has bizarre energy, is all. Have not felt anything like it."

137

"What do you mean?" Hak and Annie asked in unison.

"She is not a Vinder. But acts like one. She has a lot of energy. I am not saying it like it is a bad thing! Bah! Enough of this talk. How are you feeling, Annie?"

"Much better. Thank you. I never thought I would see this well again!"

"Eh. How come you never had that healed up when you were young? You really walked around that blind the whole time?"

"It's a long story," Annie said quickly.

"Ah, I bet it is a good one," Saiso said, pouring himself a cup of tea.

"Did you deliver my message?" Hak asked Saiso.

"Aye. Both of them."

Annie gave Hak a questioning look, but he turned from her and poured tea into two cups. Annie gratefully took one from him.

"Well, if you do not want to tell me your story now, that is fine. I suppose you want to get to the council before they send out a search party. I'm sure that guard remembers you were here by now. I am not so good at mind spells. And you did not exactly sneak in to Meda very quietly. Showing up half dead on your horse. Bah! You might as well have thrown a saint's parade while you were at it."

"Thank you, Saiso."

The old man shrugged and sipped his tea. "I owed you one, Hakayatas. I guess we are even now."

"Yes."

"Fair enough." Saiso pulled a long bone pipe out of a pocket inside his robe. He packed in some brown-colored substance and pointed his finger at the pipe. A small flame sprang from his fingertips and burned the contents. Annie watched with a mix of fascination and envy.

"Is that tobacco?" she asked eagerly.

"Pardon?" Saiso gave her an odd look. "Never heard of that. This is nontak weed. It is similar to naroh weed, but it does not muddle the mind."

"Can I try some?"

"Annie!" Hak said. "Do not be rude!"

Saiso laughed. "It is fine. If a lady wants to smoke, who am I to stop her?" He handed Annie the pipe. She puffed at the mouthpiece eagerly. *It tastes better than tobacco, whatever it is.* After a few seconds she felt even better. *They might not have a name for nicotine here, but if this isn't the same thing, it's damn close!*

Annie handed Saiso the pipe and leaned back, sighing with contentment.

The old man set his cup down and stood. "There is clean water in that basin over there. Feel free to wash up and get out. This is not an inn, you know."

"Thank you again, Saiso."

"Bah." The old man shuffled out of the room and shut the door.

"Annie? How are you feeling, truly?"

Annie pulled at her tangled hair. "Better than I have in days, I guess."

"Are you well enough to talk to the council?"

"Yeah, might as well face it. I'm eager to see what kind of answers they have for me. I'm really excited to go home. I don't really feel like teasing death again."

Hak looked at the ground sadly. "I am sure I will find some answers."

CHAPTER NINE:

THE COUNCIL

AFTER EATING AND cleaning up, they said good-bye to Saiso and his family. Annie felt great wearing her comfortable jeans and old gray hoodie. Her hair was brushed and pulled back by her purple bandana. The air outside was cool and crisp, and Annie was grateful to stretch her legs and walk for a while. Even the simple act of walking felt like a miracle after yesterday.

Hak had polished his dented armor as best as he could, and wore it proudly. The streaks of dried blood were gone from his leg plates, and a clean dark blue cape hung behind him. He held his helmet lazily under an arm, and tugged at the scarf he used to hide his scars.

"Where are the horses?"

"Saiso's son took them to a stable for us. I think it would be easier for both of us to walk this morning. Enjoy the cold air and the scenery."

Annie sunk her hands into the pockets of her hoodie and frowned. *Hak seems like he's up to something. I can feel it.*

Tia trotted happily alongside of them, staying within inches of Annie's hand. They walked along the streets underneath the massive cliff and made their way to the enormous waterfall in the distance. Annie was surprised to see a grand structure built around the edges of the waterfall. It had long circular towers and countless windows with stained glass and balconies.

Annie gaped and pointed at it. "Is that . . . a castle?"

"Yes, that is King Halona's palace, and home of the great mage council. It is the heart of Meda, and this part of the eastern kingdoms. King Halona's rule stretches from the eastern sea, across this mountain range, and all the way over to the Shafani Sea far in the west."

"But how did they build a palace under a waterfall?"

"It is *behind* the waterfall, Annie. It is all one structure that is built deep into the Dohl Mountains. You will see soon enough. We just need to finish climbing this street."

She puffed as they walked uphill, but felt glad for the exertion. *I feel like I'm making the final march to the end of my adventure,* Annie mused. *I'm going to get my answers, and I'm going to go home. Or maybe I'll find out I'm already dead. This still seems like a crazy dream.*

I've really only had the chance to hang out with Hak. And that innkeeper, Odal. It will be good to meet other people, and see what I can learn. I'll be happy to get away from Hak. Yeah, keep telling yourself that, Annie.

She blushed fiercely as she remembered her vivid dream of Hak kissing and fondling her. *Not going to complain, sex dreams are fun, but holy shit . . . It's wrong on so many levels!* Annie watched Hak's back and shook her head with amusement. *But he sure looks good without a shirt on. Even with those awful scars. Oh man, I am so stupid sometimes . . .*

Two small men waddled past them at an easy pace. Annie blinked and tried not to stare. *No. A man and a woman.* They were wearing simple peasant clothes and wide leather belts. But one was wearing a dress. The man had a great puffy beard. Their faces looked swollen, their noses were huge, and their eyes were unnaturally large. *They aren't midgets! They're . . . oh my god!*

"Hak!" Annie tugged eagerly at his cloak. She stood on her tiptoes and whispered near his ear. "Were those *dwarves*?!"

Hak laughed. "It is not polite to stare, Annie. And yes, they are dwarves."

Annie watched with amazement as the couple walked down the street and disappeared into a building. *Just a regular couple out for their morning stroll, maybe. Wow!*

Hak talked in a hushed voice as they continued up the hilly streets. "They are the Dohlen dwarves. Their ancestors were the first dwarves, and they made their home under the mountain range near Meda. To hear the dwarves talk, they were the first two-legged creatures to roam Tahldia."

Hak gave her a sly smile. It was eerily like the one she had seen in her dream. She felt herself blush and looked at the ground.

"They are great drinkers and partiers. I think you would get along very well with dwarven culture. They can be loud, blunt, and they love to tell crude stories. But they are great builders, and they helped shape the castle you see here."

"You said all the dwarves in the western world had been killed. Are the Dohlen the last of their kind?"

"No. There are several clans in the east. Some are not as friendly as the Dohlen. There is a chain of islands to the far south. Many of the mountains there are still alive with fire and molten earth. I think the harsh landscape bred a harsh people," Hak said.

"The Fier dwarves are mean, and often attack first and ask questions later. They have very little honor in my eyes. The Lohlen in the far north, near Feldall, are the complete opposite. They share the wooded mountains with elves. They would not attack you even if you attack first. They are very shy."

Annie gaped at everything as they passed. The cobblestone streets were lined with tall stone buildings roughly three stories tall. Clotheslines hung between the alleys, and there was a sense that she was wandering through an antiquated European town. There were storefronts with large glass windows that held a variety of wares. She saw food, trinkets, jewelry, plants, furniture, and clothing. She felt her heart beat painfully in her chest, but it was from the sheer amazement of the world around her. Annie found herself smiling happily the entire walk.

Maybe I can go home in a couple of days. I want to explore Meda as much as I can. There is so much to see and do here! Annie's eyes watered. *Part of me wants to go home and try to find my family . . . the other part of me wants to explore. Real magic! Dwarves and elves! Dragons! Children and old men who can make fire with a snap of their fingers! I've been through a lot the last two weeks, but I think that good things are in the future.*

Annie smiled at the people on the street as they passed. Some looked at her questionably, especially if they noticed the skull and ravens printed on her hoodie. Yet if she smiled and gave them a slight nod, they returned the courtesy. Meda citizens seemed to be genuinely happy folk going about their lives at a leisurely pace. There didn't seem to be a fear of attack, or plagarne, or wild mercenaries who could shoot lightning from their hands.

Flowers and clothes hung from balconies, and other than the occasional whiff of horse manure or chamber pots, the town was clean and well cared for. Annie didn't see trash or litter anywhere.

Children played in the streets with balls or one another, and Tia ran up to give all the children a quick lick with her tongue. Sometimes she would try to steal the ball to play fetch.

They took a turn off the main road and walked toward the center of town. The houses were larger, and built together like small apartments. Each building had a large yard with a simple wooden fence and gate. She saw toys and gardens scattered throughout these yards, and young women holding babes and talking under the tall trees.

Hak opened the gate for Annie to one such yard, and closed it behind him. A child kicked a leather ball at Annie, and she deftly kicked it back. *I wonder if they have soccer here?* She laughed at the thought and looked around the yard.

Seven wooden doors opened into the yard. The stone building seemed ancient, but well maintained. The window shutters were painted bright hues, and clothes hung on the railings.

A woman shrieked. Annie ducked and looked around, her heart suddenly pounding in fear. She saw a young woman in a pale blue dress running toward them. Her long brunette hair was curled and twisted into a loose braid, with several flowers poking out. Her green eyes were wide and shining, and her mouth was curled up in an ecstatic smile. She sprinted to Hak and wrapped her arms around him tightly.

"Ahhhhh! You are back! It is so good to see you!"

Hak returned the hug fiercely. He bent his head down to the woman and picked her up in a larger hug. His eyes were closed and he buried his face in her hair. Annie felt her heart clench for a moment.

"I told you I would be back," Hak said, smiling.

"I received your message. Thank you!" She stood back and held his arms to get a good look at him. "What were you doing at Saiso's? Is everything all right?"

"Minor, I assure you."

Annie snorted.

The woman turned and looked at Annie curiously. "I am Nivya Shoreleon, of Osmek." The dainty woman took Annie's hand and bowed slightly. Her hands were perfectly manicured and decorated with many small bands of gold.

Annie gave her an awkward bow. "Hi. Uh, I'm Annie. Armstrong. Of Oregon."

Nivya beamed at Annie. "What a wonderful name you have there! But apologies, I do not think I have heard of Oregon. Is that near the Snow Seas? How did Hakayatas find you?"

"It's a long story," Annie said dryly.

Tia was excited to meet Nivya as well. The hundred-pound dog jumped up on Nivya and tried to lick her face. Hak quickly reached for the scruff of the dog's neck, but Nivya simply laughed. "Oh it is fine, Hakayatas! You know I love dogs!" The woman bent to scratch Tia's ears. The dog was wagging her tail so much Annie thought her butt would fall off.

"How is Viv?" Hak asked, looking around.

"Oh." A sad look washed over Nivya. "She . . . she finally passed to Alhena."

"I am sorry to hear that. She lived a very long time, and had wonderful people to watch over her. Viv had a good life."

"Yes." Nivya nodded with a sad smile. "She was a good dog."

"That's Tia," Annie said, feeling left out. She bit her lip and watched as Nivya played with her dog. *I don't like her and I don't know why. Crap . . . am I getting jealous? Over what? Her beauty? Her charm? Or the fact that Hak is staring at her like she's a goddess?*

Annie shoved her hands into her pockets so she could discreetly grind her nails into her skin. *Stop thinking like an idiot, Annie!*

"Please, join me under the tree. Can I get some tea or some food for you?"

"No, thank you. We cannot stay long," Hak said. They walked over to a quilt spread out under a leafy, flowered tree. Nivya scooted a few heavy books out of the way and straightened the blanket before they sat down.

Hak picked up one of the leather-bound books and inspected it with a smile. "Some light herbalist reading? It is a nice morning for that."

"Yes! Just the basics, you know. I have a sordid novel for later." Nivya gave Annie a quick laugh and a wink. Tia walked between the women and sprawled on her back, begging for belly rubs.

Nivya was all too happy to ruffle the dog's fur as she talked. "It has been many turns of the moon, Hakayatas. Seasons come and gone. How goes your mission?"

"It has been very hard, but I think I have discovered a few things that the council can use. I am hoping I have found the key to getting my magic back."

"Oh, that is wonderful news!" Nivya beamed at him, and turned her beautiful smile to Annie. "And you, my dear? Have you been enjoying the city? I hear it is your first time here."

Annie nodded slowly. *I wonder what was in that message Hak sent her. I wonder how much he told her.*

Nivya didn't seem put off by Annie's sullen response. She gave another warm smile to Annie and turned her attention back to Hak. "Will you be off to the south next?"

"I would imagine so. It depends if the council deems me worthy."

"Oh, they would be fools to think otherwise!"

"You seem well, Nivya. I am glad to see you are studying and happy."

Sadness flashed briefly across Nivya's face.

"Aye. Life has been very good." The young woman lifted her sleeve and held out her arm so Hak could see the gold and silver bracelet with an intricate design curled around her wrist.

Hak looked crestfallen. "Oh! Well . . . congratulations, dear friend!" He forced a smile and asked, "I assume you are keeping the bracelet?"

"Yes. I think so. It would be a good match. His name is Kier Woodstan. His family owns a very nice herb shop near the falls."

"Ah. You finally have your shop!"

Nivya gave a soft chuckle. "Not like that, Hakayatas. But yes, I imagine I will help run the place someday. Perhaps when I am old and gray. Kier has two wonderful older sisters and a younger brother. They are sweet and kind. That is the kind of family to marry into. But yes, I am happy he is not a tanner or farmer. It will be a good match, and my father is ecstatic."

Annie picked at a blade of grass, listening to them talk about the weather and the upcoming festivals. *I'm ready to go. I want to see this mage council already.* Annie watched Nivya and Hak carefully. The body language and the dynamic had changed between them. Hak appeared sullen, and Nivya seemed thoughtful. There was a long, awkward silence.

"Hak? Shouldn't we meet with the council already?"

Hak turned to Nivya. "I apologize if she appears rude. She grew up with dwarves."

Nivya's eyes grew wide. "Oh?"

"He's kidding," Annie said. "I just lack manners. I'm sorry, I say what I think."

"It gets her into trouble a lot," Hak added. Annie stuck her tongue out at him.

"Well, if you are going to the council, would you like me to watch your dog for you, Annie?"

Hak nodded. "That would be kind—"

"What? No, Tia is staying with me."

Nivya looked wounded by the response. "Dear, they do not allow just any person or creature into the palace."

Hak agreed. "It is best if Tia stays here, Annie."

"Your darling dog will be safe with me, I assure you. My neighbors have several children who love dogs. They will give her plenty of exercise here in the yard."

Annie growled but said nothing.

Hak and Nivya exchanged glances, and Hak said "Annie, we will not be gone long. Just the afternoon."

Tia scooted up against Nivya and licked at her hands until the woman gave the dog another scratch behind the ear.

Annie sighed. "Fine, I guess. But don't let her out of your sight. I worry she'll run off. This is a weird place for her."

Nivya clapped her hands together. "Did you hear that, Tia? I get to play with you all day!" The dog wagged her tail in response. "If you are gone longer, it will not be an issue, Lady Annie. I still have several of my dog's old toys and her bed. I am sure Tia will feel right at home."

"It's cool. I'll be back as soon as I can. I have a feeling Tia will enjoy it here." *Yeah, she won't have to worry about ripping anyone's throat out.*

Annie shuddered at the thought and gave Tia a long hug. Hak stood and offered his hand to Nivya, and then Annie. When they were all standing once more, Hak awkwardly scratched at the back of his head and stared at the brunette.

"Oh, Hakayatas. You will do fine. Do not worry so." Nivya gave him a long hug. Hak looked sad as he embraced her.

"Now, Tia. You have to stay. You can't follow me. I'll be back. You stay." Annie repeated it over and over. It was the same phrase she had often told Tia when she would leave for work in the morning. The dog stopped wagging her tail and whined. As they turned to leave Tia tried to follow. Annie turned on the dog and said sharply, "No. Stay!"

Tia gave another whimper and sat down. Nivya knelt by the dog and soothed her with a few words. *I hate to admit it, but Tia is safer with her than she is with me and Hak.* The thought bothered Annie to no end.

"You planned that out, didn't you?" Annie hissed.

"Pardon?"

"You knew we needed to dump Tia somewhere before we went to the palace."

"Yes. But I also wanted to see my friend before I saw the council." Hak didn't sound happy about it, so Annie didn't press him any more.

They left the yard and walked back to the main street that climbed toward the palace. The shops and homes became more grandiose as they walked closer. The stone buildings were chiseled with patterns, and the polished wooden doors were intricately carved by talented hands. The storefronts had finer clothes and other wares, and the citizens they passed wore silks and velvet. Many of them turned their noses up at Hak and Annie as they passed.

They reached a tall marble wall decorated and carved with countless figures. The rose-colored rock ran the length of the palace grounds, and stood in stark contrast to the gray hues around it. Men fighting dragons, dwarves holding hammers, and strange creatures that Annie could only guess at were carved deep into the wall. It appeared to be more decorative than defensive, but Annie guessed that the wall still kept out plenty of intruders.

Two men with large shields stood at the gate. Their armor was white and polished to a brilliant glow. The swords at their hips appeared to be detailed with gold and silver. The faces underneath the helms looked extremely hard. Annie felt a tickling sensation inside her head. She frowned.

The guards stepped out in front of Hak and Annie and wordlessly looked down at them. Annie gulped and tried to hide behind Hak's large frame.

Hak held up his left hand, fingers spread. "Hakayatas Flamefeather and Annie Armstrong."

"We know. They have been expecting you," said one of the guards. He didn't even bother to look at Annie. He turned abruptly on his heels and walked through the gate. She gave Hak a questioning look, but he ignored it and tugged on her sleeve.

"Come along, Annie. And please . . . do not forget your manners."

She wrinkled her nose at him, but said nothing. They passed through several courtyards that lined the castle grounds. The sound of the waterfall was almost deafening at one point. Annie looked up and saw the stained-glass windows and balconies, but no stairs or ladders leading to them.

The main part of the palace must be inside the cliff. All of those rooms must open up to the inside somehow. She stared up at the dizzying layer of rooms and windows. They seemed to reach all the way to the top of the cliff, several thousand feet above her.

They walked up a marble staircase that ran the length of the cliff behind the waterfall. As they neared the top, Annie could see large golden doors and several guards standing still as statues. The guards silently stepped aside as they passed. Annie noticed that Hak was sweating and biting at his lip.

Inside the golden doors was a cavernous chamber lined with marble pillars that stretched high above them. They were draped with paintings and many were carved to resemble various creatures such as serpents, bears, and men. Annie noticed a few people who were dressed simply walking about the room carrying trays of food or bundles of cloth.

"To the left and above are Halona's royal audience chambers. To the right are the council chambers. In some ways the palace is split into two sides— one for politics, and one for magic."

The guard escorting them took a sharp right and led them up a staircase, deeper into the cliff. Despite walking into a mountain, Annie was amazed at how well lit the hallways were. Strange crystals glowed in the ceiling, giving off plenty of light. It looked like someone had thrown thousands of penny-size diamonds against the ceiling and they had stuck there like stars. Annie gasped and found herself wanting to take one home with her. The effect reminded her of Christmas lights.

"How do they glow?"

"Hush, Annie," Hak said. His voice sounded thick and strange.

A door opened at the end of the hallway and a tall young woman was standing there. Her robes were a luxurious deep red, and her black hair was carefully curled and tucked into a beautiful cluster at the nape of her neck. Her eyes were very large, and the irises shone like purple sapphires.

Annie gaped. She was perhaps the most beautiful woman she had ever seen. She saw that the woman's ears were sharply pointed as well. *Is that an elf?*

The tall woman looked at Annie and gave her a sly smile. Her purple eyes seemed to flash when she blinked. Annie felt her head itch and she scratched irritably at her ears for several seconds before she realized that the elf was touching her mind. Annie didn't like it one bit.

Hak placed his hands over his heart and gave the woman a deep bow. "Peace of the stars be upon you, Wise Diana."

Then Hak shot Annie a glare. She jumped and quickly mimicked his bow. The courtesy fell awkwardly from her lips, but the elf tipped her head respectfully.

"Welcome back," the elf said in a thick accent to Hak. "I see you have brought a friend."

Annie's brain tickled again. She scratched at her head irritably and gave the elf an angry look. The elf laughed, obviously delighted at Annie's discomfort.

"Ah, very interesting," she said, still smiling at Annie. Her purple eyes seemed to glow the longer Annie stared into them.

"I see you have not regained use of the current, Hakayatas," The elf said.

"Not yet, Wise Diana." Hak's tone was respectful, but Annie saw that he clenched his jaw. He was sweating and looking past the elf nervously. Annie felt a chill. *Hak is usually so guarded with his emotions. Why does he appear so troubled? It seems like he could come unglued any minute.*

"Peace, Hakayatas. There are some here who will hear you out. You *do* have some allies." She touched a smooth hand to Hak's arm. Annie noted that the elf's fingers were almost comically long.

"And you, my dear Annie. There is much we need to talk about."

Annie brightened for a brief moment, but one look at Hak's troubled expression and she withered. *Something is very wrong here.*

"Shall we?" Diana asked, still smiling.

They walked down a long, brightly lit hallway. The stone walls were carved in intricate patterns, and Annie found hundreds of different scenes etched deep into the rock. Entire armies of men fought other men and dragons, and she saw elaborate castles and beautiful women of all species. Small crystals glowed within the carvings and gave off an eerie light. It created the impression that the castles were lit and full of miniature people. A dragon's flame glowed with thousands of red crystals the size of ants.

Annie reached out to touch one of the crystals, but Hak quickly grabbed her hand. His fingers seemed to swallow hers and they squeezed tightly. Annie recoiled and jerked her hand back with a wounded expression. Hak ignored her and stared at two golden doors at the end of the hallway with apprehension. A man and woman made of flame were etched into the doors.

With a flick of the elf's wrist, the doors swung open into a brightly lit chamber. It was as if the sun shone down into the depths of the mountain and illuminated the white marble walls with rays of light. Bright green ivy covered the walls like a blanket. Annie could not find the source of the sunlight, and assumed the ceiling was somehow imbued with magic.

A polished marble table circled the room, and Annie counted six figures seated at it, facing the open floor in the center. A seventh seat sat empty near the door. The elf made her way to the chair and sat down with a simple grace. Annie spied a larger chair at the end of the chamber that loomed above all the others. It was gilded and covered with precious metals and glittering gems. It reminded her of a throne. It was empty.

Annie felt seven pairs of eyes stare down at her from the high table. She instinctively edged closer to Hak and swallowed nervously. She expected to be probed right then and there, but even the elf stayed away from her mind. She tensed and waited for someone to talk.

Hak abruptly knelt on the floor with his hands over his heart. He bowed so low his long blond hair almost grazed the floor. He gave Annie a strange look out of the corner of his eye, and she quickly followed suit, awkwardly kneeling before the seven figures as she tried to calm her rapidly beating heart. The light that shone from the ceiling suddenly seemed too bright, and the faces seemed to loom over them.

"You have been gone long," said a deep voice.

"Too long," said another.

"We have been waiting," said a woman in deep blue robes.

An ancient woman seated at the center of the table leaned forward slightly and scowled. She was tiny and covered in wrinkles. Her silver robe was more intricately designed than the other council members. Long silver vines embroidered the silken cloth. Her hair was a wild white halo, and she wore numerous rings as well as a strange silver circlet on her brow. She must have been the oldest person Annie had ever seen. She did not talk, but stared down at Hak and Annie as if they were insects.

"Hakayatas brings us news. And strange tidings," said Diana. "Hakayatas, would you please tell us of your quest, and why you have brought this . . . woman with you?"

"I have made the pilgrimage to the northern Felian mana points," Hak said in a thick voice. "I walked for many turns of the moons on Mount Felia, saying the prayers of the stars at each mana point. I walked to all the points according to the moons and the council's direction. Nothing happened for many new moons. At Ikti's full light, I waited at the southern point for an extra day."

"Why?"

Hak hesitated, and then said, "I had seen a star shoot from the dragon's eye. I considered it a good omen."

"Bah! Shafani superstition!"

"You were not to waste a day!" someone said.

"Ridiculous," said a voice.

"You have a cycle to keep."

"Balance must be maintained."

Hak kept his eyes on the floor, and Annie saw him clench a fist. "It was not just any falling star. The star was a large, brilliant blue flame. It could very well have been an Ikti'osha."

Someone in the room gave a snort.

"I waited at the southern point another day. I prayed at the crystal for an extra night."

"And then?"

"Bah. Nothing happened. He wasted an entire turn of the cycle!"

"Fool."

"Hear him out," Diana said. The elf's voice rang through the air like a delicate bell.

"It was not a few hours after I left the point that I was delayed by plagarne," Hak said. Everyone in the room tried to talk at once. Hak waited until the criticism waned and sucked in a deep breath.

"The plagarne were crawling all over the mountain. Some sort of magic had clearly agitated them. I was delayed because there were so many. I waited for their numbers to dwindle. It was midday before I could walk toward the next mana point."

There was another round of angry murmurs. The old woman at the head of the table held up a hand and the room quickly hushed. Hak waited patiently until he had the council's attention before he continued. Diana and the old woman were watching Hak and Annie with interest.

"I had to stop and fight many plagarne to continue on. By that point I felt cursed to fail the quest. I had already wasted a full day and night at the wrong mana point. But then I heard thunder, despite no clouds being in the sky. The noise echoed across the mountains. I was then struck with a dilemma: Was it another sign? Do I follow the sounds of cloudless thunder? Or do I travel to the mana point?"

Hak paused and sucked in a deep breath. "It was then that I heard a woman scream. It was coming from the direction of the mana point I had just prayed at. I returned to the area and found this woman trapped atop a stack of boulders. The plagarne had cornered her and were extremely focused on her.

"I slew the plagarne and . . ." Hak paused and bit his lip. "I was unsure at first of this woman's true form. I tied her up. Through interrogation I learned that she comes from another planet called Earth. She said that she woke inside the crystal and did not know how she got there."

Silence. The council members stared at Annie with open mouths.

Finally an old man in a brown robe slapped his palm against the marble. "That is impossible!"

"This is what she claims," Hak said. "She has proven herself to be very resourceful. She has an odd assortment of items from her home world to prove her strange background."

"What kind of magic do you use, girl?"

"How did you use the mana points?"

"This is warlock magic," hissed another old man.

"Madness."

Annie swallowed and said, "I don't have any magic. I just woke up here. And I want to go home. This place is crazy."

Hak turned bright red and glared at Annie as if she had jumped up on a table and flashed her breasts at the entire council. Annie's knees hurt from kneeling for so long, and she was getting impatient.

Some of the council members sputtered at her outburst. The elf and the old woman at the center exchanged a look and smiled.

"She lies right before us."

"In the grand chamber!"

"Tongues have been burned out for lying in here," said one of the old men.

"I'm not lying!" Annie said.

"Bah!"

"We will need to have a look."

"She has mana and she tries to tell us she does not!"

"It pulses from her!"

Hak gave Annie a thoughtful look and a smile tugged at his lips.

Diana rested her chin on her long fingers and watched Annie. Her violet eyes flashed brightly every time she blinked. "Yes. Magic surrounds her somehow. She may not be attuned. Or she could be brainwashed. Instead of spending the entire day arguing, perhaps we should dive in and see what we can find."

"Aye. I am very curious," said the old man in brown robes.

"Girl, we will be entering your mind."

"Yes. Do not try to hide anything from us."

"We will know if you speak true."

"Let us read both of them at the same time."

"Excellent idea. Let us see if their tales match."

"Bring them both into the current."

Annie was painfully aware of every eye in the room staring at her. She was kneeling less than a foot from Hak, and she turned to give him a pleading look. She was suddenly very afraid. Hak looked back at her coldly, as if he did not know her. Her panic and dread seemed to grow like a cancer.

The elf touched Annie's mind first. She heard Diana's gentle voice whisper inside of her mind, *"Do not be afraid. Peace be upon you."*

Suddenly, Annie felt as if she had stuck her head under the pounding waterfall outside. A great flood of emotions and sensations tore through her. Her head itched as thought it were covered with bug bites and fleas. Annie clenched her fists and resisted the urge to begin scratching wildly at her scalp.

Annie began recalling strange memories for no reason. She saw sudden flashes of her childhood that she had forgotten about, and the memories dashed within her mind without a conscious decision on her part. She was three years old and hiding from a tornado in her parent's basement. She remembered being nineteen, and sitting in the back of a friend's car watching the Colorado mountains glow with the orange haze of sunset.

She remembered a night walking home drunk from the bars with Patrick and her roommates. Annie and Patrick had just met and were discussing the comic book characters Wolverine and Deadpool. Annie found it strange that the memory was somehow stronger than usual. She had barely remembered that night, let alone what they talked about.

Annie remembered Hak's lesson about mind control and the idea of two pools of water merging. She knew that while the council members were in her head and watching her past, she could also try to catch glimpses of theirs. She felt strange emotions that she could only guess came from the men and women surrounding her. If she focused on one particular sensation, she could push her mind toward the source.

She saw strange faces and memories that were not her own. She thought she saw a young elf girl playing with a ball of fire between her tiny hands. She saw children being born, and people on their deathbeds.

She saw a young blonde girl with yellow eyes who looked about ten years old. She was covered in blood screaming, and holding out her hand.

Annie shuddered and looked over at Hak. He wore the same cold expression as before.

She saw someone's memory of a great ballroom. She was in their body, reliving the memory like a happy dream. The person was dancing with a beautiful young woman who looked like a queen. Annie saw long, slender fingers reach out and gently stroke the queen's face. A great golden crown rested on top of her blonde-silver hair, and she smiled lovingly at her dance partner. Annie felt a brief emotional longing as the recollection faded.

Then someone pulled a memory from Annie of when she was painting with her neighbor. When Annie remembered Mr. Wilson's face, something sharply bit her mind.

Annie gasped as a faint memory brushed against the edges of her mind. The memory vanished before it had come fully into focus, like a dream that escapes upon waking. It was a familiar sensation. Annie pushed her mind against the others, trying to swim after the strange thought in the great tangle of memories and emotions.

Annie saw a street that could only have been from Earth. But it was not her memory. The cars looked very old. The person was remembering walking down a cobblestone sidewalk with a young woman pushing a baby carriage. A boy called out to them in a strange language and held out a newspaper. A picture of Hitler was on the front page. Annie's heart clenched. She pushed her mind in the direction of the memory, but it was yanked away from her.

Has someone here been to Earth? Who had that memory? Annie looked helplessly up at them. Their faces were unreadable, and frozen with concentration.

Annie felt more memories pulled from her brain. The council watched Annie pack her car with camping supplies, and saw her hand reaching for Tia ... and then that horrible flash.

Then they took her memories of the crystal, running from the plagarne, and getting choked by Hak. Diana gave Hak a frown. He kept his eyes on the ground.

They watched as Tomas grabbed her and caused a blinding blue light.

These are Hak's memories! Annie was fascinated to see herself from someone else's point of view. She watched as she fell limply from Tomas's grasp and he whirled on Hak. Hak swung his sword into Tomas's shoulder, and the mercenary seemed to vanish into the shadows.

Hak screamed and ran to Annie's unconscious body, thinking she was dead. He turned her over on her back and begged her to wake up. He was crying. He was so distraught in the memory that Annie felt tears flood her eyes. *He does care about me!*

Suddenly a memory from Annie flowed through the collective pool of their minds. She was sitting by the campfire watching Hak sleep. Annie felt her face grow hot with embarrassment.

They pulled all of her memories from sparring, talking while riding through the plains, and the attack at the hot springs. Annie barely remembered the attack, but somehow the council pulled a clear memory from her head.

Suddenly the current of minds shifted and began pulling away. The resulting emptiness surprised Annie. She had never realized how quiet her own thoughts were until she had eight other minds and their cumulative emotions to deal with.

"Yes."

"You did well, Hakayatas."

"Very well."

Hak cleared his throat. "Thank you. As you can see, she is the sign you wanted me to search for. The mana points are alive, and she is proof."

"Yes."

What is he talking about? Annie wrinkled her eyebrows together and gave Hak a searching look. He avoided her gaze and watched the old woman in front of him. She was the only one who had not spoken aloud since Annie had entered the chamber.

Her voice was frail and raspy, but she spoke with authority. "Yes, Hakayatas. This means that mana points are connected with the currents once again. There is hope for you yet to regain your magical abilities. You bring us this woman as your sign, yes. You have done well, yes. But what do you expect of us now, hmm? What do you want us to do with her?"

"Whatever you need to, Wise Aiyana. I believe she is the key for the mana points. She is in your hands now."

"Yes," said one of the councilmen.

"She will be useful," Diana said.

"Very useful indeed."

"We will have to run more tests on her," said Aiyana, her wrinkled stare narrowed as she looked down at Annie. "She is *interesting*."

Annie felt her heart sink. *What? Did I . . . just get sold out?*

"Hak?" she asked, fear squeezing her voice. Her heart started pounding in her head. She looked at him as if for the first time.

He kept his eyes on the ground and said, "I am sorry, Annie."

"Wait, *what*!? Hak, what's going on? What are you *doing*?" Annie's shrill voice echoed through the large chamber. She ignored the startled looks from the council.

"Annie, mind your manners!"

"No! You mind *your* manners, asshole! You didn't say anything about this the whole fucking time to me!? Are you just going to give me to these people and not explain that I was just some stupid piece to your quest? *I trusted you!* You promised me you wouldn't hurt me! You promised me I would get to go home—"

Annie felt a prickling sensation in her throat. She kept moving her mouth, but nothing came out. She looked up at the council and saw that one of the old men was glaring at her and had his fingers squeezed together in front of his lips. *That bastard took my voice!*

"I apologize, Wise Aiyana. She is very spirited."

The old woman looked down at Hak contemptuously but said nothing. Diana was smiling.

Annie tried to scream at Hak but nothing came out of her mouth. Her lips moved helplessly. Finally, she held up her hands to him as if to ask, *"Why?"*

He looked at her coldly and said, "I am sorry. But you need to stay here with the council. In a way, you *were* the quest."

It doesn't make sense. He . . . he betrayed me! Annie felt tears burn in her eyes and silently roared at Hak. She swung her right hand out and punched the scar under his eye as hard as she could. The resulting shock of pain shot up her arm.

Annie thought she heard the elf laugh. Then the old woman was pulling at her mind. She caught an image of Aiyana standing in front of her, and the apparition said, *"Have patience, child."*

Annie ignored them. She hated them in her head. She hated Hak. She mouthed another silent curse at him and loudly beat at his armor. The cold metal hurt, but Annie did not care if she broke all of her fingers. Her face was contorted with silent screams. Hak did not try to defend himself. He looked miserable.

Annie felt someone else push at her mind, and her entire body tingled. All of a sudden something grabbed her wrists and her hands were jerked away from Hak. Annie gritted her teeth and tried to fight the invisible person wrestling with her body. She pushed the strange magic away and reached for Hak's throat, tears streaming down her face.

"My, my . . . look at that."

"Incredible!"

"Yes. She is strong."

Annie was thrown back by a blast of air. Her hands were pressed against the floor, and then her knees and feet were stuck as well. It was as if the white marble floor had turned to glue. Annie cursed silently and struggled to lift her hands for a few moments. She couldn't move them at all. *Great. They stole my voice, stuck me to the floor, and Hak sold me out like a fucking idiot.*

She sobbed and stared up at the ceiling, not caring that the light blinded her. She felt herself screaming at the top of her lungs, but only silence met her ears. She pressed her forehead against the cold marble floor and choked on her soundless cries.

"You were right."

"A little too spirited."

"Apologies," Hak said. "She is a good person, please be patient with her! She has a gentle heart."

"Is that why she just tried to choke the life out of you, Hakayatas?" Diana asked, a wicked smile playing at her lips. "Or would that be because you choked her first?"

"She is a good person. Please do not harm her."

"Wild as a Vinder," said the man who had silenced Annie and glued her to the floor.

"Girl, you will need to learn your place here."

"Yes."

Annie wanted to clench her hands into fists and charge at the council, but her fingers were soundly stuck to the floor. She gave everyone in the room a feral look.

"Aye. Even now she thinks to commit violence in the chamber."

"Perhaps it is a blessing she is not attuned."

"Yes."

Diana cleared her throat. "I think that we need to deal with the girl later. The reason we are here today is to judge Hakayatas Flamefeather and his quest to the Felial Mountains. Not the actions of a wild young woman."

Aiyana nodded.

Diana said, "Hakayatas, I believe you have done well. I believe that I speak for the council when I say you have earned the right to wield magic once more. Your actions with this girl have shown us that you are ready. It is time for your final quest."

"Thank you, Wise Diana."

"The council will need to meet this evening to discuss the events of the day. However, bear in mind that you must prepare for the Fieriel Senefal."

The old man who had silenced Annie leaned forward and said, "Aye. You should prepare well for the south."

"Our council will provide you with the appropriate armor," said another mage.

"And we will return your magiel."

Hak let out a gasp and gave a deep bow. "Thank you!"

Aiyana held out a small silver box. Hak took a few shaky steps forward and took it reverently.

"Do not worry. They are all there."

"You will need them for the Fieriel Senefal."

"Pardons wise council, but how am I to use them? I am not even sure which one belongs to me."

The council members exchanged looks and shook their heads. Diana said,

"I am sorry, Hakayatas, but that knowledge has been lost to us."

The old woman said, "The scrolls were destroyed long before I was born. It was considered black magic. It has been five hundred years since someone attempted to bind magiel. Only myth and legend guide our instruction now."

"Yes. You will need to use care, Hakayatas. It is a dark art."

"We know that magiel can be bound at the heart of the current."

"Yes. Every nation has a legend about it."

"There will be a dragon at the gate. He may know."

"Bah. A dragon will not waste his time talking with you," said the man in the brown robes.

"I think when the time comes, you will know what to do with them, Hakayatas," Diana said gently.

"Keep the stars in your heart, and you will find a way."

Aiyana said, "Remember that your heart must be pure and good. It is said that one who attempts Fieriel Senefal will have a battle with darkness. It will be a fight unlike any you have ever had. It is said that impure hearts have never left the heart of the current, and become part of the darkness."

Diana looked at each council member and let out a laugh. "Oh, this is delightful." She looked down at Annie and gave a wide smile. "My dear, this has been an interesting day, yes?"

Annie seethed at the elf, and tried to pull her hands up once more. She mouthed the words, *"Fuck you."*

Diana just grinned.

One of the mages stood and said, "Hakayatas, we have prepared your quarters for you. Please meditate on the day's proceedings, and we will meet back here in one week. It will give us ample time to study what we can, so that we might aid you to the best of our abilities."

Diana nodded gravely and said, "We would like to see you succeed, Hakayatas. We will do what we can to help you." The tall elf stood and touched a finger to her temple. A moment later two palace guards entered and stood before Diana.

Annie gaped. The men were as tall as Hak, but much leaner. She saw their eyes flash brightly when they blinked.

More elves?

Diana waved a hand at Annie and said, "Please show this woman to the fern quarter. I have prepared a room at the end of the hall. She is very wild and might try to run. Do not let her escape."

Annie felt the pressure on her body release and heard a moan escape her lips. The guards picked her up by the arm and shoved her forward. Annie growled and turned to look at Hak. "You're a fucking asshole, you know that? I hate y—"

And then her voice was gone once more.

"Too soon."

"Yes."

"Maybe a night without a voice will do her some good."

"Teach her some manners."

A guard gently placed his hands on her shoulders and urged her to turn toward the door. Annie wanted to gnash her teeth and scream and charge them, but she slumped her shoulders and stared at the floor helplessly.

They escorted her out of the room and into a maze of staircases and hallways. They climbed until Annie became so winded she had to stop. She leaned against the railing of a tall marble staircase and panted for several seconds. The guards exchanged looks and one went to pick her up.

Annie tried to scream, *"No! Don't touch me!"* but her voice was still missing. She pushed furiously at their long fingered hands and tried to gesture that they just needed to wait. Finally, they relented and simply stared at her until she caught her breath.

They traveled up several sets of stairs and eventually turned down a long stone hallway with stained-glass windows. They stopped at the last room, opened the door, and unceremoniously shoved Annie into the room. The door slammed behind her, and Annie heard something heavy scrape against it. They had locked her in.

She looked around at the room and gave a small gasp. There were elaborately designed carpets across the marble floor, detailed paintings hung on the walls, and the furniture was covered with fine bloodred velvet.

There were polished wooden dressers, ornate vases, and a large bed with curtains. Annie took a few shaky steps toward the stained-glass window and tugged at the latch. The glass panel swung inward, and Annie cupped her hands to her face in shock. She was near the top of the cliff, and had a view that took in the entire Dohl Valley. The sun was setting and cast a soft golden light across the wooded valley.

Meda was below. The people were so small that they looked like insects walking around, and the yards of the larger apartment homes were small green patches.

Tia . . . Annie felt her heart clench. Fresh tears burned in her eyes. *I know she is in good hands, but I want her so badly right now. She's my only true friend here.*

Annie ground her teeth and turned from the beautiful view. *A dog . . . is my only friend . . . .* Hak's betrayal made her sick. She missed her friends and her family. She missed getting hugs. Usually when she was this sad, she made herself feel better with a tub of ice cream and a movie with friends. Or a bottle of whiskey.

She paused and realized those days were most likely gone forever. *Is anyone even alive? Is anything even left of Earth? Is it just one big smoking wasteland with nuclear fallout everywhere? Even if I got home, would anything ever be the same?*

Annie walked to the bed. She wasn't tired, but she felt like crying for the rest of the day. She threw herself on the bed and was surprised to find a wonderful, comforting feeling. The mattress was stuffed with feathers. She sank in, and let the tears come.

Annie opened her eyes; the sun was gone and the room was dark. *I must have cried myself to sleep.* A soft glow radiated from the city below, yet it was barely enough light for Annie to spot the person standing above her. Two glowing purple eyes stared at her.

Diana?

"Would you like some light? Or do you prefer dark rooms for some reason?"

Annie moved her lips, and was sad to discover her voice was still missing.

"Oh that's right. We are supposed to be teaching you a lesson," Diana said dryly. "Firiel."

A lantern on the oak dresser lit itself. Candles along a stone shelf on the wall also caught flame. The small hearth near the window crackled to life. The room was suddenly much brighter.

"Is that better?" Diana asked. She was wearing the same long red robe as earlier, with gold-trimmed waist and cuffs. The material shimmered softly in the firelight. Her luminous purple eyes flared.

Annie nodded.

"Do not worry. I can hear your thoughts if you do it right. You just have to think it *loudly*."

Annie crinkled her nose as she tried to understand what the elf meant.

"You had no problem screaming your thoughts earlier. Gods . . . even after Mau silenced you, I could still *hear* you. You have quite the foul tongue, has anyone ever told you that?"

Annie watched as the elf retrieved a tray piled with food from the top of the dresser and set it down on a small table next to the bed. It appeared to be some roasted meat and vegetables. The last thing Annie wanted was food.

I just want to go home, she cried silently. *Hak told me Meda was full of magic. That jerk said there would be answers here.*

"Well, he may be right. Perhaps we can help," Diana said.

Annie gave a start and stared at the elf. *How are you hearing my thoughts?*

Diana laughed and said, "My dear, you really have no idea how anything works, do you? Of course I heard those thoughts. Although, technically, the council thinks you should not be allowed to communicate with anyone at all. Stupid punishment, in my opinion.

"Now . . . I have brought you some food, and some fresh clothes that I think will fit you. You will need to properly groom yourself for the morning. I will send someone up first thing. I would like to spend the day with you."

I want to go home! Annie screamed in her mind.

Diana pursed her lips and blinked. "My dear, there is much we need to discuss. Remember, I saw your thoughts today. I know that this has not been easy on you. I know you feel hurt, lost, and sad. It is not my desire to inflict further injury on you. But you are an . . . interesting human. I think we can learn things from each other that might be pleasant surprises."

I don't want you guys to hurt me again. I didn't like you in my head earlier. And I sure as fuck don't like it right now.

"Annie, I may be the most tolerant of all the council members, but my patience does have a limit. You need to learn many things if you are to stay here."

Just let me go home. Or let me die. I don't want to be some weird lab rat for you guys to probe and dissect. I would rather die than spend the rest of my life having old men read my mind and having the ability to control my body against my will.

Diana laughed. "So melodramatic! No, we will not be dissecting you. We want to talk with you. And yes, there may be a bit more searching within your mind, but that cannot be helped. I think you have suppressed some memories. There seems to be much more than what we saw today.

"But no, we will not hold you here forever. Gods, that would get very boring. And no one will control your body again if you can behave like a normal human."

I'm not some monster!

"No? Beating Hakayatas and wanting to choke him? My dear, you went absolutely ballistic earlier. I saw into your mind. We all did. You were ready to kill him. You lost complete control of yourself."

Annie sneered and looked at the floor. *I have a bad temper, so what? I don't care. If you saw that in my mind, you also saw why I was so angry. You knew exactly how I felt because you were in my fucking head.*

"I know dear," the elf said sadly. She rested her long fingers on Annie's shoulder and gave her a gentle squeeze. "I know that hurt. It could have been handled much better. I know you care for him."

No! Fuck that guy. He's an asshole.

Diana shook her head and grinned with amusement. "Well, whatever helps you get some rest tonight. Please eat something, and help yourself to the items in the small washroom. It is just behind that curtain there. You have a long day tomorrow and you will need to get some rest. And be sure to drink the fae water on the dresser. You are very dehydrated right now."

It's probably poisoned or something, Annie thought irritably, as quietly as she could.

Diana laughed. "Oh, it is not poisoned. It has some mild herbs that will soothe your mind like a nice glass of wine. But I assure you we are not poisoning you. Oh, and if you were trying to keep that last thought to yourself, you will have to try harder. You are as easy to hear as if you are talking aloud."

Ugh. This sucks. Get out of my head.

"We will work on this, I think," Diana said thoughtfully. She turned to the door and paused, as if listening to something. She let out a sigh. "It would appear you have company approaching. Please do not tear him apart. We need him alive."

Diana walked out without another word. Annie heard Hak's deep voice greet the elf in the hallway, and a moment later he poked his head tentatively through the doorway.

Annie's first instinct was to hurl something at his face. Instead she waved him frantically away. She went so far as to shake both of her middle fingers at him, but she suspected the insult was unknown in his culture. He slowly entered the room and shut the door.

Annie was frustrated to no end. *Just get out! Leave me alone and never talk to me again!* she thought angrily.

Hak gave her a sad look but said nothing. He nervously looked around the room and tugged the scarf around his neck higher. *Oh right . . . he doesn't have any way to read my thoughts. Ugh. What's he going to do now?*

Hak took a chair from the wall and sat it next to the bed. His manner was very slow, as if he were approaching a wounded animal capable of striking.

"Still no voice, Annie?"

She tried to growl. She felt her throat vibrate with the effort, but no sound came out.

"Maybe you could give me a moment to talk then? Please?"

She sat on the rumpled sheets and watched him furiously. Her fingers twitched and she tucked her knees under her chin. She pulled herself, and her resentment, into a tight ball.

"I was not . . . I did not think that . . ." Hak paused and scratched at his head. He pulled at the scarf again. He looked miserable. "Let me try again. I concealed my intentions because I thought you would not willingly follow me to Meda. Initially, I believed you were a spirit, and then an insane person babbling about waking up in a crystal. After a while, I realized you were the sign I was meant to find.

"The quest was to make a pilgrimage to the mana points. I had been there for two seasons. I would walk to Feldall and grab supplies on the new moon. At the full moons, I had to be at the points, praying. There was a very strict schedule in place for pilgrims that stated where we needed to be for each of the full moons. I saw a strange comet one night, and took it as a sign to stay. And thank the gods that I did stay one extra night. I found you the next day."

Yeah, I kind of got that already.

Hak shifted uneasily in his chair and glanced at Annie. She tried to bore holes in him with her stare. She clenched a fist but didn't move.

"I think that the crystals pull in power from the stars. It is said that the warlocks used the crystals to travel to different parts of Tahldia, but it has never been known for anyone to travel from a different planet. That idea is absolutely ridiculous. Yet, here you are with your dog and your stories of Oregon.

"I knew that I had to bring you back to the council, Annie. I had to. You somehow got transported. It proves that we can still use those crystals. And that means the place I need to go to next will work correctly. I need to bind the magic back to my body. You see, the crystals are all connected, like the roots of trees, deep within the earth.

"There is a cave in the south called the Fieriel Senefal that was once known as the heart of the current. The main root of the tree, if you will. All magic is said to come from this cave. However, the magic has been dead there for many generations. Many of the crystal points on Tahldia no longer work. I believe Voltay may have had something to do with it, but no one really knows. The cave is not easily accessible and it is very dangerous, so not many have tried to investigate.

"It is said that at the heart of this cave is the largest of all the mana points. All of the energy from the smaller crystals supposedly flows to this center."

Annie gripped the bed sheets and bared her teeth at him. *Why would I give a fuck what you need to do next?*

"Annie. It was never my intention to deceive you! Yes, initially, I just wanted to turn you in to the council and be done with it. You were rude, loud, and you had a knack for getting into trouble. But I came to understand the person you are, and I realize you are gentle, kind, and caring. I . . . began to like you.

"That is why I dreaded the last few days. I wrestled with the notion of telling you everything, but I feared you would run away. I feared that you would not understand if I told you the truth. So I felt that it would be easier to keep it from you. That was a horrible mistake."

Annie gave a silent sniffle and wiped a tear from her eye. *No, no, no, I'm still mad at you. Everything would be so much easier if I could just hate you . . .*

"I want to come clean now. With everything. I do not want to hide anything else from you." Hak pulled out the silver box Aiyana had given him. It was square shaped, scuffed and scratched with wear, and Annie could make out a small dragon etched on the lid. The square box was only a few inches across and deep. Annie eyed it with reluctant interest.

Hak let out a tired sigh and said, "I want you to have the full story. I should have explained it before, but as I said, I was not expecting events to unfold as they did. And part of me worried that I would never get these back."

Hak gently opened the lid and showed Annie the contents. Eight crystals the size of thimbles sat on a blue silk pad in the bottom of the box. In the firelight, the dark gems appeared black, and they had a strange purple glow within them. Annie reached out to touch one, but Hak pulled the box away by several inches.

"Look, but do not touch. I am not sure what would happen if you touched them. You have strange abilities, Annie."

Annie frowned and stared at the gems. The longer she looked at their soft glow, the more that she felt the gems were *alive*. The glow seemed to throb and pulse. She was uncertain what Hak was showing her, so she held her arms out in a questioning manner.

"These are magiel. Some call it the cursed crystal. One of these gems has my mana trapped within it. I do not know which one."

Annie let out a silent gasp and stared at the circular welts that lay in the middle of his long scars. *Those crystals are huge! That must have been so painful! But . . . how did he get these?* She made more questioning gestures with her hands, pointing at Hak's scars and back at the crystal.

"One of these gems was placed inside of me and drained my mana," Hak said slowly, trying to understand her gestures. "I took them when I escaped. That was another thing I kept from you, Annie. I did not tell you that when I left my prison cell, I did not escape immediately. I went to the chamber where they had drained me. It was a stroke of dumb luck that the gems were still there.

"I was not sure which gem they used for me and which gems they used to drain others, so I took every gem I could find in that room. I imagine the attack came so suddenly Voltay and Bingen did not have time to hide them. Perhaps they were too busy fending off the attack, or hiding larger, more sinister things.

"I kept these when I escaped Shafan. I stowed away on a trading ship and came to the eastern world. I told you that the mages of Meda had power over me, yes? That they made me do quests and had me under their heel?"

Annie gave him a small nod. She was unsure what to think of the situation.

"When I approached the council for the first time, they read my mind and saw what I did while I was in the Shafani army. They took the magiel from me the moment they saw them in my memories. It was their way of holding power over me and ensuring I would behave, and do whatever it took to get them back," he said, his lips tightening into a sneer. Hak closed the box and placed it back in his pouch.

"I will be honest. I am not sure that I can get my magic back even with these gems. Supposedly I will need them, but no one knows what I really need to do when I go south. I am frustrated beyond belief."

Annie waved a hand at Hak. *Welcome to the club!*

"Since no one knows what I need to do, I feel that I might not make it back from Fieriel Senefal. I might die trying to bind these magiel back to me. I do not want to leave with things weighing on my heart. I regret not telling you everything from the beginning. I do care for you, and I want you to know how sorry I am . . . I want you to know that I wish things could have been different between us."

Is he actually confessing that he has feelings for me? For a brief moment, Annie's heart clenched with uncertainty. A very small part of her wanted to comfort and hold him, but a much larger part of her wanted to slap him.

She fought with her emotions, and grew angrier and angrier. She remembered how cold Hak had been toward her in front of the council, and something inside of her snapped.

It's too late! I'm stuck here! You lied! Annie leapt off the bed and shoved Hak. She tried to push him off his chair but the large man was as easy to move as a mountain. He gave her a wounded look.

"Please, hear me out, Annie. I did not mean to hurt you."

Annie jerked at the words. Something about the way Hak said it unhinged her. She had a flashback of her last fight with Patrick. *"Annie, I didn't mean to hurt you,"* he had said. She had caught him with another woman, and thrown him out of the house.

They're all the same, Annie told herself. *You'll always get hurt if you get close Annie. Don't get close. Don't get hurt.*

Her throat trembled with an inaudible cry. *You stupid men always lie! Get out!* Annie pointed at the door furiously. Part of her wanted to hit Hak once more, but the other part of her realized she could not lose her temper again.

"Please, Annie . . ."

She saw a tear trickle down the scar on his cheek. Annie set both her hands on his shoulders and pushed with everything she could. Hak stood and let her move him toward the door.

"Annie."

Annie gave him another shove and he was at the door. Hak reached into a pouch at his hip and pulled out her smartphone. He held it out to her and she hesitated.

"I asked Aiyana if I could bring this to you. I told her it would put your mind at ease. I thought a little music could get you to smile."

Annie snatched the phone from Hak and pointed at the door again. Hak tried to reach out to her with his hand, but she smacked it away.

Hak frowned and stared at the floor. His lips worked uselessly for a moment, and then he said, "I am so truly sorry, Annie. I will not bother you again. I hope that you find peace, and your home. It . . . It was truly a pleasure traveling with you and getting to know you."

Hak left without another word. A heartbeat later a guard appeared in the hallway, shut the massive wooden door, and she heard something heavy scrape against it.

Assholes! Every single one of them!

Her mind boiled with confusion and anger. She pulled at her hair and, for once, was thankful that she could scream as hard as possible and no one would hear. She paced the room several times before she caught sight of the pitcher of water on the dresser. She found metal goblets next to it. Ignoring them, Annie picked up the glass pitcher and drank heavily.

Like a glass of wine, eh? Something to dull the pain. She found the water extremely sweet and satisfying. It had a hint of peppermint and something else she didn't recognize but found tasty. She took a moment to breathe and then drained the pitcher. She slammed it back onto the dresser, the thick handblown glass denting the wood.

Annie felt drunk, and she was grateful for it. She swayed for a moment as the world spun around her. Her anger cooled like a dying ember. She could still remember Hak's face, his words, and gave another silent roar of frustration. *I hate him! I don't care what happens to him! He tricked me!*

Annie stumbled toward the bed; the haze of intoxication twisted the world around her. Her anger was gone and in its place a deep worry began to fester. Suddenly she felt aware of her small place within the universe. A strange urge to transcend her past mistakes and embrace a new sense of self-awareness began to grow within her. In the slow and fuzzy world of fae water, everything and nothing made sense.

A sense of realization chilled Annie's blood. *Oh god . . . he's going to die on that stupid quest . . . he's gone. Forever.*

Tears streamed down her face. Annie dove onto the bed and wrapped herself up under the covers. She turned on her phone and found that it was paused in the middle of an album she and Hak had last listened to by the campfire.

It was a mix of acoustic guitar. Hak had told her he liked it.

She hit play and cried herself to sleep.

Annie woke to a soft knocking and a gentle prickling in her mind.

She curled up and pulled the covers over her head. She tried to shout that she didn't want anything, but only a silent breath of air passed her lips.

Stupid mages . . .

Someone stepped into the room and said, "Ah, yes. Many of them can be stupid."

Diana? Annie hesitated, and then pulled the blanket down to her chin to look at the elf. She was wearing the same silken robe, and wore an intricate line of silver and gems in her black hair. *So what are you doing here?*

Diana raised an eyebrow and motioned at the open door with her hand. A young, skinny elf tiptoed into the room and stared at Annie. Her long, pointed ears poked out of a braided mane of black hair that drifted close to the floor. Her large eyes were the same hue as Diana's, and flashed just as bright when she blinked. She wore a white robe trimmed with silver and gold thread. In her tiny hands was a tray of food. She looked like she could have been around eleven, but Annie wasn't sure how elves aged.

So, what do you want? Please don't fuck with me and lie to me like Hak did.

The young elf gasped, and Annie glared at her.

Oh, so you're in my head, too, huh? How do you like it? Annie imagined herself turning into a green skinned monster and flinging the two elves out of the room as if she had superhero strength. She felt her scalp tickle as the elf tried to keep hold of her thoughts.

Yeah, that's what I thought. Don't get too comfy in my head. That goes for you, too, Diana.

"Annie, allow me to introduce my niece, Iriel. I hope you do not mind her here, she is in training. Hak taught you that trick, yes?"

Sending scary imagery back to the person trying to sit in my head? Oh yeah. I've watched every horror movie ever made. You guys don't even want to know what I can think up.

Annie thought Diana would cringe, or berate her for her bad manners. But Diana laughed. Her delicate voice was hypnotic. "Oh, Annie. This is just delightful. I am glad you learn so quickly. Ah, and I see you like the fae water."

Diana picked up the pitcher and looked at it thoughtfully. "My, my . . . It seems you enjoyed it greatly. I thought you would perhaps have a cup or two, not empty the entire pitcher. But you did not eat."

Not hungry.

"Do you often neglect to eat?"

I eat fine. I just didn't feel like it last night.

Diana glided over to the bed and sat on the edge. "Let me ask you something. When you are under stress, do you often feel *full*? As if you have plenty of energy to spare? You can go days without eating. In fact, food makes you feel ill when you are anxious. This is correct, yes?"

Yeah. But isn't that what stress does to everybody?

The elf looked distracted. "Yes. Of course."

Annie watched as Iriel busied herself with tidying up the room. She took the empty pitcher and disappeared behind the curtain. A second later Annie heard a sound that startled her.

Is that running water? You guys have running water here?

"This is not some simple countryside inn, my dear. This place was built with magic."

Iriel walked back into the room with a full pitcher and set it on the large table by the window. She pulled a bundle of blue and brown herbs from a pouch at her hip and set them out on the white cloth.

"You need to eat, Annie. You have a long day ahead of you."

Annie felt her stomach clench nervously. *I'm not hungry! How can I think about food at a time like this? What are you guys going to do with me?*

"Eat," the elf said sternly. She leaned forward and stared at Annie with her fascinating purple eyes.

Annie's head itched all over. She felt her fingers drift toward the food, but she jerked them back with surprise and glared at Diana. *No.*

Diana said nothing. She stared deep into Annie's eyes and blinked. Her eyes gave a soft flash, and Annie felt compelled to pick up a bowl of warm oats. Annie was too tired to fight the elf's mental prodding, and she had a feeling she wouldn't win, anyway. She dug her spoon into the thick white substance and took a bite. It reminded her of oatmeal. It was sweetened with honey and milk, and had odd little yellow berries in it that she did not recognize.

"Very good, Annie. You are strong. It is remarkable that you have not had any training."

What are you talking about? You guys keep saying that shit but it doesn't make any sense.

Diana sighed and asked, "Do people not use magic where you are from?"

Nope. I didn't believe magic was real until some asshole shot me up with lightning. Oh wait, that's right, you saw my memories. You know everything about me, so why ask questions?

"I don't know *everything* about you, Annie. Just what I saw yesterday. And believe it or not, I would prefer to talk with you, instead of holding you down and forcefully digging around in your head."

So, what's the deal? Why do you keep acting like I can use magic?

"Annie. You *can* use magic. It is an odd form, and it is very raw, but you seem to have some defensive abilities. You can resist spells remarkably well. That *asshole,* as you call him, should have killed you with that lightning blast. Any normal person would be dead."

Diana's words took the breath out of Annie. Her fingers trembled and she dropped the spoon. Instead of smearing the velvet sheets, the spoon and bits of food stopped and hovered just an inch above them. Diana was staring at the floating spoon. She waved a hand and set the bits of food onto the table in a neat little pile. The spoon floated back to Annie and placed itself into her bowl.

That was cool!

Diana laughed and said, "How would you like to learn how to do that? Make things float? Cast barriers to block spells? How would you like to learn how to never get shocked by lightning again?"

Annie gaped. *Hak said I couldn't learn magic. He said I was too old. And what the hell are we even talking about! The fact you are asking me if I want to learn how to make items float . . . ? This is just crazy!*

"Annie, my dear. Every human, dwarf, troll, and elf has the potential to use magic. It is an innate ability we all have. We are all born from the current. It creates our very souls and feeds our lives. Without magic, we would not exist. Now, not everyone who is born can control magic. Sometimes it is just at the edges of a life and only serves to keep our hearts beating and our lungs moving."

That's crazy! I took an entire year of cellular biology, I know what makes a heart beat and lungs move. It's red blood cells and hemoglobin and a complex assortment of scientific facts.

"There is a difference between giving your lungs and heart oxygen, and giving them life. Have you ever known someone to die of a broken heart? Or someone who is incredibly happy, and therefore healthy? The current affects your mind, and your mind affects your body. Think about people who are rotten to the core as they age. Their bodies grow sick and wither. A happy person usually ages much better. This is the very basic concept behind the current that flows through your body and mine."

This just doesn't make sense.

"It will in time, I think. I wish I could give you all the answers right now and send you on your way, but it is not so easy. I think you have many questions for us now, yes? Perhaps we can reach a mutual understanding through shared knowledge. As a member of the council, I want to know how you used the crystal points. As an elf and a scholar, I want to know a little about your world and how raw magic works. I have always wanted to study the raw forms of current.

"You see, Tahldian children with extremely strong currents are picked out at an early age and trained. Not all succeed in becoming a mage. Not all of them would have been able to resist the control spell Mau put on you yesterday."

Diana gave her a smile and shared the memory. Annie was not prepared for Diana to charge into her head. The shared image seemed to flow into Annie's brain like an unbidden dream and form a vision from Diana's seat in the council chamber. Annie saw herself hitting Hak and screaming at him. Annie felt ashamed to see herself so angry. She looked insane.

She saw the old man with the puffy white beard and brown robes. He looked, comically, like a mean Santa Claus. Annie watched through Diana's mind as Mau flicked his wrist, but Annie kept hitting Hak. Mau furrowed his eyebrows together and uttered a curse. He raised both his hands and seemed to concentrate intensely on Annie. He squeezed his hands and yanked, and at the same time Annie saw herself being pulled off Hak.

Then she saw herself lunge for Hak's throat. Mau seemed to be giving every bit of his attention to controlling her. He stood and pushed his hands out in front of him, and a blast of air knocked Annie away from Hak. Then the old man waved his hands down and flattened them to the marble table with an angry intensity. His hands twitched as Annie writhed, and Mau struggled to keep her glued to the floor. Annie felt amusement and satisfaction seep from Diana's mind.

"That was funny, yes? Did you see his face? Mau was not expecting that at all."

Annie blinked away the vision. She felt disgusted with the way she had behaved. She remembered Hak's sad face staring down at her as she hit him over and over.

I looked like a rabid animal.

Diana patted the blanket and said, "It is all right. You were very frightened. And Hakayatas was a fool for not telling you."

Annie shook her head. *I hate to admit it, but I think he was right. If I had known what you guys were going to do with me, I would never have left Feldall.*

"And then what, dear? Spend the rest of your days wandering around, lost and wanting to get home? Find a greasy old farmer and settle down to have a house full of children? You are not like that, yes?"

Annie sighed.

"You should be thankful that you found Hakayatas and he brought you

169

here. You are in the best place possible. We will see to it that we can send you home, if you would like. I have no desire to keep you here forever, Annie."

Wow. I really lost control yesterday. I know I have a bad temper sometimes . . . but that was the worst I've ever been.

Diana patted Annie's shoulder and gave her a beautiful smile. Annie found herself liking her.

Diana said, "My dear, you have been through a lot. You're worried about your home and your family. You have been under a great amount of stress, and you finally cracked from the pressure.

"Worry not about the past. That is your first lesson from me. Dwelling on painful things in your past clouds your current, and makes you ineffective. Accept what has happened to you and learn from it. And then let the past go. You must learn to live in the moment. You and Hakayatas must both learn that lesson."

Diana stood and strode over to a chair piled high with cloth. She pulled a dress out of the pile and showed it to Annie. It was frilly, lacy, and pink, with a strange, narrow waist that reminded Annie of something she had seen in a Renaissance painting.

"Do you like this color? It was difficult to find something so late in the day yesterday. I think it will do, for now. Why don't you change, and Iriel will groom your hair. And then I think we should take a walk down to the gardens."

Ugh. Do I have to?

"Would you prefer to spend the rest of your days crying in bed?"

I dunno. Kind of. This is just so much to take in at once. I still can't believe I'm here sometimes.

"Remember to live in the moment. You cannot change your past, so do not exert any energy worrying over it. That clouds your mana current. Just accept that you are here and that the rules are a little different. You might begin to enjoy yourself."

Do I have to go with you?

"Listen, Annie, I do not want to force you to do anything else today. It is bad enough I had to make you to eat like an unruly child. I would prefer that you fed and dressed yourself. You are a young lady and I expect better courtesy from you."

Whatever. Annie pulled the covers off and stood. She felt amazing, despite crying the entire night. Her body felt fresh and full of energy.

Did you guys dose that oatmeal with some kind of magic crap?

"Just a few herbs to give you some energy. You are too tiny and too dehydrated from your journey. You need all the help you can get."

Can you at least warn me if you're going to feed me drugged food?

"Fair enough. I will warn you next time. But please bear in mind that imbuing food with herbs and spells is very common in the palace. It would be easier on you if you just expected it to happen. It is not done with ill intent. It is just a part of culture here in Meda."

Fine. Where's the bathroom?

"Ah, wonderful. A bath would do you some good. It is there, behind the curtain."

I meant a toilet . . . or chamber pot . . . whatever you guys pee in.

"Same room, dear."

Annie walked to the large heavy curtain and pulled it back. Annie sucked in her breath in wonder. She was shocked to find a marble tub so large she could lay in it, a deep sink with a simple metal spigot hanging over it, and something that resembled a wide-lipped chamber pot made of marble.

After she relieved herself, she stood and was shocked to see that there was nothing in the pot. *Is that magic too? It just . . . disappeared?* Annie walked over to the sink and turned the water on. The water disappeared at the bottom.

There's no plumbing here! Annie gave a silent laugh and clapped her hands together. *Okay, magic can be pretty cool sometimes. It's not all lightning and body control!*

Iriel poked her head into the room and looked at Annie cautiously. "W-wise Diana wanted me to show you how the faucets work to pour a bath. Cold water comes from this tap here, and I will heat the water with some simple magic. Is that okay, Lady Annie?"

Annie nodded, suddenly feeling a little guilty for trying to scare the elf child out of her head earlier. *Poor thing is just some young apprentice trying to figure out her place in the world. And then they stick her with me.*

After a few moments the tub was full and steaming. Iriel hung a towel on a hook and added some herbs to the water. The humid air was thick with the aroma of sweet flowers. Annie spied a lumpy white bar of soap next to the tub and smiled. She wasted no time sliding into the hot water, and relief seeped into her sore muscles. It was her first real bath in two weeks. She spent a long time scrubbing the dirt off her body and washing dust and grime from her hair.

Annie wrapped a towel around herself and tentatively poked her head out of the bathroom. Diana and Iriel were sitting by the window, gesturing silently to each other.

"Do not be shy, dear. We elves are not as bashful as Shafani. You could dance around this room naked and we would not care. The body is a wonderful thing, and you should not be ashamed of it."

Annie walked into the room and looked around at the elves and the clothes. Iriel hopped up from the chair and pulled a few silken garments out for Annie.

Underwear huh? Annie found the cloth soft, but not stretchy. *I miss elastic.*

"You will have to explain this *elastic* to me sometime."

Are you seriously just going to hang out in my head all day? It's really annoying, Annie said in her mind as she slid the clothes on. Iriel helped with the dress, which had a white ribbon that ran up the back like a corset. She pulled the strings on the back tight, pushing some of the breath from Annie. She wrapped a lace shawl over Annie's shoulders and used a golden clip to hold it in place.

"We must wait a full day before I can give you your voice back. Until then, yes, I am going to be listening in. There is a difference between being receptive to your thoughts, and just charging into your head and taking them by force. I prefer not to do the latter."

"Please sit here," Iriel said softly, urging Annie to a chair in front of a small table and mirror. The small elf began combing out Annie's hair and humming a simple tune. Annie found the gentle motion of the small hands running through her hair very soothing, and she had to force herself to keep her eyes open. Annie watched as Iriel used magic to dry her hair and style it into simple curls that draped over her shoulders. She placed a silver band behind her ears to keep the curls out of her face.

Okay, I will admit, Iriel, this is really nice. I feel normal for the first time in weeks. Even better than some mornings back home. My hair looks great, and that bath did wonders for me. Thank you.

The small elf beamed down at Annie. "You are very welcome, Lady Annie."

I don't mean to sound rude, but I'm curious. How old are you?

"I have seen twenty-two summers."

How? You look like you're eleven!

Diana laughed and said, "Elves do not age as humans or dwarves do."

Iriel stood back and let Annie inspect herself in the mirror. She almost didn't recognize herself. She looked like a royal courtier out of an oil painting. Despite her tears and troubles, she looked well rested. *Dang, even I think I'm pretty. Ha! You guys did really well cleaning me up.*

"You look like a new woman. It feels good, yes?"

Yeah. I feel pretty good, thanks to you guys. But . . . why are you being so nice to me?

Diana looked perplexed. "Why wouldn't we be?"

You guys seemed pretty cold yesterday. I thought you would throw me in a prison cell.

"Oh dear, no! We have a protocol we follow in the chambers. Everyone is so pompous. We might seem a little stiff and imposing, but that's just politics, yes?"

Annie paused, and then asked, *Do you guys not get along? I mean, is the council a united body of mages, or is it split up into political parties? I got the sense yesterday that you guys don't agree on a lot of things.*

"Hmmm, you are observant. Yes, the council often disagrees. But that is how balance is maintained. You can't have a unanimous ruling body. There is a side and point of view to every issue."

Is everyone okay with me being here?

Diana hesitated for a brief moment, and then said, "I will not lie to you, Annie. There are a few here who wish you would leave. Mau, for one. He thinks you are a waste of time. He is convinced Hakayatas will die on his quest and finds you too wild to keep around. He thinks once Hakayatas is dead, there will be no reason to bother with any of this."

Annie shivered.

"Do not worry, Annie. I think you and Hakayatas can patch things up. And I have hope he can return safely."

Ugh! Stop it! I don't want to patch things up with him.

"Do not lie. I saw your memories."

Annie blushed furiously. Despite herself, a brief memory of her dream floated to the surface. Hak had been fondling her . . . .

The young elf let out an embarrassed gasp. Diana laughed.

Oh my god! Get out of my head right now! Please! I can't control what I think all the time! Please oh my god I can't believe you saw that! Annie's cheeks turned a dark red and she clamped her hands over her face.

Diana tried with an effort to contain her laughter and said, "You are as prudish as that Shafani! We will work on that today. It will be a good lesson. I think it will be useful for you to practice how to block people, and hide particular memories from even the most prying mage."

Please.

As Iriel ushered them out the door, Annie reached out and grabbed Diana's soft red robe.

For the love of god, do not *share that memory with anyone! You got that? I'll die from embarrassment.*

The tall elf turned to look down at her and gave her a mischievous grin. "Oh, I would not think of it," Diana said, giggling. "You are a funny human, Annie."

They spent the entire day working on magic in a garden near the waterfall. It was a lovely wooded patch carved deep into the side of the cliff, with a multitude of flowers, fountains, green moss, and beautifully strange songbirds. Diana and Annie were seated on a white marble bench by a small fountain, and Iriel busied herself with her own studies nearby, lifting droplets of water from the fountain and gently twisting them into various shapes.

The best part of the day came when a messenger arrived with a letter for Annie. The wax seal had already been broken, and she imagined the mages were keeping a close eye on her. Nivya's handwriting was very elaborate and curvy, but Annie could make out the words:

"Hakayatas has told me of your predicament. Please know that Tia is in very good hands, and has plenty of food and a warm bed. She really loves to curl up with me in the evenings as I study. Do not worry about her. Do not feel rushed to return, and I will see you when you are able."

The letter lifted the last nagging weight off of Annie's shoulders. Annie missed Tia horribly, but knew that circumstances prevented her from keeping Tia at her side. The dog would quickly get in the way of any teaching, and would make an immediate mess of the palace garden.

Relieved to know that Tia was safe and happy, Annie focused on her training with Diana. She was frustrated that she didn't know *how* she was able to push back at spells. And Diana was visibly frustrated with Annie as well. Sometimes Annie could push Diana out of her head with very little effort, but other times, the elf had an easy grip on her mind.

After a simple lunch in the garden, they practiced with a sort of invisible arm wrestling. Annie would try to push against an invisible force holding her wrist down. More often than not, when Annie got angry she succeeded in breaking free of the hold.

"You do very well, but you *must* learn to harness this energy you create when you are mad. That is the key. You have to turn that energy inward and combine it with your current. Then you can grab hold of it and use it. Knowing a word for a spell is but a small part of casting magic. It is a matter of will power. We must forge your will, and direct it accordingly."

You aren't making much sense! Annie felt the pressure on her arm release.

"You have raw mana energies, Annie. These seem to float just out of reach from you most of the time. You do not seem aware of them at all. Do you know, Annie, that mana energies spike when someone is under a lot of stress, pain or fear?"

Yeah, Hak told me about that.

"And do you find yourself sometimes light-headed and dizzy from this stress? Is your heart pounding in your head and do you feel like you could faint? The world seems to fade a little, yes? Do you ever have the sensation of tunnel vision?"

Annie felt her heart clench when she remembered how weird her body had reacted when she heard the news about the nuclear explosions. Her whole body had boiled with adrenaline.

"Yes, that is good. Right there. Whatever you just hit spiked your current. Now we need to find a way to reach that point without you fainting or soiling a pair of undergarments."

Did I somehow . . . Is that how I got here? Annie shared the memory with Diana.

"I do not know how you did it without training or a crystal point on Earth. But it appears possible. That memory is potentially one of the most frightening things that anyone can witness. That is an immense amount of stress. You come from a very strange place, Annie. I cannot imagine living in a world where entire cities can be wiped out in a heartbeat and millions can die in an instant. That is worse than anything Voltay or Bingen could do to Tahldia."

Do you believe Hak then? About them being demons?

"Of course, Annie. You forget I am an elf. I have lived nearly four hundred and twenty-two summers. I saw them rise to power in Falishan. I saw the dwarves and dragon eggs wiped out. It is only fanatical humans and their ridiculous superstitions that float the idea of Voltay and Bingen being divine beings. I know better. Many do."

So why did Hak feel like you guys didn't believe him?

"Hak is referring to King Halona and his family, dear. They are the ones who make decisions about going to war. The mage council, however . . . we are divided on what to do.

"Let me warn you—these kind of politics are *very* improper to talk about. It would be unwise of you to bring them up at the dinner table."

So . . . people just ignore the dangerous country across the sea?

Diana looked sad for a moment, and carefully said, "Most humans see what they want to. Many elves are the same way. The citizens of this kingdom would rather dance at parties and spend the treasury on frivolities. They hire enchanters for toys, not weapons. I cannot complain, they have built a magnificent city here. But I also feel Medalia is ripe for the taking. Shafan has not been aggressive with the eastern kingdoms because they have had plenty of resources. Now . . . I hear they are running out of zythil and many key components to running an army."

So you fear war, is that it?

Diana nodded and then caught herself. She pursed her lips and then said, "This is improper, Annie. And these kinds of worries will cloud your mind and distract you from training. Come, let us work on your blocking some more."

Is Meda safe?

"Yes, of course, dear. Now, pay attention. I want you to focus on that adrenaline you feel when you are upset. Let us try and get you to harness that. Calmly."

It was easier said than done. Annie failed miserably. She felt Diana's frustration through their mental bond, despite the elf's calm demeanor. Annie could not resist any spells while calm. It was only when she got angry that she succeeded. Notwithstanding her failures, Annie found herself liking Diana's company and patient tutelage. She had originally thought Diana was stuck-up. But she discovered the elf was mischievous and playful, and seemed to enjoy Annie's company as well.

The sun was low in the sky when they left the garden. A stark shadow from the western cliffs slowly consumed the valley below. They walked along several staircases and pathways cut into the side of the cliff. Annie tried very hard not to look straight down as they climbed. They passed a large dirt terrace with target dummies and an assortment of weapons on the wall.

Eight men were sparring in the center of the terrace. As Annie and Diana walked by, Annie's jaw dropped. Hak stood in the middle of the men, swinging his sword as he dodged their blows. And yet the men Hak fought didn't seem real. They flickered as if they were some sort of illusion.

Annie looked around and spied three old men in robes waving their arms about from the comfort of the shade.

Diana grinned and said, "You do very well, Hakayatas!"

Hak paused, and the strange images he was fighting vanished. The mages gave a slight bow to Diana and she returned the courtesy. Hak bowed to Diana and Annie, and then froze when he recognized Annie. Hak was standing a good fifty feet from her, but she could still see the shock plain on his face. Annie self-consciously picked at the lace cuff on her pink dress.

Diana gave Annie a grin and said softly, "Illuyuah worden. You have your voice back, Annie. If you would like to say something, you may."

Hak stared at her with hopeful eyes from across the yard, and they exchanged a long silence. A strange longing emotion tugged at Annie's heart and made a tight knot in her chest. She gritted her teeth and thought, *I don't even know what to say anymore.*

Annie turned and walked inside the nearest entryway, not caring where her feet took her. Diana had to step quickly to catch up with her.

"I thought you would at least have a pleasantry to give him, Annie."

Nope. And I really don't want to talk about it.

"Ah, you prefer to use mind speak. That is promising."

I won't lie, it's pretty handy to talk with someone and not be overheard. Annie turned sharply on her heels and glared up at the tall elf. *You walked us by that training yard on purpose, didn't you? You wanted me to see him.*

"Do not be so angry, Annie. He meant you no harm. And I know there is a part of you that would like to talk to him."

Get out of my head, Diana.

"But my dear, I can see this miscommunication happening between the two of you. If you would just talk to him—"

Out! Annie thought furiously. She felt her frustration and anger flare. Suddenly the gentle prickling sensation that she had grown used to evaporated. The elf had finally retreated from Annie's mind.

Annie cleared her voice and found the sound odd. She said, "I can be angry with him if I wish. It is none of your business how I feel about someone else."

Diana looked wounded, and placed her long fingers over her heart. She gave a slight bow. "I apologize, Annie. Humans are just so odd at times with the way they treat each other. Your lives are so short, and so much time is wasted. I was simply trying to help."

"Well, I don't need help like that."

"If it is any consolation, you did well pushing me out. Fine work, Annie."

Annie snorted and kept walking. She walked the maze of hallways and staircases for several moments, wondering where they were within the cliff. Diana seemed content to follow Annie and let her explore.

The hallways became more polished and elaborate as they walked, and Annie found a carved arch in the hallway that led to a small balcony. She heard laughter echo in the nearby room, and her curiosity pulled her toward the sound. The balcony was set high up in a large room overlooking rich red carpets, gold statues, and numerous oil paintings. Annie saw several young men talking amiably with one another.

One of the men wore an intricate crown of gold vines on his black hair. Even from the distance of the balcony, Annie could see the man was handsome. His face appeared young, but the defining edges of age were beginning to carve deep lines in his cheekbones. He had a sharp, hawkish nose and pointed chin. Diana quietly joined Annie's side and watched the men banter.

"That is King Halona, Annie."

Annie raised an eyebrow. "What? He looks really young to be a king."

Diana nodded and said, "A sad tale. His father passed two summers ago, and he had the crown forced upon him at the young age of twenty. He has done very well, despite hardship. You will never meet a more pleasant and kind human. He is a good king, and I am very proud of him."

He's gorgeous, Annie thought. She was happy to have that thought to herself. Diana had not tried to pry back into Annie's head once she had been pushed out. The young king turned to look over his shoulder and spied the two watching him. He gave them a warm smile and Diana quickly bowed. Annie jumped to follow suit.

The king gave them another grin and returned to his conversation. There was a playful air about him. Diana gently tugged at Annie's sleeve and said, "Come, we must return to your quarters. You have had a very long day; you need to eat and rest. You will find that using the current will greatly increase your appetite. You have done well today."

"You guys still aren't going to dissect me, eh?" Annie asked dryly.

Diana gave her a smirk and said, "No, I think not. But you still have a lot of questions to answer. All in due time, dear."

Diana bid Annie farewell at the entrance to her room. Annie was annoyed to see that the council had placed two elven guards outside of her door. Their eyes flashed quietly within their visors. *They still don't trust me. That's fine, I barely trust myself. I don't know what I'm doing anymore. This place feels like a dream.*

Annie walked to the window and pulled up a chair. She was content to rest her chin on the windowsill and watch the sun set. She felt completely at peace as she watched the city lights twinkle below. The town was surprisingly well lit, and Annie suspected the streetlamps she saw were also imbued with magic.

Annie heard the bar against her door scrape upward, and Iriel poked her head into the room. She had a small cart with her.

"Hi there, Iriel," Annie said, trying to be as kind as possible. She felt bad about frightening the young elf earlier that morning. Annie felt a soft prickle itch behind her ears.

"Lady Annie, I have brought dinner and wanted to give you a moment to clean up."

I'm not really hungry, despite Diana telling me I would be. "Thanks, Iriel. Feel free to leave it by the bed."

"Pardon? No, you have company tonight, Lady Annie. Please clean up. And . . ." The elf looked at her feet and blushed. "Wise Diana has told me to tell you to 'mind your manners.'"

Annie chuckled. "Okay, fine. Who's coming to dinner?"

"I cannot say, or Diana will be disappointed with me. She wanted it to be a surprise."

Annie frowned. *Oh, shit. What did Diana do now? If she's trying to force me to have dinner with Hak I will tie those tall ears of hers behind her head!*

Iriel gave a squeak at Annie's thought and hurried to wheel the cart into the room, avoiding Annie's eyes.

Annie went and washed up. When she walked back into the room, she found the table had been covered with a fine red cloth, and several plates of food were sitting on it. A small pitcher of wine and a vase of flowers sat in the center, and the room glowed warmly with candlelight. The dirty towel and socks she had left on the floor were gone.

This place looks like it's set for romance. I'm going to kick that elf's ass!

A beautiful young voice spoke clearly in Annie's mind, as if a woman were standing right next to her. The voice said, *Please don't. Elves by nature are just unbearably mischievous. You must get used to their little games. Diana meant no harm.*

Annie turned to the doorway and saw the old woman Aiyana hunched over a wooden staff. Annie froze. She knew she was supposed to bow, or say a courtesy, but shock ground her mind to a halt.

Aiyana looked at Annie and pointed at her throat. She once again heard a young voice say, *I hope you do not mind me talking to you in this manner. I am old, and it hurts to talk aloud. Diana told me you are very agile with mind speak.*

"Wow. You sound really young."

Aiyana gave a dry cough that could have been a small laugh. Her light brown eyes twinkled in the firelight. *My dear, I do not like the sound of my old voice. I prefer to use the one of my youth. That is the pleasure of living to be over a hundred years. I can do as I please.*

Annie watched as the old woman shuffled over to the table. Her silver robes shimmered warmly in the firelight as she adjusted the long sleeves. Annie helped Aiyana sit in a chair, and pushed it closer to the table for her.

Thank you, dear. You are very kind.

"You don't think I'm some sort of monster?"

My goodness, no. You are different, but differences are not bad things. Often they are just misunderstandings.

Aiyana helped herself to some bread and pointed at Annie. She said in Annie's mind, *You are quite the enigma. I have many serious questions for you, and I expect honest and detailed answers. But first, we must have some music. It has been so long since I've heard recorded music. Will you play some on that odd device of yours? If you have anything with a piano, that would be lovely.*

"Uh, sure . . . just one moment." Aiyana's words didn't quite sink in. Annie walked over to the bed and retrieved the smartphone from the nightstand. Her heart was pounding in her chest. She felt compelled to do everything the old woman said, but she was not sure if that was from mind control or a desire to please the council leader.

Annie found an hour-long piano concerto that she thought would satisfy Aiyana. She set the phone carefully on the dresser and sat down as a beautiful melody filled the room.

It is a true wonder what they can do with technology on Earth, isn't it?

Annie felt her chest tighten. "Y-you! It was your memory I saw, wasn't it?"

Aiyana frowned and cocked her head at Annie.

"I'm sorry, I don't mean to sound rude. But—"

My memory? What memory? The young voice inside Annie's mind had a dangerous edge to it. *What do you mean?*

Annie was about to explain the old street she had seen, and the newspaper with Hitler's face, but Aiyana barreled into Annie's mind with a brute force that made Mau seem like a weakling. The sensation of her brain swelling made Annie feel sick. Aiyana saw the memory Annie was talking about, plain as day.

The old woman sighed. *I didn't think you saw that. You're good, Annie. Let's cut to the heart of the matter, shall we? I am old, and I do not like wasting time on pleasantries and stupid courtesies. I think you are the same, yes? So let's get to the point, child. I saw your memories of Joe Wilson. I want to see more.*

"Why?"

Aiyana's eyes glittered dangerously, and she plunged deep into Annie's mind. Annie's childhood seemed to flash before her eyes. Annie gasped and gripped the table. Aiyana yanked every memory from Annie that was remotely related to her odd neighbor who had known about Tahldia. The mind reading was so intense that Annie couldn't make a complete thought before it was pulled apart again.

Finally, Aiyana leaned back in the chair and released her strangling grip on Annie's thoughts. Annie exhaled and took a few deep breaths, her head tingling. Much time had passed, and the food was cold. Annie saw tears streaming down Aiyana's wrinkled cheeks.

Annie scratched at her ears and tried to regain focus of her mind. "Wise Aiyana? Are you okay?"

Aiyana patted at her eyes with a cloth and let out a small sigh. *He's dead. He got hit by a car and his mind was never the same. He lost his grasp on the current. He couldn't make it home. His brother couldn't find him. He lived out his days . . . teaching young children to paint and use the current. He got cancer, and there wasn't a healer. He's gone.*

Use the current? What does she mean? Joe never taught me magic!

If Aiyana heard the thought, she didn't say anything. Her raspy wheezes alarmed Annie, and she reached across the table to hold Aiyana's wrinkled hand. Carefully Annie said, "Who was Joe Wilson? Really?"

His real name was Mazaska Iktomas Atokal. We called him Maz. He was my grandson.

A cold chill seized Annie. *The man I grew up next to was . . . Oh my god!*

Don't faint on me, Annie.

"This is just . . . I mean, how did you . . . how did he . . .?"

Aiyana patted the pockets of her robe and pulled out a long, elaborately carved bone pipe. With a shaky flame on the tip of her finger, she began smoking.

My gods . . . Do you know, we searched for years, both on Earth and Wesah. We looked everywhere until the mana points began to die one by one . . . It was unlike Maz to leave without a word. And stranger still for him to never return home. I think he fled from hunters. But I always knew he was alive. Somewhere.

"My mom said he was hit by a car when I was a baby. She said he was walking across a street and someone ran a red light. But I never got any other details about it. I just knew that was why he limped. I didn't think anything was wrong with his head."

Aiyana took another puff from her pipe and said, *He couldn't heal himself. He probably had some blasted Earth doctor try to heal him. Bah! Earth doctors are all a bunch of idiots. All science and no heart. They don't even know about the current.*

Annie felt Aiyana's anger and sadness through their mind link. She couldn't help feeling her eyes mist a little. They sat for many minutes and Annie looked sadly at her full plate of food. Aiyana stared at her. Annie felt confusion and then amusement bubble from the mind bond with the old woman.

You miss smoking, yes?

Annie nodded.

Aiyana gave her a smile and placed some stringy dried leaves that looked like black tea into the pipe. She floated it over to Annie. Annie put the pipe to her lips and tried to take a drag. Aiyana pointed her finger and a small flame suddenly hovered in front of Annie's face. She held the pipe to it and lit the strange, aromatic herb. It was not like the brown stuff Saiso had shared with her. Like the fae water, it made her feel tipsy and thoughtful.

How about some wine? The pitcher rose off the table and filled their goblets. Then both cups lifted off the table and hovered before them.

A toast.

Annie reached for her goblet and toasted against the one that hung before Aiyana.

To Annie Armstrong. The first, and possibly last, Earth girl on Tahldia.

What does she mean by last?!

My dear, you left a nuclear holocaust. Do you really think there is anything worth going home to?

"I-I-I need to find my family! My friends!"

My dear, you are in denial. Face it. Your parents lived in Atlanta. And it was

181

bombed. I saw that news in your mind. Even if I could get you home, it would be foolish beyond belief to go back there. The invention of nuclear weaponry is the main reason I came back to Tahldia.

If anything is left of your country, it is likely a hostile place full of radioactivity. I doubt there would be electricity or petrol. People may be killing one another for food or fresh water. Imagine all the Americans with all their guns shooting one another. Surely law and order has crumbled.

The words thrust deep into Annie's heart like a hot sword. Her lips quivered and she buried her face in her hands.

You know I am right, yes?

Annie began sobbing. Aiyana calmly floated the pipe back to her wrinkled hands and waited for Annie to compose herself. She couldn't find the will to try to speak as she gasped for air, so she said in her mind, *I have to go home! I want to go home!*

Denial. You and I both know it. Earth is not an option, Annie. You are not accepting the full range of your thoughts on this matter. Deep down, you know the life you used to live is gone forever. And besides, you can't even control your current, let alone create a complex burst of mana energies to hop from one planet to the other. If only mind control allowed us to train someone properly . . . Alas, it does not. Only you can learn how to control your mana current.

Listen, Annie. Maz taught you magic. Why he blocked those memories after each lesson I will never know. But it appears the connection remained in your subconscious. Your project with work, and your life, reflected his teachings. Perhaps he thought someday you would remember, but I can't say for sure. But you have the ability, Annie, to use magic. You will relearn it. And if you want, you can go to Wesah someday. That world has more technology.

Annie wiped away her tears with a napkin and said, "Whoa, whoa, whoa... *What?* There's another civilized planet somewhere?"

Yes. There are three worlds the warlocks know about.

Annie's eyes bulged. "Are *you* a warlock? Was Joe—I mean Maz, a warlock?"

Of course.

"Hak said they were all gone!"

Not quite, dear. But our numbers have diminished greatly. And the dozen or so warlocks that sought refuge on Earth are probably dead if they didn't escape in time. Fools. They were probably trying to save others and not themselves. They had married and settled into a quiet life on Earth.

It would be wise of you, dear, to not tell Hakayatas that I am a warlock. I believe that he changed sides . . . But I would never tell Shafani scum who I really am. I'll bind that thought, so you cannot communicate it with him. He can't know about Maz, either.

"Whatever. I'm not talking to him anyway. But . . . I mean, how is this even possible?" Annie felt as though her brain were going to break.

Annie, you enjoyed the cinema, yes? Aiyana packed more herb into her bone pipe and floated it across the table. Annie took it gratefully and gave Aiyana a funny look. "Cinema? You mean a movie, right?"

I want to share some memories with you. Please bear in mind my memories, when shared on purpose, are very strong. It is a little like going to the cinema, yes? Except that you are in the body of the actor.

"Yeah. Sure."

Let me share with you a brief history of my life. Perhaps it will help.

CHAPTER TEN:

REFUGE

I WAS SIXTEEN when my world changed forever. . . .

Annie felt Aiyana's memories flow into her mind. The palace room melted away, and was replaced by a grove of beautiful trees.

It was autumn, and the air was smoky and crisp. Annie could feel a gentle breeze on her skin. Aiyana's long black hair fell along Annie's shoulders in the periphery of her vision. The skin on her hands was young and smooth. A small silver bracelet with several emeralds hung around her wrist, and numerous silver rings encircled her fingers. A handsome teenage boy stood in front of her; he had shaggy black hair that drooped over his yellow eyes.

He wore a smile as he picked up a pile of golden leaves with magic and hurled it toward Annie. Or rather, Aiyana. It was a strange sensation to be in someone else's memory and share their body. Annie felt Aiyana's happiness with the memory in her own mind.

Aiyana ducked and let out a giggle as she picked up her own pile of leaves and hurled it at the boy. Annie felt so alive within the memory. She could feel the dry leaves in her hands, and strange desires drifted through her mind. The teenagers chased each other around the grove, stealing kisses between trees and using magic to jump extraordinarily high and swing from tree limbs. It was a dizzying sensation for Annie as the couple floated near the canopy.

"Ai, we must get back."

"No! You're still it!"

The boy pulled his arms at the air and Aiyana felt herself yanked through the grove into his arms. "We must go. Or your father will kill me."

"Oohhhh! Don't pull my current like that! You worry too much, Ikto!"

"Your father is a big man, Ai, I do not want him to send me home with a panicked chicken stuck to my head again."

Aiyana let out a delighted giggle and kissed the tip of the Ikto's nose. "Oh, fine! I think he did that more for amusement, though. He does approve of you, you know."

"One more kiss."

The teenagers giggled and nuzzled each other for a few more minutes. Annie felt a stab of sadness touch her emotions from out of nowhere. And then the world exploded just beyond the grove. The hot shockwave knocked the kids out of the air and threw them to the ground. The memory was so vivid that Annie felt dirt grind into her face, and Ikto cover her protectively.

"Aaaah! What has happened?"

"Aiyana! The village!"

"Mom! Dad! *Oh gods! Seiri! Faiy!* Ikto, get off me!"

The boy rolled over and they jumped to their feet. Burned bits of leaves floated down all around them like black snow. Smoke billowed across the sky. They could hear more explosions and shrieks of terror coming from the distance. Something horrible roared in the distance; it sounded like tearing metal.

"Mana hunters!"

Aiyana exchanged a look with Ikto. They held hands and their rings glowed, burning their skin. They lifted high off the ground, above the trees. They stopped above the canopy and floated there, staring at the remains of their burning village. There was so much smoke and fire that Aiyana could not see anything remaining of her home.

She wailed and began to fly forward, but Ikto grabbed her wrist and jerked her back.

"They found us, Ai! You know we can't go back!"

"Ikto—"

"Your dad would want you to run! We must flee! Do not make me force you!"

"But—!" A fireball flew out of the sky into the center of the burning village. The air was full of terrible screeching.

"Listen! They have wyverns! Come on!"

Aiyana and Ikto zipped through the trees. Their feet never touched the ground. Her jewelry was sizzling against her skin with the magical exertion. Her heart raced and tears streamed into her dark hair. Something roared behind them and a tree next to Aiyana shattered in flame.

"Run! Go!" Ikto forced his will into Aiyana and she kept flying forward. Then he stopped and turned, and held his hands out before him. A great snake with scrawny wings flew out of the smoky sky. The wyvern's scaled snout was flecked with dark red liquid. A saddle strapped behind its head held a man wearing full armor. He wore a black tabard with three moons on the front. He raised his glowing hands at Ikto.

"Iktomas! Noooo!"

Aiyana broke his pushing spell and flew to his side.

"You idiot!"

"Fool!"

"Up!"

The ground exploded below them as they flew higher; hot embers and rocks whistled past their ears.

"Ai! We must be quick or we'll run out of energy! You distract the wyvern, I'll get the rider!"

Aiyana pointed her hands at the enormous serpent and let out a howl of rage when she saw the blood on its lips. Her fingertips began to glow white and all of her jewelry sizzled against her skin. The serpent reared its head back and opened its mouth. A blast of orange flame rocketed toward Aiyana's face. She flattened her hands against the air and a blue translucent bubble enveloped her. Fire poured around her. The bubble pressed toward her hands from the pressure of the blast, but it did not break.

When the flame dissipated, the wyvern saw the woman floating before it and gave a frustrated roar. Ikto was at the wyvern's left side, and had his own shield up against the man shooting lightning from his hands. The blasts were pushing dangerously against Ikto's barrier, threatening to break it.

Aiyana wound her arm back behind her head and flung her arm forward like she was hurling a baseball. A ball of light flew from her hands and hit the strap holding the saddle in place. The light seemed to melt into the wyvern's flesh.

A fountain of blood sprayed from the side of the creature's neck. Its metallic scream was deafening. It jerked its head wildly and the saddle slid precariously toward Ikto's side of the beast. The lightning spells ceased as the rider struggled with the straps that held his legs in place. Aiyana did not give the man a chance to free himself.

She balled her hands into fists and the jewelry on her body nearly blinded her with their glow. She flung her hand forward over and over.

The first ball of light hit the man's armor and bounced off, but the second ball of light hit him on the hand, and the third hit him in the head. He melted in the saddle.

Aiyana's world spun and she fell from the sky.

Ikto swept down and grabbed her, and placed her gently on the ground far away from the distracted wyvern. Ikto hugged her and asked, "Are you okay? You are crazy! When did Faiy teach you that?"

"Worry about that later!"

They watched as the injured wyvern shook the saddle off of its head. It had no need to fight the tiny humans anymore, since it was free from the mind control of its rider. It soared up into the sky and disappeared into the smoke.

Ikto turned to Aiyana, tears streaming down his cheeks. "My heart, we must flee. It is too dangerous here."

The forest around Aiyana turned black and faded as the memory was withdrawn from Annie's mind. Her body felt numb and heavy.

Annie heard Aiyana's voice say, *The fate of all warlocks. I know how you feel, Annie. My life changed forever that day. I lost my family, my teacher, and my friends. I do not know what happened to them exactly . . . It is likely many of them were captured by hunters and drained of their mana. I have spent my entire life hoping that my family met a clean death in battle. I have prayed to the stars that my mother and youngest sister were not tortured, raped, and drained. Draining mana is the blackest magic, as I am sure you are aware, after talking to Hakayatas. You do not want to see that man's memories. Ever.*

Before Annie could say anything, the blackness that surrounded her exploded with greens and browns. It was as if Annie watched an oil painting bloom to life.

She was back in Aiyana's memory, in an older body, with a black haired, yellow-eyed toddler in her arms. His mouth was open and he appeared to be shrieking, but no sounds came out. Aiyana had surely silenced her grandson's cries with magic. An older Iktomas stood nearby, streaks of gray running through his shoulder-length hair. He was standing next to their child, Faiya, who was just beginning to show her second pregnancy. She held her small belly and gave a frightened look to the sky. They were once again in the woods, although Annie recognized the mana oaks immediately.

It is not the same place, dear, she heard Aiyana say in her mind. *It is similar to the place where you woke up, but this is far north and west, by the Snow Sea. Shafan has just invaded the last country on the continent, and is winning. We were fools, and stayed too long. My daughter, Faiya, has just lost her soul mate. My eldest son is also dead. I think you do not need to see that memory, yes? He blew himself up when hunters surrounded him. He took out three of them. I wish I could*

187

block it from my own mind.

The family looked around in complete silence. The baby squirmed and silently screamed. No birds sang, and the air was heavy and still. Faiya reached out with her hand and said something that soothed the baby. It clung tighter to Aiyana and looked about with dulled eyes.

We were trying to escape this day, Aiyana said, as the memory unfolded. *We had been at a safe house in Ayrelen when the hunters came. What could we do but run? They had a half-demon among them.*

Annie felt apprehension grip her as the family began running, using magic to quicken their pace. It was like watching a sped-up horror movie and the victim runs through the forest with the camera bouncing and jostling. A small silver bracelet glowed on Faiya's wrist. It was shaped like Annie's bracelet, but much smaller and covered with emeralds. The sadness of the memory chilled Annie, and she struggled to pull her mind away from the vision.

Watch, Aiyana said sadly.

Men in black armor flew through the woods toward the family. Their dark tabards flapped as they zipped between the trees; the three moons embroidered on the front were the only spots of white on the figures. A few links in their chain mail glowed like small white flames.

They were equipped with zythil, Aiyana said angrily.

Aiyana handed her grandson to Faiya and yelled, "Take Alomas and go! It is not far!"

Faiya gave her mother a grim nod and ran ahead at an inhuman speed. Aiyana swung her arms around and sent a blast of white-hot light into the nearest man.

"You must go, too!" Ikto said, deflecting a blast of lightning.

"Not without you!"

"Do not make me force you, Ai!"

Annie watched in fascination as the two warlocks began hurling white fireballs at the men. Lightning sprang from their armored hands and splintered the massive tree next to Aiyana.

The hunters and warlocks danced in a dizzying frenzy between the trunks, darting, shooting magic and deflecting it. The forest began to burn all around them. Aiyana and Iktomas were linked to each other's minds in battle, and used the flow of their combined current to make quick work of the armored men. Soon there was one large armored figure left. Their magic seemed to disintegrate before it reached the strange black-and-green armor.

The figure was taller than the other men, and the armor was a grotesque exaggeration of spikes and sharp curves. Green runes were etched in the black breastplate. A long row of spikes that reminded Annie of a Mohawk raced down the back of the helm. Within the deep slit on the front of the helm, Annie could make out two large, glowing green eyes. She felt an almost overwhelming flood of despair and sadness emanate from Aiyana's mind.

Ikto threw a bright flash of light at the hulking figure. "Bingen!"

The half-breed demon batted away Ikto's spell as if it were a toy. The eyes flashed brightly within the dark helmet.

"Is that all you have?" the demon asked. The oily voice was strange to Annie, as if several men and women were hissing the words in unison. "I was expecting more from you two."

Ikto and Aiyana gripped their hands together, and wound them over their heads like synchronized dancers. The combined ball of light flew forward and stretched until it was a flat disc of brilliant energy. It cut through every tree around Bingen. The forest seemed to moan with splintering wood. The runes on the black armor glowed greenish yellow for a moment before fading. The hulking figure let out a maniacal laugh.

Ikto and Aiyana turned and flew in the direction of the mana point. They pulled up the earth and brought trees crashing behind them. It took less energy to rip a mana oak down than to try to create a blast strong enough to puncture Bingen's enchanted armor. They needed to slow down the demon any way they could as they approached the point. They could see Faiya standing before the strange crystalline structure among a distant grove of trees. It was glowing brightly.

"Run, Aiyana. Get to the point. Or try to jump into the current as close as you can. I'm going to rupture it behind you!"

Annie felt hopelessness and frustration boil from Aiyana's mind. Ikto frantically began removing his jewelry. He handed it to Aiyana and gave her a sad smile.

"I love you with the brilliance of all the stars, my heart." Ikto reached over and quickly kissed her lips. "Faiya will need you. I will be waiting for you in Alhena."

"I love you, too, Iktomas." Aiyana was sobbing, but did not argue or try to stay. She spun in the air and flew toward the mana point. Toward her daughter and grandchildren. She swept her arms around her family, daring to look back.

Bingen appeared between two trees, the strange eyes flashing brightly.

She saw her mate between her and Bingen. Aiyana felt Ikto's mind leave hers as he raised his glowing hands above his head. Bingen did the same.

"Mother!"

"It is time to go!"

"But Dad!"

"No!" Aiyana pushed her mind into her daughter and rendered her powerless. Her mouth hung open and the panic on her face was replaced with a dull stare.

"Forgive me, Faiya. You do not need to see this," Aiyana said. She wrapped her arms around her family and began chanting strange words in her head. Annie could not understand what she was saying, but she remembered the horrible tunnel-vision sensation. The world seemed to spin and grow heavy. Annie felt sick watching the world tremble and bend.

Aiyana gave one last look at her soul mate. There was a strong urge to reach out and caress his mind just one more time. Iktomas was bent over as if ready to pounce at Bingen. The ground all around them began to crack and glow white.

"Fool!" the half-breed demon shrieked.

"You can't have my family! And you can't have the point!"

The ground trembled and erupted in hot light. Everything turned white and Aiyana was blinded. There was a whooshing sound, like ocean waves or the steady pulse of blood in her mind. Then the sounds ebbed away. There was a strange sensation of flying through nothing. Her body heaved up and down with the bizarre twists and turns of flight.

Aiyana compelled her family to cling to her as they sped through the white world. She couldn't tell what was up or down. She heard a low rumble and saw a black swirling mist far in the direction they had fled from. It looked like a black hole.

Annie said in her mind, *That's how . . . the light . . . I didn't see a bomb, did I? I saw the current!*

Aiyana ignored her. *I had enough zythil on me to transport everyone with ease. However, Iktomas did not want us followed. He destroyed the point once we went through. He blew the ground up around the crystal, disconnecting it from the heart of the current. We both knew that rupturing the ground would create a huge explosion of mana. We thought it would kill Bingen.*

The memory faded and everything grew dark around Annie. She felt her eyes burn with tears.

Aiyana said, *I will speed things up a bit. You know your own world's history, yes?*

"Yes."

Annie saw several quick glimpses into Aiyana's life on Earth. For the first time, they lived without fear of mage hunters or half-breed demons. She and her family settled deep in the mountains of northern Europe. Maz was born without any difficulties. Aiyana healed her family and used the brief peace to train her grandchildren in the arts of magic, music, and Tahldian history.

It was a lonely time in their lives, but they tried to be happy. Faiya struggled the most; many days she would not get out of bed. If losing both her brother and soul mate had injured her heart, losing her father had broken her. She did not speak out loud again.

Maz and Alomas grew, and Aiyana trained them in a meadow every day. At night, she went into the woods and prayed to the stars, but never said the words that would transport her home. Her happiest memory was the day she brought home an old piano from a flea market. Aiyana had compelled the merchant to deliver the piano, and then erased his memory and sent him back to town. The boys spent every evening trying to play the alien instrument.

Annie watched as the family endured World War II. They used magic to trick the soldiers that came asking questions at their door, and created wards around their small cabin that sparked fear in any human who approached. Aiyana spent many nights sitting on a tree stump outside the house wearing all of her zythil. She spent months watching the night sky with trepidation, living in constant fear of a plane dropping bombs on them.

She saw the Holocaust unfold in Germany. They sat out the war in relative peace, but Annie could feel the fear rise in Aiyana when the Americans dropped their bombs on Nagasaki and Hiroshima. The citizens of Earth as a whole bothered her. She regarded them as disdainfully as she did the Shafani.

Earthlings stole, lied, and cheated constantly. They did not believe in magic or herbalism. Faiya's extravagant gem-studded zythil bracelet drew stares. One day while in the city, she had to use magic to protect herself from being mugged. She had to cloud several minds at once and barely got away.

That evening Aiyana melted down some silver jewelry with magic. She carefully wrapped the glowing bands of hot metal over Faiya's small bracelet and its brilliant gems. Once the metal had been cooled and shaped, Annie recognized the bracelet as hers immediately. She felt a tinge of bewilderment.

Yes, child. You wear my family's bracelet. Maz gave it to you when he was dying, yes?

Annie didn't respond. She was still stuck in Aiyana's memory of the small cabin. Aiyana pulled the memory away from her.

Take some deep breaths. It will help.

The palace room seemed small, cold, and dark in contrast to the sunlit cabin. Annie became aware of the silence and glanced over at her phone. The candles had burned low, as if several hours had passed.

Annie leaned on the table for a moment and took a few breaths. She stared at the thick silver bracelet on her wrist as if seeing it for the first time. There was a small white scar underneath.

"It . . . burned me when I came here."

Yes. A pity you didn't know how to heal that. I could not destroy that bracelet; it is priceless and useful. Covering the zythil in silver was a sloppy job, but it did the trick. Gems are not as common on Earth, yes? Zythil is almost indestructible, and the best thing I could do was cover it with something so it wouldn't stand out. The power within it is still easily retrievable. If anything, the silver works as a mild conductor for the magic enhancement.

"Maz had told me the bracelet belonged to his mother. On my last visit to the hospital, he told me to keep it."

Yes.

"What happened to Faiya?"

Long ago, she vanished in the night. Ten months later, her current grew quiet. She has passed on to the stars. So many of the warlocks have, Annie. Hunters no longer burn villages to the ground. No. There are too few of us. They come like spirits in the night. Right under everyone's noses. Nowadays, people just . . . vanish. Warlocks must merge quietly into society, and be on constant guard. They must never show anyone just how powerful they are. Most people assume they are extinct.

Annie took a long drink of wine and tried to collect her thoughts. Finally, she asked, "Why did you come back?"

As I have said, Earth ended up being more dangerous than Tahldia. I cannot deflect a nuclear explosion. Maz and his brother, Alomas, needed proper training. They needed to meet other apprentices and mages. Earth was not a good influence on their youth. Your entire planet festered with a bad energy. It was corrupt and polluted. The Cold War frightened me enough to come back here. It was only a matter of time before . . . well, before things ended.

Alomas listened and obeyed like a perfect grandson, but Maz was a difficult child. Maz and I fought often about Earth. It had been his home the first twenty years of his life, yes? He had grown attached to your culture. He loved jazz and rock music. He even schemed at ways to build his own piano on Tahldia.

We found our way to Meda and settled here under the guise of regular (but slightly more powerful) mages. The spells passed down in warlock culture have remained our secret. Diana knows I am a warlock, but not the others. I have firmly blocked them from ever seeing that in my mind. I had to go so far as to feed Mau several false memories.

I know Maz snuck back to Earth several times against my wishes. Sometimes he brought Earthlings here. But one day he never returned to Tahldia. I went to Earth once to try to find his mana energies, but I couldn't find a footprint of his current anywhere. If only I had known he had been injured and unable to travel home.

The mana points are in chaos, Annie. What Iktomas did sped up a catastrophic series of events that led to the death of the mana points. It is like the blackouts we had in Europe. Basically, Iktomas blew up a power station that fueled several others. All the lights simply went out.

Annie chewed at a fingernail. "But you can travel between worlds without mana points, right? I mean, Earth doesn't have any that I've ever heard of."

There is much you probably didn't know of Earth. But yes, they existed in Norway, Africa, Australia, Greenland, and I even heard of one in Wyoming. Though I only visited the one outside of Oslo.

You do not need to be at a mana point to travel, but it makes things infinitely easier. If you try to travel without one, it is easy to be lost in the void forever. It is like launching a boat from a dock versus the middle of the ocean. Sailing down a narrow river is easier than adrift in a vast sea, yes? If you leave at the right place, the current will carry you.

You traveled without a mana point, but the current picked you up and carried you to one on Tahldia. That is a miracle for someone who doesn't consciously know what they are doing. It would be like tossing a babe in a basket into the middle of the ocean, and hoping it finds the shore. Yet, here you are.

"And Maz just disappeared one day?"

I think he was fleeing hunters. I wondered why he left so suddenly, and with no trail. It had to be Bingen. Alas, I was too busy with the politics here to pay much attention. He was a grown man, and he made his own choices, as much as I hated them. Stubborn as his grandfather. By then, I had climbed the ranks of the council. I was determined to make a change from the inside out.

Annie, this country is in denial. I cannot force my will on the Halonas and compel them to make war. No, that is too messy. I have been biding my time. When that Shafani Hakayatas showed up . . . well, I decided to use him.

Annie's eyebrows wrinkled together. "Use him? What do you mean?"

Child, that man is full of anger and desire for revenge. I will use that against the demons to the best of my abilities. Hakayatas was a renowned mage and soldier before the demons turned on him. His power was unequaled. Did you know that? I will help him get his mana back, and send him on a quest we both desire. Revenge. For my family, and his.

Annie felt a chill and stared at her plate of cold food. "You want him to take that suicide mission."

Do not worry yourself with him. He is Shafani.

"But he's still a person."

Aiyana watched Annie carefully with her pale brown eyes. She smoked her pipe quietly and blew strange snakelike figures with the smoke. Her eyes were glassy, unfocused, and her eyelids drooped lazily. She appeared to be mildly intoxicated as she contemplated the smoky shapes that blew from her lips.

Child. It appears my grandson taught you magic, but you have forgotten. How would you like those memories back? How would you like to become powerful?

"I don't know. I don't know what I'm supposed to do anymore."

Aiyana's wrinkles flexed around a strange, crooked smile. *Perhaps I do.*

Without warning, Aiyana flew deep into her mind. Annie felt as though her brain were being stretched apart like putty. Annie gasped and her eyes watered. The tingling sensation became so painful that she started seeing little white floating stars fill her vision. The balls of light zigged and zagged before her, sparkling painfully.

Aiyana left Annie's mind as quickly as she had jumped in. Annie's fingers twitched and she gripped the tablecloth tightly. Her stomach lurched and her vision was blurred. She looked at the window, thinking she would be sick.

I am sorry. I had to try.

"What the hell! That was almost as bad as a lightning spell! Don't do that again!"

Bah! It appears I taught my grandson too well. I am sorry, but I cannot unblock your memories so you can see them. I was trying to show you what I saw. Your blocked mind is like a barred door, and I can see a small glimpse of him tutoring you through the keyhole. We must open that door. It is a strange thing, reading minds and seeing memories, yes? It is something warlocks are especially talented at. Not even the council can see Maz within your mind as I do.

I see a few memories that you can't, but the spell is bound in such a way that I cannot show you. It would cause you too much pain. The rest of your memories of learning magic are so well hidden that not even the council could pull them out of you. Stubborn Maz. He locked that door well, whatever his reasons.

"So you can see memories of Maz and I, but you can't show them to me, is that it? It would basically break my brain?"

Yes. I can catch flickering images of him within your mind. I saw you at his piano, talking about the star songs. Mind spells are powerful, and you must have a delicate hand. I was trying to untie a massive knot of magic in your brain. One wrong move and I could render you stupid, mindless, or insane for the rest of your life. I will not risk that with you. These memories must come back on their own. And I think I know a way to do that.

"How?"

Aiyana gave her a considering look through a puff of smoke. *There are a few places you could visit that might help. I must think on this. I will not make a hasty decision tonight. But there are ways to attune you with the current. Similar to what that blasted Shafani must do.*

Annie felt her stomach turn. Finally she asked, "How did Maz teach me magic and block my memories? You said he couldn't use the current."

My dear, you are comparing something like space travel to minor surgery. Both are complex and require much skill and many tools. Blocking a memory is something a warlock can do with barely a thought. But traveling between worlds . . . Well, my dear, that requires full connection with the current. If you get hit in the head hard enough, it can disrupt the current one uses for magic. The vast ocean of mana becomes but a trickle.

It was easy for Maz to teach you the words, songs, and meditations, and block your memories. But he could not plunge into the void to travel back to Tahldia. It takes full use of his current to travel.

You must learn to be stronger, Annie. Do not waste time overthinking life. Take it as it comes. Use your stress, control your current, but do not let it cloud your mind. I will have Diana work with you more on barriers. And possibly healing. Has she tried to teach you that yet?

"Healing? No."

It may be too difficult for you to pick up in a week, but you should know the ideas behind it. Let us use our time wisely. I have much to think about. Aiyana stood and reached for her gnarled wooden cane. Annie helped her to the door.

The old woman reached a wrinkled hand to Annie's face and spoke some words that Annie instantly forgot.

You do not need to talk about this night. Do not try. To do so will cause you immense agony. I have blocked this memory from all prying spells. If you try to tell anyone, you could lose your mind from the pain.

"Who would I tell?" Annie asked, feeling light-headed.

Hakayatas, of course.

"I doubt I'll talk to him again. Don't worry."

Aiyana squinted her eyes up at Annie and gave her a sly smile. *I am just covering my tracks.*

"Um, Aiyana?"

Yes?

"Thank you. I mean, for sharing everything with me. I think I need some time for all of this to settle in my brain. This is just so crazy . . . but I know how I got here. I know I'm not dead, or somehow in heaven. Things make sense for once. Kind of."

Aiyana patted Annie's arm. *My dear, that is why I came tonight. I saw a frightened Earthling who missed her old life. She had been hurt, and the truth hidden from her far too long. I had to ease your mind somehow. You were so sad and confused. You deserved the truth. As much as I can give you. Even if you can't tell anyone about tonight.*

Put your mind at ease, Annie. You live here now. Perhaps later you will go to Wesah, but for now, Meda is your home.

Aiyana gave her a wicked grin. *We will try to give you comforts, and in return I am sure you can think of some way to make yourself useful. While you have been through much in your short time here, I would like to assure you that magic can be used for good. There are healers who can cure bad eyesight, cancer, and broken spines. The air is clean, the water pure, and the wine is delightful, yes? I am sorry you lost your home, but be at ease here. Enjoy life, and the moment, for what it is. Great things will be in your future. Your destiny is here, in Meda.*

Aiyana swept her hand at the door to open it and shuffled out of the room. Annie saw the elven guards sitting across from each other in the hall. They were playing some strange game on a circular board, similar to checkers but with dozens of multicolored stones. They stood quickly and gave a bow to Aiyana, but didn't look in Annie's direction.

She closed the door and paced around the quiet room until the sky began to lighten. She couldn't seem to organize her thoughts, and fell into the bed with a huff. Her mind ran in furious circles.

It's not a dream. I am not dead. Did I really see a bomb, or was I getting swallowed by the current? Why did Aiyana avoid that question? Does that mean Earth is okay? Does she know something I don't? Is she hiding something from me? Ugh . . . . My mind is just all fucked up from spells, and there is some old crazy warlock who wants to use Hak as a weapon. And I can't tell him.

CHAPTER ELEVEN:

HEALING

"MY, YOU ARE exhausted today."

Annie moaned as Diana sat down on the bed next to her and pulled the blanket away from her face. Iriel sat a tray of fresh fruit and the strange oatmeal on a small bedside table and darted away. Annie could hear her clearing the larger table by the window.

"Long night, Annie? Did you and Aiyana have fun?"

Annie sat up and rubbed her eyes. *God, was I only asleep a few minutes?*

Annie felt her scalp prickle. She focused her eyes on the elf and asked, "Do you have to?"

"Just making sure everything is still in there," Diana said with a chuckle.

"Yeah. We talked a bunch."

"Oh? I am curious."

Annie opened her mouth, but small white stars began to painfully flow through her vision. Her stomach twisted.

"Ah, she blocked most of it, did she? Clever woman, she is."

Annie poked experimentally at her thoughts. There was not any pain from recalling the night before, but if she even thought of talking about it, her vision blurred.

"She told me some of last night over breakfast. Honestly, how that woman goes without a full night's rest, I'll never know. Aiyana mentioned that she wanted you to learn healing. That will be challenging, I think."

"Why's that?"

"Healing can be the most difficult tier of magic to teach. Some of the spells are the most dangerous to use."

"Dangerous?"

Diana nodded and said, "We will go over all of this today, yes? First you must eat, bathe, and prepare for the day."

"You're like a mom."

Diana gave her one of her dry smiles and said, "I look forward to the day when I do not have to mother you. You must learn how to eat, sleep fully, and be ready each day. Honestly, how did you survive so many years on your own?"

Annie bristled and said nothing. But Diana plucked her memories with ease. Annie had spent countless mornings eating stale bagels, chain-smoking, and slaving away in her cubicle half asleep.

"I am sorry. You were not happy in your old world?"

"Don't want to talk about it," Annie said and grabbed the bowl of oatmeal. She began shoveling the food into her mouth, ignoring the elf's stare.

"Well, today, we will live in the moment. I will need your full attention, so be ready."

They spent the majority of the afternoon in the palace garden. Annie tried not to let her eyes wander, but the view was simply too tempting. Hawks lazily circled about near the waterfall, and strange flying mice would dart away from them to scurry into small cracks in the rocks.

Diana had to call Annie's attention back several times, but she remained patient.

"I know it is hard to teach you something without practicing on an injury, but you must learn the ideas behind it."

"Yeah, but don't people study healing their entire lives? How am I going to grasp this in a week? Why does it have to be a week? Am I going anywhere?"

"No. Just . . . you must try to learn it quickly, that is all. You need to at least understand the concepts of repairing an injury. Now, pay attention."

Annie turned to face the elf, and Diana took her hands.

"I want you to focus on your breathing. Feel the breath filling your lungs, and feel that energy escape your lips as you breathe out. Seek out the current and feel your breathing flow with it."

"It feels like I'm breathing," Annie said dryly.

Diana gave her a disapproving look, but said, "Imagine I am injured, and you are grasping at my current. You might feel pain, you might not. I want you to use your mind, Annie. Imagine you have hands of pure light and love, pulling my pain away when you take a deep breath, and then breathing the pain out. Long, slow breaths. Yes, that's it. Now use your *mind*, Annie.

"You want to see the current within me. You might find it weakened, depending on how bad the injury is. You will want to grab the current and take my pain. If it is a bloody sword wound, I want you to imagine that the bleeding stops. Breathe in, and imagine sucking that damage out of me. Breathe out, and imagine blowing the pain into the wind."

Annie felt clueless about what she was doing, but she tried to imagine everything Diana told her.

"Now, Annie, if the wound is particularly grievous, or lethal, it is best you do not attempt this. You can injure yourself beyond repair, or lose your current within that of the person you are trying to heal. That is to say, healing drains you, and can kill you if you are foolish. No life is more important than your own. Remember that."

Annie tried to focus on her breathing, and asked, "So, are you feeling anything yet from me?"

"No. Not yet."

Annie tried to imagine somehow joining herself to the elf, but nothing happened for several long minutes.

"Do not become discouraged. This can be a process. Do you know how to tap into the power of your bracelet yet?"

Annie stared at the elf in shock.

"Yes, of course I know most of your past. Aiyana does not hide much from me." The elf gave her an eager grin and said, "Don't you know? Aiyana and I practically run this part of the palace. Nothing escapes us."

"I don't understand."

"I am young, but Aiyana is very old for your kind. She will pass in a few years, perhaps, and I will be the one to carry on her wishes. At least, the ones I see fit. We try to be as honest with each other as possible. And our . . . politics, I should say, are in agreement."

Annie wanted to ask about Hak, but a sudden flash of pain zipped through her mind. *Maybe Aiyana didn't tell her that? Ugh. Why is magic so difficult and weird?*

"Now, back to your bracelet. It is a lovely thing, yes? Rather large and clunky, but the zythil inside will surely be powerful if it came from Aiyana's family."

"Do you think she wants it back? It's an heirloom or something, right?"

"She seems to think that you should keep it for now. Aiyana is extremely powerful, and has plenty of zythil of her own. As do I." Diana held up her hands to show Annie several diamond rings. The metal holding the gems appeared to be bright silver, and almost seemed to radiate its own light.

"You keep it for now. You need all the help you can get. Now, Annie, let us focus. Please." Diana massaged Annie's hands with her long fingers and closed her eyes.

"Compassion and clarity are key for healing. Oftentimes healing must happen under stressful circumstances. Someone has fallen or been cut, and they might thrash about or cry. Do not let that bother you. Focus on clearing your mind of everything in the moment except stopping the bleeding. If someone's heart has stopped beating, focus on applying pressure to that four-chambered muscle and imagine it beating once more.

"You must use your imagination. You must be brave. You must be confident. You must think about the injury and how to heal it. Connect with the current, and use it.

"What if it's a really complex injury? Like the brain, or a broken bone?"

"Ah, good questions. And yes, those require much skill. Healers must learn the anatomy of the body and surgery to be fully effective. That can take years. However, for the time being, simply try to connect with the current, Annie. We must develop your spiritual side."

And so Annie spent the entire day trying to connect with the current, and learning the ideas and techniques behind healing from Diana. It was frustrating work, and Annie couldn't seem to get anything right. She felt like a failure as they walked back from the garden.

Annie felt a new prickling sensation in the back of her mind, and somehow knew it was Aiyana before the young voice spoke. *My dear ladies, I would like a moment of your time. Alone.*

Yes, at once, Wise Aiyana, Diana said in their minds.

Annie looked around but didn't see the old woman. "Where is she?"

"She is inside, dear, in a small room on the way back to yours."

Annie felt Aiyana fade away from her mind and shuddered. *Maybe I am getting better at this, if I can tell who is in my head before they speak. Ugh . . . I wonder what that crazy old woman wants.*

"Are you okay, Annie?" Diana asked.

Annie jumped. *She didn't hear those thoughts!*

"Yes. I missed something. You actually blocked a thought from me. Very good!"

"I don't know how I did it, though. I just . . . sort of did."

"You have good instincts, and practice makes a skilled person. Keep at it, my dear. And do share that thought with me, if you want."

"I just . . . I wonder what she is up to."

"Knowing Aiyana, she is up to one of her schemes. Come along, Annie."

They walked up great staircases and long hallways that seemed familiar to Annie. The inside of the palace was so large she wasn't sure if she would ever get her bearings. But she was learning to recognize statues and paintings, and used them as if they were street signs.

They turned down a dark hallway and Diana waved a wooden door open with a graceful flick of her wrist. Aiyana was sitting by the fire with an orange cat in her lap and a book resting at her side. For one brief moment, she could have passed as someone's normal great-grandmother. She looked up at Annie and gave her a warm smile.

Annie couldn't help herself, and thought, *What are you up to?*

Diana gave her a sharp look. An awkward silence followed Annie's thought, and then Aiyana laughed.

Diana said, "I promise, she was good earlier. She managed to block a thought!"

Ohhh, wonderful. I knew she would start to get the hang of it. Still a long ways to go, though. I sense she failed the healing arts thus far.

"It could be a while," Diana said.

Come in and make yourselves comfortable. Aiyana waved a hand and two large, cushioned chairs slid from the wall. They would have been too heavy for Annie to lift. She gingerly sat down between the elf and the old warlock in front of the fireplace.

You are tired, yes? Care for some tea? Perhaps some naroh smoke? A teapot floated over to a small hook that held it over the fire.

"You like showing off to the Earthling, yes?"

Bah! I am old and I don't feel like moving. Here, Annie, I got this for you.

A small bone pipe appeared on the table.

"What the! How did you do that?"

Diana said, "It was just invisible. It was there the whole time."

You take the fun out of everything, Diana.

"I just want her to know what's really going on around her."

Fine then. I can get straight to the point. Aiyana fluffed the pillow behind her back and settled deeper into the chair. She gently stroked the cat in her lap and gave Annie an odd, crooked smile.

Annie, how would you like to become powerful? Very powerful?

"I think you asked me this already. . . . I, um, don't know. It would be rad to make objects appear, and to heal someone who is hurt, but I'll be honest with you, Wise Aiyana . . . you sound like you're up to something."

Aiyana and Diane both laughed, and the old woman said, *Ah, I like you. Blunt and honest. You care not if you sound rude. I like that in a person. You get to the heart of the matter.*

Aiyana leaned forward and fixed her pale brown eyes on Annie. *I want you to go with Hakayatas to the Fieriel Senefal.*

Diana gave a start and placed her long fingers over her chest. She looked at Aiyana with wide eyes.

"Wait, *what? Why?!*"

"Wise Aiyana, I fear that . . . that would be . . ."

'Unwise,' dear? That is what you want to say. Both of you. I can sense it. Bah! Listen closely, Annie. You must go with the Shafani.

"No way! I just got here! I like having hot baths, a toilet, and a feather bed to sleep in!"

It is the only sure way.

"Sure way for what? Why me? Why do I have to go?"

Aiyana motioned for her to be silent. Irritably, she asked, *Do you want Hakayatas to live or not?*

"What?"

Diana was boring holes into Aiyana with her glare. The old woman stared back, and they seemed to be silently arguing. Diana's eyes flashed angrily and she gestured at Annie with her hands. Annie tried to open her mind to them, to catch whatever they said, but she met silence.

Diana frowned and folded her arms against her chest and stared into the fire.

Aiyana turned to Annie, her eyes flickering brightly in the firelight. *You, my dear, are the key to the points. You breathed life into the ones north of Feldall. You might very well be the key to the one in the south.*

"No. Noooo way. No fucking way. I'm not leaving."

Aiyana leaned back with a shrug. *Then he dies.*

"*Why?* Why do you have to be like this?"

"Wise Aiyana, I know you mean well, but surely this isn't fair—"

Do not question me on this matter, Diana. And as for you, Annie, he goes on that quest whether you leave with him or not. I just fear that the crystal point will not work for him.

"If it doesn't work, then why can't he just come back?"

Diana shuddered and said carefully, "There are things in that cave . . . that . . . well, the current must be working. . . ."

What the elf means to say is that you have the ability to work the mana points. You can connect to the current, while Hakayatas cannot. You need to turn the point on, so to speak. Hakayatas needs it to work so the magiel can be used. If the point isn't on, he will most likely die from the attempt. Also, your current flows stronger when he is near you. You seem to affect each other in a way that is strange but powerful. You must go with him and aid him. You must turn the point on. And you just might become powerful in return. That is all I will tell you.

"B-b-but, I don't know how I did it the first time! I have no idea what I'm doing!"

It is said that light must be shed on the darkness.

"You might not need to do anything. I—" Diana stopped and turned to look at Aiyana. They gestured angrily at each other in silence.

"You guys are being really rude, you know that? I'm right here."

"Annie, please consider what Aiyana is asking of you." Diana sighed.

"Dude, this is blackmail. I don't want Hak to die, but I don't want to die, either! I want to stay here."

And do what, Annie? Maybe we do not need to waste our time training you, yes? Perhaps you would like to find a place of your own with your dog and settle down to find a trade. You are getting too old for marriage, but perhaps you know how to cook or mend clothes? Surely you can find a shop that will hire you.

"Ugh. You know I don't want to settle down. And I hate working. Quit this blackmail stuff."

Diana looked uneasily at Aiyana and back to Annie.

Aiyana pointed a finger at Annie and said, *Do not misjudge my kindness for endless charity. We all have roles we must play as we flow through the current of life. Diana should be spending her time studying herself, not training helpless Earthlings.*

Bah. I saw promise in you, Annie. My grandson surely did. Now is the time for us to find out what that is, yes? There are things you must do, whether you want to or not.

Annie gasped and said, "You're just using me! Just like Hak—" She felt a sharp slap on her face, but neither woman had moved.

Diana's eyes flickered with alarm to Aiyana. Annie felt tears burn her eyes, but she gritted her teeth and tried to ignore the stinging sensation on her cheek.

You're rude and act like a spoiled child. You're a lazy drunk. And your mind is a complete disaster. Grow up, child. Embrace your potential. How did such a lazy Earthling ever get here?

Diana looked apologetically at Annie, and said to Aiyana, "Give her time to think on it. Let us give her a choice, instead of forcing her."

"I have to decide if I want to help Hak or not . . ."

Forget that Shafani for a moment! You are also making a decision about power, Annie! This is your destiny! Think of the power you might unlock within your mind at the Fieriel Senefal! The heart of the current is said to work miracles. . . . You have three days to decide.

Annie felt a strange emotion wrap tightly around her heart. Suddenly, she thought of Hak's smile, and watching him sleep by the campfire. She remembered laughing and sharing music with him. His eyes always softened when he talked about the stars. She remembered him holding her when she had been injured.

Annie's eyebrows crinkled together. *Are they feeding me those thoughts? Is she trying to muddle my emotions?*

Aiyana simply watched her with a smile.

You're using me, Annie thought sadly, not caring if they heard it. *Well, it won't work!*

Annie stood suddenly and said, "May I be excused?"

Diana looked surprised, but Aiyana waved her hand dismissively. *If she does not want to be proper or social, we cannot tame her. Bah. You may go, Annie. But please, take the gift with you. There is some naroh smoke in the small pouch next to it. Take it, mull your thoughts over with an open mind, and decide. I know you will come to the right decision.*

Annie grabbed the gift and ran from the room. She let her feet carry her through the hallways as tears streamed down her cheeks.

Diana touched her mind and asked, *Are you all right, Annie?*

Yeah, just fucking great. You knew about this, didn't you?

I had my suspicions Aiyana would go this route, but I did not believe it would happen so quickly. Honestly, I was hoping this wouldn't happen.

Why does everyone lie to me? Why does everyone hide things from me? I am tired of everyone hurting me the second I start to trust them! I just need to stop caring.

Diana tried to send some calming emotions to Annie, but she pushed them away with her anger. *Just stop! I need time to think!*

Well Annie, eat a good dinner and get plenty of rest. I will have Iriel send some fae water to you. Smoke, drink, whatever will soothe you. Would you like me to send Hakayatas to visit—

No!

Very well. I will see you in the morning, Annie. Just remember to live in the moment.

Easy for you to say!

Annie stomped down the hallway to her room, not even looking at the guards nearby. She kicked the wooden door open and stormed into the room.

Iriel was at the nightstand and gave a squeak as she stomped in. Annie muttered an apology and walked into the washroom.

"Would you like a hot bath, Lady Annie?"

"Yeah . . . please."

The small elven child busied herself with the fae water. Then she quietly filled the tub and heated the water. She added perfumed oils and a few flower petals, and bowed as she left the washroom.

"There is fresh bread and butter on the table, Lady Annie. I hear there are roast quail in the kitchens tonight. I will send some up within an hour, is that acceptable?"

"Yeah. Thanks."

Annie watched her shut the door and heard the bar scrape down to lock it behind her. *They still think I'm going to run. Well, I have more reason to run now than I ever have!*

Annie paused and tried to feel around in her mind for anyone else. She was unsure half the time if someone was listening in on her thoughts. It angered her. She tried to remember the lessons about mind-blocking as she sat the pitcher of fae water next to the marble tub.

She retrieved her lighter and picked up the delicate bone pipe Aiyana had given her. She sneered, but took the pipe and the herb into the washroom and shut the curtain.

There was a small stained-glass window next to the tub, and Annie opened it to let in the cool evening breeze. The sky was brushed with a brilliant palette of oranges, reds, and bright pinks. She could hear birdsongs and the waterfall.

Don't cry. Don't cry. Don't cry. They can hear you.

Annie stripped and stepped into the hot water. She purposely filled her mind with thoughts related to what was around her, in case someone eavesdropped on her.

Interesting white marble. I wonder how they mine it and shape it? I wonder how the enchantments that work my toilet happen. Diana said enchantments are just long-term spells used in place of a repetitive job. I wonder if they have a plumbing enchanter and a tub enchanter, or if the hands that made this bathroom are one and the same.

She took a deep chug from the pitcher and then lifted the pipe to her lips. She watched the sun set over the forested valley and fought her tears as her train of thought crumbled.

Remember your training about mind-blocking, she told herself. Annie took several deep breaths, but felt her mind buzzing pleasantly. It was difficult for her to maintain focus.

She tried her best to hide her thoughts, but she wasn't sure if she was succeeding. *They say I can use magic, but I have no idea what I'm doing! I don't want them in my head anymore. I'm terrified they're just using me like some sort of guinea pig. I need to get out of here! Maybe I can get to Feldall again. Or hitchhike with some caravan farther south. I need to get Tia and get out of here.*

She slunk deeper into the tub until the water was just below her nose. She breathed in the flowery aroma of bath oils and thought about escaping for a long time. She drank the entire pitcher of fae water, though she suspected it was not as potent as the first night.

Diana is nice, but she must think I'm an asshole. Aiyana is just . . . crazy. She has her own agenda. I don't care about power. I don't want to be some great wizard or whatever. I just . . . I just want to live. I want to explore. Yeah . . . I want to explore this entire world. Just me and Tia. Maybe I can find another handsome swordsman to travel with. One who isn't a big idiot with a death wish.

She felt the tears run down her cheeks into the water, and looked up at the starry sky. *Oh, Hak, you love the stars as much as I do . . . I've never seen so many. There isn't any pollution here. Tahldia is perfect. And yet, I'm miserable. I wish I knew what to do. I don't want you to die. . . .*

Annie heard the wooden door to her room creak open, and from beyond the curtain she heard Iriel's delicate voice ask, "Lady Annie?"

Annie raised her head a few inches and said, "Yeah?"

"There is some roasted quail and tanna root with honey here for you on the table. A-are you all right in there? May I get you anything?"

"Can you heat this water again? It got cold. Please."

Iriel poked her head through the heavy velvet curtain and looked around the room. She gave a long stare at the empty pitcher on the floor. Finally she walked over to the foot of the tub and placed her hands in the water. Her fingers gave off a soft orange glow.

"Your skin will be very wrinkled if you stay in the water all night."

"It's okay. Maybe make some more fae water?"

"Ah, pardon, Lady Annie, but I am not sure you need any more."

"Ohhh, c'mon, please? I need all the help I can get, right?"

"But you will get intoxicated!"

"Good," said Annie. She sighed as the water near her feet began to warm up.

"Please tell me if this gets too hot."

"More fae water? Please? Did you know that Aiy—" Annie jerked and almost threw up as white-hot pain flashed through her mind. Iriel gave a small squeak and jumped back.

"B-be careful, please. Do not trouble yourself so."

"Just give me something so I don't have to think. I'm a bird in a cage that can't fly even if someone opened the door for me. Trapped forever in drama and bullshit. Yeah, that's hot enough. Thanks, Iriel."

The elf gave Annie a frown, but stood, filled the pitcher in the sink, and walked out of the room.

Annie let herself sink back into the water. *I just want to fly out of this cage and be free.*

She sat in the tub long after Iriel left. When she finally stood, the room spun pleasantly around her. She took a small white robe from a hook in the wall and walked into the bedroom. The hearth was crackling softly, and lent a gentle red illumination to the room.

Annie sat down at the table and ate her food quietly. The strange tanna root Iriel had mentioned appeared to be some sort of sweet potato with purple flesh. The roast quail was delicious, and Annie savored every bite. She washed down the dinner with most of the second pitcher of fae water. Her mind was dull, and she was happy she couldn't hold a straight thought.

She stared around the empty room and then looked out the window toward the falls. The spray of mist seemed to glow softly with the city light. She thought she saw bats or some other strange winged creature hunting in the night.

Annie had thought that she would enjoy a night to herself and her thoughts, but she began to feel increasingly lonely. The room seemed too large, dark and empty for her tastes.

"I wonder where Hak is right now . . . Big idiot . . ." *I can't believe I miss him.* Annie sighed heavily and dragged her feet to the large feather bed. She pulled the blankets over her shoulders and curled up in a tight ball. After a moment, she reached over and grabbed a spare pillow and hugged it tightly.

Annie dreamed about the cliff again.

The forest around her was on fire. Annie stumbled as a tree crashed down in front of her. She turned and ran, but found her legs heavy and clumsy. She thought she saw shapes in the fire: a large feline the size of a horse, black shadowy forms with green eyes, and plagarne. She tore through the burning forest, struggling to breathe in the smoke, and found herself on the edge of a cliff.

The Dohl valley was below, and everything was red and aflame. The sky was choked with black smoke and Meda was crumbling. Strange shadows that changed shape contorted in the sky. Annie stopped just short of the cliff's edge and looked behind her to see a flickering red and orange wall.

A screech erupted from within the inferno, and a great hawk soared out of the canopy. Its body was the size of a station wagon, the feathers were tendrils of flame, and the eyes burned white.

A phoenix?

Annie felt her body clench with fear as the yellow bird dove toward her. It was almost upon her when Annie took a step backward. Her foot found only air. She lost her balance and fell toward the flaming valley below. The bird was screaming and flying at her as the ground rushed to meet her. Large talons made of molten rock reached out for her.

Annie jerked awake and tore the sweat-soaked covers off. The room was unusually hot. She looked at the open window and saw the red sky. Her heart skipped a beat. She ran to it, feeling as if she were still dreaming. She let out a deep breath when she realized it was only the sunrise.

She sank into a chair by the window and began biting at her nails. *I keep having that dream. Fire. And falling. Is it supposed to symbolize something? I wish I had Google so I could search for the meaning. Maybe Diana will have some sort of magical insight.*

Annie reached for the leftover bread on the table, tore off the stale end, and discarded it. She nibbled at the hunk absently while she watched the sun rise over the valley. Eventually she made her way into the washroom and cleaned herself up.

She felt her head itch, as though fleas were crawling across it. She scratched at her scalp, and somehow she knew it was Diana. A soft presence washed over her thoughts.

Ah, you are awake. Wonderful!

Yeah. Slept pretty good last night.

Well, I hope you are hungry. Big day today!

Oh, great. What are you plotting now?

You'll see.

The prickling sensation faded away and Annie rubbed her head. She was about to slide out of her simple white robe when she heard the door scrape open.

"Are you clothed?"

"Yeah, one second, Diana."

Annie tightened the robe around her and walked into the bedroom. She found the door wide open. Two guards entered carrying a large ornate chest. It was black with golden figures etched into the lid. It easily could easily have fit three people inside.

"What's this?" Annie asked as the guards set the chest down.

"Oh, you will love it, do not worry."

"Good morning, Lady Annie," Iriel said, beaming as she walked into the room with a tray of food. On her heels was a middle-aged woman who appeared to be human. Her graying hair was woven into a loose bun of braids and ornate silver leaves that hung above pale shoulders. Her blue eyes were flecked with bits of silver and green, and she had meticulously drawn black lines along the edges of her eyes.

She gave Annie a slight bow that jingled numerous baubles and gold chains around her wrists. "I am Evera Dohlomai. I am here to fit you."

Annie felt her chest tighten and she stared at the black chest with renewed suspicion.

"*Fit* me?"

"Annie, dear, Evera is a seamstress here in the palace. She has excellent taste in fashion and I think you two will get along quite well."

"Oh. More clothes?"

"Yes, Annie. You cannot have just one dress here. Truth be told, I wish we could have a lovely day shopping down in the city, but I fear that we can't waste any time. So Evera was kind enough to bring us some of her wares. I will have her measure you for new boots and more sturdy clothes as well. Something that will be easy to travel in. But for now, we want to see how pretty we can make you."

Annie narrowed her eyes. "What's the occasion?"

Evera's eyes widened and she glanced at Diana. "Oh! She does not know?"

Diana fixed her glowing eyes on Annie and smiled. "I believe our dear guest here has been so busy studying and talking with council members, I have not found the time to give her a formal invitation."

"Invitation?"

"My dear, there is going to be a feast in two days! You have been invited by the council and King Halona himself!"

"What?"

"Yes, my dear. You."

"But . . . why?"

Evera gave a small bow and said, "There has been some talk of a beautiful stranger residing on this side of the palace. It is said you have come very far. It would be wonderful for you to attend and meet the curious."

"Wait . . . this party is for me?"

Diana's eyes flickered to the floor sadly. "No, dear. It is not a party for you. But you have been invited, and you must attend. There will be many who would like to meet you. I wanted to tell you last night, but . . . well, we just didn't have time."

Annie squinted at Diana, but the elf returned the look with a frosty air. *I will tell you everything later. Not in front of this commoner, yes?*

Annie tried to push her sense of foreboding away. She reminded herself to live in the moment as Evera busied herself with strange measuring ribbons. She showed no modesty as she wrapped the ribbon around Annie's breasts and hips, and jotted down some numbers on a scrap of parchment with a red quill.

Evera walked over to the large chest and swung the lid open. It was stuffed to the brim with an assortment of colorful dresses. Evera and Iriel began placing the dresses on the bed. Some were lace, while other patches of color looked silky. They were all beautiful in a strange way. The cut of the dresses seemed to closely mimic Renaissance or ancient Greek garb. The cloth was meant to drape heavily and cover the chest and legs, but often came with a sash to secure around the waist.

Evera had Annie remove her shift, then wrapped an odd corset around her and pulled the strings in.

"Ugh, do you have to? I can't breathe in this thing."

Diana chuckled. "But Annie, dear, this is the fashion."

"Men like skinny chicks where I'm from, too, but that doesn't matter to me. How am I supposed to do anything with this wrapped around my lungs?"

Evera paused and gave Diana an uneasy look.

"This is just for a night, dear. You will look amazing, trust me."

"I don't care how I look," Annie muttered.

They spent the better part of the morning fitting Annie with various dresses. She particularly liked one puffy dress with a soft silver lining and a golden lace veil that ran over the silken fabric. It gave the impression the dress was woven with gold leaves and vines swirling over the silver. It was low cut, and accented with pearls and blue gems.

"Yes, that is perfect." Diana nodded approvingly and gave Annie a proud smile. "You look like royalty, Annie."

"Aye. It fits her just right. She is about the same size as the king's sister. I won't have to take up the measurements at all. Long as she wears her undergarments, it will fit like a dream."

Great, Annie thought. But she still smiled and gave a small twirl. The dress caught the light and shimmered softly. The blue gems twinkled and gave the impression of falling rain on the golden vines.

I've got to admit, this isn't so bad. I don't have to wear a corset every day, so I guess it's okay for just one party. I've only been here a few days and I'm already invited to one. Cool.

Annie carefully slid out of the silver and gold dress and handed it back to Evera. She sighed with relief as the corset was removed. Evera gave her some simple flat sandals that were mostly ribbons. The only real part of the shoe was the sole, while the ribbons gracefully snaked between her toes, around her heel, and up her legs in a style that reminded her of ballerina slippers.

At least they aren't uncomfortable like high heels, Annie thought.

Evera had Annie walk around the room some and adjusted the ribbons several times. Finally she removed the shoes and set them to the side.

"You will look like one of Halona's long-lost sisters. It is just amazing how well these fit you. I will work on the traveling clothes and bring them back in two days. And I will also bring some cheek and eye paint."

Eye paint?

Evera shuffled out of the room, beaming with delight. The guards entered, picked up the chest, and followed her down the hall.

"Two days, huh? Hak leaves in three days, right?"

"Yes."

"And you think I'm going to go with him?"

"It is your choice, Annie. Give me more time with Aiyana. I do not want to force you to go with Hakayatas."

"Do you really think he will die on that quest?"

"Do not worry yourself with such thoughts, Annie."

"That's a *yes* where I come from."

Diana hesitated, and then turned toward the fresh food on the table. "I did not say such a thing. Hakayatas is a strong human. I believe in him. Come, let us eat breakfast and work on your healing and blocking meditations."

"What does it mean to dream of fire? And falling?"

Annie brought the memory of the dream into the forefront of her mind.

"Very good, Annie! You are better at pushing. But yes, that is a disturbing dream."

"But what does it mean?"

"Fire means change. Falling means a loss of control. As for the kayatas bird you saw . . . very strange."

Annie gasped and said, "Kayatas . . . that is the bird Hak is named for, right? It's called a phoenix where I'm from."

"It is a creature of myth that brings destruction and renewal."

"So my dream means I'm fearing change and a loss of control. And something that represents Hak is chasing me off a cliff. Is that it?"

"I would not interpret it so literally. But that is one way to look at it. And the images you showed me . . . that bird might have been trying to save you. You never truly know with dreams."

"Do you guys take much stock in dreams and their meanings on Tahldia?"

"Yes, we do. But we often meditate on them for days. There is meaning within meaning. Dreams come from the current."

"I have another question. Something that's been bugging me."

"Please ask."

"What is the difference between a warlock and a mage?" Annie asked, half fearing that some sort of mind block would cause her pain.

"That is a good question, but I do not know if I can have a proper answer. That is like comparing an infant to a skilled swordsman. In simplest terms, it is a difference of blood."

"Like genetics? Breeding?"

"Yes. Warlocks have a natural ability to mold mana currents to their minds. They are very powerful. A warlock's skill is unique to the family line, and passed down to their offspring."

"Skill? What can they do?"

"Hmmm, well . . . some warlocks were renowned for flight, viewing the future, or twisting rock like water in a stream. It is said that long ago, there were a few warlock leaders who could control the undead, or summon fearsome beasts from beyond the stars. Those warlocks were the most dangerous."

"But they look like regular people?"

"Yes."

"How can you tell if someone is a warlock and not just some mage?"

"They are usually taller than most, and have thin builds. Some scholars say yellow eye color is the hallmark of a warlock. But that is not always true, yes? Look at poor Hakayatas; he is definitely not a warlock. To assume someone is a warlock because of yellow eyes is like assuming someone with dark skin comes from Taui.

"Warlocks lived throughout Tahldia long ago. They normally breed with soul mates. But some have bred with regular humans, and some of the traits, such as height and yellow eyes, have made their way into the regular population. But that is extremely rare. Warlocks are not very fertile, Annie. Aiyana's family was a special exception."

"Maybe Hak had some distant relative a long time ago that was a warlock?"

"It is possible. But if he had any real power, he would have been hunted down and killed long ago. There are very few left alive that we know of."

"Why are they all dead?"

"That is a long story. If I must summarize, I will say that the warlocks were once a very proud tribe. They often used their powers for black magic as well as the healing arts. They were an aggressive people long ago. They caused many of the ancient wars. Shafani myth states that the world broke into three continents because a warlock lost control of his summoned beast. Stories meant to scare children.

"Of course, most humans only focus on the negative side of things, twisting reality with superstition. When I was young, there were still many warlocks, but they were feared and mistrusted. A very misunderstood people."

"Ironic."

"What's that?"

"Well, Aiyana hates the Shafani. She fears and mistrusts all of them, it sounds like. And yet she is a warlock."

"I would not point that out to her, Annie."

She snorted. "Wouldn't dream of it."

"A warlock is very powerful, Annie. When they try to merge with regular society, they hide their true strength. The council seems to think much of Aiyana's power comes from the zythil jewelry she wears. But that is just part of her illusion. She doesn't need magical enhancement to do anything the council can do."

Diana rested her narrow face against her long fingers and stared down at the pipe on the table for a long while.

Finally her large purple eyes flickered to Annie. "You smoked a lot last night, yes?"

Annie paused with a spoon of oatmeal halfway to her mouth. "Yeah. So?"

"It is interesting, yes?"

"What do you mean?"

"Well, it seems Aiyana knew you would enjoy that all too well. And Iriel has informed me that you have quite the thirst for fae water."

"It's the best stuff I've ever had. It's a million times better than whiskey. And I don't get sick or hungover."

"Yes, well . . . you should not grow so attached to fae water. You like getting very intoxicated, yes? That is not a good habit, Annie."

Annie frowned and began eating again. She kept her eyes on the oatmeal. *Oh my god, she is totally going into mom mode again.*

"Annie, I have a question for you. I have seen into your memories some, yes? But I am curious to know how long you have been muddling up your mind with intoxicants."

"Hey now! That was just a short experimental phase in college."

"I am referring to the smoking and drinking. You started drinking young, yes? A few years after your teacher died?"

"My teacher?"

"Maz. Aiyana told me he taught you magic. You were very close to him, yes? And you began drinking heavily after he passed to the stars."

"So? I wasn't hurting anybody."

"You had trouble at home as well. Difficulties with your parents?"

"My stepdad and I didn't always get along, but it was never bad. He didn't beat me or anything." Annie paused and felt her face twisting into an angry grimace. *At least, not really.*

"What about your real father?"

"Screwed us over. Ran off on my mom before I was born." Annie laced her tone with sharp edges. She didn't like to think about those early years, and her mother's emotional state. Her mom had spun wildly between depression and fury. If there had been a spark that caused Annie's distrust with men and most people, those years were the flint and tinder.

"I see. Many problems with family. And you drank an excessive amount."

"So?"

"You were hiding your current. Aiyana told me that you were taught magic, but the memories have been blocked from you. I can imagine that would be stressful, yes?"

"Honestly Diana, I don't remember anything of the sort. Wasn't that the point? I don't remember being upset because of my lack of magic."

"Of course you don't, dear. But subconsciously, I think you were trying to muddle your connection with the current. Something deep within you was hurting, and you hid from that."

"I didn't know I was hiding from anything."

"Hmmm. It is a theory. Regardless, getting intoxicated constantly can ruin your connection. You must be more careful."

"No more booze?"

"I did not say that. But do not be so eager to reach for fae water when something troubles you. Learn to face it with a clear mind, and accept the current's energies."

"You make it sound so easy."

"I think you will find it easier with time. It feels good to dull the senses, yes? I have had plenty of experiences with too much wine and dancing myself." The elf gave Annie a mischievous grin.

"Well, okay, fine. I'll try and take it easy on the fae water and this weird herb stuff Aiyana gave me. But I am going to have a good time at that party."

"Just do not make a scene."

"No way. I won't dance on any tables, okay? Just a few drinks. Oh man! I'm going to a party with a king!" Annie grinned and clapped her hands over her reddening cheeks. "I mean . . . what do you say to a king?"

Diana let out a delighted giggle. "We will have to work on social graces just a little. Maybe tonight after training, I can show you a few dance steps, yes?"

"That would be awesome."

"You are a funny human, Annie. I have grown fond of you. You have transformed since arriving. You seem . . . happier."

"A little, yeah."

"But Hakayatas bothers you, yes? You are worried."

"Hey now. That's getting a little too nosy."

"Why do you hide what you feel, Annie?"

"Dude . . . please. Let's change the subject."

"Why not just talk to him? At the very least, say what you have been thinking?"

"Diana." Annie laced her tone with venom and glared at the elf.

"You drink to hide from your current. You fool your own brain into hiding what it thinks and feels. You just like to hide, Annie. It is not healthy for your spirit to do such contradictory things. I will not push you any further on the matter, but please, bear in mind that these behaviors prevent you from reaching your full potential. You hold yourself back. At the very least, make peace with him."

Annie glowered at her plate and tried to stare holes into it. She bit her lip and was proud she held her temper in check.

"Annie, I have seen into that man's mind. He has been worried for you. He yearns to talk to you."

"Ugh! Diana, *please*!"

The elf gazed at Annie coolly.

Annie looked at her food for a long while. Finally she whispered, "Is he a good guy, Diana?"

"Of course he is, Annie. He is one of the better human men that I have met. You already know this."

Annie felt her lip twist into a small smile, but she said nothing.

"He scared you when you first met him. But he has proven himself to be a good companion, yes? He has a good heart. Do not be scared to love, Annie."

"Whoa, whoa, *whoa*! I didn't say anything about love!"

"You can love someone without wanting to mate with them, Annie. Elves give love freely. There is no shame in that. If only humans learned how to do it half as well."

"He thinks about me, huh?"

"Yes." Diana gave her a smirk. "Very much."

"Crap." *No brain, no. Don't get all mushy and stupid on me.*

"Come, let us go to the gardens for a while. Put these thoughts away for now. I have more surprises for you."

"Oh, goody."

They spent another long afternoon practicing different forms of meditation. After many hours, Annie still felt as though she was unable to do anything without getting frustrated and angry. Diana was patient as always, and Annie was grateful for it.

Toward the end of the afternoon, Diana insisted on teaching Annie a few dance steps. They were easy to follow, but Annie still felt herself stepping on the elf's feet half the time. Diana encouraged her and beamed proudly as Annie perfectly recited several proper greetings.

"I wonder what you guys would do about break dancing."

"What is that?"

Annie pushed a memory to Diana. She had to admit, she was finding it easier.

Diana laughed at the memory of three dancers Annie had seen at a club five months back. "My my, that is . . . rather interesting. Were those people well?"

Annie let out a deep laugh. "Oh man, I wondered sometimes. But yeah, I'll try not to attempt that at the party."

"Might be for the best."

They walked back into the castle and made their way to Annie's room, laughing and sharing memories with each other. Diana shared a few memories of a night dancing in the forest with dozens of elves and dwarves. There were strange instruments and everyone seemed to be drinking wine and laughing.

"Man . . . I want to explore this world so bad. That looks like fun."

"Someday, yes? It would be fun, I think, to take you home and introduce you to my brothers. My family comes from the mountains in the far north."

"Near Feldall?"

"Yes."

"Diana?"

"Yes, Annie?"

"Can you help me get out of here? Please? Can you take me to your homeland now?"

"I am afraid I cannot do that, Annie. But I appreciate the trust you bestow upon me to confide such a risk. I will not mention to Aiyana you said that."

"You seem cool, Diana. I just don't trust that old woman. She's using Hak. How do I know she's not using me?"

"She means well, Annie. Keep in mind that she thinks this trip is for your own good, as well as for Hakayatas. You want to explore Tahldia. The Fieriel Senefal is supposed to be one of the five wonders of the world. Why not venture to a place that few ever get to see?"

"Because it sounds deadly as hell?"

"There are risks, yes. But you would see a great many sights from the back of a griffin."

"A griffin? Seriously?"

"They are fun to fly on. I will take you by the stables tomorrow. They are very sweet creatures. Loyal and fierce in battle."

"Wow . . . okay. I'll check them out. But that doesn't mean I'll go with Hak."

"Of course not, dear."

They opened the door to Annie's room and she gasped. Tia practically knocked her over. The dog ran in several excited circles around the room, wrinkling the carpets and nearly knocking over the small nightstand by the bed. Nivya was sitting at the table with a book. She stood, walked over to Annie, and took her hand.

"I hope you do not mind, Annie. Diana said you missed her and—"

"Oh my god, thank you!" Annie gave Nivya a fierce hug. She squeaked with surprise but returned the embrace.

"She is happy to see you, yes?"

Tia bounced around the room and pushed up against Annie's legs. She reached down and hugged the dog for a long time. She scratched her ears and buried her face into the soft black fur.

"Annie, dear, Aiyana has been kind enough to ensure you can have Tia here for a night or two."

"Your dog has been such a wonder, Annie. She curls up with me each night and accompanies me on my morning walks. She has been a joy to have. After Viv passed away, it has been a blessing to have Tia around. I will be happy to watch her anytime for you."

Diana reached down and touched Tia's nose. The dog eagerly sniffed her long fingers and then sneezed.

"Iriel also loves dogs, Annie. She will be happy to watch over Tia while you train with me. I just felt that you needed something to cheer you up and ease your mind."

"Oh man, thank you. Really. I half felt that I wouldn't see her again."

"I should be getting home," Nivya said. "I have a practice tomorrow that I must study for."

Annie hugged her again. "Thank you so much, Nivya. I really appreciate it."

"I will leave you as well, Annie. I imagine you will want to eat dinner and rest by yourself. Tomorrow will be another long day. Think on all we talked about today, yes?"

"Sure."

They shut the door. Annie turned and looked down at her dog. Tia's tail wagged furiously and she jumped up and tried to lick Annie's face. She danced around the room for several minutes, letting Tia chase her. She collapsed with her on the floor and wrestled with her. The dog weighed almost as much as Annie, and had an easy time wiggling out of her grasp.

Annie laughed and spent the rest of the evening scratching Tia's ears and giving her belly rubs. She lived in the moment, and did not think too much about the intimidating days ahead.

The following day Annie took a long walk with the elves and Tia, and then spent the entire day studying. With only a small break for dancing lessons, Annie was forced to try to learn magic in the garden. She felt like a failure by the end of the day once again.

She also felt increasingly anxious about the council and her decision. She knew that the day after the ball, they would meet in the council chambers. She dreaded the day with increasing pressure in her chest.

Despite all the trouble that she had gone through, she also found herself missing Hak. She missed his smile, and his deep laugh. She still, on occasion, thought of kissing him. Annie knew Diana was right. She needed to talk to him, and soon. She feared she would never see him again.

At dinner that evening, Annie looked over the plate of roasted vegetables and fresh bread and fixed her eyes on Diana. "I want to talk with Hak. Can you bring him here tonight?"

"I am afraid I cannot, Annie. He is training deep within the mountain right now."

"Oh."

"I am pleased you want to get some weight off your heart, however. You will see him tomorrow at the ball. After all, it is being held in his honor."

"Really?"

"Oh yes. The Fieriel Senefal is a most important mission. He will get a hero's send-off."

"The way he talks, I thought no one liked him."

"That is not true. Some of the council members do not like him, but King Halona thinks highly of Hakayatas, despite him being Shafani. A true credit to how gracious the king can be. And Hakayatas is attempting something that has not been done in a hundred years."

"What's going to happen down there? What is it?"

Diana's eyes flickered to her food, and she bit her lip. "We will be discussing it in the council meeting soon enough. We have all been busy studying ancient texts and trying to discern the meaning of them."

"You said something lived in that cave he has to go to."

"Ah . . . yes."

"What is it? A monster?"

Diana hesitated, and didn't meet Annie's gaze. "It is said a demigod resides at the heart of the current."

"A demigod? Is that like . . . a demon?"

"No. It is a neutral entity. It is neither light nor darkness. It is neither good nor evil. It is something born from the current with a will of its own."

"What does he need to do?"

"Annie. Focus on the moment. Trust in your destiny. You will find out at the meeting. I know Mau and the other council members have not left their studies since the day you met with them. We will be pooling our knowledge together tomorrow. There is much information that has been lost to time."

Diana refused to say any more about the subject. She busied herself after the meal with the new dress and shoes Annie was to wear the next day. She doted on her and tried to put her mind at ease, but Annie couldn't help feeling a horrible twisting sensation deep in the pit of her stomach. She thought she knew what she wanted to do. She thought it would be easy to say no to Aiyana. But her thoughts washed over one another like the pounding waterfall outside.

What do I really want out of life?

All of her emotions swirled together in a churning, white-water rush. She curled up in a tight ball on the bed and wrapped her arms around Tia. Annie found it almost impossible to sleep that night.

CHAPTER TWELVE:

DECISIONS

"DO I HAVE to wear this?" Annie asked as Iriel tied a corset around her. The small elf blinked uneasily and wiped a strand of black hair from her violet eyes. She looked over at Diana, who was standing by the window.

"It is the fashion, dear." Diana pulled the front of her velvet dress down slightly to flash her own black corset. She gave Annie a wicked grin.

Diana made Paris runway models look like clumsy oafs. She seemed at ease in her ankle-length red gown embroidered with hundreds of small dark crystals. Her black hair was curled tightly against her head and held in place with a silver tiara made in the shape of a dozen feathers.

Diana poured a glass of wine and handed it to Annie. "We should have a toast, my friend."

Iriel smiled shyly as Annie took the heavy handblown glass. Diana poured a glass and held it out to the young elf, and then poured one for herself.

She raised the glass high and smiled. "To Annie Armstrong, Hakayatas Flamefeather, and the Fieriel Senefal. May fate and the stars smile upon you, now and forever."

Annie bit her lip, but raised her drink against theirs. She gulped the wine down, placed the nearly empty glass on the table, and let out a deep breath.

Iriel took a small sip and went to retrieve the silver-and-gold dress.

Diana said, "Do not worry. I know you are still undecided. It is still all right to toast good fate, yes?"

Annie made a face and slipped into the dress Iriel held out for her. She was still annoyed that she had to return Tia to Nivya earlier that day.

"Annie. Live in the moment, my dear. You will have fun tonight," Diana said.

"The council meets tomorrow?"

"Yes . . . My, those blue gems look so nice on you. They match your eyes. Let me fashion your hair and paint your face myself."

Diana pulled up a chair with magic and sat Annie down in it. She brushed out Annie's hair and hummed to herself gently.

"You guys have been the only nice people here. Thank you, Diana."

"What? Aiyana was not nice?"

"I don't trust Aiyana."

"What about that woman Nivya, who watches over Tia at this moment? And Hakayatas? Many people care for you, Annie."

"Yeah, Nivya's a blessing to have. Tia is safer with her than me right now." Annie closed her eyes and enjoyed Diana's calm brush strokes. "And Hak . . . I still think he's an asshole for not telling me everything. But . . . you're right, I want to talk with him."

"You will forgive him, then?"

"I didn't say that."

"Talking is good."

"I wish he didn't have to go on that quest."

"It is all his heart desires. We could not stop him from going if we wanted to. He wants his mana back."

"It's stupid."

"No, dear. To be powerful and to feel the current within you is to truly feel alive. You can feel the power of the stars flood your body. To have that cut off is like a living death. Now, open your eyes, Annie."

Annie looked in the mirror and gasped. Her hair was curled and magically enhanced to stay in place. Somehow the elf had created an effect like hairspray to give the curls a stiff hold. Diana placed a small silver band around Annie's head to keep the hair out of her face, then flashed one of her mischievous grins and put a small bag on the dresser. "You have had your face painted before, yes?"

"You mean makeup?"

"What a strange name for it." Diana pulled out a small vial of beige paste and began brushing it against Annie's cheeks with a small bit of magic.

"Hey speaking of strange, I have a question."

"Yes?"

"Diana is a lovely name, don't get me wrong, but I'm wondering how you got it."

"Ah. I was named for an elven queen who lived long ago. It was said that she brought peace to the humans and elves."

"Huh. It's a really common name on Earth."

"You have known many Dianas? That is interesting. Perhaps the first Diana was not from Earth?"

"What?"

"Maybe the name was introduced to Earth, Annie."

"I wonder how. I thought only warlocks could hop around."

"Careful how freely you talk like that, my dear. You are privy to some information that most would not believe in. The knowledge of world-traveling has been gone for millennia. Those who still know about it prefer to keep it a secret. But yes, there was some mingling between planets a long time ago. Warlocks opened the gates."

A million questions bubbled up in Annie's mind. "Whoa, really? When was this, exactly? Why did they stop? Is this why we share a common language? Is that why beasts like griffins are seen in ancient myth—"

Diana sighed and held up a hand. "Stop. That is a story for another time, Annie. The elves guard such secrets closely. It is so complicated that I would not know where to begin. It is not a happy tale. I would not trouble you with it this evening. You must live in the moment tonight."

"So our worlds were connected once. We shared knowledge and language —"

"Annie." Diana's tone was firm. There wouldn't be a discussion about old secrets.

Annie sighed and closed her eyes as Diana traced over her eyelids with a small black stick. When she opened her eyes again, she was shocked to see how far the eyeliner went. It was almost comical, like the ancient Egyptian art she had seen.

"You are not used to *makeup*, yes?"

"It's a little more than I would usually put on, but it's cool. When in Rome, right?"

"Rome?"

"It's just a saying. It's a city on Earth."

Diana gave her a funny look and put the bag away. "Hmmm. When the time is right, I would love to talk Earth history with you, Annie. The name Romen is quite common here as well."

"Please. I want to know more about our histories! If you won't tell me about how our worlds were connected, at least tell me about your home. And like, all the stories elves have. I want to hear about what it was like growing up an elf."

"Ah yes, soon enough."

"We need to have a girl's night sometime soon, Diana. Please?"

"What do you mean?"

"It means we sit around and eat really rich food, gossip and play games, and wear the most comfortable clothes ever. No corsets!"

"I would like that, I think."

"Iriel can come, too."

Iriel brightened and said, "I think that would be nice. We all have been training very hard. I want to hear more stories of Earth . . . Diana has not mentioned them to me." There was a slight edge to her voice, as if the elf may have been annoyed at being kept in the dark about Earth's existence.

"We will have to plan a night then, to have fun and be silly. I think I would like that very much. But as for rich food, I think we will find many culinary delights in the ballroom. Are you ready to go, Annie?"

Annie bit her lip and looked at the last inch of wine in her glass. She finished it off, took a deep breath, and looked at her strange reflection in the mirror.

"Yeah. Let's do this. How far is the ballroom?"

"It is at the very top of this cliff."

"That's a long walk!"

"No, we will take the lift."

"You guys have elevators here?"

"Uh, I am not sure what that is, Annie. We have what is called a lift. A small room that moves up and down a shaft. It was a dwarven concept using rope and pulleys, but we use enchantments these days to power them."

"Cool. That will make things a little easier tonight. These sandals don't really have any padding to them."

"Just remember, the moment is all that matters. Focus on what will make *you* happy."

The ballroom was a large, cavernous chamber close to the top of the cliff. Crimson silks outlined with gold were draped over the glittering, mica-flecked stone walls. Several balconies opened to the green valley below, and the sky was awash with the fading colors of the sunset. The warm glow from the sky seemed to melt into the torchlight in the room. There were several crystal lights that hovered in midair and gave off a soft yellow flame. Annie was mesmerized by the enchantment.

On the other side of the room, a small band played a happy melody. The sound of flutes, violins, and a large string instrument that sounded like a bass guitar flooded the room. Nearly a hundred people had gathered to feast and dance, and the room was full of talk and raucous laughter. Men and women garbed in periwinkle, forest green, cobalt, and fuchsia seemed to float along the red-and-gold carpets. Annie found it challenging to follow all the conversations around her, and tried not to gawk at a table of dwarves near the balcony.

Farther down the walls she could see a dozen tall, well-muscled people with rich, varied shades of chestnut skin sitting at a round table. Their faces were all high cheek bones and sharp angles. The women wore green and yellow silks cut daringly low at the bodice and high on their chiseled thighs. Half of them had very short hair shaved in tribal shapes. Annie could easily see the bright jade tint of their eyes in the soft torchlight. Diana had told her the stiff-backed, confident people were emissaries from Taui. They kept stealing furtive looks at Annie, and she felt her stomach curl uneasily when her eyes met theirs.

Annie was pleased to sit between Diana and a tall man with a well-trimmed goatee and black hair. He appeared to be around Hak's age, with just the smallest hints of silver in his beard and subtle wrinkles in his sun-browned skin. Annie found it difficult to make eye contact with him. Aiyana and several council members were sitting at the end of the long table. Her face was stern, and she seemed to be mind-speaking to a sullen-looking Mau. Aiyana reached out with a bejeweled hand and patted his arm; he glared distastefully at the full wineglass in his gnarled fingers.

Annie stole several glances down the table at Hak, who was seated next to the king himself and one of his sisters. She tried to catch his eye several times since he had entered the ballroom, but he kept his attention fixed on the king. They ducked their heads together in a spirited conversation while the king's sister watched with amusement.

Hak was clean-shaven, with his long blond hair tied back in a fancy blue ribbon. It matched his dark blue jacket that was embroidered with golden thread and white lace cuffs. The collar was high and frilly enough to cover most of his neck scars. Annie found the formal attire goofy-looking on the tough man. But she admitted that he seemed genuinely happy.

Annie's head prickled suddenly, and she turned to look at Diana. The elf was purposefully watching the musicians as she spoke in Annie's mind. *Do not worry, Annie. I am sure you can steal a dance with him later.*

Who said I'm worried? Annie gave Diana a small grin. *I'm here to have fun.*

Of course, dear.

What's the name of the guy next to me again?

He is Layn Halona'tak, dear. A distant cousin of Gaeric's and the dragon general for the air guard. He looks grumpy, but he will not bite you.

Annie giggled. Layn turned to her and gave a small smile. She blushed and quickly turned her eyes to her half-finished dinner. The meat had been soaked in wine and unfamiliar herbs, and the vegetables were roasted and buttery soft, but Annie felt the meal lacked something. There wasn't enough salt and spice in Median cuisine to suit her taste.

Layn patted his lips with a napkin and said, "So, how have you enjoyed Meda so far?"

"It's really nice. There's a lot to see and do here."

"I hear you have traveled far?"

"Yes, my lord."

Annie knew the drill. Diana had given her some lessons on etiquette, but more important, what *not* to say. By now, everyone knew she had traveled from a place called Oregon, but Diana and Aiyana had dismissed it as a small village deep in the mountains near the border with Taui. They had urged her to be as vague as possible, and to change the subject quickly.

"Will you be staying for the Saints' Day feast here in two weeks?"

"I believe so. Tell me about Saints' Day."

"Ahhh, it is a wonderful event. We dress up in the guise of our favorite saints. There will be much dancing and giving thanks to the stars. I have had my Orionus costume prepared for months now. His sword is always so difficult to replicate. What is your saint, Annie?"

"Ah, I never really thought about it."

"Surely you have a saint! Everyone has one, you know."

Annie hesitated and glanced at Diana. She was chatting with the woman next to her about the latest fashion trends in Osmek. Annie turned back to Layn and bit her lip. After an awkward pause, Layn's eyes softened with a smile.

"What does Annie mean, if I might be so bold to ask. It is an unusual name, yes?"

"It means grace . . . uh, graceful, I think." Annie resisted the urge to pick at a fingernail.

"Ah, that is delightful. A fitting name for such a fine lady."

Annie felt her face grow hot and reached for her wine. "Um, thanks. Thank you, my lord."

Servants bustled about them, refilling goblets and clearing away dirty plates. Annie allowed them to fill her goblet for the second time.

Remember not to drink too much, Annie.

I won't, Diana, don't worry. I don't want to do anything stupid. I'm a pro.

Annie drank deeply the moment Diana turned away. She felt tipsy, and was glad for it. *I feel like a fish out of water here,* she thought to herself.

Diana discreetly jiggled a finger and moved Annie's wineglass several inches away with magic. *You must save room for dessert. I think you will be pleased to know that Hakayatas had a say in what they would be serving tonight.*

Annie reached out with her hand and pulled the wineglass toward her. *Oh?*

Trust me, you will like it. Oh, here it comes now!

Annie watched nervously as a young servant lowered a small plate onto the table in front of her. The dessert was some sort of black cake covered with a red glaze.

Oh! No way! Is that chocolate?

Diana laughed and gave Annie's shoulder a small squeeze. *It is a common delicacy where you are from, yes?*

Yeah. It's my favorite thing to eat! Annie tentatively took a small bite and sighed with ecstasy. The red glaze reminded her of tart strawberries, and the cake was on par with her favorite bakery. It appeared that there was not a shortage of sugar, cream, or butter in Meda. She caught Hak watching her from the end of the table; she gave him a huge grin and pointed at the cake. He smiled warmly.

Diana lightly tapped her plate. *It is good, yes?*

Oh man . . . you guys are never going to get rid of me.

Imagine all the cake you can have if you return triumphant.

Annie stopped chewing and gave Diana a careful look. *Did I say I was going?*

No. But I can sense the turmoil in your heart.

Hey. I'll figure it out. Aren't I supposed to be living in the moment?

Annie, dear, are you . . . getting drunk?

Nope.

Diana shot her a flat stare.

Whatever. It's cool, Diana. I'm having fun. Living in the moment, you know. Annie tried to imagine pushing Diana out of her head. She then tried to imagine stuffing her thoughts deep down and covering them. She pulled in her awareness and imagined setting up a wall around her mind. Then she thought, *I don't know what I want to do. The fact I'm unsure is really unsettling . . . Why is it so hard to make up my mind?*

"You're getting a little better," Diana said, returning to her cake with a frustrated glare. She watched Annie wolf down the cake and the rest of her wine in silence.

"I have a good teacher," Annie whispered. "I think it's a lot of instinct, too."

A burst of laughter from Hak's end of the table drew her attention.

Halona stood and the music ceased. The chatter and laughter in the room quickly hushed.

"Illuyeh ata. I would like to thank you all tonight for coming. Stars shine on Lohel'ein, Dohlen, and Taui. I am honored to be with you this fair evening! Let us toast to the travelers among us! As you are all aware, I am not the sort to bore you with long-winded toasts, so please! Continue to feast and drink, and let us dance! The stars watch over all of us tonight, and always."

The room erupted in cheering and toasting.

"Ata'vierna Gaeric Halona!"

"May the stars bless your path!"

The music began again and several people made their way to the center of the room.

Annie leaned over to Diana and whispered, "I thought this was a party for Hak?"

Annie could almost feel the elf knock at her mind, tentatively poking at her thoughts to gain entry. It felt like a gentle push inside her temples. Annie imagined lowering the mental barricade.

It is *a feast for Hak, dear,* Diana said in Annie's mind. *But the Fieriel Senefal is not a known custom to those here who do not practice magic. As you know, Hakayatas is rather shy about his past, and I am sure he is content not being the center of attention. Many here do not know his story. Hak prefers to keep it that way. Halona honors this, yes?*

I guess. It just seems weird to me.

Annie dear, this room has seen countless feasts in your lifetime. They have a feast every week. This is a casual affair, yes?

Annie laughed. *Casual? This is pretty fancy for me.*

You haven't seen a real feast yet. Wait until King Halona gets married. That will be a party to gossip about in old age.

Annie watched as the empty space in front of the musicians filled with dancers. She watched in amazement as two elves swirled about each other effortlessly. They seemed to float above the floor as they moved to the tune. She noted that the dwarves and Tauians did not leave their tables to dance. They seemed content to watch and drink among themselves.

A tall man with a pinched face approached the table and gave them a bow. "Wise Diana, honor me with a dance this evening."

"Eryt, the honor would be mine. Please excuse me, Annie." Diana seemed to float away from the table, one arm intertwined with the lanky man. She looked back at Annie and gave her a wink. *This guy is such a bore.*

Good luck with that one, Annie thought to Diana. She glanced around the table awkwardly, and tried to catch Hak's eye. He was talking with Halona again.

Layn asked gently, "My lady, are you well?"

"Huh? Oh, yeah. I mean, yes, my lurd. I mean, l-lord! I, uh—" Her face burned with mortification.

"Would you honor me with a dance?"

Annie looked at her empty glass and then took the half-full one Diana had left behind. She finished it in one breath. Layn watched her with amusement.

"Yeah, let's see if I can dance without stepping on your feet. My lord." Annie hated the way the word sounded. She felt the corset squeezing tightly against her stomach. *I am just not good at this formal stuff. I'd rather have the common room at Odal's inn.*

Layn raised an eyebrow at her and led her toward the other dancers. Annie's nervousness melted away as she remembered Diana's lessons. They danced for several minutes as Annie perfected the simple toe tap every seventh step.

"You have not stepped on me once, my lady! You dance with grace." He spun his arm over her head and dipped in a low bow. Then he took both of her hands and guided her between the other dancers.

Annie glanced back over to where Hak had been seated and saw that the table was empty. Her eyes darted around the room, and she found him dancing with Halona's sister.

Annie sighed and let Layn carry her through another song. She felt the sweet buzz of wine eating away her worries and fears for the evening. The room spun pleasantly around them, and she let herself float away on a sea of music and laughter.

"Cousin, will you allow me to cut in for a dance?"

Annie turned and felt her heart clench. King Halona stood behind them, a warm smile on his lips. He was wearing his crown and some fur-trimmed clothes that were the color of a glacier. The light blue robe was open in the front, revealing a black velvet tunic and pants lined with gold thread.

Annie gave a nervous bow as Layn kissed her hand and melted into the crowd.

"I hope you do not mind my interruption," the king said as he took her hand and placed it on his shoulder. Annie blinked and stared up at him.

"It is an honor, my lord. I mean, your grace." Annie winced and bit her lip. *Was that the right word to use? Ugh, I sound like an idiot.* She glanced over and saw that Hak was now standing and talking with several men at the edge of the room. He caught her gaze for a brief moment, and then turned back to the short old man next to him.

"Hakayatas will be a hero, yes?"

Annie gave King Halona a searching look.

"He is going to the Fieriel Senefal. It will be a wonder when he returns. There is so much I am curious about. I wish I could see the place myself."

"Why don't you?" Annie asked, and then caught herself. "I mean, is it possible to go there, your grace?"

"Sadly, I cannot. There is much I would like to see of the world, but the council keeps me rather busy these days, it seems. I hear they have been talking with you?"

"Yes, your grace. They have been very . . . kind."

"That is good to hear. You must know that you are welcome to stay here as long as you like."

Annie gave the king a searching look. "I am?"

He grinned and nodded. His hands gently squeezed hers. "I have been told you have traveled very far, and need a new home. Wise Diana has told me some of your predicament."

"What did she say, your grace?"

"She merely informed me that you had lost your family, and that you had been wandering, lost, for a long time. Hakayatas found you and brought you here, yes?"

Annie winced at the mention of her family. "Yeah."

"I apologize, that was rude of me. Surely you have been sparring with questions since the moment you arrived in Meda. In my haste to ask my own, I lost my manners. Please know that I would like to help you, if I can."

"I would like to stay here, your grace. Meda is a beautiful city, and I want to visit the libraries and learn more about history and magic."

"Is that so? That's wonderful you want to study. Let Diana know if there is anything your heart desires, and she will see to it. She is like a second mother to me. She has been helping my family since my father's father."

I wonder what she does? I thought she was only involved with the council? Or maybe it's the same thing? Geez, I wish I could just fire away with my questions and not sound like a complete idiot. If I have to give him another honorific I think I'll barf.

Annie let the king spin her around into another slow set of steps. She focused on the strange five-three-five pattern her feet made and allowed herself a smile as she remembered Diana's patient instruction.

"My lady, I hope you will be attending the Saints' Day feast as well."

"Oh, don't I need a costume?"

"You do not have one? I will have to talk to Lilai. I imagine she has several spares. My sister never seems to stop collecting Aquaria costumes."

"That would be kind of you, your grace. I hear it will be a very fun party."

Halona gave her a merry laugh. The song ended, and Annie gave him a deep bow. Suddenly the king didn't seem like such a daunting figure to her. The pale man struck her as kindly, like a boy next door. She nervously wondered if she had done anything to offend anyone yet.

I'd like to go one night without drama. It would be nice.

"My lady, it was an honor." The king clasped her hand gently for a moment, gave her a slight nod, and melted into the crowd.

Annie stood there for a moment, not sure what to do. She picked at a nail and looked around. Diana was intertwined with an ebony-skinned elf in an exquisite emerald dress. They were gazing intensely at each other and smiling like old lovers. Her silver hair was almost long enough to touch the floor. Annie watched them wistfully for a moment, and then looked around quickly for Hak.

Did he leave already? Where did he go? The guy is the size of a tower, how could he just vanish?

Annie slowly backed away from the other dancers until she felt the wall behind her. She tried to look aloof, but inside her heart was racing. *Maybe talking to him was a bad idea.*

Then she caught sight of Hak's ponytail as he made his way through the throng toward the balcony. She took a deep breath and forced her legs to move in that direction. She walked out on the wide balcony and found Hak leaning against the railing, his back to her.

"I-i-it's a nice party."

Hak turned his head at the sound of her voice and gave a sad smile.

"What are you doing out here? Can I join you?"

"Of course. I just needed to get away from the politics for a little while."

"It's a nice view," Annie said hesitantly, looking at the steep drop and feeling dizzy. She saw a soft shimmer in front of her and tentatively reached out. Her hand found a firm, invisible surface a few inches away from the railing. It glimmered brightly as she pressed against it.

Must be there to keep the drunks from falling off. Magic is so cool.

She stood there awkwardly for a moment, and then leaned against the marble railing. She avoided Hak's eyes, tracing her finger along the invisible barrier and marveling at the soft light her hands created as she stroked the surface.

"You look nice, Annie."

"Ah, thanks."

She bit her lip and felt him staring at her. Her stomach did a small twist. The music in the room started up into another slow melody.

"Um, Hak? Do you want to go in there and dance?"

"I need some fresh air. It is too stuffy inside for my tastes."

"Oh . . . okay."

"But we can dance out here, yes?"

Annie smiled as Hak took her hands and placed one on his shoulder, and the other on his waist. His large hand encircled her cinched waist, and Annie felt herself blush.

"I really suck at dancing. Be careful, I might step on your feet."

"I think I will suffer through it just fine. I am not well-practiced myself."

She giggled despite her nerves and burning cheeks, and let Hak lead her in a gentle but clumsy dance. She stepped on his foot, and he bumped into her hip. Annie tripped and almost fell over, but Hak caught her. They looked at each other and laughed.

"You're as bad as me!"

"Oh come now, you do well, Annie."

She giggled uncontrollably for a moment, and pressed her forehead against Hak's velvet coat. *Big, stubborn oaf . . . It feels so good to be around him.*

"Have you had much to drink this evening?"

"I haven't started singing on a table yet, have I?"

Hak laughed and twirled her into a slow spin. "That would be a sight to see."

"Someone actually called me graceful this evening." Annie laughed, remembering the first time she had talked to Hak about the meaning of her name. He had teased her.

"Well, I think you are becoming quite graceful. Meda seems to suit you."

"I like a lot of things here. But . . ."

She looked up at Hak and found her tongue tied up in knots.

"You are still homesick, yes?"

Annie shook her head. The wine was making it hard to talk. "It's not that. Yeah, I miss home. I still find this whole thing about Tahldia being real . . . it's crazy. But . . . I just, I feel awful. For yelling at you. And . . . I don't know . . ."

Hak paused and looked down at her with soft eyes.

"I owe you an apology, Hak. You saved my life. You brought me here. It hasn't been all fun and games, and I really wish you had told me the truth. But a part of me is ready to admit now that I might have just run away from you if I had known everything."

"I did not want to hurt you."

"I know. I can see that now. I mean . . . I have a bad temper. And I've been really stressed out. I just . . . I've never seen anyone die before I came here, and I saw you cut someone's head off. My own sweet dog tore out a man's throat! And then the mages poking around in my head . . . I just became kind of . . . unhinged. I snapped."

"I was just doing what I thought was right at the time. I realize things

231

should have been done differently."

"Let me ask you a question." Annie sucked in a deep breath. Their dance had dwindled to short, nervous footsteps, turning slowly under the moonlight. She felt her heart squeeze nervously under her corset.

"Shoot."

Annie grinned up at him. "You're picking up my slang pretty well."

"What is your question, Annie?"

"When we were attacked at the hot springs . . ." She trailed off and tried to fight off the mind numbing effects of the wine.

"Yes?"

"When we were attacked, and you practically carried me to Meda, did you . . . did you save my life because you care about me? Or did you save my life because I was a part of your quest?"

Hak let out a heavy sigh and gave her an anguished look. He paused their dance and looped his other hand around her waist. "Annie. How could you ask such a thing? Of course I care about you. I did not want you to be in pain."

"But wasn't I crucial to the success of your quest? They keep saying I'm some sort of key."

"Annie. I saved you because you're special to *me*. The council had nothing to do with it."

"I just started thinking . . . I felt like I was only important to your quest. That's all I was good for," she slurred.

"Do not say such things. We had many bad nights traveling, yes? But we also had many good nights."

"You consider me a friend then?"

"Of course. You no longer think I am an asshole?"

"You act like one at times, but . . . I forgive you."

Hak let out his breath and pulled her into a tight hug. She buried her face in his velvet coat and inhaled the scent of lavender and mint.

"Thank you, Annie. Your forgiveness is an honor."

Annie looked up at him and bit her lip. "Do you have to go on that quest, Hak?"

"Yes, Annie."

"Will I see you again?"

"I hope so."

Annie looked down at his coat for a moment and fixed her gaze on one of his gold buttons. She took in a deep breath and said, "I hope so, too. I want to go on another adventure with you. A safe one. I want to go do fun things like festivals and this weird Saints' Day thing everyone talks about. I want to visit the elven kingdoms. There is still so much I don't understand about your world. In a way, you've not only been a friend, but you've also been a great teacher."

"You learn quickly. Wise Diana says that you have learned mind-speaking very well. She thinks you have some well-hidden defensive abilities. I have long suspected that, but because I cannot use magic, I couldn't test my theory."

"I don't know how I do any of it, really. It's so frustrating."

"The day we met with the council, and you . . . attacked me . . . Mau had a very difficult time controlling you. He fears you, Annie."

Annie looked up at Hak with wide eyes. "I am so sorry about that! And I think I disgust Mau more than frighten him."

"You were scared, Annie. It is all right."

"No, it's not all right! I lost my temper and I hit you. A lot. I feel like a horrible person."

Hak gave her another hug. "I forgive you, Annie."

Annie returned the embrace fiercely. She didn't want it to end. *He just feels so good to be around . . . I feel high around him. Geez, am I drunk?*

"Hak?"

"Yes?"

Annie was still holding him, aware of his hands around her waist, and she gazed up into his strange yellow eyes. Her heart started racing wildly when she realized what she wanted to do. She shoved her anxiety away, reached her hands up to Hak's head, and brought his face down to kiss her.

She had to step up on the tips of her toes to reach him. She felt his body tense with shock for a brief moment, and then his arms were around her and his sun-chapped lips pressed into hers. For one brief minute, Annie felt her body buzz with energy and pleasure. Then Hak gently pulled away, sighed, and placed his hands on her shoulders.

"Annie . . . I am sorry, but we cannot do this."

Her chest felt as if it were suddenly filled with ice.

"I like you, Hak," Annie said in a quavering voice. She reached up and grabbed his hands and gave them a slight squeeze.

"Annie, we are friends. Nothing more."

"But . . ." *But Diana said . . . I thought he . . . He said he liked me!*

"You are a lovely woman, Annie. You are spirited and intelligent, and I know we will be good friends. But nothing more."

Annie tried to swallow and avoided his gaze. Her chest throbbed painfully. *Oh my god, I'm an idiot!*

"Are you well, Annie?"

She looked up at his handsome face and blurted, "I just want to kiss you again." Almost instantly she recoiled at her drunken admission.

Hak exhaled, took a step back, and removed his hands from hers. "We are too different, you and I. I have a destiny to fulfill with the Fieriel Senefal, and with those monsters in Falishan. I must stop them before they hurt anyone else."

Annie crossed her arms tightly against her chest and tried not to tremble. She looked out over the darkened valley and imagined flying away from her embarrassment.

"You are a good person, Annie. But I cannot allow myself any distractions as long as I have a duty to fulfill. Besides that, I am Shafani. I have no honor and no country right now."

"But . . . neither do I."

"We must remain friends, Annie. Nothing more. I . . . do not want to cloud our friendship. I care for you as a sister." He paused and looked uneasily around them. "I should probably go back inside. Please, excuse me."

Annie ground her teeth but said nothing. Her eyes and cheeks burned as Hak walked away. She turned, leaned against the railing, and put her face in her hands. She remained frozen for several moments.

Stupid!

She took in several shaky breaths and heard a high-pitched whimper escape her lips. She let her tears dribble down her cheeks as she tried to stay quiet. The last thing she wanted was anyone seeing her cry. The more she fought it, the easier the tears came.

Why am I such a drunken idiot? Why did do that? Why?

She wiped the back of her hand against her nose and sucked in a shaky breath. Too upset to move, she looked up at the stars and the three moons. "Are the stars really gods? Can you guys hear me? Do you even care?"

She sniffled and wiped irritably at her face. *What a stupid thing . . . stars with divine powers . . . They're just balls of burning hydrogen.* She jumped when a long-fingered hand rested on her shoulder.

"Are you well, my dear?"

Annie turned and looked up at Diana. Her purple eyes were filled with concern.

"I'm an idiot."

"No, no you are not." Diana hugged her. "Do you want to talk about it?"

"No."

"Do you want to go inside and get some more cake?"

"That definitely won't help. I . . . I want to go back to my room."

"Why, Annie, we have only been here a few hours."

"I just . . . don't feel like being at this feast anymore."

"Let me tend to your makeup first, yes? You have smeared the eye paint." Diana placed her warm fingers on Annie's face and began to gently swirl them against her cheeks. Annie felt a cool tickling sensation.

"There. You do not want to have smudges."

"Thanks."

"Shall I have Iriel prepare some fae water for you?"

"No. I need to force myself to deal with this."

Diana gave Annie another hug. "I am sorry. Human communication is just so *strange* sometimes."

"I thought . . . I thought he liked me."

"He does, Annie."

"Not like *that*. He just wants to be friends."

Diana's eyebrows wrinkled and she pursed her lips as though she had tasted something sour. "Well, my dear . . . there is no dishonor in that. Perhaps that is what it must be. You and Hakayatas make a good team. You will get past this, yes? Live in the moment, and do not worry yourself. There are plenty of men in there who would like to dance with you. Wouldn't you like to meet them? Layn in particular could not keep his eyes off you."

"I'm drunk. And I'm really frustrated right now. That's a bad combination. I should probably go back to my room before I embarrass myself further."

"As you say, Annie. I think I can usher you out of here. Eryt is rather drunk himself and I can't seem to get him away from me. I would enjoy a walk."

"Thanks, Diana."

"Here, we will take the side door and pass the servants' quarters. We will use their lift. We will not run into anyone."

Annie followed Diana through the ballroom to a narrow hallway. She kept her eyes firmly fixed on the swirling hem of Diana's dress. They walked in thoughtful silence for many minutes. As they approached the lift, Annie mulled over her conversation with King Halona. Suddenly she grinned and turned to Diana. Annie clumsily caught the elf's arm.

"Yes, Annie?"

"I was thinking. Halona said I could stay here. He practically said I could have whatever I want."

"It is true," Diana said slowly, "that Gaeric wants you to feel comfortable in his kingdom."

"Who would win in a battle of wills? Aiyana, or the king? Couldn't Halona override the council?"

"Ah, that is a tricky question." Diana paused as the door to the lift opened and a woman carrying a tray stepped out.

Annie's mind prickled. *The council and the king will work hard to come to an agreement. Discord is frowned upon, Annie.*

So? He's the king! I want to stay here. I want to hang out in your libraries and learn all I can! Maybe he can find me a job that isn't cleaning or mending clothes.

It is not so simple, Annie. If Gaeric talks with Aiyana, he will side with her. She will tell him it is a matter of security for the kingdom.

How?

They stepped into the lift and the door closed. Annie could feel them slowly descending.

"Annie, Aiyana believes you and Hakayatas could unlock some answers that will aid us in our plight with Shafan. She will most likely talk with Gaeric and convince him to agree with her. She might be doing that at this very moment."

"Why?"

"It is in her best interests to see Hakayatas succeed. And you are a part of that plan."

"I don't want to be a part of *anyone's* plan!"

"I know. But think about your friend for a moment. You want to help him, yes? I sense that even though your evening did not go as planned, you will not discard the friendship."

"No. I guess I have to be happy to be his friend, and leave it at that. But I'm scared." Annie gave Diana a pleading look. "I don't want to go to some strange place and die."

"Fear of the unknown is a normal trait for humans, Annie. Do not worry yourself over what might happen in the future. I have confidence you two will return."

"I never said I was going!" Annie crossed her arms and let out a huff. "What if I went, though? What if I went to the Fieriel Senefal? Could I get my wishes fulfilled?"

"What would that be, Annie?"

"I want to live comfortably here. I don't want to be homeless. I don't want to be rich, but I don't want to worry about how I would pay for food or lodging. I want to explore. Couldn't there be some sort of financial incentive for me to go on that stupid quest?"

Diana smiled and petted Annie's hair. "That could be possible. I think with the riches of this palace, it would be an easy thing to give you some gold to live off of for the duration of your short human life. I like that you do not want to seem overly greedy. You simply want to study and explore. That is admirable. I would encourage this idea before the council."

"I still don't know if I would go, even if you guys gave me all the gold on Tahldia."

They stepped out of the small lift and walked toward Annie's room. She sighed when she saw the two guards playing their odd board game by her door.

"Think about everything tonight, my dear. Tomorrow will be a long day, and you will need to make your decisions soon, yes?"

"You know, on second thought, I think I do want some fae water tonight."

Diana laughed and clasped Annie on the shoulder. "I think I can do that. Just for you."

Annie slid out of her dress and corset, and curled up on the top of the covers, dizzy from the fae water, the wine, and her emotions. The room spun wildly and she went into the washroom to vomit. She drank some more fae water and crawled back into bed.

Annie tossed and turned the entire night. She kept reliving the memory of when she kissed Hak, and the moment when he had returned the kiss. For just one brief second, he had wanted to kiss her. It had felt so good. She growled and hugged a pillow.

Just friends. You big idiot. Why the fuck does that bother me so much? Why do I care so much for you? I don't know who the bigger idiot is anymore. I was afraid I would piss someone off tonight, and I did. There's nothing worse than being mad at myself and wishing I had done something differently.

Her mind drunkenly swirled the thoughts together and she let out a small, helpless moan. She kept remembering the kiss. *I don't want him to die . . . I don't want him to die . . .*

"Annie, my dear! You must wake up!"

Annie cringed as the windows were opened and light splashed into the room. "Ugh. No way."

"Come along, it is time."

"For what?"

Diana gave an exasperated sigh and yanked the covers off Annie. "The meeting is in an *hour!*"

"Crap . . ."

"Iriel has been trying to rouse you."

"Sorry."

"You had too much wine last night."

"Ugh. I had too many emotions last night."

"Well, there is that, too. Your head hurts, yes?"

"That's an understatement. This is why I prefer whiskey over wine."

"Here. Let me try to cure it. I will not heal all your hangovers. I believe you need to learn a lesson, but this morning is not the time. You need your wits about you. Here, drink this."

Annie sat up in bed and took a warm mug from Diana. She sniffed at the vapors wafting from it and made a face. The mug held what looked like bright yellow cider.

"Ugh. What is this?"

"Aya fruit blended with needle flower. It will help sharpen your senses. Drink."

Annie made a face as she took a sip. The hot fruit juice was extremely tart, and reminded her of sour grapes.

"This is awful."

"More awful than your headache?"

Annie groaned and finished the mug. Iriel took it from her and scurried away.

"I have a robe for you this morning."

"A robe?"

"A training robe. I think it will help your cause to wear the white and silver markings of a student."

Annie scratched at her head and stretched. She already felt a little better. She visited the washroom and cleaned her arms and face. Iriel was waiting patiently for her when she returned, the robe held out.

It was a soft fiber, not unlike a mixture of cotton and silk. The white sleeves were extremely long and cuffed with silver embroidery. Annie found herself constantly trying to push the sleeves out of the way.

"You are to walk like this." Diana stood and loosely crossed Annie's hands in front of her. Her palms rested on opposite wrists in front of her solar plexus, and the sleeves slid down to cover her hands. "It is a star song meditation pose, and should help you find inner balance."

"I'd rather just wear my hoodie."

"Not today. And let us not be so angry this morning, yes?"

"I'm not angry. Just tired. And really nervous."

"Let us try and eat quickly, and make our way downstairs. We do not want to be late."

Annie forced herself to eat the strange oatmeal as Diana instructed her on the rules of the council chamber and how the meeting would play out. Iriel busied herself with Annie's hair as she ate, pulling it into a simple bun with a few dangling curls. Annie was tense, and found it difficult to eat. There was too much on her mind to keep a focused thought.

Before she knew it, they were back in the long dark hallway with the glittering statues in the walls. She saw the golden doors in front of her and sucked in a shaky breath.

"Peace be upon you, Annie," Diana said softly, and waved her hands to open the door. The blinding white light of the chamber spilled over them. The council was already seated, and King Halona leaned back in the large throne that overlooked the chamber.

Hak was standing in the center of the room, but Annie almost didn't recognize him. He wore brilliant red armor that shifted to a dark orange hue as he moved. His spaulders were emblazoned with the angry eyes of some feral beast. A new sword hung at his back, and a twisted red helm rested in one arm.

He turned to Diana and Annie and gave them a deep bow.

"Peace be upon you, Young Flamefeather."

"Peace be upon you, Wise Diana."

"You are late, yes?" said Mau, leaning forward slightly. The old man was wearing the same brown robe that he had worn the first time Annie had seen him. He really did remind her of an angry Santa Claus.

"We are just in time, I believe," Diana said as she glided to her seat.

Don't forget to bow, Annie. Especially to Halona.

Annie grudgingly gave a small bow to the council, and a deeper bow to the king. "Peace of the stars and the red dragon be upon you."

Mau sat back, impressed. "Well, you are tame after all."

Annie gave a small inclination of her head to Mau, and then stood awkwardly behind Hak.

"Step forward, Annie," Aiyana croaked, motioning for Annie to stand next to Hak. She did so. She caught Hak's eye and gave him a timid smile. She was relieved to see him return the grin.

"Hey," she whispered.

"Why are you here?"

Annie froze. *Does he not know about Aiyana's plan?*

Diana cleared her voice and said, "We have summoned you here today to discuss our findings in the libraries."

Mau cleared his voice and said, "I have found many interesting scrolls that talk about the demigod Nuda."

There was a gasp from Halona, and he leaned forward.

Annie made a face and turned to look at Diana. "Wha—"

Annie! Do not speak out of turn.

What's Nuda?

Patience, Diana hissed in her mind. Annie felt a strong wave of frustration radiate from the elf's mind.

An older woman seated next to Mau adjusted the sleeves on her long blue robe. She said, "I have also found a reference to Nuda. It appears he is a part of the cycle of the points, and mainly resides within the Fieriel Senefal. Scholars write that the entire cave is one single mana point."

"Could it be possible the girl's appearance was related to Nuda?"

"It is doubtful. Most likely coincidence."

"And we are certain Nuda will be present?"

Aiyana said, "There are two halves to Nuda. Currently, the cave is dormant. If Hakayatas were to walk in there without magical aid, he would only find the dark half of Nuda, who is insane and would easily kill him. If someone were to use magic," Aiyana glanced at Annie, "they could summon Nuda's light to create a pool of mana. Only then could there be a fair fight. You need the current flowing through the point to find balance."

Mau stroked his white beard. "It is said that Dark Nuda will attempt to take several forms before showing his true strength. Both sides of Nuda will test the person who approaches. But the darkness will fight on the physical plane, while Light Nuda will fight within the current."

Aiyana gave a grave nod and cleared her throat. "Yes. It was written that Nuda became insane when split by the dragon Razahlahn, but he plays fair when both sides of him are present. His light will flow into Hakayatas and there will be a battle within the current itself. Hakayatas, you must be prepared to fight two battles."

"Pardon, Wise Aiyana. But how am I to ensure that the current will be flowing when I enter the mountain? How will I have a battle within the current, if I am unable to grasp it?"

"The current will flow all around you within the heart of the crystal point, Hakayatas. The scrolls say that there will be a pool of pure mana that you must step into. When this happens, both sides of Nuda will appear. If the mana pool is not there, his darkness will consume you."

Hak shook his head and gave Aiyana a confused look. "But how will I know if the current even works? You say the mana point is dormant! I was not guaranteed it was possible the last time we spoke."

What the fuck are they talking about? Diana? Hey! Diana! HEY! Annie tried to send the thought only to Diana, but a few of the council members appeared startled and stared at her.

Diana shook her head and squeezed the bridge of her nose.

Hak caught the pause in conversation, and the stares Annie received. He gave her a searching look, but said nothing.

Mau sneered. "You are rude, child."

Hak gaped at Annie. "What did you just think?"

Annie felt her cheeks burn. "Nothing!"

"It does not matter." Aiyana's frail voice rose above the muttering of the council. "She has gifts, and I for one, am very interested in seeing what would happen if she were to go to the heart of the current."

"Bah! That would be ridiculous!"

"She is not attuned."

"She is not even from this planet. She does not deserve to see the heart of the current."

Hak stepped forward and bowed. "Pardon, wise council, but are you suggesting that Annie leave with me?"

"She has the ability to grasp the current, Shafani. The crystal point within the heart will respond to her. You need to balance the light and the darkness."

"I don't even know how to use the point!" Annie blurted.

Hak shook his head angrily. "Pardon, wise council, but I need to do this alone."

Aiyana gave him a scathing look. "With what magic, Hakayatas?"

Diana cleared her voice and said, "I believe we should not force anyone to do anything they do not want to do. Young Annie here is not a slave. We should treat her with more respect."

Mau's white beard twitched as he glowered down at Annie. "Bah. She acts like a Vinder."

"You have grown too close to that Earthling, Diana," Aiyana said. Her narrowed eyes sparkled dangerously.

"What is in it for her?" Diana shot back, waving her hand down at Annie. "Surely we could find some compensation for all of her troubles. She has been through a lot, and I think it is only fair that we give her some sort of reward if she is successful."

Mau leaned back and stroked his beard thoughtfully. "It might make her more docile."

Halona's deep voice rang out over the chamber. "I would be interested to know what Lady Annie would desire as a reward."

Diana folded her hands in her lap and straightened in her chair. "She wants to travel, to explore our world. She wants to study and better herself. I think that is very admirable, yes? We should provide a small trust for her, so that she can pursue these dreams. She has been through enough, in my opinion."

Annie watched Halona and bit her lip. He seemed to be considering the offer. Aiyana was glaring at Diana. In fact, several council members gave the elf a scandalized look. Hak stared straight ahead. Annie could hear him grinding his teeth together.

Halona nodded his head. "I trust your counsel, Wise Diana. I think that a reward can be put in order. I know what it feels like to desire knowledge and exploration. I support this."

"Very well." Mau waved a hand dismissively. "She goes with him, and can collect herself some money later. Bah, what a greedy thing."

Annie chewed at her fingernail, but said nothing.

"Annie, will you go with Hakayatas?" Diana gave her a sad, almost pleading look.

Annie felt all the eyes in the room staring down at her. The chamber seemed too bright and stifling. She felt an overwhelming urge to flee. Most of the stares were incredulous or thoughtful. Diana looked sad. Aiyana was smiling. Hak was gripping the helmet in his hands so hard they were shaking. He looked furious.

Aiyana said if I don't go with Hak, he could fail. I don't want him to die. I don't want to go on this quest. Maybe I should have been fried by a nuke. No . . . I can't think that way.

"Annie?"

In the end they never really gave me a choice, did they? They just danced around courtesy and pretended I had a say in this matter. In the end, they will use me just like they are using Hak. I'm just a puppet that moves in the direction of the strings that are tugged. Now I can understand how they used him.

"Annie, do not do this," Hak said, his frown deepening.

"It is not your decision, Hakayatas. Girl, what do you say?"

"I don't feel like I have a choice," Annie said, keeping her eyes on the floor. "But if there is a chance I can help Hak, and make sure he stays safe . . . if I can live out the remainder of my life in peace and quiet, without concerns for money . . . well, that would be nice. I'll do it. I'll go."

Hak sputtered and looked wildly around at the council. "We cannot let her enter the heart of the current! This is my quest, and mine alone! If I must have someone to summon the current, call upon a gifted mage or apprentice. But not her!"

Aiyana held up a finger and Hak paused. The old woman pointed it at Annie, but kept her stare on Hak. "You will need her, yes? You are drained. She can touch the current. Nuda will be appeased if the current feeds into his darker side. This is the only way to ensure that the mana pool will be there."

"Hear my concern! It is too dangerous for her!"

Diana looked down her nose at Hak and said, "It is too dangerous for anyone. Yet you will both go. The odds will be much better if there are two of you. Annie is a strong and intelligent woman. She has made her decision."

Annie sensed another round of protest boiling inside him, but his mouth worked uselessly. Hak sighed and his shoulders slumped.

Mau brushed at his robe irritably and gave a small grumble. "Now, do you want to hear about what we learned, or not?"

"Yes, Wise Mau," Hak forced through clenched teeth.

"The ancient dragon Talsierling, hatchling of Tahlrahzen, hatchling of Razahlahn, is still thought to inhabit the mouth of the Fieriel Senefal. The

Fier dwarves have a superstition that Talsierling's sire, Tahlrahzen was the dragon that created the mountain where the largest mana point in the world sits. Bah, that's dwarven mythology for you. We understand that Talsierling will not give you any trouble as long as your intent is pure. He has done well to guard the mana point from evil."

The blue-robed woman nodded gravely. "You will find that the interior of the mountain is a maze. We do not have a map, but there are markers within the cave that should light the way. Again, one of you must use mana for them to work."

Hak gave a small bow. "Please explain, Wise Isa."

The old woman in the blue robes pointed at Annie. "I think that if this woman here touches the wall, the correct runes should illuminate for you. Your path will be lit. She may need to recite an incantation."

"What incantation?"

"We do not know."

Mau picked at some lint on his robe. "The girl will think of something, yes?"

Annie's eyes widened in horror. *"How?"*

Aiyana nodded. "The Earthling shall prove very useful for you, yes? Her mere presence might be enough to awaken the crystal point at the center of the mountain. It has worked before, why not again? If she can summon the current, a pool of mana should appear in the heart. And more than likely, both sides of the demigod Nuda will appear as well."

"How will I use the magiel?"

"That, we could not discover."

Hak sucked in a breath, the disappointment plain on his face.

"Hakayatas, the concept of magiel is sinister. All teachings have been burned from the pages of history. It is a dark art from the days of demons and warlocks, and our need to hide that knowledge also destroyed our ability to study it. We could not find any texts on how to return your mana to your body. However, there is a slight chance that Nuda might be willing to help you if you pass the test. That is a chance we must hope for."

Annie looked around at the council members helplessly. "I-is this Nuda guy good or evil?"

"Both."

"Neither."

Annie stared at all of them and heard a crazed giggle escape from her own lips. "Well, which one is it?"

"Nuda is both light and darkness, fire and water, the void and the current. Ultimately, Nuda protects the heart of the current, and he will give a fair test to those he deems worthy. Nuda is two creatures in one, Annie. When both halves are present and connected with each other, Nuda is pure balance."

So he's a yin-and-yang-type deity, huh? "It doesn't really make much sense. But as long as Nuda doesn't hurt me, I guess I shouldn't worry about the details, right?"

"Nuda will likely not even bother looking at you," Mau said to Annie. "The demigod will only be interested in the person who steps into the mana pool. That is who receives the test."

"Yes. The test will be part strength and part mind. Take care, Hakayatas, to keep your sword sharp and your armor on. If you can successfully spar with Nuda's dark side, he will take your mind into the current."

"And then?"

"And then, we do not know exactly. The scholar Aulin'ock said it would be a battle on the white plains. Most accounts of the light binding are hard to decipher. They say you will have a fight within your mind, inside the current, against Nuda's light side. We think that Aulin'ock's description of the white plains refers to the current itself. The ancient texts say that you must 'aim for the light within the light and take the heart.' The translation may be weak, but it mentions a fight within your mind. I have faith you can win a battle of wills, Hakayatas, so please do not worry."

"I worry about the magiel. I do not know what to do with them."

Aiyana gave him a small nod. "They were created with blood and energy, and it is possible they can be dissolved the same way. I would recommend that you keep the magiel against your body at all times. I had my attendant create a small pouch for you to wear around your neck, next to your heart. It seems like the best place to keep the magiel. At least, until Nuda says otherwise."

Isa waved her hand at Hak. "Perhaps Nuda will not even bother with this one, yes?"

Diana stiffened in her seat and said coldly, "I have faith that these two will succeed. We do not give them enough honor or credit."

"I agree with Wise Diana," King Halona said. He shifted his weight on the throne and rested his chin thoughtfully on one hand. "It is fascinating to hear about this long-lost knowledge. And even more fascinating that a demigod still dwells within the heart of the current. While it seems very dangerous, if there is anyone capable of fighting a demigod to regain their magic, it is Hakayatas. And I have no doubt that Annie will prove herself resourceful." Halona turned to Diana and said to her, "Please contact Irikohln, and tell him that we need more armor. Something that would fit a person her size." Halona swept his hand at Annie.

Mau nodded. "Give her a sword, too."

Diana looked off into the distance and closed her eyes for a moment. Her eyebrows drew together, and after a moment her face relaxed.

"I get my own armor? Really?" Annie clapped her hands together.

"How can you seem so pleased, Annie?" Hak asked her coldly. His mouth was twisted into an ugly frown.

"I'm just trying to live in the moment, dude. I didn't—" Annie felt a sharp bite of pain in her mind and grimaced. She glared up at the council. Aiyana was looking down at her with a crooked smile, a wrinkled finger pressed against her lips.

Hak caught her glare at Aiyana and his frown deepened.

He leaned down to her and whispered, "I do not want you to go. It is too dangerous."

"It's been decided Hak. And . . . I think I can help you. They seem to think so, anyway, so just . . . just don't be mad at *me*, okay?"

Hak straightened and stared gravely at the council.

"You leave in three hours," Aiyana rasped. She leaned back in her chair and folded her arms against her chest. She looked as though she would accept no arguments.

Annie choked and her heart throbbed painfully. "What? So soon?"

Aiyana looked down her nose at Annie and said, "Yes. So soon. And you need to go to the armorer immediately. Diana, take your pet to Irikohln and have her fitted with something suitable."

Diana bristled, but replied softly, "Yes, Wise Aiyana. I will have Iriel gather her necessary belongings and provisions."

"But what about my dog? What about—"

"Tia will be safe, I assure you. I will personally check on her while she stays with Nivya."

Anxiety pressed heavily against Annie's chest. *No, no . . . this is happening way too fast! I don't know if I can handle this!*

King Halona stood and placed his hands over his heart. "I will see to it that one of my personal griffins will escort you on your journey. Qualisk is fast and noble, and will watch over you. I wish you a swift and safe journey, Hakayatas and Annie. May the stars and the moons guide you and bless your path. I will chant your names in my star song this evening. I will see you two back here soon enough."

Gaeric stepped down from the throne and everyone in the room gave him a deep bow. He left the room without another word. Isa left with Mau, their heads bent together in spirited conversation.

Diana walked over to Annie and placed a hand on her shoulder. "You are trembling, dear. Do not be afraid."

"I'm terrified."

Annie felt her head prickle and a soft blanket of peace washed over her.

She didn't fight Diana's emotional push. She welcomed the chance to calm down and think clearly. She sighed with relief as her anxiety fled.

"Here, we must go to the armorer, and quickly. Hakayatas . . . I will see you at the dock. Please know I will be praying for you."

He gave her a stiff nod and muttered some gratitude. He turned his glare toward Aiyana. She was the last person sitting in the room. She had her chin resting in her hands and was watching them thoughtfully.

"Good luck and blessings on your success, Hakayatas. I think you two will succeed where one would fail. Take comfort that you have such a spirited friend for the journey. She will help you immensely, I know it."

Annie felt a chill at the words. *Something doesn't feel right. She knows more than she is telling us. She has to!*

Diana tugged at Annie's white robe and ushered her out of the room. Annie had to jog to keep up with the long-legged elf as they walked quickly through the palace.

Diana! Can you hear me?

Yes.

What the hell is Aiyana up to? I think she knows more than she admits.

I have that feeling as well.

Serious? You don't know anything? You promise me you aren't hiding anything?

Annie. You are my friend, and if I knew something more, I would tell you. Warlocks are the most secretive of all the two-legged creatures.

They stopped in Annie's room first.

"Place anything you need on the bed, and Iriel will pack it for you."

"I could just take my backpack."

"No, dear, we have a special bag made just for you. It is enchanted, and will be very lightweight. Iriel is on her way with it."

"Oh. Okay." *So they did assume I would just go along with their plan!*

Annie didn't have time to dwell on it. She set about grabbing a few items that she had carried with her from Earth. She pulled out her flashlight, tested it, and put it on the bed. She also set aside some spare socks, her headband, the lighter, the pipe, a small bag of toiletries, and, after a moment's hesitation, her sketchpad and a mechanical pencil.

The traveling clothes that Evera had made for her were waiting on the nightstand. Annie was pleased with the brand-new leather pants and the dark green tunic. They fit well and were surprisingly comfortable. The wool was of a high quality and didn't itch. The leather boots, however, were much too tight and stiff.

"I can't wear these, Diana. I'm sorry, but they're too tight and will hurt my feet. They need to be broken in."

"We do not have time—"

"Let me wear my old hiking boots. Please? They're comfortable, and they remind me of home. I want a good-luck charm."

"Fine, wear your odd shoes. But I have the true good-luck charm." Diana reached into a red silk pouch at her hip and pulled out a simple silver necklace. She fastened it around Annie's neck and gave it a tug to make sure it was secure.

"This was a gift from my brother, Raun. Do not lose this, Annie. I hope . . . I hope it will help you."

"Is it . . . ?"

"Yes, it is about eighty percent zythil. It is very rare to get a zythil alloy. You need dragon's fire to create it."

"Whoa."

"I hope you will not need it. But a little boost to your abilities cannot hurt. Between this necklace and your bracelet, you should be fine. I expect you to come back in one piece and return this necklace to me. Now, let us get moving to the armorer. I'll have Iriel meet us at the dock."

"Wait, there's one thing I want you to do!" Annie ran over to the dresser. She had given a very brief tutorial to Diana about how to play music on her phone. The elf had been entranced with the technology, and managed to understand it surprisingly fast.

"You remember how that blue solar panel works with my phone, right?"

"Yes."

"And do you remember how to choose music on it?"

"Yes."

"I want you to keep it safe for me. Enjoy some music from my world. But be careful of the heavy metal."

"Thank you, Annie."

"Oh, and this." Annie pulled a yellow tennis ball out of the drawer. She had forgotten that she had shoved it into the bottom of her backpack when she was leaving her house.

"What is this?"

"It's called a tennis ball. It just bounces. It's Tia's favorite toy and she'll bring it back to you if you throw it. Please take that to Nivya for me. I think they would have fun with it."

"I promise."

"Thank you."

"It's time for us to go, Annie."

Annie closed her eyes for two breaths and steadied herself. "I know."

They walked out of the room and Annie paused. She turned and looked back at the stone room she had come to think of as a second home. It wasn't her bedroom in Oregon, but it had sheltered her and she had enjoyed most of her stay. Even with the drama, she had felt safe within these walls. She would miss the hot baths, and the feather bed. She knew she would miss the view, and the way the sunlight hit the stained glass and scattered the colors across the rugs on the floor.

She let out a heavy breath and closed the door.

The forge was a cavernous, hot room deep within the cliff. Irikohln was a fat dwarf with wild black hair and an ugly burn on the left side of his face. The scars gave him half a beard.

He did not waste time with courtesies. Before Annie even had a chance to gape at him, he spun her around backward and motioned for his tall human attendant to place some chain mail over Annie's head. The teenage boy jumped when the dwarf gave a command.

The mail dangled two feet past her waist and gave decent protection. Annie tried to raise her arms and some of her hair became tangled in the links. She gave a small yelp as the armor pulled her hair.

Irikohln sighed in irritation. "You'll have to keep you hair away from that, eh? How's it fit?"

"Good, I guess. It's a little heavy."

"Ugh. You can't start complaining now, girl. You don't even have all the proper bits on. Sig, would you grab that breastplate over there? Aye, that's the one."

The boy hefted a large bronze piece of armor, but hesitated. "Are you sure —"

"Yes. This is on Halona's coin purse, not ours, Sig. Give 'er the best." The dwarf shot Annie an apologetic look. "Pardon, but our best is meant for lads. I have not crafted for a woman in a long time. This oughta fit ya though."

They buckled the breastplate over the chain mail and let go. Annie's breasts felt squished within the armor cage. It was not painfully heavy, but it was not as comfortable as her favorite hoodie.

Then they fastened some spaulders, leg plates, and gauntlets with open fingers onto Annie as well. *How did Hak move around for two whole weeks in stuff like this?*

Diana stood back and looked Annie up and down. "Iriel will have some gloves for you in your pack. You'll want to wear something soft underneath those gauntlets. I think the outfit is complete."

"Nay, yer forgettin' the most important part." Irikohln rapped his thick knuckles against his head. He waddled over to a low wooden table covered in helmets and plate armor, and retrieved a small helm with a pointed visor. It gave Annie the impression of an eagle's beak.

"Right, here we go." Annie knelt and the dwarf slipped the helmet over her head. He adjusted its leather strap under her chin, and lifted and closed the visor a few times.

"How does that feel, girl?"

"It's heavy."

"Ha! Is that all you say? It is some of my lightest armor. Costs a pretty pinch as well. The king must like you to have me give you my best stock."

Diana gave Annie a sly smile. "It is very interesting."

"How so?"

"Do you not recognize the bird? Here, look at your reflection."

Diana held out a polished piece of metal so Annie could see her reflection. The helm was circular in shape, but the front came to a point several inches out from her face. The visor resembled a flat beak, complete with two nasal slits. Annie could see feathers patterned in the helm.

"It's an eagle?"

"It's a kayatas bird, Annie."

Annie shivered despite the heat of the forge.

"You do not like the armor?"

Annie rotated her arms, bent her knees, and then adjusted the helm once more. She felt stiff and awkward. She pulled the gauntlets off and flexed her sweaty hands. "It's nice . . . Kind of hard to see with the visor down . . . but I mean . . . thanks."

"Best we got fer a little head like yers. Keep that strap tight when you fly, or yer likely to be very uncomfortable. It's my best helm, but still a little too loose for my liking. I don't have time for proper adjustments."

Diana nodded with approval. "It will work. What about a sword?"

"Aye, she can fight, eh?"

Annie lifted the visor and took in a deep breath of air. "Um, not so well."

"Hah! I have something I was making fer my friend's young nephew. Seein' as how my friend still owes me money, I won't mind partin' with it. Halona said he would pay for it all, yes?"

Diana gave the dwarf a cool smile. "Yes, he will."

"Right then. Well, it is unfinished, but it's the right size for her. I wanted to make the pommel all fancy and inscribe some runes on the blade. Get an enchantment or two. But seein' how yer in a rush, I think you won't mind the missin' details."

Irikohln handed Annie a sword in a scabbard. She grabbed the simple black pommel and clumsily unsheathed it.

She hissed as the firelight caught the blade. "It's beautiful."

"Of course it is, I made it, didn't I? It's light, yes?"

Annie lifted the sword a few times and smiled. "Very light."

"I will send Iriel with payment later, yes?"

"Fine by me."

Diana held out her hand. "My dear, let me see that sword."

Annie handed the blade, pommel first, to Diana. Diana ignored the pommel and gripped the naked blade with both of her delicate, long-fingered hands.

Annie gasped, but Diana hushed her. The elf stared intensely at the blade and began singing something in an odd, slippery language. Diana's eyes glowed as bright as two purple flames. The blade began to shimmer in response. Annie's eyes widened as she saw fine lettering appear on the sword. The words flashed a delicate purple light.

Diana released her grip on the sword, but it hovered in place.

"Trust me," the elf said as she took Annie's right hand. Diana dragged Annie's palm along the edge of the blade. Annie cried out and tried to jerk her hand away, but some unseen magic had her hand glued to the sword. Diana kept singing. With two long fingers, the elf smeared Annie's blood along the length of the blade. The lettering flashed once more, and the runes disappeared. Annie felt the magnetic tug of her bleeding hand release from the sword. The glow cooled until only forge light filled the room. She looked down at the blood dripping from her palm and felt bile rise in her throat.

Diana took Annie's hand again and massaged it gently in a circular motion. She chanted something in the same slippery language as before, and Annie's hand prickled and turned to ice as the cut healed into perfect pink skin. The new skin was tight and itchy. Diana closed her eyes and leaned against the table. She rubbed her temples and grimaced. "Take your sword, Annie."

Annie grabbed the hilt, but kept her eyes on Diana. "Are you okay?"

"Yes. That just . . . took a lot out of me. But you will find that sword greatly improved, yes?"

Annie looked down at the sword in her hands and tried to find any visible changes. It felt much lighter, but the surface appeared unchanged. "What did you do?"

"I inscribed the prayer of the dragon's eye onto your blade."

Irikohln let out a deep breath. "Aye, girl, yer gettin' all sorts of fancy things today."

"What does that do?"

"The sword *knows* you, Annie. That blade will never draw your own blood. Even if someone takes the blade from you, they will not be able to strike you. The sword will be too heavy to lift for those with ill intent. It will also resist most elemental spells."

Annie felt Diana creep into her mind. The elf said, *Do not think yourself invincible. If a demon finds you, you run. Do you understand me? You run. Do not forget our training.*

Annie let the dwarf buckle the scabbard onto her hip and thought, *Don't worry. If I find a demon, I'll definitely be running!*

Diana looked down at Annie and her face twisted with sadness. The elf stepped forward and gave her an awkward embrace. Annie returned the hug gently, aware of her armor and visor sticking out. She felt the open connection between their minds tense. She felt fear and anxiety radiate from the elf.

You've been a good friend, Diana. Thank you for helping me back there in the chamber. Thanks for the dresses, and the lessons, and putting up with all my stupidity.

You are not stupid, and don't ever think that way. I will see you when you get back. We must have our girl's night, as you say.

Annie laughed and gave Diana one more squeeze. The elf patted Annie's helmet and smiled. "Shall we, my dear? It is time to go up to the docks."

They thanked Irikohln and made their way to the lifts. The ride to the top of the cliff was awkward and silent. Annie unabashedly bit her nails and tried to take deep breaths. She put the gauntlets back on and made a face at the cold metal brushing her wrists. Diana leaned heavily against the wall of the small room until they felt it come to a stop.

The door opened and sunlight spilled in. Wind howled into the lift and whipped at the elf's hair. Stray strands of hair danced around inside Annie's helm and tickled her nose and lips. Diana put her hand on Annie's back and gave her a gentle push. They walked out onto the top of the cliff, and Annie felt her breath catch in her throat.

She gaped at three large wooden airships resting in metal stands. The docks jutted from the cliff like long horseshoes with iron support beams underneath. They resembled large wooden galleons with an empty envelope of fabric stretched from stem to stern. The ships appeared unoccupied, and a lone guard stood watch.

Wow! Those things are huge! I wonder what else is here that I haven't seen yet?

The large mountain she had seen from afar when she and Hak approached Meda was right before her. The unobstructed view left her speechless. The snowcapped mountain was larger than any she had seen in the Rockies. It was the first of several mountains that ran like jagged teeth into the horizon.

"This way, Annie."

Diana led her to a large, windswept courtyard the size of a city block. A small crowd had gathered around a griffin that was easily the size of an elephant. It was a soft orange and brown color. A black band of feathers ran along the edges of the eyes and the long beak, giving it the appearance of a mask.

The griffin was laden with armor and several large leather bags. The council stood around it, and Hak stood before it, placing items in a smaller bag strapped between the beast's front legs. The creature remained still as stone, but Annie could see the thick muscles tense in the feline legs. Her heart began beating painfully in her chest.

I'm really going to ride on top of that thing? The world began to slowly spin around her. She gripped Diana's arm and let out a small whimper.

"Can you, like . . . put one of those calming spells on me? Please? I'm kind of freaking out right now."

"Have you ever flown before, Annie?"

"Yeah. But we had this thing called an airplane. I just . . . This is a bit much right now."

Diana cupped her hands around Annie's cheeks and hummed a soft tune. Annie felt her anxiety and fear melt away. Her heart slowed, and she felt like she could breathe again.

"Thanks."

"You need to take care, Annie. Only you can conquer your fears. I wish I could help you more."

"Me, too."

"May every star and moon in the sky bless you with peace and good fortune, Annie Armstrong. Return safely, so we can go and dance with the men once more."

Annie giggled at Diana and gave her another hug. The elf kissed Annie quickly on the lips, and then closed her visor.

Hak watched them approach and nearly dropped the blankets he was holding.

"Annie? Is that you?"

Annie walked up to him and spread her arms out. "Ta-da! Check out the armor!"

Hak gaped, and his lips worked helplessly for a moment.

"It's cool, huh? Not nearly as heavy as I thought it would be."

"Wow."

"Is that all you can say?" Annie hid a huge satisfied grin behind her visor.

Diana stepped forward and held a small pouch out to Hak.

"What is it?"

"A few trinkets to help you along your way. And two minor potions that prevent infection. If one of you gets hurt, be sure to drink it. It will prevent festering wounds. Alas, I do not have access to stronger healing tonics, but this will do."

"Thank you, Wise Diana."

The elf gave Hak a slight nod as her eyes narrowed and flashed brightly. "Do not let anything happen to her, or I will send cold wraiths to haunt you to the end of your days. Understood?"

"Yes. Of course."

"Good. I *will* see you two return successful. Has Iriel brought Annie's belongings?"

"Yes. I have strapped them in already. Here are her gloves."

Diana took the black leather gloves from Hak. "Excellent. Annie, I made sure you will have at least a few comforts. Be sure to search your bags well. Put these gloves on now. It will be cold up there."

Annie gave her gauntlets to Hak to hold. She slipped the soft gloves on and found that they fit well and were very warm. Hak handed her the gauntlets one after the other as she slipped them on. It felt good to have a buffer of leather between her skin and the armor. "Thank you, Diana."

"You are welcome, Annie." The elf turned to the council members and nodded gravely. "We should bless them. You know we must."

"Of course," Aiyana croaked. She hobbled forward with her cane and stood in front of Annie. The other members of the council encircled Hak and Annie and held hands. The wind furiously whipped their multicolored robes around them.

They sang in unison in a strange language. The song chilled Annie's heart and she felt goose bumps prickle down her arms and legs. Even Aiyana's raspy old voice sounded young and different.

Her armor began to lighten, and her anxiety and fear disappeared altogether. She felt warm and cozy and safe.

The council bowed deeply to Hak and Annie and let go of one another's hands. Isa and Mau reeled from the exertion. Diana looked ill but determined to stand straight.

"Your armor is now stronger."

"You will be warm up in the sky."

"And you will have the ability to breathe easier up there, for short periods of time."

"Still, it is unwise to fly too high for too long."

"Please note this enchantment will last until Maule's next phase. It will wear off when that moon is at its fullest."

Diana took their hands and kissed them in turn. "May every star and moon bless you with good fortune. I will see you two soon, yes?" Her purple eyes shimmered with tears. The tall elf bowed deeply, and the council melted into the waiting crowd.

Annie looked awkwardly up at Hak and gave a nervous laugh. "We're seriously doing this, aren't we?"

"We will talk later. In the air."

"Is everything okay?"

"Hush. We will talk later."

Annie made a face at him and turned to give her farewell to the king. She tried to ignore Aiyana's smug grin. She couldn't tell if the old wrinkled woman was proud, or simply happy to be rid of them.

Hak turned and looked up at the enormous griffin. The beast focused a large eagle eye on the man in front of him.

Hak made a noise that sounded like a bark. "Daka!"

The beast immediately flattened itself to the ground so they could climb on. Hak went first, easily scaling the large creature. He sat down in the long saddle and offered his hand to Annie.

"Grab the buckles on the neck strap and step up. You will not hurt him."

Annie swallowed and eyed the griffin warily. It returned the same uneasy stare. Finally, she sucked in a deep breath and pulled herself up a few feet. She tried to grab Hak's hand, but slipped and grabbed a feather. The griffin gave a sharp squawk. Sighing, Hak grabbed the back of Annie's breastplate and hoisted her up to sit behind him.

"These are for your legs, Annie, so you do not fall off while we fly. Pay attention to how I do this, in case you need to quickly untie yourself."

Annie watched as Hak buckled her legs tightly against the saddle. Three straps held each leg firmly to the saddle. The stiff leather was molded for the legs to rest against it, and Annie found it much more comfortable than horseback riding.

"Is that tight enough? How do your legs feel?"

"Like they're tied to a giant saddle."

"Is your helmet securely on?"

"Yeah."

"Are you ready?"

"No fucking way."

Hak let out a deep burst of laughter. "Neither am I. But this is our fate, yes?"

"I don't believe in fate," Annie said flatly.

Hak laughed again and grabbed the reins. "You. Of all people! Arra!"

The griffin quickly stood. Annie gasped and gripped the saddle as the beast lurched underneath them.

She started to raise a hand to wave good-bye when Hak made three sharp whistles. The griffin turned and ran toward the edge of the cliff. The creature tucked his wings in tightly, and jumped high into the air. The wings spread out and he pushed higher.

Annie watched with growing apprehension as the ground raced away from them. She felt a chill run down her spine, and wrapped her arms tightly around Hak's waist as the beast moved beneath her.

"You all right back there?"

Annie couldn't speak for several minutes as her heart raced wildly. After a moment she shouted into the wind, "Oh. Just great. I'm in full body armor, flying on a beast that is half lion and half eagle, on my way to a cave with demigods and dragons. Just. Fucking. Great."

"Do not get sick on me."

"I think I'm going to keep my eyes closed the whole way."

"You will miss the view. You said you wanted to explore."

"I figured it might feel a little different."

Hak's deep laughter echoed within his helm. He reached a hand back and gave her knee a pat of encouragement.

The air felt colder. Annie reluctantly opened one eye and looked down. They were just below the clouds, and the entire world seemed spread out below them. She was glad that they were both wearing armor. She felt that she could squeeze Hak's waist as tightly as her muscles would allow, and she wouldn't hurt him.

The wind was whistling loudly through her helmet, and Annie found it hard to hear Hak talk as he pointed out features in the landscape. They flew along the western edge of the mountains that raced south from Meda. Annie had a basic understanding of plate tectonics from a geology class in college, and the mountain range didn't make sense to her.

There were no foothills at the base of the mountains. No signs of earthquakes or continents colliding. The mountains just seemed to explode out of the ground and tear into the clouds in a long line far into the southern horizon. The land around the base of the mountains was flat and covered with a dense forest.

Several streams and lakes glittered in the afternoon light. While Annie tried her best not to pee in her pants from fright, she gradually found herself more comfortable as the flight wore on. When the griffin's wings caught an updraft, he would coast and the ride became smooth.

However, every time the griffin flapped his wings, Annie felt her stomach lurch uncomfortably with the movement. She was thankful that she had had a light breakfast that morning.

Just breathe and think of this as the most epic adventure of my life. Just try to think of the next three days as camping and hiking and exploring old ruins . . . Ugh. I'm on the back of a griffin. In armor! Going on a fucking quest like I'm in some sort of video game or comic book. This . . . This is just fucking crazy!

Annie sighed and allowed her arms to loosen around Hak. Her muscles were stiff and sore from gripping his waist. She felt slightly more comfortable in the saddle. Her legs were strapped so tightly she no longer had the fear of sliding off.

Hak must love to fly; he seems like he's in a better mood. It just . . . It feels really good to be around him. I don't know what it is. I guess I still like him . . . but I'll never try to kiss him again. He's right, we're way too different. He's a cool friend, but he has too many issues.

When this stupid quest is all over with, I'm going to take an entire week to sit in a hot bath, eat chocolate, and smoke the finest stuff Aiyana can get me. I'm not going to move, or think, or try to understand one thing about this damned planet. I'm just going to relax and catch up on sleep. Maybe curl up with a good book and spend the whole day in that awesome feather bed with Tia!

They flew south for hours, and the landscape barely changed. The flat expanse of forest became patched with little farms and fields as they passed small villages and cities. None were comparable to Meda. For the most part, the countryside was wild and uninhabited. The long line of mountains in the east looked like it continued forever.

CHAPTER THIRTEEN:

FLIGHT OR FIGHT

THE SUN WAS a few hours from the horizon when Annie felt Hak jerk in the saddle. He turned and she could see his yellow eyes flash alertly behind his visor. He was staring at a mountain they had just flown by.

He shouted something, but the wind smothered his words.

"What? What's wrong?"

"I said wyverns!"

Annie whipped her head around and the wind caught the loose helmet. The strap dug painfully into her chin and she felt as though the helmet would pull her head from her shoulders. Annie removed one hand from Hak's waist, pushed the helmet back down on her head, and held it there. She attempted to look again in the direction Hak pointed.

At first she didn't see anything on the mountain. Just a few low-hanging wisps of mist at the tree line. Then she saw long serpentine shapes crawling out of a crevice. They poured out of the mountain, twisting and climbing over one another.

Annie felt her heart jump as she watched the creatures. There were a dozen or so of them swarming on the rock. And then Annie saw an enormous wyvern pull itself out of the crevice. It looked as long as a ten-car train. It stretched its wings and looked up in their direction.

Oh shit! That must be the mom!

"Hang on!" Hak jerked at the reins, and the griffin flew faster, gaining elevation.

The large wyvern launched itself off the side of the mountain and flew toward them. The offspring were right behind it.

Annie wrapped her sore arms around Hak and pressed her helm into his back. She shouted, "What the hell is going on?"

"It is a nest! We can lose them if we fly higher!"

They flew into the clouds; water droplets collected and streamed through Annie's visor. The temperature dropped rapidly as they cleared the cloud. Annie sucked in her breath at the expanse of white before them.

Annie remembered sitting by the window on long plane rides and watching the towering pillars of clouds that had poked out of the white sea below her. She had always wanted to reach out and touch them, to fly through them.

The reality was vastly different than her daydream. She could see the tops of the mountains now. They poked through like small islands to their left. The air was cold enough that the water droplets on Hak's back froze. The griffin began panting.

The large wyvern broke the cloud's surface moments later and shot toward them.

"It's going to get us!" Annie shrieked, feeling dizzy from fright.

"No! It is too cold up here! It will not keep up for long!"

Hak was right.

Annie watched as the wyverns began struggling to flap their translucent wings. They seemed to grow lethargic, and the griffin began to pull ahead.

Annie felt a little calmer. *Of course! They're cold-blooded!*

It was not without a cost, however. The griffin was making strange, low-pitched noises. It almost sounded as if he was weeping.

"Is he okay?" Annie shouted against the frosty wind.

"He will be fine! I am sure King Halona's own stock will have plenty of enchantments."

Annie frowned and didn't feel reassured. Ice crystals were quickly forming along all of the feathers, and the griffin was panting noisily.

There can't be enough oxygen up here for him! Annie realized with alarm. She felt fine, however. She wasn't dizzy, or even terribly cold. But that didn't stop the panic from boiling up in her chest. It just didn't seem right to her that everything was freezing around her, and she felt warm.

After several agonizing minutes, the large wyvern collapsed into the clouds and disappeared. Annie waited impatiently for them to descend, but

Hak kept them above the clouds for a frustrating amount of time.

At last they descended. When they broke through the clouds they were farther from the mountain range. The landscape was still heavily wooded, and scattered with dozens of small sparkling lakes.

"Are you all right?"

"Yeah! Dude, that was crazy! I think I'm stuck to you, though. I can't move my arms."

"It will melt."

"Have you done that before?"

"Yes. Long ago."

Annie bit her lip. *There is still so much I don't know about him. I wonder what he did when he was a general? Maybe I don't want to know. . . .*

The thought made her shiver.

They flew for another hour before landing on a small island in a lake. Annie half fell, half slid off the beast. Her armor pinched her when she landed, and sore muscles howled at her. Hak dismounted with ease and removed their bags from the beast. He handed Annie her bag and a large bundle of blankets. Then he patted the beast's haunches and pointed out at the forest beyond the lake.

"Loorak. Loorak ik murtack."

The beast rose, gave a low squawk, and flew off across the lake.

"Hey! Wait! Where's he going?"

"Do not worry. I told him to go catch dinner."

"And he'll just . . . come right back?"

"They are intelligent creatures, Annie. He will know we are here. A griffin must eat. Especially if it is to travel hard."

"What does it eat?"

"Pygmy whales. Deer. Fae elk. Or just about anything it deems worthy. It is not like we can carry enough food for the beast. Do not worry so much, Annie. We will be safe here."

Annie looked from the shore to the dense forest behind her. The trees were choked with thick, twisting vines. Annie walked forward and heard something move away from her in the underbrush. She paused and swallowed uneasily.

"Any weird shit in these woods I need to know about?"

Hak laughed. "No. Small rodents, perhaps? Mau told me there were some ruins on this island. We will find good shelter here, and a chance to have a campfire without being seen."

"You think we're being *followed*?"

Hak hesitated and looked at the ground.

"Dude. Answer me."

He looked up at her; his blond eyebrows were creased with worry. "I will not lie to you, Annie. I would be a fool to think we are *not* being followed."

"You think Tomas is still after us?"

Hak nodded.

"Great."

Hak hefted the bags onto his shoulders and walked toward the forest. "Best not to think about it, Annie. Hunters have been after me for a long time. I have had good luck thus far."

"Hey! Don't jinx it!" Annie ran after him.

As they walked through the thick forest and climbed over fallen logs, Annie continued to pepper Hak with questions.

"How long have they been after you?"

"Since I escaped."

"How many encounters have you had with them?"

"Several. Tomas must be the replacement for the last one that tried to catch me. His name was Desch. He was good."

"But not good enough. You killed him, I take it?"

"Yes. He was a skilled swordsman, but not a very skilled mage. Most of his gear was enchanted, but Desch could not cast a decent fireball to save his life."

"But Tomas . . ."

"Tomas is zyl magi."

"What's that mean?"

"He is a skilled mage, with plenty of zythil enhancements."

"So they're, like, the super skilled assassins then."

"Yes. That is a good way to put it."

"But you hurt him. He wasn't with his cronies that attacked us at the hot springs."

"Only because you broke his barrier somehow. But yes, it is all very strange. I have wondered why he was not present at the hot springs. He should have been healed by then and leading the attack."

"So you still think he is out there."

"Oh yes. And he is very upset with us, I think. I am sure Bingen is controlling him, and that is a fearsome master to have."

Annie felt a brief shiver run down her spine. Hak looked over at her, but it was hard to read his expression behind the visor.

"It will be all right, Annie. We are safe here."

Annie looked around in wonder. She realized that the thick vines and moss were covering ancient rock walls. Stone stumps that rose out of the ground might have been hearths at one point.

"Where are we?"

"The name of the city has been lost to time. No one has lived here for hundreds of years."

"What happened to it? Why did everyone leave?"

"Most likely war wiped the city out."

Annie had a brief memory of Earth and trembled.

Hak found three intact walls that would serve as adequate shelter. The dense canopy above obscured most of the sky. Hak nodded to himself and removed his helm. Annie dropped the blankets and struggled with the leather strap under her chin. She pulled the helm off and took in a deep breath.

"Time to gather wood and have ourselves some dinner, yes? I am curious to see what the council packed for us."

Annie busied herself with picking up all the dry wood she could find. Hak cleared away a spot in the corner of the walls and started stacking the wood that she brought him. As the sky darkened, the air grew chilly and foggy. Annie handed Hak her lighter, and before long, they had a warm fire and unrolled the blankets.

Annie began pulling items out of her bag and was happy to see her flashlight, extra socks, and sketchbook. There was a loaf of herbalist bread, more of the dried oats that she detested, and some dried meat. She also found a velvet pouch, a large water skin, and a small note with a wax seal.

Annie broke the seal eagerly and read the letter. Diana's long script was hard to decipher, but Annie read the words carefully.

My dearest Annie,

I hope that this letter finds you well and smiling. I hope that big oaf Hakayatas has not done anything too stupid in my absence.

Annie let out a giggle and then hugged the letter to her chest. Hak gave her an odd look, but she continued to read.

I know how much you despise the grain meal, Annie, but please bear in mind we had it prepared by the palace herbalist. It will give you much energy and stamina, so be sure to eat it. And yes, I know I sound like a mother.

There is also some fae water and chocolate for you. Alas, as much as I would love to pack you some wine or naroh smoke, I want you to have a clear mind for the duration of this journey. Use the fae water sparingly. You must be alert at all times. A few drinks before you fall asleep should leave you well rested. I imagine that griffin travel has not been kind to your body.

When you come back, we shall feast and dance. You are such a delightful friend, Annie. Your spirit and energy is an enchantment all on its own. Be strong and be

261

brave. You are already so smart and fierce. I will see you soon.
May the stars and moons bless you always,
Diana Loraldin'ar Mieree

Annie sighed and hugged the letter to her chest again. "I miss her already."

"Who?"

"Diana."

Hak made a face. "Diana? Really?"

Annie set the letter in her lap and tilted her head at Hak. "Why? What's wrong?"

"Nothing! She is just . . . It is strange you two get along so well, I think. She has always been very formal and imposing with me."

"Maybe she accepts me for who I am. She always made me feel okay . . . to be me. I didn't have to put up a front with her, like I did with so many others in the palace."

Annie opened the small velvet pouch and smiled at the small lumps of chocolate wrapped in thin paper. *Even if she is an elf, and a part of that stupid council . . . I really think she wants to be a friend. I really hope she is not using me like Aiyana. No, I can't think that way! I've got to start trusting people, or I'm going to go crazy.*

Hak split the loaf of bread with her and shared some of the cheese he had packed. It was a very simple dinner, but Annie felt thankful for it. It might not have been roast quail with a fancy wine, but it was a meal split between two friends.

Annie sighed and stared at the bread. "Hey. About last night . . ." She hesitated and picked at the seeds on her bread. She knew there would be no easy way to say it, so she took a deep breath. "I was drunk and being dumber than normal. Sometimes I get a little too friendly when I'm drunk. I'm sorry if I made things weird between us."

Hak watched her for several moments while he chewed. Finally he nodded slowly. "I am glad that we can be friends, Annie."

"You're right. We're way too different. And I was drunk and kind of acting on impulse. It just . . . It feels good to be around you. I feel safe."

"You are safe for now, Annie, but the days ahead will be dangerous. I am very upset with the council's decision."

"Hey, that wasn't my idea!" Her head ached when she said it.

Hak gave a low growl and set the bread down. He placed his hands on his knees and glared at the fire.

"I do not understand why they wanted you to go. Why *you*? Why not a mage? Why are they sending a girl who can barely understand the concept of magic?"

Because Aiyana wants me to get powerful. She thinks something is going to happen to me down there. She wants my memories of her grandson to come back. Or maybe she is hoping I die. That old woman is using us both!

Annie opened her mouth to say as much, but white stars flashed painfully in her eyes. She dropped the bread into her lap and grabbed her head.

"Annie! Are you all right?"

That mind-fucking bitch!

Annie pointed at her head and whimpered.

"Do you have a headache?"

She shook her head fiercely, which made the stinging sensation worse. She sat for a minute, taking in deep breaths and waiting for the dizziness to subside. Suddenly, she remembered her sketchbook and put it in her lap. She dug out her mechanical pencil and found a blank page.

She started to write Aiyana's name. She got through the *A* before her arm started convulsing. She tried to hold down her right hand with her left and write the word, but her hand shook harder. Stars began flooding her field of vision and her head throbbed.

Annie howled and threw the sketchbook into the darkness. She pulled her knees up under her chin and gritted her teeth to keep herself from crying.

"Someone has blocked you. I am going to assume it was Aiyana, based on the power of the spell. Do not feel the need to try to tell me anything more, Annie. I do not want you to hurt yourself."

"I'm . . . sorry."

"Let me ask you one very important thing. I hope you can answer me."

Annie looked at Hak and cringed, fearing his question would cause more pain.

He gave her a flat stare. "Are you here to sabotage my quest, hurt me, or kill me?"

"No! Never!"

"Good."

"How can you say that, Hak?"

"It is curious that someone would go through the trouble of blocking your speech specifically about our journey. You know why they are sending you, perhaps, but you are not allowed to speak freely. As long as you will not hurt me, or impede my quest, then I have to hope for the best and trust in the stars. It is not worth the trouble and pain I would cause you to find out their reasons."

"I hate it, Hak. The mind stuff. They just jump into my head and see everything."

"I know."

"Could you do it? Could you jump into someone else's head and force them against their will to do something?"

"At one point in time, yes, I could."

"Did you ever kill anyone that way?"

Hak's eyes widened and he grimaced. "That is an improper question, Annie."

"That a yes? Don't worry, I definitely don't want details."

"I am not the person I used to be. In many ways." Hak stared sadly down at his hands in the firelight. Annie joined him in staring at the scars that snaked along his palms.

Hak whispered, "I hope to get my mana back. I want to at least have a chance to do some good with my powers before I die. To make up for the horrible things I had to do. I was an animal, once upon a time. A puppet."

"I'm sorry, Hak."

"It is not your fault, Annie. Those demons used me."

Annie felt her eyes burn with tears. *Everyone uses us!*

Hak put his arm around her and gave her a small hug. "Do not cry, Annie. They no longer control me."

Annie let out a small whimper and put her face in her hands. *We're just controlled by someone else! You big idiot!*

"What is wrong?"

"I'm sorry. I just . . . you've been through a lot."

Hak patted her back. "Everything will be all right. You will see."

Since when has Hak ever been the cheerleader of our little party? Annie thought bitterly.

"Are we keeping watch tonight?"

"I have been debating it. We need as much rest as possible. With the fog that will roll in from the lake, I do not think anyone will be able to spot us. We should both get as much sleep as possible tonight. I am not sure where we will be camping after this. It all depends on how quickly we travel."

"Two days south to the Fieriel Senefal?"

"Yes."

"What's it like?"

"I have never been there. But the maps show it as a chain of mountains in the southern sea. We will pass seven islands, and two islands with a small bridge of sand between them. The following island is supposed to be it. There will be a cave on the side of the mountain. Mau assured me that we would find it. He said, 'Even a big idiot like you cannot miss it.'"

Annie giggled. "Mau is kind of an asshole."

"You think most people are assholes, Annie."

"That's true. Here, you want some chocolate?"

"Please." Hak took two small lumps from her and savored them slowly. Annie chewed hers as she slid out of her armor and placed it next to her. Once she had the chain mail off, she burrowed between her two blankets and edged closer to the fire. She was happy to discover that the blankets had been enchanted somehow with warmth. It was almost as pleasant as her electric blanket on Earth. She was painfully aware of her fatigue and the sharp pain that coursed through her muscles.

"Do you want a little sip of fae water?"

"No, thank you. I prefer to sleep as light as possible."

"Suit yourself." Annie popped the top off of the small waterskin and drank for a moment. She found it difficult to resist a second sip of the sweet liquid. Finally, she forced herself to put the half-full waterskin away.

"Good-night, Hak. Sweet dreams."

"The stars watch over us tonight. Our dreams will be sweet."

Annie looked over at Hak's face illuminated in the firelight. His yellow eyes glowed with the flame and gave him an unearthly appearance. He caught her staring at him, and he gave her a soft smile. It was enough to put her mind at ease. The cold fog rolled in thickly that night, but Annie was warm within the enchanted blankets, and she quickly fell asleep. She dreamed of Meda crumbling, and a bird made of flame chasing her as she fell from the ballroom balcony in her silver dress.

The next day was a blur. They flew over many more forests, and the strange red Tauian desert that lasted for most of the day. The long line of mountains in the east continued snaking south into the horizon. That evening they camped at the southern edge of the crimson desert in the shadow of a cliff. Hak would not allow a fire that night, and the temperature dropped rapidly after the sun went down.

They brought the griffin up against the small hollow in the cliff to keep the wind out. Hak insisted on keeping watch for most of the night. He told her he was unable to sleep anyway. He paced back and forth and kept his eyes fixed on the north, and a few times Annie wondered if she was connected to his mind. His anxiety seemed to radiate from him in waves.

The next day was full of rolling grasslands that changed into a dense tropical forest with blue and white trees. Hours melted together as Annie found herself entranced by the changing landscape. But a sense of dread festered within her, and she found it difficult to make small talk. She made it a point to stare at passing buttes, forests, and lakes, and pushed the worrisome thoughts to the back of her mind.

Hak seemed absorbed in his own concerns as well. That night they camped next to a beach. The sea spread endlessly before them to the south. It reminded Annie of the time she had been to Hawaii on a family vacation. Fat leaves and fruit dotted the branches, and there were birds in every hue of the rainbow. The air was sweet with the fragrance of tropical flowers, and Annie picked a few to put in her hair. She rubbed a few petals against her skin and tried to wipe away the musky smell of the griffin.

The tropical setting was beautiful; Annie thought it was almost romantic. She glanced over at Hak and shook her head ruefully. She was simply happy to be his friend, and she welcomed it like warm sunlight on cold skin. She might never understand the strange connection she felt with him, but she would count it as a blessing. She found herself dreading the next day, and fearing for both of their lives.

I just need to live in the moment. I can't think about tomorrow. I need to remember what Diana said about love. I should give love freely, as a friend. He's probably terrified right now and needs a friend more than ever. The best I can do is keep his mind off tomorrow. I just have to keep us distracted and happy.

It was an enjoyable night. They didn't need a fire in the temperate climate, but Annie wished they had one just for the ambiance. She yearned for the acoustic playlist on her smartphone. She liked camping with Hak, and she loved to hear his stories. There was a peaceful simplicity in sharing tales under the stars. She wanted to ask him about his family and his childhood, but she knew from experience it would sour the mood.

She urged him to tell her the stories of Tahldia. Hak smiled and waved his hands around as he told her a children's tale called "The Princess and the Five Hatchlings." He seemed at peace, even if he glanced northward several times.

He seemed to enjoy storytelling immensely, and even more so when Annie laughed at his jokes. In turn, she told him the story "Sleeping Beauty" and tried to describe the magic that was animation. For emphasis, she drew a stick figure on the corner of the pages of her sketchbook. Each page had a different pose as the figure ducked and jumped over a pencil-dot ball. She flipped the pages and loved the look of wonder on Hak's face as he watched the drawing come to life.

Annie kept first watch, and at Hak's instruction kept her eyes on the north. He was convinced they were being followed, even if he didn't talk much about it. His nervousness, and careful choices for campsites, made her wary. Annie wasn't sure she would be able to fall asleep anyway, so she settled on a pile of boulders several yards from camp that was just high enough for her to see over the tree line.

She glanced over at the griffin huddled under the palm trees, and the figure sleeping against it, and sighed.

I could be dead this time tomorrow.

The thought hit her so suddenly she winced and curled up tightly. She sat there with her chin pressed into her knees and her armored arms wrapped around them. Her eyes burned and she shook her head angrily.

Live in the moment. Live in the moment. Look around you. Look at how beautiful this place is! You will come back here someday, Annie. Don't give up. Don't give up. . . .

Annie wiped at her cheeks irritably and forced herself to take several long, deep breaths. Her eyes caught a flicker in the distance, as if an object had passed between her and the nebula in the north.

She froze, eyes wide and clenched hands trembling. She blinked, then stared long and hard at the horizon.

I know I saw something. But what? Just a creature out hunting? Do I go and wake Hak up?

No. He needs to sleep. He has a big day tomorrow. In fact, I should just stay up all night and let him rest. He is the one who will be fighting tomorrow. Not me.

Annie flattened herself against the rock and stared anxiously at the northern horizon until sunlight illuminated the east.

Hak was not happy with her keeping watch the whole night. But Annie knew that he had had a hard time falling asleep. He had tossed and turned most of the night. She refused to hear his admonitions that morning. She made sure he had a full meal, and kept the conversation light. She could see the fear in his eyes, the dark hollows encircling them like lost hope, and felt her heart sink. She didn't have nerve to tell him about the shadow she had seen the night before. Surely it had not been a threat.

Before they took off, Annie tucked several tropical blooms into her breastplate. Hak teased her, but she insisted that they smelled good. She wanted all the good luck and peace she could get.

They flew over the ocean for an hour without seeing land. The thought of endless ocean made Annie nervous, but she kept her thoughts on all the things she wanted to do when she returned to Meda. She refused to give in to her fear, despite its constant gnawing. She refused to give up.

After a while, Hak pointed to their left at an island far into the distance.

"That's one! Just six more to go!"

Annie could see another island far in the horizon. *Man, this is going to take all day!*

She sighed, stared out at the endless ocean before them, and leaned against Hak. She was no longer scared of falling off, but that did not stop her from wrapping her arms around Hak and holding him. She took in a deep breath, cleared her mind, and tried to lose herself in the soft energy that seemed to ebb between them. She rested her head against his back and managed to doze off.

She awoke to the griffin furiously pounding its wings. The rolling motion it produced threatened to make Annie sick. Hak was jerking at the reins and making urgent commands at the beast.

"What's going on?"

"Behind us!"

Annie pressed her helm to her head and held it there, and turned as far as she could in the saddle to look behind her. She saw three large serpents far behind them against the blue sky. The wyverns looked odd to her, as if their heads were deformed. She squinted, and then gave a gasp when she saw something metallic glint in the sunlight. The figure looked familiar to her just then. She had seen an armored wyvern and rider in Aiyana's memories.

"There are people on them!"

"Yes!"

"Can't we fly higher? Get us out of here!"

"Our mount will die before theirs! I fear there is a demon riding among them!"

Every inch of Annie's skin prickled with goose bumps. She grabbed Hak tighter with her one arm, but kept her other hand on her helm. She stared with growing apprehension at the three figures behind them.

"How many more islands?"

Hak shouted, "We have two more to pass! Hang on!"

After an hour of hard flying, the griffin was laboring to keep his pace up. The shadowy figures behind them kept their distance, however. Annie guessed they were three or four miles back, but she couldn't be sure.

"Are we going to lose them?"

"No! Enchanted wyverns will be faster than an enchanted griffin!"

"Then why aren't they attacking us?"

"They want us alive, Annie! That must be the only reasoning behind it. They cannot get us easily over the open water. They will not risk the magiel sinking!"

"Fuck!"

"You can say that again. Just hold on. If we can get to the Fieriel Senefal, we have a chance!"

"But isn't there a dragon there? Are we just going to barge in with a demon at our heels?!"

"That is the plan!"

"This is fucking *insane*! You hear me? We are *so fucked* right now—"

"Keep calm Annie! Just be ready for anything!"

They kept their altitude, but Annie thought that the griffin was slowing. Hak kept urging him on, but his long pointed tongue hung out of his foaming beak. His labored breathing alarmed Annie. Pungent sweat matted his fur and feathers. *Hak better know what he is doing!*

Finally, they saw it, a gigantic brown mass that loomed in the distance. As they got closer Annie could see that the mountain was composed of several smaller peaks clumped together. The land was barren of all greenery. The slopes were sharp and serrated, like knives poking out of the ocean. In the center, a large mountain rose out of the choppy water. Its red and brown peak rose high into the cloudless sky, and in the center of the slope, Annie saw the cave.

Even from their great distance, she could make out the large terrace that led to a gigantic black maw. Several city blocks could easily fit on the flat surface, and not even the dams Annie had seen in Oregon could block the entrance to the cave.

Annie felt her chest clench tightly. *I've seen that! It was a painting in Mr. Wilson's house!*

Annie wanted to tell Hak, but she feared that Aiyana had blocked that from her. She forgot about their pursuers for a brief moment and gaped at the mountain ahead of them.

Suddenly blood and fur burst behind the saddle and a horrific screech split the air. The griffin lurched wildly to his right, and Annie felt her stomach jump as the world began to spin around.

Annie felt her head prickle. But it was not the soothing sensation that she had felt from Diana, or even Aiyana. It felt like thousands of needles had driven into her mind and were scratching her brain.

A dozen oily voices seemed to whisper in her mind all at once. It was the voice from Aiyana's memory. *Land. Or you will die with the next blast.*

"*Hang on!*" Hak jerked the reins and steered the griffin toward the mountain in front of them. Annie glanced back at the griffin's wounded torso. His back leg hung useless. Blood oozed over exposed bone, charred fur, and flaps of torn flesh. Annie felt bile rise in her throat. She pressed her helmet into Hak's back and tightly shut her eyes. She tried to shut out the pained moans the griffin uttered as he tried to remain aloft.

After a moment of blindly reeling in the air, Annie dared to open her eyes again to peer over Hak's shoulder. The mountain was much closer. They were flying over small jagged rocks near its base.

Annie felt the intense pressure of the demon on her mind once more.

Land!

Annie tried to push the presence away. It felt as though a sharp-edged anvil were sitting on her head. She tried to remember every lesson Diana had taught her. She gritted her teeth and puffed out her chest and tried her best to push the monster from her mind. It was like trying to push her head against a wall covered in nails. Every attempt made her scream in agony.

Hak struggled with the buckles on the leather straps on his legs for a second, but had difficulty with his heavy gauntlets. He pulled a dagger from his waist and began cutting the straps.

"What are you doing?!"

"Trust me! Just hang on!"

"You're crazy!"

"I have to hurry! If we are still tied in when we land, we will be crushed! Qualisk is dying, Annie! He has lost too much blood! Squeeze as tight as you can with your legs and just *hold on!*"

Hak turned and began cutting the straps from Annie's legs. Her heart raced wildly in her chest and she felt increasingly dizzy. She wrapped her arms around Hak's waist and held him as tightly as she could. She pressed her legs into the saddle and began feverishly praying to anything that would listen.

The cave entrance raced toward them. Now that they were over land, Annie realized just how fast they were going. She gripped Hak tighter and let out a long scream as the griffin sped toward the ground.

Annie shut her eyes again as Hak yelled, "Be ready to jump!"

The poor beast was not even able to land on its feet. They flew into the ground and slid across the terrace toward the cave. Annie rattled in her armor as the world spun and crashed around her. The struggling mount thrashed wildly as it left a bloody streak across the terrace. Annie lost her grip on Hak and she was thrown from the saddle.

The world flashed bloodred and white with pain as she rolled across the dusty terrace. She came to a stop in the orange dirt and felt her body freeze with shock and fear. She took in a deep breath and coughed as she inhaled the dust, and felt her ribs ache. Everything hurt. She struggled onto one arm and saw Hak trying to pull their backpacks off the thrashing beast. He managed to grab them before the creature squawked and rolled over onto his back, kicking his legs at the sky. Annie grimaced as she watched the beast writhe in pain as he sprayed blood everywhere.

The wyverns were closing fast. They dove toward Hak and Annie, and she could see a great figure riding the lead serpent. The armor was a sickly green and black, and the helm was covered with a black crest that ran backward like a Mohawk. The helmet opening was split and twisted in the shape of a *t*.

Ominous yellow-green eyes glowed brightly within the visor, and around them Annie could see a hint of bone white skin.

The demon raised a glowing hand at them, but suddenly his mount reared wildly. The armored figure dropped his hands to wrestle with the reins, but the wyvern struggled to get away.

The ground began shaking. Giant rocks fell from the cliff that encircled the terrace. Small pebbles danced across the surface with the tremors. Annie tried to stand as the ground heaved around her.

Annie screamed, "Earthquake!"

Hak tried to run to her, his steps wobbly with each quake. He was screaming something at Annie, but she couldn't hear him over the screeching wyverns and the rocks that fell onto the terrace.

She looked up and saw their enemy flying away, their mounts twisting against the commands of their riders. Despite the ground shaking around her, she jumped to her feet and raised a middle finger defiantly at them.

"Wooo! We did it, Hak! Fuck those guys!"

A shadow fell over her, and most of the terrace. Annie's body went cold with sudden understanding of the long-necked silhouette. She turned her head slowly toward the cave and found herself staring up at the massive black belly of a dragon.

It could have filled a football field. Its girth took up most of the cave entrance, and its long neck reached as high as a ten-story building. Black spikes as thick as tree trunks ran from its head down the length of its spine to a long tail that disappeared into the cave. She could have used one of his black scales for a shield.

"Annie! Do not move!"

Hak was standing frozen ten yards from her, his hand reached out to her helplessly in an effort to enforce his command. Even from that distance she could see the whites of his eyes flash with panic behind his visor.

The dragon took a step and the ground shook. Its black and silver talons were easily eight feet long and a foot thick. They left great gashes in the red rock as the creature approached. The beast bent its neck and brought its head down to Annie.

The teeth were as long as her body. The eyes were alive with fire; red and yellow irises blazed brightly in the dark face. The scaled snout curved back in an angry grin and its mouth opened fifteen feet from Annie. It let out a deafening roar that tried to blow the helm off her head and lifted the chainmail around her waist. She fell onto her butt and held her hands out before the gaping maw. She saw two rows of teeth on his top jaw, and three rows of teeth on the bottom.

Annie felt herself screaming, but the dragon's roar drowned out everything. Its breath reeked of decaying meat and a strange acidic odor. Her legs trembled violently, and Annie realized she'd wet her pants.

At once the dragon snapped his mouth shut and let out a great snort that blew more dust up around Annie. Her ears were ringing painfully. The beast leaned closer and almost touched her. The nostril that sniffed her was large enough to stick her head in. She sensed an ancient power from the beast. And also a hint of amusement.

A deep gravelly voice, almost impossible to understand, rolled into her mind. It was slow, and ancient, and Annie felt compelled to ignore all else.

You will suffice.

The dragon turned his head from Annie and bent down to Hak. It roared again, but Hak stood defiantly against the blast. The gust of dirt rushed all the way across the terrace to the twitching griffin. The dragon closed his mouth and curved his neck to inspect Hak from every angle, sniffing and blowing dust up all around them. Its lip curved back to expose the rows of glistening white teeth. It almost looked like a smile.

Yes. Good. Kayatas born anew. You are worthy. Welcome, hatchling. Mageli'okta urkta. Mageli'okta urkta.

A screech from above caught their attention. Even the great dragon whipped its head up and stared at the three wyverns circling high above.

She felt the prickly demon trying to dig into her head again. She felt compelled to walk away from the dragon and the cave. Then she felt another presence creep into her mind. It was not nearly as strong as the demon's, but it felt dirty and greasy.

Come to us . . . I look forward to dancing with your pretty dead body, Annie.

She knew the voice. *Fuck you, Tomas!* Annie screamed back, and tried to push the disgusting man from her mind.

Oh, I look forward to it.

The dragon stared up at the wyverns and opened its great mouth. Its teeth glinted with a white glow that emanated from the inside of the mouth. The belly of the dragon made a strange roaring sound, like jet engines before takeoff.

A great jet of flame shot from the dragon's open mouth and seemed to cut the sky in two with its brilliant white and blue light. The blast poured out of the dragon's mouth for several seconds. The wyverns shrieked and bucked at their riders, who seemed to have difficulty controlling them in the presence of the dragon.

Mageli'okta urkta, the dragon said once more in their minds. And then he stretched his wings and pushed away from the terrace. The gust of air pushed Hak and Annie against the ground and scattered dust and rocks away. The dragon soared toward the wyverns. They screeched and split up.

Hak ran to Annie and he jerked her off the ground by her breastplate.

"We have to run! Hurry! While they are distracted!"

Hak pulled her in the direction of the massive cave, carrying their two small bags with him.

"*Faster!*"

"I'm *trying!*"

They reached the mouth of the cave and paused to look back. The three wyverns were quickly outmaneuvering the larger dragon. One wyvern managed to zip past the dragon and flew toward the cave's entrance. The dragon roared and, whipping his head around, opened his jaws. Annie watched as the depths of his mouth began to glow white-hot, like a star being born in front of her.

Hak jerked Annie toward the interior of the cave. "*SHIT! RUN!*"

They ran deeper into the dark mouth of the cave and Annie heard the great rumble from the belly of the dragon. A second later flame spilled onto the ground nearby. They continued to flee as the flames illuminated their way but stayed mercifully out of reach. A wyvern screamed and fell silent.

"Fuck! I hope that was Tomas!"

"I hope that was Bingen!"

"That was Bingen?"

"Yes. I will never forget that voice."

The dragon's flame disappeared, and the cave fell into darkness. Hak paused and Annie ran right into him. All was black, and the only sounds were their ragged breathing. And the winged monsters fighting outside.

Annie felt Hak press a bundle of leather and cloth into her arms. Her pack. "You have that odd thing, the light? In your bag?"

"Th-the flashlight? Yeah."

Annie dug around and felt for the small plastic light with trembling hands, and slid her fingers along the length of it to find the switch. She flipped it on and waved the light against the black walls around them.

"Ah. Thank the stars," Hak said.

Annie handed him the flashlight with a shaky hand. "Here. I don't feel so good."

Hak took it and started walking down the large tunnel. "You did well, Annie. You did very well with the dragon."

Annie slung the pack on one shoulder and let out a shaky breath. She walked after Hak and felt her wet leather pants rub against the inside of her thighs. She was too shocked to feel embarrassed.

CHAPTER FOURTEEN:

THE HEART OF THE CURRENT

THEY WALKED IN silence for a few moments as Hak shone the flashlight on the walls around them. They came to a giant split in the tunnel. Their flashlight was not bright enough to illuminate either one. Hak sighed and began searching the walls at the juncture.

The flashlight found a strange black script on the wall. It was the size of a billboard and faded with time.

"Come here, Annie."

"What is it?"

"Our sign."

"What's it say?"

"'Darkness within darkness. Light within light. Say the words and you shall find truth.'"

"The fuck does that mean?"

Hak paused and stared up at the wall. He tilted his head and read the script aloud several times to himself. He turned to Annie and his yellow eyes shone with excitement.

"The words Tarsierling said."

"The dragon?"

Hak gave an exasperated sigh. "Yes, Annie. The dragon."

"Magiel oka something . . . right?"

"Mageli'okta urkta."

"Mageli urkta."

"Mageli'okta urkta."

Annie sighed and tried again, "Mageli'okta urkta."

Nothing happened.

"Reach for the current, Annie. You trained with Diana, yes?"

"Of course I did! But that doesn't mean I know what's going on!"

"Say it again."

"Mageli'okta urkta."

"Again, Annie."

"Mageli'okta urkta."

"Try putting your hands on the wall."

"What good is that going to do?"

"Are you even trying to reach for the current?"

Annie gritted her teeth and snarled at Hak. "Of course I am!"

"Do it!"

Annie put her hands against the wall and repeated the words. She tried to feel aware of her breathing, and searched her mind for some deep-down energy. Nothing happened for several minutes.

"Damn it, Annie. *Try.*"

"I am!" Annie shouted, losing her patience. She took in a deep breath, mindful of the blood pulsing in her body, and focused on the words. "Mageli'okta urkta!"

A small blue light appeared far down the tunnel to the right. It was faint, but they could see the glow in the ceiling of the cave.

"You did it!"

"How?"

"I do not care! Come on!"

They walked down the tunnel toward the light. After several long minutes they passed under it. A strange glowing rune was etched into the ceiling.

Annie stopped and looked up at it. "What does it mean?"

"I do not know. It is just a letter. Come on, keep moving! I can see another light farther down this tunnel."

"Do you think we need to know that?"

"What?"

"It's a letter. And there are more of them. Hold on." Annie reached into her backpack and grabbed her sketchbook while Hak impatiently looked on.

"What are you doing?"

"This reminds me of something I saw in a video game once. Call it a hunch, but I'm going to write these down. Maybe they spell something."

"Perhaps. It cannot hurt to write them down. Good thinking, Annie."

They continued down endless tunnels, writing down the runes as they passed. The letters did not mean anything to her, but Hak could say them properly. That was all that mattered to Annie.

As they walked deeper into the mountain, the cave walls began glowing different hues of blue, green, and violet. The strange patches of light seemed to move in places. Annie dared to get a closer look, and was shocked to find strange creatures not unlike the sea anemones she had seen in aquariums. They slowly waved their inch-long tentacles in the air and gave off a soft light. It was almost enough to see by without the aid of the flashlight.

"What are they?"

"I do not know. I would not touch them if I were you, Annie."

Annie leaned closer and blew on a glowing purple creature with waving tentacles. The moment her breath hit it, it stopped glowing and tucked itself into a tight ball.

"Whoa! Cool!"

"Come along, Annie." Hak's voice sounded thick and strange.

"Are you okay?"

"We must hurry."

He had already walked several yards ahead of her. She jogged to catch up with him.

"You didn't answer my question. Are you all right?"

"Just nervous."

"You can do this, Hak. I know you can."

He sighed and said nothing. They walked for a long time. Without sunlight, Annie was unsure how many hours passed. They kept following the runes down twisting corridors. The tunnels were growing narrower, and the rune light was bright enough to help them find footing. Soon the tunnels became just wide enough for a large bus to pass through. The dragon couldn't reach this part of the cave.

I understand now why Aiyana wanted someone who can use magic to come along. Without those runes, anyone could get lost down here and probably die of starvation. Even with just a flashlight, it could be easy to take the wrong tunnel and get lost. This is pretty scary. I would hate for the batteries in my flashlight to die right about now. I couldn't imagine getting lost down here.

Annie felt her heart skip a beat. *What if Hak dies down here? What if I can't find my way out? How would I get out? Oh shit, the griffin is dead! We're trapped here! Oh my god . . . no . . .*

Annie shook her head and pulled her helmet off. She felt hot, but her skin was clammy with cold sweat. She was getting claustrophobic, and started to feel dizzy. She reached for Hak's arm and leaned against him as they walked.

"Are you well, Annie?"

She gave an uneasy chuckle. "I'm . . . just trying to live in the moment. I'm trying really hard not to overthink everything right now."

"Take a sip of water, and splash some on your face. Take deep breaths."

Annie did as he suggested, but her hands were shaking and the strange sensation of tunnel vision seemed to creep at the edges of her mind. Her vision became fuzzy around the edges. She thought she heard the delicate notes of a piano. *I'm going crazy*, she thought.

"It will be all right, Annie. Just do not faint on me."

"I'm trying."

Hak paused and reached down to hug her. She dropped the helmet and returned the embrace. The metallic sound seemed to echo down the tunnels.

"Hak, I'm really scared."

"So am I, Annie, so am I. At least we have each other."

She sighed and hugged him tighter. "You have the magiel right?"

Hak patted the front of his breastplate where his heart was. "They're under my tunic. Aiyana made a special pouch for me to wear crafted from zythil and silver."

"Do you know what you need to do?"

"I wish I did, Annie."

She picked up her helmet and they continued walking. Annie took several long, measured breaths and tried to think happier thoughts. She thought of playing fetch with Tia, and Diana and Iriel laughing in the garden. A warm bath. A feather bed. Dancing with Hak. Annie's heart ached, and she was having a difficult time pushing her fear down to a manageable level. Then she heard the piano again. Five notes rising, five notes falling, and then repeating several times.

"You hear that?" she asked, looking around.

"Hear what?"

Five notes up, five notes down.

"You don't hear that music?"

The wide-eyed look Hak gave her was proof enough that only she could hear the piano. She shook her head, and the sound disappeared.

"Are you well, Annie?"

"Yeah . . ."

His gaze lingered on her for a moment longer, and then he looked down the tunnel. They saw a rune ahead of them unlike the others. This one was white and embedded in the floor. Hak began walking faster.

They reached a large hollow made of blue and purple crystal. It reminded her of the crystal point she had woken in, but on a much larger scale. The chamber could have held a large house. Stalagmites and stalactites made of cobalt crystal encircled the room like icicles, and the white rune shimmered brightly within a depression in the center of the hollow that was roughly thirty feet in diameter. Everything in the crystalline chamber glowed with the light of the rune.

Five notes up. Five notes down. There's that strange melody again. Where's it coming from?

Along the rim of the depression, Annie saw several large mounds of crystal the size and length of people. The uneven ground was littered with the lumps. The beam of the flashlight fell on one of them, and Hak and Annie gave a simultaneous gasp.

There were skeletons within the crystal mounds.

"What the . . ."

Hak swept the flashlight past the crystalline tombs and gave a startled jerk.

"By the gods!"

"What! What is it?"

"T-the ceiling—"

He pointed the light at the dark ceiling above the depression in the crystal floor. It was as if the darkness absorbed the light. Then Annie saw that the shadow covering the ceiling was boiling and moving on its own accord. She dropped her helmet and sketchbook.

"What the hell?" Annie's voice cracked. "H-H-Hak? What is th-that thing?"

"I think . . . that is Nuda."

Annie hadn't been sure what to expect of a demigod. She had toyed with the notion of Nuda being a creature made of fire, or humanoid. Maybe even a monster composed of several different creatures, like a griffin or some other mythological beast. She was not expecting a frothy black blob that boiled and moved like animated oil.

"Annie, what does your book say? What runes have we passed?"

Annie picked up the sketchbook and handed it to Hak with shaky hands.

He looked at the rune in the center of the chamber, and then back at her sketchbook.

"Dani'shal soli'shal murdi'shal holi'shal."

"What does that mean?"

Hak shook his head. "This . . . This is the ancient language of the stars. I think it means 'the dark, the light, the death, the life.' What an odd order for those words."

"Why is that?"

"Death before life."

"Diana said all life and death are intermingled. That we are all a part of the current, even if we cannot grasp it."

"She is wise, Annie."

Hak had Annie repeat the ancient words several times in a hushed whisper. Something hissed within the boiling mass across the room. Annie's heart raced wildly as she saw a black skeletal hand reach out from the mass that was Nuda. Its clawed fingers seemed to scratch at the air and reach toward them.

"Repeat the words, Annie. You can do it."

"Dani'shal soli'shal murdi'shal holi'shal!"

The skeletal hand paused, then melted back into the wall. The entire mass started to boil angrily.

"Again, Annie! Reach for the magic!"

She jumped, grabbing Hak's hand and squeezing it. "D-d-dani'shal!"

Several skeletal hands reached out of Nuda and clawed at the center of the chamber. A sickening gurgling noise emanated from the demigod as it grew, filling the ceiling.

"Annie, for the love of the stars! *Keep saying it!*"

Annie squeezed his hand tighter and closed her eyes. She tried to focus on her breath, but her heart seemed to be seizing up in her chest.

"Dani'shal! Soli'shal! Murdi'shal! Holi'shal!"

The noises stopped. Annie dared to open her eyes. The hands withdrew back into the oily mass.

The ground gave a small shudder, and the light within the rune on the floor pulsed brighter. A strange milky white substance poured out of the rune and filled the crystalline depression in the floor. Annie couldn't tell if it was water or a very thick smoke. The pool of light shimmered and pulsed with energy. The black mass was motionless. Almost as if it was waiting.

"Oh my god . . . Is that?"

"That is the mana pool Aiyana spoke of. This is the heart of the current."

"W-what do you need to do? Are we supposed to step in that?"

Hak turned to her and placed his hands firmly on her shoulders. He stared down at her and his lips worked uselessly for a moment. He shut his eyes and took a deep breath.

"Annie, you must stay right here. Behind one of these pillars. Do not—under any circumstances—attempt to walk into that pool. *No matter what happens to me.* Do you understand? Promise me."

Annie shrank under his intense stare. "Y-yeah. I'll stay here. But what if —"

"You must not go into that pool! I do not care if I am in pain or dead. If something happens to me, use the runes to find your way out of here."

"I won't leave you, Hak!" *It's not like I can leave here anyway!*

"Annie. Stay right here. *Please.* Nuda could kill you. I cannot bear the thought of something happening to you. This is for me, and me alone. Do you understand?"

Annie's eyes burned with tears, and she nodded numbly. Her lips quivered as she stared up into his beautiful yellow eyes.

"Hak, please be careful!" Annie choked on a sob and threw her arms around him. She fought the urge to crumble into a wailing mess on the floor.

I have to be strong. I have to be brave for him!

Hak returned the embrace fiercely, and stroked her head with an armored hand. Then he stood back, placed his hands gently on her cheeks, and stared deep into her eyes. "Do not worry, Annie. I can do this, remember?"

"Yeah. I know you can do this."

Hak brushed some hair out of her face, bent down, and kissed her forehead. He gave her a sad smile, and closed the visor on his helm.

"Do not move from here, Annie. This will be over soon."

Hak strode toward the pool of light. The glare bounced off of the crystals in the room and glinted sharply everywhere, except for the strange shadowy mass on the ceiling. Nuda absorbed all the light that came near it.

Annie helplessly slid down onto her knees next to a stalagmite and clenched her fists, taking several deep breaths. She fearfully put her helmet back on.

Hak's red armor caught the light of the pool and shone eerily. He stepped into the depression, and the white smoke curled around his knees. The strange white vapors churned and glowed brighter, and the shadow on the ceiling boiled furiously. It gave off a strange, low wail. Suddenly, four red eyes flashed within the black mass.

The oily demigod called Nuda detached from the ceiling and began circling the mana pool like a black tornado of shadows, skeletal hands, tentacles, and eyes. It spun viciously around Hak, kicking up dust and bits of white vapor.

The whirling vortex condensed in the pool several yards from Hak and tightened into a humanoid shape. Nuda flashed black and white, and flickered like an old image from a movie projector. The demigod shifted into a thin, sickly elf with haunting green eyes and pointed teeth, and then a huge, bearded man with yellow hair. The shapes shifted with every beat of Annie's panicked heart.

He took the form of a child with yellow hair and eyes, then Tomas, and then Aiyana, and then Mau. His form flickered once more and he was Diana. Another shift and he was an image of Annie, except his skin was a sickly dark blue that flashed with patches of white. The false Annie gave Hak a twisted grin and cackled, and Nuda shifted again, this time to a mirror image of Hak, except for dark skin and strange, black eyes. He was armored exactly like Hak, and stood in Hak's frightened stance. Hak took an unsteady step back and drew his sword. Nuda mimicked his actions precisely. It was like Hak stood before a mirror, except the reflection was something out of a horror movie.

"You dare challenge me, Hakayatassss?" The voice was raspy and strange. It was not unlike the voice of the demon Annie had heard. It sounded like it was composed of dozens of voices hissing in unison.

"I have come to take the test. Dani'shal soli'shal murdi'shal holi'shal. The dark. The light. The death. The life."

"Yoooou are the dark. Yoooou are the light. Yoooou are the death. Yoooou are the life." Nuda cocked his head and gave a scratchy chuckle. "You think you are wooorthy?"

"That is for you to know."

Nuda let out a wild laugh that was far too warped and loud to come from a human body. It echoed through the chamber and back down the tunnel. He edged closer with the sword held out in front of him.

"Yooou. Are very. Braaaave."

"I seek your guidance, Wise Nuda. I seek your help with binding."

Nuda sliced his sword through the air between them impatiently. "I knoooow what yoooou sssseek, Hakayatassss."

Nuda swung the weapon down. Hak angled his sword up and blocked the blow. Annie squeaked, but they didn't seem to hear her over the clash of ringing steel. She hugged the stalagmite tightly and felt herself becoming dizzy with fear. But she was not frightened for her own safety. She stared at the two Haks in front of her with wide eyes.

"Let usss . . . ssssee if you are woooorthy."

Nuda struck at Hak again with lightning speed. Hak parried and dodged these blows with ease. It was strange for Annie to watch two Haks fighting. If Nuda's skin had been a normal color, she might not have been able to tell them apart.

Hak lunged at Nuda and tried to stab him in the head. The demigod slid away fast as a snake, and then turned to counterattack.

For several minutes Hak barely dodged Nuda's blows in time; the demigod seemed to playing with him. It was all Hak could do to block the blows and parry while Nuda attacked, pushing Hak around the pool.

Their feet kicked up the strange white vapor. While it looked like water, it acted like very heavy smoke. It would spray out and slowly fall back down with each step and swing.

Hak swung his sword high over his head and brought it down at Nuda's face. The demigod vanished and reappeared behind Hak. Annie let out a bloodcurdling scream as Nuda arced his sword at Hak's neck.

He tried to dodge, but the tip of the sword caught his helm. It flew off of Hak's head and disappeared into the milky white pool. Hak rolled to the right and stood, parrying the next five blows Nuda made. His yellow eyes flashed with determination.

Suddenly Annie understood. *Nuda is trying to push him out of the pool! And Hak seems to know it! It's all he can do to avoid the blows and keep himself standing in the pool!*

Nuda lunged with his sword and Hak blocked the blow. They pushed against each other for long, agonizing seconds. Nuda let out a strange, raspy noise that might have been a laugh. Hak's foot slid closer to the edge of the pool. Annie knew that if his foot hit the edge, he would lose his balance and fall, or Nuda would cut him in two.

Hak roared and pushed back against the demigod. Nuda's black eyes flashed red as Hak put his weight into the thrust. Nuda backed up several feet and Hak regained his footing.

The demigod roared with laughter. "Yoooou think to kill a god? Haaaaaaah! I sssseeee it in your mind."

Nuda swung his sword and deflected Hak's next blow. The swords screamed as they slid against each other. Nuda quickly twisted his sword in the other direction, and Hak's weapon flew from his hands, away from the pool.

"Yoooou cannot kill a god. Nooooo. You are a fool to think sssssoooo."

Hak looked helplessly across the chamber at his sword. Annie stood, thinking to retrieve it for him, but he shot her a look and shook his head. He stared at Nuda and raised his hands in defeat.

Nuda's helmet melted into smoke and blew away. His sickly blue skin twisted as he grinned at Hak. Nuda wore the same scars as Hak, but his teeth were pointed like a wolf's. His black eyes glistened with excitement. It was one of the most disturbing things Annie had ever seen.

The sword in Nuda's hands melted away. He raised his hand up in front of him and curled his fingers at the ceiling. Hak floated off the floor, panic shining in his eyes.

"YOOOOU. CANNOT. KILL. A. GOD."

Hak struggled against the invisible force that pulled him up toward the ceiling. Long tentacles of white vapor from the pool clung to his legs and feet. Nuda tightened his hand into a fist and shook it. Hak twisted in midair and screamed in agony.

Nuda laughed.

Annie stepped forward, her heart pounding frantically. She thought her heart would burst from all the panic she'd felt in the last few hours.

Hak was choking and writhing in pain, and his legs kicked helplessly far above the pool. The white tendrils of smoke still clung to him. Annie took another shaky step forward, wondering what she could do.

Hak choked and his wide eyes found her far below him.

"No . . . Stay Annie. Please—" he managed to croak.

Annie wrung her hands. Hak looked like he was dying. He jerked and struggled in the middle of the air and there wasn't anything she could do. *I can't reach him if I want to.* The white vapors of the mana pool churned and stretched upward in fresh tendrils that curled around his body.

Nuda was still laughing as he watched Hak thrash about. He gave a wicked grin up at the struggling man. Suddenly he changed into the black oily mass that had been on the ceiling, and it shot up into the air and flowed into Hak's body along with several of the white tendrils.

Hak kicked wildly and convulsed as the smoky demigod poured into him. As the last trailing bit of smoke melted into Hak, he fell still and his eyes rolled into the back of his head. He hung silently, his head tilted back, his eyes blank. His skin began to turn blue and then black.

Annie whimpered and dropped to the floor. She punched helplessly at the stalagmite. She looked up at Hak, motionless twenty feet above the pool, and watched as the tendrils of white vapor continued to reach up and twist around his legs.

She looked up at him, panic and fear shredding her heart into pieces, and waited.

Hakayatas fell through an endless white void.

He twisted in the air and looked around in panic. The last thing he had seen was the cave. His helmet was back upon his head, and he no longer felt any pain or exhaustion.

Have I failed? Am I dead?

He flailed in the air for a moment, and then forced himself to concentrate. He tried to remember his training in Falishan.

This must be the current. Think. Bingen once said that the void between worlds is white. Warlocks knew about it. Could this be it? Or am I truly dead? Is it the same thing? I thought that the afterlife was supposed to hold all the stars in the sky.

Hak scanned the endless abyss around him as he fell. Far off in the distance he saw a black speck.

A soft feminine voice spoke in his mind. *Fly to it, Hakayatas.*

Hak gaped and looked around. "Who is there?"

He received no answer, but felt like someone was watching him. He focused on the black shadow far into the distance and began rowing his arms, propelling himself toward it. It was like every dream he had ever had where he was falling or trying to fly. The world seemed slow and thick, and he could push himself through the air as though he were swimming. He willed himself to fly faster, and found that it worked.

Perhaps this is the place of dreams? It feels . . . familiar, somehow.

Hak noticed outlines in the white void around him. He saw the faint form of distant hills and grass, but the world was bleached a brilliant white. The small black speck he had seen from afar soon grew to be an enormous mountain of writhing hands, tentacles, eyes, and teeth. It was Nuda, but immensely larger and more powerful. It pulsed with the slow and steady rhythm of a beating heart.

Is that black mountain Light Nuda?

Hak landed in the glowing white grass near the writhing monstrosity. He looked down at his scabbard and heaved a sigh of relief.

I may have lost my sword on Tahldia, but I have one here! Has Nuda given me a second chance? What game does he play at?

The black mass ejected a long shadow that resembled a snake. It roared and hurtled toward Hak.

Hak took a step back and pulled his sword from his scabbard.

How do I fight a shadow?

The massive snake dove for him. He spun his sword upward and plunged the blade into the gaping maw. The creature fell apart in a rain of black ash that disappeared as it fell.

It can be slain like a spirit! How is this possible?

Nuda let out a roar that seemed to fill the white void. The mountain of faces, teeth, and tentacles ejected several strange figures that ran toward him.

"By the gods . . ." He gaped at the hulking black figures that ran toward him. Some were ogres, others trolls, sharp-edged golems, and some were shapeless and covered in clawing hands and eyes. Still others loped along the ground on several dozen legs.

Is this part of the test? Am I . . . have I failed? Am I in the hell Bingen spoke of? Hak shook the doubts from his mind. He raised his sword at the approaching shadows, growled, and ran through the tall white grass to meet them.

His sword met no resistance as he sliced through the charging horde. The shadowy monsters began to grow larger. Hak observed that blows through the torso or neck were the only kind that could make the monsters vanish. He swung his blade down on a long black tentacle, only to watch as it grew back twice as large.

Hak also discovered that the shadows could hurt him. A large troll plowed into him and knocked him to the ground. The troll's tusks snapped within inches of Hak's face. He thrust his sword upward into the troll's chest, and it burst into small black bits of ash.

Still the monsters poured out of Nuda's shadowy body. The white world around him seemed to fill with the dark, teeming shadows.

Will this ever stop?

Hak slashed and chopped at the never-ending horde. He tried to remember what the council had said about Light Nuda.

"Look for the light within the light," Aiyana had said.

I cannot give up! Hak thought frantically, slashing his way through a group of ogres. *I cannot stay here forever!*

Hak slowly fought his way toward the writhing black mass.

Am I supposed to attack Nuda? How?

As if reading his mind, Nuda flung out a long tentacle. It slammed it down on the ground where Hak had been standing a second ago. It slid toward him, scattering bright white bits of grass like sparks. Hak thrust his sword out at it, cutting it in two. Another tentacle sprang from the other side of Nuda and hurtled toward Hak. He jumped back and swung his sword wildly at it.

This is impossible! He just keeps attacking! I feel like I am not even hurting him!

Nuda spit out another ogre, but Hak was close enough that he charged forward and sliced it in two before it had fully detached itself from the demigod.

Hak felt as though he'd been fighting for hours, but he suspected time moved differently in the current. He felt like he was dreaming. He did not feel tired, but he grew weary of the abominations that burst from Nuda. No matter how many shadows he cut down, Nuda created more.

Hak focused on Nuda as much as he could between attacks. Just after a large burst of monsters, Hak saw something shimmering within the mountain of shadow. Hak cut down the monsters, and stared intensely at the point where he had seen the flicker of light.

Within the dark writhing mass, a large white heart pulsed. It reminded Hak of drawings he had seen of a dragon's eight-chambered heart. The muscle glowed with the brilliance of the sun. Shadows quickly covered it again as Nuda shifted.

There! But how do I reach it? Do I charge in? Or is it a trap?

Diana's words at the council meeting flooded into Hak's memory.

"It will be a battle on the white plains. Most accounts of the light binding are hard to decipher. They say you will have a fight within your mind, inside the

current, against Nuda's light side. The ancient texts say that you must 'aim for the light within the light and take the heart.' I have faith you can win a battle of wills, Hakayatas. . . ."

He swung his sword down on the nearest shape and tried to cut into the side of Nuda. A shadowy face reached out of the mountain and took the form of Annie. Hak hesitated and watched in horror as her face twisted in a silent scream. Her clawed hand grabbed his armored wrist and tried to yank him toward her. The mouth opened wider to reveal several rows of long sharp teeth. Hak shuddered and shut his eyes as he plunged the sword into the figure.

Another hand began pulling him away from where he had seen the heart. He twisted and hacked at the arm, but several more took its place.

The light within Nuda flashed amid the writhing shadows. It was only ten or fifteen paces away. Hak's mind reeled with panic as more hands and tentacles reached out to grab him. The mountain was swallowing him.

I cannot let them overwhelm me! I have to get to the heart!

He pushed himself through the wriggling mass, slashing his way blindly toward the heart. Almost immediately he was nearly overwhelmed by shadows that grabbed and pulled him. He struggled to walk forward as a tentacle grabbed his boot. Another long black hand whipped out like a snake and wrapped itself around Hak's helmet.

He swung his sword wildly as he felt himself fall backward just a few steps from the heart. The white muscle was covered in silver veins that pulsed with the rhythm of the mass around Hak. The shadowy tentacle around Hak's helm pulled, and he screamed in frustration as he tried to keep his balance. He resisted with every muscle in his body, and slashed at a pair of hands reaching for his breastplate. He let the helm slip off his head and suddenly his upper body was free once more. He grabbed the hilt with both hands and whirled his sword around, driving the shadows back.

He raised the sword above his head. Dark hands and tentacles crawled all over him, yanking his face and pulling his hair, trying to tear him away. Hak gritted his teeth and growled with determination. He plunged his sword into the heart.

It vanished.

The dark hands around Hak's face and body melted away. The ground shook, and a strange howl filled the abyss. It reminded Hak of the eerie sounds the wind had made while it gusted through the miles of canyon west of Falishan.

Nuda exploded around Hak. The shadowy mountain burst away from the center and pressed the white grass down. Flecks of black ash fell around him, and faded into nothing. Hak fell to his knees, breathing hard. He stared up at the limitless sky and gave a prayer of gratitude to the stars, wherever they were.

He stood and looked around the field. Nothing remained of Nuda. The world was white and pure once more around him. He felt like weeping with relief.

He heard a man's deep voice inside his head. *Thief . . . Kin-slayer.*

Hak whirled and saw eight ghostly figures standing behind him. They were all tall and emaciated. Their robes and skin were white and their eyes glowed a brilliant yellow. One of the figures was taller than the rest, but was transparent. Hak could not make out his or her features.

They encircled him and walked closer. Hak felt panic rise in his mind. *The light within the light! Are these . . . is this Nuda as well?*

Hak crouched and held his sword out before him, trying to make the figures stop. A thin, ghostly woman with waist-length white hair waved her hand at Hak's sword and it vanished. He gaped and stared at his empty hands, and then back at the figures encircling him.

"Stop! Stay back!"

One of them hissed. *Hunter . . .*

His armor vanished, and his clothes. He stood vulnerable and naked before the figures. Their power and control over the current frightened Hak.

He dropped to his knees and held his shaking hands out in front of him. "Please. I beg of you. Have mercy!"

They grinned and reached for his bare chest.

Annie had been watching Hak for several long, agonizing minutes. His still form hung above the mana pool. His skin was bluish black and his eyes stared blankly up at the ceiling. He hadn't moved since Nuda had entered his body.

Hak twitched suddenly. His arm jerked up and clutched at his chest. His head flew forward and his mouth opened. He vomited blood everywhere.

"Hak!"

Annie stood and took a shaky step forward. Black smoke began to pour out of Hak's armor. His skin slowly returned to its normal color. Blood dripped from beneath his breastplate. The last wisps of the demigod Nuda poured out of Hak and retreated into the cracks in the cavern ceiling, vanishing completely.

Hak convulsed, and blood started seeping from the corners of his mouth. His eyes still stared blindly upwards, and he let out a chilling scream that echoed throughout the chamber.

And then he fell. His armored body crumpled with a loud clang and the white mist covered him.

Annie rushed forward, but stopped at the edge of the pool.

Hak forbid me from stepping into that. But he's dying! He needs help! Is this all a part of the quest? Has he failed? If I step in there, will I die?

Annie felt as if her heart would burst from agonizing doubt. She hesitated at the lip of the pool and stared down at Hak. His eyes were closed, but his hands and legs jerked violently. After a few seconds of thrashing, he fell still. The vapor began to cover him, and then the white smoke turned red.

Fuck it! I'm going to die down here anyway! He's my friend!

Annie tore off her helmet and gloves and jumped into the pool. She ran to Hak and waved the smoke away so she could see his face. She half expected Nuda to pour out of the wall and kill her, but nothing happened.

The vapor in the pool dissipated. The rune that illuminated the pool still glowed brightly. Annie knelt down and tried to pick up Hak's heavy upper body.

"Hey! Hak! Can you hear me? *Hey! Wake up!*"

She shook him and opened one of his eyes with two fingers. His pupil was dilated and didn't react to the white light of the rune.

Oh my god! There's so much blood! Where is he bleeding? How did he get cut?

Annie frantically searched around Hak's body for any signs of injury, but couldn't find any. There was too much blood dripping from his armor. She slid her right hand under his breastplate and chain mail and felt warm, sticky wetness everywhere. She felt the magiel pouch, but couldn't find any tears in his skin. He felt unnaturally hot, and his face was drained of all color.

She pulled her hand out and found it covered in blood. Her body grew cold with fear.

"Hak? Hak? Come on, answer me! *Wake up!*"

Annie placed two fingers along the scar over the vein on his neck. Her whole body was shaking, but she pressed firmly against his neck and tried to feel for a pulse.

Then she placed both hands against his neck and waited to feel something.

Anything.

There was nothing.

Annie jerked her hands from his neck and shuddered.

"*No—*"

Hot tears blinded her. Her heart felt like it was pumping shards of broken glass through her chest.

She grabbed his armor again. "*Noooooooooooo! Haaaaak!* You can't die on me! You can't leave me! Haaaaaaak!"

She slapped his face and beat at his armor. She bent down and screamed just inches from his closed eyes. *"Don't leave me! You have to stay here!"*

Annie felt her whole body grow numb. Shock threatened to pull her senses into a dark undertow where fear would conquer them. She pressed her forehead against Hak's face and took several deep breaths.

I can't faint. I can't lose control. Damn it, Annie! Think! Remember what Diana said about healing!

Annie sucked in a shaky breath and tried to remember her healing lessons in the palace gardens.

"You want to see the current within me. You might find it weakened, depending on how bad the injury is. You will want to grab the current and take my pain. If it is a bloody sword wound, I want you to imagine that the bleeding stops. Breathe in, and imagine sucking that damage out of me. Breathe out, and imagine blowing the pain into the wind. Compassion and clarity are key for healing. Oftentimes healing must happen under stressful circumstances. Someone has fallen or been cut, and they might thrash about or cry. Do not let that bother you. Focus on clearing your mind of everything in the moment except stopping the bleeding. If someone's heart has stopped beating, focus on applying pressure to that four-chambered muscle and imagine it beating once more.

"You must use your imagination. You must be brave. You must be confident. You must think about the injury and how to heal it. Connect with the current, and use it.

"Now Annie, if the wound is particularly grievous, or lethal, it is best you do not attempt this. You can injure yourself beyond repair, or lose your current within mine. That is to say, healing drains you, and can kill you if you are foolish. No life is more important than you own. Remember that."

Annie placed one hand on Hak's breastplate, and slid her right hand underneath it to rest against his heart.

Breathe the pain in. Breathe the pain out. How can I heal when I don't know what I'm doing? No, I can't think that way! Diana told me I must always be confident and brave. But . . . if I succeed, will it kill me?

She looked around the strange cavern and shook her head. The griffin was dead. There were demons and a dragon outside. She was doomed no matter what.

I have to be brave. I have to try, even if I don't know exactly what I'm doing. I have nothing to lose.

Annie took several measured breaths and tried to reach for the current within her. She tried to imagine healing Hak, but nothing happened.

"Who are you?" Hak whispered, watching as the ghostly figures walked around him and examined him. He felt like a cornered fae elk with wolves circling for the kill.

A ghostly man to Hak's left hissed in his mind, *Thief should know.*

"I am no thief. I swear to you upon the stars!"

You stole us. But you saved us, said a woman's soft voice. She knelt down to eye level with Hak. Her face was wispy and strange, and her translucent skin flowed and moved as though her body was full of white smoke.

You are a kin-slayer, said the man.

Hunter . . .

He does not remember, said the woman.

Two more ghostly figures crouched in front of Hak and examined his face. *He does not have much time left here.*

Yes. We must be quick.

The woman kneeling before Hak brushed a strand of hair away from his face. Her large yellow eyes were the only drop of color in her white smoky body. Her sharply chiseled face twisted with sadness.

My poor son. You do not remember anything.

"Who . . . are you?"

You brought us here.

We are the magiel.

Hak gaped up at them, eyes widening in astonishment. He looked up at the tall, silent figure who had not spoken. The one who did not appear to be fully formed into the shape of a person. He felt a familiar energy pulse from it. *The current is truly the place of lost souls and dreams!*

"Are you . . . me?"

The wispy figure stood silently.

That is you, kin-slayer.

"Why do you keep calling me that? Why do you call me son? What do you want from me?"

Because you hunted and killed your own . . . you hunted me down and you took me to Falishan.

You remember, and yet you do not.

"I . . . I remember the things I did. I am not proud of it! I was told to find criminals!"

Is being a warlock a criminal? Is a man sound asleep in his home with his family a criminal? The ghostly man sneered down at Hak. *Did you know that after you took me, hunter, they sent someone after my children? Used them? Drained one and trained the other?*

"Forgive me! I was following orders and I did not know you were a warlock!" Hak wept and held up his hands at the ghostly bodies around him.

I didn't want to know. I didn't want to hurt those people! I've been trying to forget all the pain I've caused! He buried his face in his hands as the voices pressed in from all sides.

Hunter. Kin-slayer.

He does not remember everything.

Do you not see he wants revenge? We can have revenge, through him, said one of the men.

This is our chance.

I see his heart. It is pure now.

Have some pity! He was tricked. He was taken and trained like the rest.

My son, I want you to remember. There is not much time!

The ghostly fingers of the woman reached into Hak's body. He felt an icy chill wash through him as a torrent of memories flashed in his mind.

She was fully formed and human in the vision. She was dressed in thick furs and trudging through thigh-deep snow. She was carrying a child in a thick blanket of fur, held tightly to her chest. A young girl was gripping her fur cloak and walking in the steps her mother made in the snow. The memory was hazy at the edges, and Hak could only see what was immediately surrounding the family. It was all thick snow and howling wind. Hak felt a wave of exhaustion within the memory.

Hak watched the foggy memory unfold. Dark shapes appeared in the forest before them, and riders wearing Shafani sigils surrounded them. A rider wrenched the infant from the mother as she fell under the weight of a binding spell. Another rider picked up the screaming girl and swaddled her in a leather blanket.

Did you ever remember? You were so young, my son. They raised you and trained you, ignorant of your blood. They stole the memories of your sister and family and fed you false ones.

The demons felt that they could raise an invincible set of warriors.

Make them ripe for the taking.

How wrong they were. The blood is rebellious by nature.

So many warlock children lost.

So many confused minds that broke under the weight.

Somehow, the truth always comes out.

Hak felt his chest tighten. He looked at the ghostly woman in front of him, and tears burned his eyes.

"Are you . . . truly my mother?"

I am what is left of her. I am her mana that they trapped in the magiel. And as it is with all mana, my spirit and soul are bound within the magic. I can speak to you here, in the current.

"I am a warlock . . .?" Hak leaned his head back and stared up at the figures around him. His lips worked uselessly and he shook his head. "No! This cannot be. The memories of Yadthra, Serah and my childhood? They were all falsehoods fed to me?"

They were never your family, Hakayatas. Just a soldier's family tasked with your adoption.

"This is impossible!"

They used my magiel in your blood ceremony, my son. I have been dead for twenty years, my heart in a box on a shelf. Unable to rest.

"Is that how I found you? They keep magiel for family?"

The secrets are in the bloodlines.

They create more magiel as we speak.

We are wasting his time. The heart has been still for too long.

Kin-slayer . . . I forgive you. Fight. Use us. Stop them. One of the men knelt before Hak and gave him a sad look. He placed his hands on Hak's chest, and then melted into his body.

Annie grunted and wailed over Hak's still form. She tried to grasp the current. Everything she tried failed. Hak's body had strangely grown warmer under her hands. It was almost too hot to touch.

Annie closed her eyes and concentrated. She removed all thoughts from her frightened mind and focused on Hak's heart. She tried to get it to beat once more. She tried to think of life flowing through him again. She imagined his body growing stronger. Her body was shaking with terror and adrenaline.

She tried to focus on a deep breath that would pull the pain from Hakayatas. Suddenly, her wrist and neck felt as though they were on fire. Annie dared to open an eye and saw that her zythil bracelet was glowing as brightly as a welder's torch.

Something's happening!

Annie tried to keep her mind focused on the thought where the fiery sensation began. The bracelet and necklace sizzled painfully against her skin. She imagined with all her might pulling the pain from Hak and restarting his heart.

She felt as though her entire body had caught on fire. She became increasingly dizzy, but did not stop. Her eyes burned so badly she felt as though they would melt from their sockets. Still, she did not release her hands and the vibrating power that radiated from them.

I have to save him! Just stop bleeding! Must . . . get the heart . . . beating!

The fiery pain was becoming unbearable, but Annie kept her mind firmly grasped on the strange, slippery feeling of the current. She felt her body connected with Hak's and felt his pain. Her chest and eyes were burning. She felt the strange pulse of his body and his current, and she grabbed it with her mind and tried to pull the pain from it.

She felt a strange energy enter her body, and her blood felt like lava.

It was too much. She heard someone scream, only to realize the strange wail was coming from her own body. The force of the spell threw her backward.

She opened her eyes and the world spun. She closed them again. The cool stone against her cheek felt like a slab of ice. *Did I black out?* She wasn't sure how much time had passed. As awareness flooded back, her stomach lurched. Annie rolled onto her chest and threw up. She opened her stinging eyes and blinked, suddenly conscious of her surroundings once more. She smelled burnt skin, and looked down at her wrist in dull surprise. It took her a few moments to get her bearings before she could remember what had happened.

She gasped and looked over at Hak. His skin shimmered like cobalt. Sucking in a breath, Annie crawled to him and tried to touch his skin, but a glasslike surface surrounded him.

It was as hard as the rock around them. Annie stared in horror at the sapphire surface that covered Hak.

"What the fuck did I do?!"

She pounded at the crystal around Hak. It appeared to be several inches thick. She looked over at the crystal tombs that encircled the chamber in growing panic. Hak looked just like them.

We failed!

"*NOOOOO!*"

Annie let out a heart-wrenching scream and beat helplessly at the rock. She felt her throat tear with the force of her wail. She fell over onto the lump of crystal and peered at the distorted face within. A pained whimper escaped her lips. She moved her hand over the spot where Hak's lips were and kissed the crystal.

I guess when people die here they just become part of the chamber. Maybe that is what Mau meant when he said the darkness would consume him.

Annie crawled on top of the tomb and rested her face against the spot above Hak's head. *Just let me fall asleep here with you.* The tears poured out of her as she stroked the crystalline surface above Hak's face.

It's over . . . I'm going to die here with him.

She buried her head in her arms and sobbed.

Suddenly she felt herself yanked up into the air. Her body jerked across the room to a large black-clad figure at the entrance to the chamber. She recognized the dark armor and the glowing lime green eyes immediately.

She hovered in shock while Bingen inspected her. He spun her in a slow circle with a casual flick of his armored hand, and she felt needles dive into her mind. The tall figure was breathing slow and deep, and reminded Annie of the dragon outside. The blazing eyes narrowed into small slits in the visor, and he waved his hand through the air. Annie flew across the room and hit the far wall. The world flashed bright white before her. She felt blood trickle down her face.

She leaned up on an elbow and watched in horror as Bingen approached the pool. The demon's body glowed with a sickly purple-black shadow. He tore off his strange, spiked helm and threw it to the ground. Annie's eyes widened.

He was really a *she*. Annie gasped. *Bingen is a female elf! At least, half of her is an elf. Damn, one really ugly elf at that!*

She had a harsh, angular face and hollow cheeks. Long tipped ears rose out of white hair that spilled down her neck in a messy braid that disappeared within her armor.

The sharp white face was contorted with fury. She growled at the crystalline tomb, and Annie saw that her teeth were long and pointed. She let out a strange, furious howl that sounded as though it were composed of dozens of screams.

"No! *I* was to kill him! Not *this*!"

Bingen curled her long fingers around one another and created a black ball of fire between her hands. She flung it down at the crystalline tomb. It didn't even leave a scorch mark. She tried again and again; each time her magical blasts grew larger and louder.

"*Worthless! Dog!*" she breathed, slamming a fireball down at the tomb with each word. "*STUPID! WORTHLESS! DOG!*"

Annie watched in horror as Bingen blasted the surface of Hak's tomb again and again, trying to break it open.

What if she breaks the crystal? Then what? I can't let her have the magiel! Not after everything Hak went through!

Annie found the strength to stand. Anger swelled inside her chest until she thought she would burst. She drew her small sword from her scabbard and charged at Bingen's back.

The demon didn't look at her. She raised a finger and Annie felt herself lift off the floor. She twisted in the air as invisible hands grabbed her wrists and pulled her arms down tightly to her side. The sword fell from her hand.

Bingen slowly turned her face to Annie and smiled. "Well. I have not met *anything* so stupid in a very long time."

The tall half-elf, half-demon turned to Annie and raised an armored fist at her. Annie felt as if a giant hand was squeezing her. She couldn't move her legs or her arms. She tried not to cry out. She didn't want the demon to see how frightened she was.

"Were you my pet's mate? Hmmm? What was my pet worth to you? Did you two breed? Produce little magical children? Hmmmm?"

Annie's temper got the best of her. "I get it. You wear all that huge armor to hide the ugly, scrawny bitch you really are. You're just a stupid skeleton with sharp teeth and fucked-up ears—"

The squeezing sensation intensified, and Annie heard a loud clang. She looked down in alarm and realized that Bingen was crushing her armor. She felt her breastplate push inward against her ribs. She heard another pop, and felt her leg plates squeezing together. Her brain felt as though a wall of needles mashed it down.

Fuck you! Annie roared in her mind, and imagined pushing the demon's control from her body. She remembered how angry she had been with Mau's control in the chamber. She seized the emotion. A burst of energy coursed through her veins, as if the very cells in her body were vibrating. She focused her fury on Bingen.

She felt her bracelet and necklace burn her already charred skin. The rage kept coming. She saw red. She ignored the pain and pushed her anger out with all her might. One arm broke free of Bingen's invisible embrace. She jerked her torso around and kicked with one leg. She writhed in midair and gnashed her teeth angrily at Bingen. Spittle flew from her lips as she cursed and raged.

Bingen's eyes widened in wonder, and a toothy grin spread across her pale face. "Hmmmm, no. This is better than I expected! Marvelous!" Bingen dropped her armored hand and Annie hit the floor. The reddish haze in her vision faded away.

The demon seemed to be talking to herself. She scratched at her chin with a long bony finger and stared down at Hak's crystal tomb. "Interesting. Yes. Combined energies. I think she will more than suffice. But it is a pity we will not have all the magiel."

Bingen pointed her palm at Annie and a black ribbon shot from her hand. Annie tried to twist away from it, but it moved too fast. It twisted around her body and bound her. She felt like a bug wrapped up in a spider's web.

"You are a wild mutt, yes? Perhaps you can be tamed. I think Voltay will like you."

Bingen grabbed her helmet and put it on. She pulled Annie off the ground and tucked her under an arm as if she weighed nothing. Annie was facing the opposite direction as the demon. She stared sadly at the silent lump of crystal in the middle of the chamber and let out a howl. Bingen hit the side of her head sharply.

"Be quiet, dog. You will either learn or you will be put out of your misery. I detest training worthless beasts such as you, and I have little patience for whelps."

Bingen raced from the chamber, carrying Annie under her arm. Annie stared at the glowing rune on the floor and the illuminated lump of crystal with Hak's body inside. Tears ran down her face and she howled.

She hoped Bingen would simply kill her.

Hak allowed the magiel ghosts to enter his body one by one. His mind felt alert and sharper than ever. He felt renewed, and reveled in the burst of current that boiled in his blood.

My son. I fight with you, and watch over you.

"Please, stay! Tell me more of my past! My family! I do not remember any of it!"

Seek out your memories in the northern snow seas. There you can catch the stars of your life. His mother's ghostly figure knelt before him. *There is no time left, my son. Even now, your body grows weak without your spirit. You will remember soon enough. Catch the stars in the north. Go back to your body. Annie needs you!*

"Annie?"

Watch over her, my son. She will bind and break—

Before she could say anything else, the ghostly woman fell into his chest and disappeared. Tears streamed down Hak's cheeks as he stared at the spot where she had been standing just seconds ago.

He looked up at the ghostly figure of himself. It had stood silently the entire time, watching and waiting.

Hak got to his feet and walked toward it, awe in his eyes. He reached up a hand to his magiel. The ghost before him seemed to sigh with relief as it reacted to Hak's touch. Hak took a hesitant step forward and allowed himself to walk into the wispy reflection.

He felt his entire body burn with newfound strength. The white abyss around him shifted and fell apart.

Hak was falling again.

His body was bursting with the current.

He felt alive.

Annie stared forlornly at the way they had come. Bingen moved at what seemed like a magical pace, quickly putting distance between them and the heart of the current. The glowing runes in the ceiling blurred as they sped past. Annie stared at the dark tunnel behind them, tears dripping off her nose and chin. She twisted in her bonds, but couldn't move a finger.

A loud crack like rock breaking rang through the cave. And then another. The runes lost their light. The noise echoed down the tunnel. Suddenly, a loud roar tore through the air and the ground began to shake. Rock and dust fell from the ceiling.

Bingen paused, and Annie felt the demon shift nervously. Her breath was ragged and deep, like a dragon's. There was another explosion in the cavern, and Bingen whirled around to stare in the direction they had come.

"What is this?"

The elf threw Annie aside, but she was still bound in the black spell. She hit the floor and rolled to her side. She tried to wiggle away from the demon like an inchworm. Bingen no longer seemed to care about Annie. A small light appeared above her head, illuminating the tunnel. She was seething and staring down the passageway, her glowing eyes wide and unbelieving. Annie's skin prickled all over.

Even I could feel that huge burst of power! What's happening?

The demon took a step back, and began swirling her hands around each other to create a large, black fireball. Annie heard a low rumble and picked her head off the ground to look down the tunnel. There was a white light coming from the direction of the heart of the current, and it grew brighter by the second.

A brilliant ball of white and yellow fire raced up the tunnel. Bingen cursed and flung her spell toward it.

Annie stared in horror and amazement as a hand reached out of the light and slapped the spell away. It burst against the rock wall.

There's a person in that fireball!

Annie felt her heart jump into her throat when she saw the tall figure within.

Could it be . . . ?

Before she could blink, the white fireball was upon them. It crashed into a green barrier that Bingen produced at the last second.

The man within the fireball raised his arms and shot several balls of light at Bingen. He looked like Hak, but his hair was white. His yellow eyes were ablaze. His face was contorted in the most vicious, hateful rage Annie had ever seen on a person. It frightened her.

But he was dead! He didn't have a heartbeat! He was covered in crystal. . . . Oh shit! Is it Nuda?!

"Give me the magiel!" Bingen swung her arms and shot black fire at him.

He laughed and batted the spells away with ease. Bingen roared, placed both her hands together, and pointed them at the blazing man before her.

He flattened his palms, pointed them at the ground, and blasted white fire down. The effect propelled him up into the air and he sailed with ease over the demon. A blast of black lightning burst uselessly in the spot the man had just been.

Annie gaped. *No human can move that fast!*

Bingen whirled on the man and flung more black lightning from her palms. The man within the white aura raised his arms up and pulled the ground up in front of him. A wall of rock blocked the lightning.

He used magic to push himself off the floor again just as a second black blast shattered the rock barrier. The man defied gravity and ran along the cavern wall, and rained rock and white fire down on the demon.

Annie's jaw dropped.

Bingen roared and sent another magical volley at the man, but it missed and exploded against the wall. Rock and pebbles fell on Annie as she felt the entire cave shake. She tried to wriggle up against the far wall and out of danger.

"Obey!"

"Never again!" The man roared, and hurled a massive blast at Bingen. The ground began to shake violently. The man within the fireball darted down the tunnel, taunting the demon.

"You! Will! Die!" Bingen hurled another spell, but she aimed it for the ceiling. The man darted forward to escape the falling rock. She grinned and opened her palms at him.

A great beam of black lightning hissed from her open hands and filled the tunnel beyond. Annie gasped, watching in awe as the man flung up a strange shield of blue light. The blast poured around him, but the continuous torrent did not touch him. The figures seemed frozen, their palms pressed before them, magic bursting from their hands.

The man grunted, and Annie could see his face through the transparent azure shield. His feral yellow eyes were full of rage. And fear.

He pushed against the constant blast like he was trying to move a boulder. He bared his teeth and produced his own white blast of magic.

The two beams of light met and pushed against each other. The man began stepping forward, roaring in hatred and exertion. The two figures hands were locked in place, their blasts of magic exploding outward in the center.

Annie felt numb with shock and fear. She tried to roll away from the two enraged figures. Bingen saw her out of the corner of her eye, and her green eyes widened. A wicked smile contorted her white face.

The man saw the look Bingen gave Annie and bellowed angrily. Bingen kept one open hand pointed at him. She turned her other palm out toward

Annie and gave an insane cackle.

"*You lose!*"

Annie screamed and tried to curl into a ball. She winced and tucked her head into her wrapped up knees. She heard a *whoosh* like flame pouring out of a furnace, and a low humming sound.

Hesitantly, she cracked an eye open and stared in shock. A small blue barrier was wrapped around her. Black flame poured around her but did not touch her.

Annie opened her eyes wide and gaped. Bingen had one hand shooting black lightning at the man, and one hand pouring flame at Annie. It hit the barriers noisily and rolled off. She looked at the man and realized he held the same stance. One hand was blasting white fire at the demon's own beam of magic.

His other hand was open and facing Annie. His fingers were curled and shaking.

He's protecting me?

The two warring figures were locked in place. They screamed and howled at each other, but would not give in. The deflected magic shot against the walls and rocks fell everywhere. They bounced harmlessly off the shield over Annie's head.

"You stupid dog! You cannot keep this up much longer. Two shields will be the end of you!"

The barrier around Annie weakened and pressed inward. The black flame was only a few inches from her face. Annie was petrified with terror and afraid that moving an inch would cause instant death.

"No . . ." The man struggled and his foot slipped back. His sweat rose off of his skin in an eerie white steam.

"*You will both die here!*"

The man within the fireball looked at Annie with wide eyes. His face twisted with fear and sadness. He set his eyes back on Bingen and let out an inhuman howl that sounded as though it were made of several voices. A light shined within his armor.

The man pushed forward and screamed, "*Noooo!*"

The light around the man became too bright to look at. It enveloped him like a white star. Annie squinted her eyes against the brilliance.

The ball of light exploded in a tight beam and pushed through Bingen's lightning. His torrent of magic hit the demon straight on, and she flew down the tunnel and slammed into a wall. The magical battle ceased, but the ground still shook.

The man walked past Annie and stepped up to Bingen. He had a white fireball in his hands, ready to throw.

The half-elf, half-demon sat up against the wall and let out a long, dry cackle. Hundreds of strange voices seemed to laugh and echo down the tunnels. Dust and small rocks continued to rain down from the shaking ceiling.

Bingen's black and green armor was cracked and glowing. Her helm was split down the middle. The cracks in her armor pulsed and glowed a bright, sickly green.

The man stopped fifteen feet from Bingen and held the white fireball before him.

"*Why?*"

"You do not make demands of me."

"Why do you do it? Why do you collect warlocks? Why do you kidnap their children?"

"Stupid human. You are meant to be slaves. You are meant to be bred and used and trained, like dogs. I do not have to explain myself to you." Bingen cackled again, but grimaced as her armor began smoking.

"You stole my life!"

"It was ours to use! You are nothing but a dog, and a dog must do as it is trained! Nothing more!"

Bingen's breathing changed. It became lower and deeper, as if she were a much larger being than the elf before them. Black smoke drifted from her skin. She flashed her pointed teeth at the man and gave him an amused smile as the cave began to fall in around them.

"You. Are. Nothing. The gate will be open soon. Your race can either obey, or be crushed."

"Gate?"

Bingen laughed, and glowing purple blood oozed out of the corner of her mouth. She looked up at Hak and her twisted smile stretched across her face. In the flashing white light of the man's waiting fireball, Bingen looked insane.

"You will die down here, dog."

The ceiling fell in, but the man yanked his hands above his head to produce another blue barrier. The rocks cascaded around him, but did not touch him. Bingen was still laughing as the ceiling crushed her.

Annie felt her bonds melt away. It took her a moment to realize she was free. She stood on shaky legs and stared around in panic. Her mind felt as though it were breaking under the shock of what she had just witnessed.

A second later the man was at her side. He was covered in dry blood and sweat, and panting heavily. He grabbed her arm. "We have to get out of here!"

Annie jerked away from him in panic and backed up against the wall.

It can't be him!

"Annie!"

"I saw you die!"

"Annie, do not lose your mind! Not now!"

"It can't be you!" she wailed. She felt dizzy, sick, and broken all at the same time.

"Annie! It is *me*! Hakayatas! You like to call me an asshole, remember?"

Before she could answer, Hak picked her up and pressed her against his chest. He seemed to catch fire again as he raced through the tunnels and falling rock. The white aura of magic enveloping them tickled Annie's skin.

It felt amazing.

Her chin rested on his shoulder and she stared behind them. The entire mountain was rumbling and caving in. They sped through the tunnels and Annie watched the strange flame around Hak in growing fascination. The tendrils of white, yellow, and red flame seemed to trickle away from them as they zipped through the cave.

Annie realized what it reminded her of and gasped. The wisps of flame that poured off Hak looked like feathers. It was strangely beautiful.

"Are you all right, Annie?"

She couldn't reply. She was too stunned by the strange vision.

How . . . ? Am I dead? This reminds me of my dream.

Sunlight hit Annie's skin, and Hak's fiery aura winked out as she turned in his arms to squint up at the bright sky. A blue bubble sprang up around the two of them as a large plume of dust and rock shot out of the cave behind them. The brown and gray cloud flew harmlessly around their shield and smothered the sun. Annie stared numbly at the magic shield, and then at the strange man. He clutched his chest and fell to his knees with a pained, tired look. He gazed up at her, sweat pouring down his face, his breathing labored and ragged.

It can't be . . .

He had the same scars as Hak, but this man seemed completely different to Annie. His long hair was white, not yellow. His golden eyes glowed softly, and Annie saw a new hardness in them.

He reached out and tentatively pointed up at her. "Your eyes . . ."

"Hak?" she managed to whimper. "Is it . . . really you?"

He gave her a soft smile. "It is me. Dude."

Annie felt her lips tremble, and she sank to her knees. Hak remained on the ground in front of her, his eyes flooded with concern. He reached out and gently pushed her hair from her face with a gloved hand.

Her eyes filled with tears as she stared at him. She let out a loud wail and threw her arms around Hak. She squeezed him until it hurt, sobbing the entire time.

"You! I saw you die! You were dead! Oh my god, you were *dead*! And I couldn't save you! I thought we were done for! You *asshole*! I thought I'd never see you again!"

Annie sobbed harder and squeezed him even tighter. She buried her face in his strange white hair and nuzzled his neck.

She heard Hak choke on a sob, and whisper into her ear, "I am sorry! I thought I lost you! Bingen almost had me!"

"You big idiot!"

"Crazy woman!"

They held each other and cried as the dust settled around them. Annie felt her heart bursting with emotions she had not thought imaginable. Reluctantly, Hak pulled away to stare at Annie.

"Your eyes . . . what happened to you?"

Annie sniffled, and gave Hak a confused smile. "What do you mean?"

"Annie. Your eyes are yellow."

She squinted at him and cocked her head. *"What?"*

"What happened to you while I was fighting Nuda within the current?"

Annie's lips worked uselessly for a moment.

Hak placed both his hands gently on her cheeks and looked deep into her eyes. "May I enter? May I see your memory? Just of the last hour or so?"

Annie shied away from him. "I . . . Wow. You can do that now, huh? Um, I'd rather you not. Please. Can't I just tell you?"

"Of course. I will never be like those people in Meda. I will never intrude upon you."

Annie shook her head and smiled at him. She reached over and gave him another hug.

"Sorry. I have to. I just . . . I can't believe you're really okay."

"Do not start crying again, Annie. It is all right. Just tell me what happened."

"Well . . . you flew up to the ceiling, and Nuda went into your body. And your skin turned black. You didn't . . . seem to be all there. You kind of went catatonic and stared at the ceiling for I don't know how long."

Annie shuddered and choked on a sob. "I saw you fall. You were bleeding everywhere, Hak. I didn't know where you were bleeding from. It was just . . . coming out of your pores. Oh my god, it was the scariest moment of my life."

Hak gave her a sly grin. "Scarier than the fight I had with that demon?"

Annie nodded and wiped the tears from her eyes.

"Y-you were dead. I felt for your heartbeat, b-but I couldn't feel anything!"

"Wait, did you run into the pool?"

Annie looked at the ground. "You were dying."

"Annie!"

"I thought . . . I thought that if you died, then what happened next wouldn't matter."

"Oh, Annie." Hak gave her another hug. "You never listen, do you?"

"No . . ."

"What happened in the pool?"

"You were bleeding, and I th-thought . . . I tried to heal you. I tried to stop the bleeding and take your pain away. My bracelet and necklace lit up, but then I blacked out. When I came to, you were covered in crystal. I thought . . . I thought I had done something wrong!" Annie took a deep breath and said, "I just sat down next to you and didn't want to move. Then Bingen showed up, and tried to break your tomb or whatever that crystal thing was. And then she tried to kill me, and then she decided to kidnap me. That's when you showed up like the fucking human torch and all that crazy shit went down."

Hak let out a loud laugh and smiled at Annie. He shook his head. "Your language, Annie. By the stars . . ."

"But that's what happened!"

Still smiling, Hak stroked a finger against the circular blister around Annie's neck, and looked at her bloody wrist. She winced as he touched the broken skin.

"May I?"

"What?"

"Let me heal this."

Hak gently rubbed at the burns and Annie felt a cold chill tickle her skin. The blood dried and the burn disappeared under his fingertips. She stared at her wrist in amazement. The skin was fresh and pink, and felt very itchy. Hak took in a deep, shaky breath and wiped his brow. He seemed exhausted.

Hak looked in the direction of the cave. "I wonder how she got in? How did Bingen get to the heart of the current?"

That would be my fault, said a deep, slow voice.

Annie squeaked and clutched Hak's breastplate. She turned and looked toward the end of the terrace. The dust had settled enough that they could make out the shapes of the landscape around them; Annie stared at the large dragon on the ledge.

The behemoth didn't return her gaze. It was calmly staring out over the ocean, oblivious to the dust settling on his scales.

The half-demon sacrificed her comrade to distract me. Disgusting, sending someone to die against their will. By the time I discovered the ruse, the demon had darted inside.

"Tomas . . . is dead?" Annie whispered.

A dishonorable way to go. His mind had no control over his body.

Annie stood on shaky legs and looked around the terrace. There was blood on the ground in several places, but no bodies. She stared in the direction of the griffin and gave a small moan. Only the saddle and a few feathers remained where the griffin had crashed.

Annie felt her heart seize in panic and she stared back at the dragon.

"Hak? How are we going to get back?"

"I do not know, Annie," he whispered.

"How far can you fly? Or do that one magic trick?"

"Not long enough, I am afraid. I am exhausted from that battle, Annie. It took everything I had to push Bingen away. I need to eat and rest."

Your mount was dying, said the dragon in their minds. *It is a dishonor to let a creature suffer. And . . . I was also hungry.*

Annie stared at the black dragon with alarm and took a few steps back.

Fear not, human. You would not satisfy my tastes.

Hak glanced around. "Is there a boat? Or anything on this island that we can take? We do not want to intrude upon you any longer, Wise Tarsierling."

The dragon rumbled, and Annie took the strange undulating noise for a laugh.

There are no boats. You are the first humans to come here in a very long time.

Annie suddenly remembered the painting in her neighbor's study. *But Maz had seen this place! He had that painting . . .* She stepped forward and hesitantly addressed the dragon.

"Did you ever see someone named Maz? Short human, no hair?"

All humans are short to me. But yes, two humans came here many seasons ago. One by that name. They went into the Fieriel Senefal and never came out.

"Annie, what are you talking about?"

She turned to answer Hak, but white stars swam in front of her eyes and her head hurt.

"That stupid mind-fucking bitch."

"Annie?"

"I'm . . . sorry. I can't tell you. Not yet. But I think you, me, and Aiyana need to sit down and have a little talk when we get back."

"Fair enough," Hak said.

"If we can get back."

"We will find a way, Annie."

You humans are so interesting. You are trapped, but you do not think to force me into taking you off the island.

Hak gaped at the dragon and gave him a slight bow. "We would not dishonor you, wise one."

It is strange how short your lives are. Your histories seem tattered. Once upon a time, your kind rode dragons. Many against their will. You are different. You are very powerful, and yet humble. I can see that you have great honor.

"How old are you?"

"Annie, do not be rude!"

The dragon let out a rumbling chuckle. *I have seen a great many things. I do not know my age exactly. But I recall the first of your kind, warlock.*

Annie whipped her head around and stared at Hak.

"Warlock?"

"I will tell you later, Annie. Do not be rude in front of Wise Tarsierling."

"But—"

"Later, Annie."

The dragon walked toward them. The entire terrace trembled with each step. He stopped before them and craned his neck down to get a better look.

You are interesting humans. You are not like the others.

Annie looked at Hak and said, "A lot happened to us inside the mountain."

I would be curious to hear your tale. Where is it you desire to go?

"Meda, wise one."

Ahhhh, the great city of Meda still exists? That is good to hear.

"Yes, Wise Tarsierling."

The dragon looked out over the ocean. *I have not left the southern seas in a very long time. I have sensed that something is very wrong with the balance of the current. I would be willing to help you, if you would tell me some of the recent human histories. It has been long since I have conversed with your kind.*

"Hak is really good at telling stories," Annie said. She looked up at Hak and gave him a smile. "I still can't believe you're here."

"Me, either," Hak said. He pulled the fist-sized magiel pouch out of his armor; dried blood flaked off of the pouch onto his fingers. "I think the zythil in this purse saved me. It gave me the extra strength I needed to fight Bingen."

Carefully, he opened the pouch and turned it over onto his palm. He gave it a shake, but nothing came out. Hak dug around inside the pouch with two of his fingers.

"They're gone!"

"Are you okay, Hak?"

He looked down at the pouch, his eyes shimmering with tears. Then he tucked it back under his breastplate and looked over at Annie.

"I think I have quite the story to share with you. But I do not really understand . . . I saw my mother in the current, Annie."

"What?"

"Let us find a way to safely ride back to Meda, and I will tell you all I know. I have new memories, but I am not sure if they make sense. I think the mind control the demons put me under really twisted my memory up."

"You can tell me when you're ready. I don't know if I can handle anymore surprises today."

Hak looked at the ground, and then back up at Annie. His eyes were full of sadness.

"When you are ready Annie, I think you should know about my past. At least, the parts I can remember clearly. There is much I have done that I am not proud of, but I think it is best if I do not hide anything from you."

She hugged him. "Hak, I don't care about who you *were*. Just about who you *are*. Life is too short to focus on the past. There's a lot I don't understand about mine. And I hope I can tell you someday. Like I said, we need to sit down with Aiyana and a giant pitcher of beer, and talk about what we all know."

"I think I would like that, Annie."

Annie grinned. "Hey, now you're like, a wizard or something! I can't believe what I saw back there in the tunnel! How does it feel?"

Hak looked down at his hands and opened and closed them a few times. "It feels amazing. I feel alive for the first time in years."

"Yeah?"

"I think . . . I think I absorbed all the magiel."

"Whoa! That means you have the power of seven other people, right?" Annie crinkled her eyebrows. "That's . . . kind of scary, actually. And a little creepy."

Hak looked grim. "I think I will now be able to defeat Voltay. For once, I feel confident."

Annie bit her lip and looked at the ground. Her heart clenched in her chest, but she said nothing.

"Well. One thing at a time, yes? We should get home. We are filthy."

Annie looked at the dried blood all over her, and her breastplate, which was dented in several places from Bingen squeezing her. She shuddered, looked up at the sky, and took a deep breath.

"Sunlight never felt so good in my life."

"Yes. I will die a happy man if I never have to enter another cave."

"You got that right."

Hak took a deep breath and walked over to where the griffin had been. A few feathers drifted away in the ocean breeze, and Annie spied their blankets and camping supplies farther away.

"How are we going to do this?"

"I will use magic to cut and rebind the saddle. We can probably strap ourselves to one of the spikes on his back."

Annie's eyes grew wide and she stared at the dragon.

"Oh man . . . No. Hell no."

Hak flashed a grin at Annie. "Are you saying that you want to stay here?"

"Ugh! I am so *through* having adventures! You hear me?"

Hak laughed and set to work with the saddle. He instructed Annie on how to hold different pieces as he bound them together. It was clumsy work, and Hak was an inexperienced leatherworker, but he did his best.

At last he held up two large straps that had held the saddle in place. They looked like giant belts. The spaces between the dragon's dorsal spikes were too narrow to accommodate the large saddle, so Hak insisted they would have to sit on their blankets.

Using magic, Hak lifted Annie up to one of the spikes and strapped her against it. He tied the blanket under her to her waist, like a giant padded diaper. She felt as though she were clinging to a large tree trunk. The small grooves on the giant spike were prickly, like bark. Hak cast a spell on the leather to ensure it wouldn't break, and gave it a tug.

"Just hold on, Annie. This will be like riding a large horse, yes?"

"Oh sure. A large, scaly horse with teeth the size of my body. Flying thousands of feet up in the air. Yeah. Just like a damned horse."

Hak smiled and shook his head at her.

She debated asking him for a calming spell, as she had with Diana, but there was something about the idea of Hak getting into her mind that disturbed her. She didn't know if she would ever give him permission to do anything to her brain. She hoped that he never imposed upon her.

I'll just have to tough this ride out. No fae water. No mind-numbing spells. I need to start being brave. I need to stop using alcohol and crap to numb my mind when I'm scared or upset. This world is strange and new to me, and I don't want to miss a thing. I can't believe I'm going to ride on a dragon! This is just so crazy. I wonder what Matt would do if he could see this.

Annie let out a sad sigh and watched as Hak tied himself to the spike behind her. *I hope Matt is still alive. I hope all my friends are still alive. Maybe that blast of light I saw was the current, not a bomb. Would I go back if I could?*

Annie lost herself in thought as the dragon rose off the ground. She gripped the spike and tried not to scream as Tarsierling jumped off the terrace.

The dragon was extremely fast, and his flight was much smoother than the griffin's had been. Annie missed the protection her helmet had given her eyes. Both she and Hak had left their helmets in the cave. She kept her cheek against the large spike to keep the wind out of her eyes, and stared out to the west as the sun began to set. She was cold, and wondered for a time if the enchantment that the council had given her was broken.

The world around her glowed with the setting sun. Annie tried to absorb everything she saw from the dragon's back, even after her arms and legs began to throb with discomfort. As they made their way over the main continent, she saw great flocks of birds rise from the trees and scatter as Tarsierling flew overhead. Herds of large animals darted and jumped through emerald valleys at the sight of the dragon. The world turned orange, then pink, and then purple.

Sometimes Tarsierling would turn his head to glance at Hak with a large reptilian eye, the corners of his mouth turned up in what could have been a grin. He would shake his head, or make the rumbling noise that she thought was a chuckle. Hak seemed to be mind-speaking with the dragon, but Annie wasn't included in the mind link. Hak was keeping his word about staying out of her thoughts.

She kept her eyes on the world below her and smiled.

No highways and traffic jams. No sprawling concrete shopping centers and skyscrapers. No factories and nuclear plants polluting this world. All those tiny farms down there look so perfect. These people are so lucky to be born in a world where healers can cure eyesight and cancer! It's amazing that so many can use magic to improve their lives!

Sure, there's a bit of backward thinking toward women. But Diana is strong and amazing. I just need to hang out with the right people, I think. I want to see the elven kingdoms, and explore some tropical beaches. Tahldia does kind of feel like home now. Maybe it always did, because of Maz.

Annie remained awake the entire night, despite not sleeping the night before. The dragon's flight was so exciting that any shred of fatigue was erased when she looked up at the sky. The brilliant red nebula that splashed across the sky still took her breath away. The clouds of stardust seemed to burst from the south pole all the way to the northern reaches, like a frozen wisp of crimson smoke speckled with a myriad of white and yellow stars. The moons lent the dark landscape a soft silvery aura that bathed the snow-topped mountains in splashes of blue and purple.

She glanced back several times at Hak. His posture, resolute at the beginning of the flight, had shifted into an exhausted slouch.

By dawn, Hak was slumped against his spike, his eyes closed. His strange white hair whipped in the wind, and dried blood still covered him.

Poor thing. He needs a break more than anyone. I hope he really thinks about that stupid revenge idea of his. I hope he doesn't get himself killed trying to take on another half-demon. I just want him to smile and be happy. That's all I want for him.

Annie was so stiff and sore by daybreak that it hurt to move, yet she still enjoyed watching the sunrise over the long tail of mountains that rose in the east.

The landscape was familiar to her then, and she realized they must be close to Meda.

Wow! We have traveled so fast!

She sat up, grimaced at her frozen muscles, and turned to look at Hak. He was awake as well, and staring around with an excited smile on his face. His eyes had cooled back to their normal yellow color, but they shone with anticipation.

They flew over a long river; Annie recognized it as the one that flowed into the Meda waterfall. More farms and villages sprouted amongst the thick forest like a great patchwork quilt.

She wanted to cheer when Meda came into view. *All I want is my dog and a weeklong nap. I need sleep. I feel delirious. I never thought I would see Meda again. I made it back! I'm alive!* She glanced back at Hak and they shared wild grins. Her heart jumped into her throat, and the emotions that rolled through her brought fresh tears to her eyes. *We're alive . . . .*

The dragon banked and flew lower. His slow, deep voice rang clearly in both of their minds.

The last time I came to Meda, they shot at me. Annie and Hakayatas, please grant me a kindness and tell the guards I am friendly. I do not like it when humans become panicked. Even now I can hear the horns.

Annie couldn't hear anything, but she assumed the dragon had much keener senses than her. She turned to look at Hak, but his eyes were closed in concentration. After a moment he opened his eyes and gave a satisfied smile.

That is good to hear, young one, said the dragon.

Annie made a face. *So he won't even try to speak in my mind? He is really keeping that promise about intruding in my brain. I suppose I should be thankful for it. I already feel a weird connection to him, I don't know if I could handle him in my mind.*

Horns bellowed through the air as the dragon alighted on top of the cliff next to the dock. The guards cowered and one ran for cover as the dragon took several steps toward the doors.

Tarsierling stepped gently between the airships and small outbuildings. Annie could hear the griffins screeching with alarm in the stables.

She felt an excited mind enter hers just then, and Diana's joyful voice rang in her thoughts.

Is it really you? Have you truly returned to us?

Yes! Where are you?

On the lifts! We will be there in a moment!

The massive black dragon stopped before the large wooden doors of the lift. A huge grin split Annie's face as the doors opened and she recognized the crowd of people within. The entire council, even King Halona, was frozen, staring dumbstruck up at the dragon.

Annie laughed when she saw Mau's jaw hanging open beneath his white fuzzy beard. Diana's hands covered her mouth in shock. Even from high up on the dragon, Annie could see her purple eyes flashing brightly.

Hak used his dagger to cut himself free. He floated to Annie's side at once and cut the strap holding her to the dragon. He picked her up and tossed the blankets and leather aside. He gently drifted down, soft as a falling leaf, and steadied Annie as her feet touched the ground.

Annie was barely standing on her sore legs when Diana crashed into her and gave her a fierce hug. Iriel ran to them and joined in the embrace.

Diana's eyes were full of tears when she stepped back.

"*By the stars*! What has happened to your eyes? You are a mess! Are you all right? By the red dragon's tears! *What has happened to you?*"

"It's a long story."

"And Hakayatas, your hair. And your magic!" Diana took a step toward Hak and hesitantly touched his arm. "You are teeming with power."

Iriel gently touched Annie's arm, her eyes glistening with tears. "So much blood." Annie's arm was still caked with dried blood to her elbow from shoving it underneath Hak's breastplate to find his injuries

The rest of the council slowly approached. They all gave the dragon an uneasy look as he sat down with an earth-shaking thud. Tarsierling seemed uninterested in the attention, picking absently at a tooth with a long black talon.

Aiyana walked up to them and leaned heavily on her cane. She and Mau were speechless for a moment. She looked at Hak, and then at the dragon, and then over to Annie. She shook her head in awe and spoke in her raspy voice. "This is truly a bard's tale, yes? Such wonder. I never thought to see another dragon in my old age. And to see this—" She poked Hak with her cane. "You and I have much to talk about. In private."

King Halona approached the dragon and gave a deep bow that swept his cloak along the ground. "I am King Gaeric Halona. You honor us all with your presence, Wise Tarsierling."

The honor is mine. I have been told Meda is in the hands of a just and good king. Much has changed in this part of the world. And it is pleasing to see good energy at work here.

The king blushed and gave the dragon another bow. "I do what I must to keep this land plentiful and in balance with the current."

It appears you do very well. The last time I was in Meda, it was during the war of the Dohlen. It is peaceful in this part of the world once more. But there is much I think you and I need to discuss, human. I have ill tidings for you.

"I will set up a meeting here, right this moment if you would like. I will summon my scribes."

That would be kind. I am eager to continue flying north to see what has happened in the snow seas. I have an old friend up there.

Diana tugged at Annie's arm. "My dear, you look frightful! Do I even want to know why you're covered in blood, or why your armor looks like it was trampled by a dragon?"

Annie remembered Diana telling her to run if she ever saw a demon. Her mind flickered to the moment in the cave when she had unsheathed her sword and charged Bingen, only to be nearly crushed to death.

"No . . . you probably don't want to hear that story."

"Aye, you have some tales for us." Mau was still staring up at the dragon.

Aiyana nodded. "Yes, my dear. Let us get that blood off you, and then we must hold council. This cannot wait."

Diana frowned. "Surely let them rest for a moment! They look exhausted!"

"The children can take a nap later. I want to know what has happened." Aiyana gave Annie a wicked grin. "But I am more than happy to propose a small feast tonight, in their honor. Best to go to bed with a belly full of wine this evening, yes?"

Annie nodded and leaned against Hak. "Just be quick about the meeting. You guys have some money for me, and I intend to start relaxing as soon as possible. Get your mind prodding out of the way so I can start stuffing my face with food and ale. After a nap, of course."

After a brief council meeting that left Annie with a raging headache, she made her way back to her room to find Tia chewing on one of the bedposts, and a hot bath waiting for her. Nivya had brought the dog as soon as Diana sent word to her. She left a letter for Annie detailing time spent studying under trees, and playing tug with an old rope.

The elves had healed Annie, of course. They cast soothing spells on her sore muscles, cramped legs, and riding blisters, but it didn't help the inescapable fatigue that weighed her down.

Annie sank into the hot water and quickly nodded off in the tub. She woke when Tia licked her face. She wrapped herself in a towel and crawled into bed to sleep a few more hours. Only the gnawing teeth of hunger kept her from sleeping away the evening. She felt like she could eat a dragon and drink an ocean of beer.

The stars and three moons shone brightly over the ballroom balcony that night. Far off, a thunderstorm rumbled on the horizon. The distant flashes of lightning added to the surreal beauty around her. The forested valley was spread out before her, the tops of the cliffs catching the bursts of light from the distant storm. Harsh shadows like teeth spread across the rock walls, only to fade back into darkness. The sky directly overhead was clear, and the nebula flared crimson and orange above the castle. With any luck, the storm would stay in the west.

Annie sighed with contentment and leaned back in the large cushioned chair with Diana. They shared the huge seat, with a bottle of wine and pitcher of beer on a table before them. Annie had helped herself to five plates of food that evening, not bothering to talk, and garnered several stares from royalty and servants alike as she shoved fistfuls of bread into her mouth. She hadn't cared. She didn't even ask what was in the stew. She just shoveled it into her mouth. She ate everything put in front of her, and asked for more. And now she could barely move. But she still found space in her belly for several glasses of ale.

They had spent the better part of an hour drinking and giggling. Annie still had a difficult time believing she was back in Meda. A gentle breeze tugged at Annie's frilly blue dress, and she tucked her legs up underneath her to get more comfortable.

"Diana, I've been thinking about something."

"And what would that be, my heart?"

Annie smiled at that, and looked down at Tia snoring noisily on the ground. "You know Tia came here when I did. But I don't think she showed up at the same point. Hak and Aiyana said there are several crystal points around the mountain where I woke up. How did she get here?"

"My dear, anything living within your current's energy was pulled with you. Imagine a river branching off into smaller streams; the current pulled you and Tia together, but you split off right before the mountain."

"I remember grabbing her collar right before I saw the light. You say anything alive within my current's energy? What kind of distance are we talking about?"

"Oh, it depends upon the person and their strength. But it would be safe to assume that the energy field would be about the distance to the door there."

Annie looked back where the elf pointed; the entrance to the ballroom was roughly twenty feet away. She gasped and turned back to Diana.

"Ben!"

"Pardon?"

"Remember when you guys saw my memories? And I was talking to my neighbor before I traveled here?"

"Ah, yes," Diana said with a troubled frown, "he seemed to be standing close enough to you."

"Do you think he came here as well? Like Tia?"

"It is said that traveling between realms requires a willingness. That is to say, you must want to *leave*. And you and this Ben were both preparing to flee, yes? Tia would follow you out of loyalty. I suppose it is a possibility he came here."

"Oh, man. I hope not. That guy would freak out. I mean, at least *I* was prepared for a world full of magic. Ben would probably lose his mind here."

Diana chuckled. "I think that you were a little unprepared, yet you have accepted Tahldia now, yes? But we must hope your friend is happy, wherever he is."

"He wasn't my friend, really. Just my crazy old neighbor. In some ways, he's like Hak. The guy had been in a war and wasn't right in the head."

"I could say *you* are not right in the head, Annie," said Hak in a cool voice.

Annie jumped and looked over her shoulder toward the ballroom. He stood grinning in the doorway wearing a long, red robe with gold-embroidered trim. To Annie, the mage fashion looked weird on him.

"Am I interrupting anything?"

Diana practically jumped out of the chair and motioned for Hak to sit. "Oh, not at all, Hakayatas. I was just on my way inside."

The elf turned and gave Annie a mischievous smile. She replied with a flat look.

Diana gave Hak a deep bow meant for an equal. He smiled and returned the gesture. "It was lovely talking to you over dinner, Hakayatas. The council is very pleased with you. Good things are in your future, yes?" Her eyes twinkled mysteriously, and she quickly walked off.

Hak stood by the chair and gave Annie an uneasy look. "May I sit?"

She smirked up at him and nodded at his robe. "Nice dress, dude."

"Ah, you are back to your old self, I see." He smiled and sat down next to her.

"The color seems to suit you. Would you like a beer?"

Hak fingered the red silk. "I would love one. Are you . . . drunk, Annie?"

"Nah, don't worry. I'm trying to keep my drunken shenanigans down to a few incidents a year. I think I've met my quota already."

Annie leaned forward and took an empty goblet from the table, filled it, and handed it to him. She refilled her drink and sank deep into the chair and sighed.

"Diana said it's the best beer in the palace. From the king's own cellar. It's good, even though it's warm."

"You do not like warm beer?"

"No way. Where I'm from we drink it cold. We have these things called refrigerators . . . they're boxes that make ice."

"Interesting."

"Yeah. You can put food, beer, whatever you want in there, and it stays cold and won't go bad. And man, cold beer is the best!"

"May I see your drink for a moment?" Hak took the goblet from Annie. He looked down at it, his brow furrowed for a moment, and then he handed it back to her.

Annie grinned. The goblet felt like ice. She took a drink and let out a happy sigh. "Oh yeah, *that* is pretty awesome. I still can't believe you can do that stuff now!"

Hak flexed his hands and, after a thoughtful moment, chilled his own drink. He tried it, and nodded with approval.

"It is difficult to believe for me as well. I feel so alive, Annie. The last few years, I have felt as if I have been walking dead through the world. Everything is clear now. I feel like I can truly see, smell and hear like I used to. It is a blessing."

Annie watched his face light up, his smile twisting the scar under his left eye. *Did I really think he was ugly? The scars aren't so bad, especially when he smiles.* She felt her cheeks grow unbearably hot, and she looked down at the drink in her hands.

She choked on some words that she knew she couldn't say, and she cleared her throat. "You look really happy, Hak. For the first time since I met you, you're smiling a lot. It's good to see."

"Yes, I am happy, Annie."

"How did your private meeting with Aiyana go?"

His smile disappeared at once.

"Crap. Sorry. We don't have to talk about it now if you don't want to."

"It is all right, Annie. She told me the truth about you."

"Really?"

"Yes. And she also showed me her past. At least, what she wanted me to see. It is strange to think I am a warlock. I can learn a lot from her."

"She really turned her attitude toward you around when she saw your memories of the current during our meeting this morning."

He nodded sadly. "Yes. She has been quite civil. While she tells me she is happy to meet another of her kind, I wonder if she already had a suspicion about me."

"She is a bit secretive. I feel like she knows stuff about me that she won't tell me."

"She says your memories have been blocked by her grandson."

"Yeah. I was hoping that something would happen down there at the Fieriel Senefal to unblock my memories. I guess it isn't as easy as snapping your fingers, though."

"She seemed displeased with you."

Annie shrugged and took a deep chug of beer. "Eh, she always seems that way. But I guess she was hoping I'd come back blasting fire like you."

"Mau suspects that you somehow absorbed some of the magiel, and that is why your eyes turned yellow."

"I'm just happy we're both alive. I could care less about what color my irises are."

"Aiyana is not so sure about Mau's theory. Perhaps in time we will find out what happened to you. Maybe if you had your blocked memories back..."

"I'll relearn magic if I have to, Hak. Look, I'm not really worried about it right now. All I want to do is sleep for a week and not move."

"She said that you can go through more rigorous training with Diana, if you wish."

"Yeah, it could be fun."

Hak let out a deep sigh. "Annie, I think Aiyana is scheming behind your back. She gives you many strange looks. And now that I have regained use of the current, I can sense her unease with you."

"I've noticed that," Annie said dryly. "Not much I can do. She promised me money and a chance to go explore this world, and I'm going to take that opportunity. And hope she doesn't double-cross me somehow. The king was present when that promise was made, so I can't imagine her finding some way to get out of it."

"You have difficulty trusting people, Annie."

"Yep."

"Do you trust me?"

It was a heavy question. Annie hesitated for a moment as something dark in her subconscious tried to worm its way through her gut. The ghosts of her past called out a warning. They were phantoms born from men who had lied to her, hurt her, and left her. She pushed the anxiety away.

Annie's posture softened and she reached out to grasp his left hand. Her

315

small hands wrapped around three of his large fingers. She studied the scars on his wrist before she looked into his eyes. "Yes. Of course I trust you. I mean . . . I'm getting better. You've been a great friend."

Hak looked down at his drink. His face seemed troubled.

"What's wrong?"

"I do not like the thought of Aiyana using you, as she did with me. She is conniving and treacherous. She has been playing with politics for far too long."

"Well, what can ya do?" Annie took a deep drink of beer and gave Hak a lopsided smile.

Hak looked at her with sad yellow eyes. "How would you like to go home, Annie?"

She froze. "What? How?"

"I think . . . I think I am more than powerful enough to take you home, if you so desire. And Tia as well, of course."

Annie leaned back and took a deep breath. She exhaled slowly and stared out at the distant thunderstorm. She pinched the space between her eyes.

"I honestly never thought I would see home again. Are you sure you're able to do it?"

"I believe so. If you can share your memories of home with me, I ought to be able to take us there."

"What would happen if it doesn't work? Would we be trapped in that weird white void?"

"I would not let us get trapped, Annie."

She bit her lip and stared up into his eyes.

"Well? Would you like me to take you home?"

His face seemed so sad to Annie just then. She could see that he didn't want her to go. And part of her was worried that the spell would fail.

It doesn't seem like the safest magic to cast, after seeing Aiyana's memories of it. And Aiyana's been practicing her weird warlock spells her entire life. Hak just found out he's a warlock. He probably needs some sort of warlock training to travel safely between worlds.

"Annie?"

But what if I could go home, risk free? Would I do it? What if I could just skip across dimensions, or whatever it is, and be back in my bed playing video games and drinking whiskey?

She frowned and stared out at the valley. *And sit in a car three hours a day, going to a job that drove me insane and coming home to an empty house every night? I would never see Diana or Hak again. Would I spend the rest of my life missing Tahldia and regretting the choice to leave it?*

Annie shook her head and fought back a few burning tears. "No."

"Annie . . ."

"Not yet, anyway. I'm not ready to go back. Not yet."

"Are you sure?"

She poked him playfully. "Dude, I am not repeating myself again. You're stuck with me. Deal with it."

Hak sighed and leaned against her. The energy between them felt as though it pulsed momentarily. Together they stared out over the valley.

She held out her goblet to him. "A toast. To magic, the heart of the current, and Tahldia."

"To your friendship." Hak smiled and tilted his cup against hers. She stared up at the great red dragon nebula splashed across the sky. She looked up in wonder at the small red moon, Ikti, and the larger moons far to the east. Thunder rumbled across the valley.

No . . . I'm not in a hurry to go home. I miss parts of my old life, but I do not think I am ready to leave this world. There is so much I can see and do here. And I think I have found some new friends that I can't live without.

Annie smiled, and pressed her cheek against Hak's shoulder. His energy felt so good to her, especially now that he had regained his magic. She closed her eyes and allowed herself to listen to the distant thunder and the soft sounds of Hak breathing.

For the first time in recent memory, she felt peace. She didn't worry about the council. She didn't fear being hurt, captured, or killed. Life's potential seemed limitless and beautiful.

She opened an eye to look up at Hak. He was smiling and gazing at the large red nebula in the sky. She grinned, and didn't want the moment to end.

About the Author

Born and raised in Texas, Crispin Young grew up on a steady diet of video games, comic books, cartoons, and watching Star Trek with her dad.

In 2001, she wandered off to the northwest in search of adventure, and received her degrees in Journalism and Environmental Studies from the University of Oregon.

One night when she was a college freshman, she looked up at the thick blanket of stars above her campfire and saw the characters of Tahldia clearly in her mind. The memories and creative inspiration of that evening followed her like a shadow through the next eight years, evolving and growing into an enormous, bittersweet trilogy. "Heart of the Current" is her first novel.

Crispin currently resides in the Pacific Northwest and works as a hardware technician, graphic designer, photographer, word wrestler and cat herder.

She dreams of being a full-time writer.

For updates on the second and third books in the series, or to contact Crispin, you can follow her on twitter @tahldia or her website www.tahldia.com